## Praise for Julie Compton

'Compton's intense, entertaining second novel involves a horrifying cover-up and a powerful new drug . . . Compton pulls off a super-satisfying resolution to this romantic thriller'
*Publishers Weekly*

'*Tell No Lies* is a strong debut from a writer who knows her law and, more importantly, can depict the ebb and flow of relationships, the conflict between love and desire and the irresistible urge to self-destruct of a "man who has everything"'
*Guardian*

'Compton adds a very sexy pair of legs to Scott Turow legal thriller territory, with this highly charged story of a young assistant DA put on the spot when his former colleague and mistress finds herself facing death row'
*Daily Mirror*

'Compton's debut is a taut, tense cautionary tale complete with courtroom drama and a surprise ending'
*Kirkus Reviews* starred review

# Rescuing Olivia

JULIE COMPTON was born in St. Louis, Missouri, and is a
graduate of Washington University School of Law. She most
recently worked as a trial attorney for the US Department of
Justice in Delaware, where she worked on some of the largest
corporate bankruptcies in the nation. She now lives in Florida
with her husband and two daughters. *Rescuing Olivia* is her
second novel.

*Visit Julie at*
www.julie-compton.com

Also by Julie Compton

*Tell No Lies*

JULIE COMPTON

# Rescuing Olivia

PAN BOOKS

First published in Great Britain 2010 by Macmillan
and in the United States 2010 by Minotaur Books, an imprint of Macmillan, New York, USA

This edition published 2011 by Pan Books
an imprint of Pan Macmillan, a division of Macmillan Publishers Limited
Pan Macmillan, 20 New Wharf Road, London N1 9RR
Basingstoke and Oxford
Associated companies throughout the world
www.panmacmillan.com

ISBN 978-0-330-45286-1

1 3 5 7 9 8 6 4 2

A CIP catalogue record for this book is available from
the British Library.

Typeset by Ellipsis Books Limited, Glasgow
Printed in the UK by CPI Mackays, Chatham ME5 8TD

Visit www.panmacmillan.com to read more about all our books
and to buy them. You will also find features, author interviews and
news of any author events, and you can sign up for e-newsletters
so that you're always first to hear about our new releases.

FT
Pbk

*For Rick, and our 'Turtle City'*

*Every life is allocated one hundred seconds of true genius.*
*They might be enough, if we could just be sure which*
*ones they were.*

James Richardson, poet

# Florida

# 1

ANDERS STEPPED off the elevator into the lobby of the ICU, and the sounds of everyday life evaporated. He still heard voices, but they were more hushed than the ones in the main lobby downstairs, and he suspected most of them up here on the fourth floor belonged to doctors or nurses. Otherwise, the halls were silent. His eyes scanned the area, and he tried to determine where he was supposed to go and how he was supposed to get there. The hallways appeared to form a large H, with the elevators in the middle. He saw only two sets of doors, one on each side of the elevator banks, each leading to one leg of the H. The doors nearest to him had an identifying plaque at shoulder height – it merely stated 'ICU'. He stepped to the opposite side of the hall and read 'ICU – Neuro' next to the other set. He pulled both handles, but they were locked.

A sense of helplessness overcame him. He was a grown man – almost thirty years old – and yet he couldn't figure out something as simple as how to visit his girlfriend in the intensive care unit of a hospital. He felt as if he was on a scavenger hunt to find something very, very important, yet no one had given him any clues to get started. It occurred to him then that perhaps the hospital prohibited visitors in the ICU. But no, no, that wasn't right either. The kind lady in the pink clothing at the reception desk downstairs would have mentioned that when he asked her which floor Olivia was on. Too bad she hadn't mentioned how he should get behind these doors once he got up here.

He heard more voices, a man's voice above softer female

3

ones, so he followed the sound down the east hall. He came to a glass enclosed room in the middle of the floor, though curtains had been drawn to block his view inside. He leaned into the open doorway, anxious to ask someone the secret code for penetrating the ICU, but when he saw who was there, he stopped.

He'd never met Lawrence Mayfield in person, but there was no mistaking that this was Olivia's father sitting on the couch against the opposite wall. The Romanesque nose and the dark waves of hair gave him away. On Olivia the features were regal, but on Lawrence Mayfield they were warrior-like, and to Anders, chilling.

Her mother was there, too, or someone Anders assumed was her mother. Though she'd chosen the most comfortable-looking chair in the room – a leather lounger with plenty of cushioning – she sat erect with both feet planted firmly on the floor. A hospital blanket draped her shoulders but underneath it her clothes screamed money.

And then there was the final person, a tall, slim black woman who sat in a folding chair just to the right of Olivia's mother. The two of them held hands.

All three faces looked in his direction and, to his surprise, two of those faces – the two belonging to Olivia's parents – hardened. It might have been a mouth closing a bit tighter on one, a cheek lifting ever so slightly into a grimace on the other, or simply a straightening of shoulders, but Anders sensed it, however imperceptible. It became immediately clear to him that they knew exactly who he was, too. The large raw scrape on his right arm, flesh exposed, provided only the first of many clues.

He nodded, his eyes on Olivia's father. 'Sir.' He managed the word by habit of manners, and as if its mere utterance set in motion a sequence of events, he finally moved to shake the man's hand.

'You must be Andy.' The flat tone of the comment told Anders that this man would not be extending his arm in greeting, and he stopped mid-step from advancing farther into the room. A sudden anger began to build as he processed the name Olivia's father had used. Only his friend Lenny referred to him as Andy. Olivia had *never* used it, so he was certain her father used the nickname in some strange attempt to be the alpha dog.

'No, sir, I'm Anders. Anders Erickson.' He almost added 'It's a pleasure to meet you' but he caught the instinctive impulse in time.

A slight smirk crossed the man's face. 'Excuse me. *Anders.*'

He waited in anticipation of further introductions, however cold, but it became apparent that none would be made. The Mayfields stared at him with accusing eyes. The black woman, though, gazed at Anders behind a veil of anguish and fear. Anders recognized it because it mirrored his own.

'Is there something you need?' her father asked, though Anders was certain the question was not intended as an offer to help.

He slowly turned his gaze back to the patriarch of the family. 'I've just come from talking to the' – he almost said 'cops', but then thought better of it – 'police. I was hoping to see Olivia.'

'Well, that's a lovely thought, but only family members are allowed to visit.'

Without thinking, he asked, 'Is she family?' and pointed at the woman next to Olivia's mother. Now *he* sounded hostile, and he regretted asking the question.

A derisive laugh erupted from her father's throat. 'Not that it's any of your business, but Makena has known Olivia since she was born and might possibly know her better than even her mother and me.'

*Her mother and I,* Anders thought.

5

Before he could respond, her father added, 'Olivia never told you about Makena?'

Anders chewed on the inside of his cheek without realizing it. He knew the point of the man's question, and he refused to give him the satisfaction of an answer, but her father had nevertheless succeeded in sowing the seed of doubt in his mind. Olivia hadn't ever mentioned Makena, and all Anders could think now was, *why not?* What else hadn't she told him?

He turned and left the room to find a nurse. At the other end of the long hall, he found a U-shaped nurse's station but no nurses, and was about to return to the lobby downstairs for help when he saw one of the doors to the ICU open.

'Excuse me!' he called.

A nurse in light blue scrubs turned at his voice and put one finger to her lips to signal 'quiet'.

'Could you hold that door, please!' He tried to shout and whisper the words simultaneously as he jogged in her direction, but it was impossible. It didn't matter; the door closed silently and the nurse made no moves to stop it.

She waited until he stood, a bit breathless, in front of her. 'Sir, I'm sorry, you're on the intensive care floor. You must keep your voice down.'

Even though she meant to scold, her voice had a soothing, sympathetic tone. She looked so young, like she could have been his kid sister. Her chin-length blonde hair was stick-straight, and her pale skin was clear and dewy. Skinny arms stuck out from the short sleeves of her top; her delicate hands held a chart against her chest. He required an angel and she was his only possibility.

'I need to see Olivia Mayfield,' he said. 'They told me downstairs she was in ICU.'

The nurse nodded to the doors behind her. 'She's in Neuro.'

'Can you take me to see her?'

Her eyes darted in the direction of the waiting room, as if

she was trying to remember whether she'd seen him in there with the rest of them. 'Are you family?'

Anders shifted on his feet. 'I guess that depends what "family" means. She's my . . . we're . . .' He fumbled for the correct term. 'Lover' sounded inappropriate, but boyfriend and girlfriend sounded too juvenile, and neither came close to describing what they meant to each other. Anders determined in that instant to propose to Olivia when he saw her. Why had he waited?

'Are you a boyfriend?' She smiled slightly. She'd seen others struggle with the same explanation. Even though he knew she hadn't intended to, she'd made him sound like he was one of many.

'Yes, we live together.' So that she didn't mistake them for mere roommates, he added quickly, 'We love each other.' He didn't care anymore how immature he sounded.

'I understand, sir. I really do.'

He believed her. When she looked down at the floor and shook her head, he knew what her next words were going to be.

'It's just that hospital rules prevent non-family members from visiting patients in the ICU. Otherwise, we'd have so many people traipsing through and our patients would never get better. I'm sure you can understand.' The pained look on her face told him that she really didn't enjoy relaying this news. He knew another, less compassionate nurse might have. 'I'm sorry, sir.'

'Are there ever any exceptions?'

She shrugged. 'Sometimes, if the family gives permission, and the doctor okays it.' She must have seen the flash of hope in his eyes. 'But . . .'

She breathed deep and he waited.

'. . . the family has made it quite clear that no one outside her immediate family is to be allowed in.'

Anders could feel his legs weakening underneath him and

7

he wondered what in God's name these people had against him. They didn't even know him, yet he was an enemy.

'I'll talk to them. I'll see if I can convince them, okay?'

She nodded sadly, and he suspected she'd already spent enough time with Olivia's father to know what he was up against. She started in the direction of the nurse's station.

'Nurse?'

'You can call me Carrie.'

'Thank you, Carrie. Can you at least tell me how she's doing?' He braced himself for a litany of privacy rules.

She paused, as if trying to decide which of them to break for his benefit. 'Look, sir—'

'You can call me Anders.'

Just her eyes smiled this time, and she came close to him again and touched his shoulder. They were friends now.

'Anders. I shouldn't be telling you anything, and I'm not sure whether this will make you feel better or worse, but she's in a coma.' He gasped. 'What I mean is, she won't know whether you're there or not.'

He looked to the ceiling to stall the tears welling up in his eyes. 'That's it? You're going to give me that information and not tell me more?'

She opened her mouth to speak, but he cut her off and began pacing the floor. 'I can't believe this is happening. I've gotta wake up soon because there's no fucking way this is actually happening.'

'Sir.' She grabbed his arm with surprising authority. 'I'm sorry. I've already told you enough to get myself fired. But you can't assume the worst, okay? Many people recover full mental and physical function when they emerge from a coma.' She paused and waited until he nodded, a signal to her that he'd regained control, however tenuous. 'I just didn't want you to leave here thinking she was lying there wondering where you were, why you hadn't come.'

*Or worse*, Anders thought. *Asking and being told a lie in response.*

He knew she offered the information to be kind, and he didn't want to direct his anger at her. 'Okay, okay. I'm going to speak to them, though, her family. Okay?'

Carrie nodded. 'There's a bell –' she motioned to a small button to the right of the door '– just press it if you don't see me around.'

She turned to go, and he called to her one more time. 'Carrie?' She looked back over her shoulder. 'Just ... well, thank you.'

She gave him a quiet smile, but it didn't look hopeful.

WHEN ANDERS returned to the waiting room, her father was alone, talking into a Bluetooth hooked over his right ear. He glanced up at Anders, but his expression remained the same; the presence of the man his comatose daughter lived with affected him no differently than if he'd been looking at a picture on the wall. To Anders's ears, the phone call consisted of all business. He caught no mention of Olivia. *All my father's business meetings were important*, Olivia had told Anders the first time she'd brought up her father. *More important than his daughter's life?* he wondered now.

Digging his hands into his jeans pockets, he fingered the necklace he'd found on the ground before the ambulances had arrived at the scene. He spoke only after he saw the man touch the device at his ear, signalling the end of the call.

'Sir, the nurse said she could allow me in to see Olivia if her family gave permission.'

'Well, Andy – Anders – I don't think that will be happening.' He reached into the briefcase at his feet, pulled out an eyeglass case, and took his time retrieving the glasses and placing them on his nose. He then pulled out a stack of papers and began to leaf through them. Anders watched in disbelief. He didn't want to believe Olivia shared blood with this man. But her father's behaviour was all too familiar, and it eroded his already shaky determination.

He stood straighter, reminding himself that this was Olivia's dad, not his own.

'Mr Mayfield?'

Her father looked up over the top of the reading glasses as if he was surprised to see Anders still in the room.

'Did I do something to offend you, sir? Is there a reason you don't want me to see her?'

The man leaned back into his chair and sighed.

'Olivia's mother and I think that you have done quite enough for her, Andy. I'm sure the two of you have had a hell of a time together – God knows I cringe to think of the details – but it's time for her to come home and be with family. If she's lucky, that is.'

For a moment Anders stood speechless, staring at him and trying to process the meaning of what he'd just said. What he'd just accused him of. If Anders had been a different sort of man, more like Lenny, he would have considered taking a swing at the guy. But if he'd been more like Lenny, he would never have been standing there discussing Olivia with her father. Olivia would have never been in his life.

'Are you saying you think I *caused* the accident? That it was my fault?'

Her father had turned his attention back to his damn papers, and he answered this time without even looking up. 'You were driving the motorcycle, weren't you?' He spoke the word 'motorcycle' with obvious contempt.

Anders snorted in disgust. 'Someone tried to run us off the road!'

'So you say. But it's interesting how there were no witnesses, isn't it?' He flipped a page. 'Not to mention no helmets. How dare you be so cavalier with my daughter's life.' Finally his eyes showed emotion, though it was only cold hate. 'Now, if you'll let me get back to my work.'

Anders's face burned, and he felt the blood pumping fast through the veins in his neck.

'Sir, I'm begging you.' Though he tried to control it, he could hear the encroaching desperation in his voice. 'Can you please just let me see her? When she comes to, she'll tell you the same thing.' He realized he'd just let slip that the nurse had told him something confidential. But if her father realized it, he didn't show it. He didn't show anything, for that matter. Anders could have been speaking to a deaf man. 'I would never hurt her. I just need to see her. I'm *begging* you,' he repeated. '*Please.*' His voice cracked with the last word.

Approaching footsteps echoed on the polished hospital tiles in the hall, but Anders heard nothing but the sound of silence coming from the statue in front of him. He turned to escape and almost knocked down Olivia's mother, who stood in the doorway in front of the other woman. 'Excuse me, ma'am,' he muttered, and as he darted past them, his eyes caught Makena's. Perhaps he'd imagined it, but he could have sworn he heard a voice, deep and grainy but distinctly feminine, telling him not to give up. Never give up.

Not that he'd planned to, anyway.


THE DAY before had started pretty much like many of the others they'd spent together. Anders woke before Olivia. The early rise wasn't new to him; even as a kid he'd woken at the break of day. He'd go fishing before school, or just hang out in the tree fort behind his house while he waited for his dad's car to pull out of the drive. Now, if he had to work, it gave him a chance to sit on the deck with her first, drink coffee and watch for dolphins in the morning surf. If he didn't have to work, well, that was even better.

He hadn't set an alarm. The light of dawn crept through the window and tapped him on the shoulder to announce the arrival of the new day. His eyes opened, and the gentle sound of the surf reassured him that nothing had changed overnight. He rolled over and inhaled the salty air mixed with the sweet smell of her sweat. He longed to touch her, but he didn't. She'd had another nightmare a few hours earlier and needed her sleep. Though she claimed she never remembered them, she always seemed a bit off the next day; an unexpected touch by him would startle her, or she'd tense at overhearing a stranger speak to his female companion in the wrong tone.

So instead he watched her sleep. He watched the flutter of her eyelids as she dreamed, he watched the rise and fall of her chest as she breathed. Every once in a while, a white tern landed on the sill of the open window and watched with him. He felt they shared a secret, he and the bird.

He knew she wasn't pretty by conventional standards, yet to him she was beautiful. Her dark hair fell against the pillow in long, kinky coils, its colour reminiscent of the black coffee she drank each morning. Her eyelashes were long, too – they were one of the few features she liked about herself – and they protected sleepy olive-green eyes. ('They're hazel, Anders,' she'd say, laughing. 'Simply hazel.') Freckles dotted the bridge of her nose and then cascaded down to her cheeks. A Cupid's bow framed her lips.

But he liked her neck the best, the way the long lines of it stretched lazily from collarbone to jaw when her head tilted to the side, away from him. A delicate silver chain with a small charm in the shape of a crane rested in the hollow. She never removed the necklace, not when she showered, not when she slept, and he'd come to think of it as just another part of her for him to marvel at. It was all he could do not to lean over and kiss that neck, ravish it until she awoke in delight and joined him in the lovemaking that had become almost a morning ritual for them. But he waited. The waiting made it all the better.

'Anders.' Her voice was hoarse. The lips formed a slight smile.

'Olivia.'

They each said it as if to confirm the existence of the other. A pinch just to be sure.

'Good morning.'

'And that it is.' He returned her smile.

She turned toward the window. 'Hmm, I can smell the ocean today.'

The tern was gone. All that remained inside the window frame's perimeter was one cotton-ball cloud against a periwinkle-blue sky.

She reached for him, wrapping her arms around his neck and pulling him close. 'Let's go for a ride today. A long ride.' She gave him a peck on the lips. 'Take me somewhere I've never been.'


HE RETREATED to the hospital cafeteria on the main floor. He told himself he'd figure out some way to get in, that leaving would be the equivalent of conceding defeat. Anyway, it'd be easier to get updates on her condition if he stayed close.

He bought a cup of coffee and dropped the change in the handmade Styrofoam tip cup next to the cash register. The cashier didn't acknowledge it. He took a seat at a table in the far corner, near a picture window facing the parking lot. The dinner hour was just beginning, and the cafeteria buzzed with the chatter of hospital personnel as they pushed their way through the cafeteria line and jockeyed for the cleanest tables.

The groupings reminded Anders of his high school days, when the jocks and the cheerleaders dared not sit with the intellectuals or the potheads. Here, he could pick out the doctors by their white lab coats over dress shirts and ties, in the case of the men – or skirts or pantsuits, in the case of the women. The nurses dressed in scrubs, mostly solid coloured but sometimes floral for the women.

The doctors and nurses stood in stark contrast to the family and friends of patients, whose hollow eyes and weary efforts to smile at strangers gave them away. They were like the walking dead, and Anders wondered how in the short span of twenty-four hours he'd managed to become one of them.


*TAKE ME somewhere I've never been.*

The irony of Olivia's request was that it seemed to Anders she'd been everywhere, and he'd never left Florida.

This wasn't entirely true; he'd visited his sister and her family in Chicago several times in an attempt to heal old wounds, and he'd taken a road trip to Southern California with a biker buddy a few years back, thinking that he'd fall in love with it and decide to stay, but he found that it had the same plastic facade that threatened to suffocate his home state.

But otherwise, Anders's life had been lived in Florida. He'd been born there, raised there, and, according to his father (who'd left long ago for New York), was wasting his life there. But Anders didn't see it that way. He liked his Florida, the part that existed away from the tourists and the snowbirds, the part beyond the sweltering cities and the burgeoning suburbs. Until he'd met Olivia and moved into her beach house, he'd lived not far from Port Orange, just south of Daytona, in a rented mobile home set on the edge of a mangrove near Rose Bay. He was about fifteen minutes from the Atlantic Ocean in one direction, twenty-five minutes from his job at the Bentley Palms Golf Resort & Spa, closer to Orlando, in the other.

That he'd moved into a mobile home horrified his parents. His mother's concern stemmed mainly from the threat of hurricanes and tornadoes, but his father simply felt that living in a mobile home was akin to living in a hole. 'You're not trailer trash,' he'd said to Anders on more than one occasion, back before Anders had stopped speaking to him completely, 'so don't act like it.' In his father's opinion, his living arrangements were unacceptable for someone of Anders's 'smarts and upbringing' – as he called it.

Anders was well aware of his own 'smarts'. At his father's insistence, he'd been IQ tested in the third grade to see if he was gifted; he'd scored 154. His teachers had requested testing again in ninth grade because despite the previous high score, his grades never substantiated his supposed intelligence. The second time he'd scored 162.

Not wanting to hurt his mom, he finally applied himself for the remainder of high school and ended up graduating near the top of his class. And though he'd dutifully filled out college applications, he ultimately declined the acceptances and scholarship offers that followed, and his mom accepted his decision graciously. Though she tried to explain the benefits of a college degree, she also knew her 'good job' arguments fell on deaf ears. She understood he had no interest in the material possessions that drove many individuals to spend their lives chasing a buck. A large house and a fast car just didn't seem like sufficient payoff to him. She argued that a degree could make it easier for him to pursue the outdoor life he loved, but he remained unconvinced. The idea of travel romanced him, but he figured he could do this without the fancy hotels and overpriced restaurants. He'd never eaten fresher fish than those he'd caught himself; he'd never found a more relaxing bed than a sleeping bag under the stars.

Olivia, on the other hand, had travelled the world. Anders didn't know the full extent of it – she didn't talk much about it and she brushed off as annoying the teasing comments from Lenny and others about her being cosmopolitan – but he knew the story of her birth, how she'd arrived in the world surrounded by African women and mosquito nets, and that told him enough to know that she'd experienced things he probably couldn't even imagine.

He jumped at the touch of someone's fingers on his forearm.

'Oh, I'm so sorry, I didn't realize you were sleeping.'

He looked up to see the nurse from upstairs standing over him. Carrie. She'd told him her name was Carrie.

'No, it's okay. I didn't realize it either.' But clearly he had dozed; blackness stared back at him now from the other side of the window. He wondered how much time had passed. He scooted to sit straighter on the hard plastic chair and managed to give her a weak smile.

'I thought you'd left,' she said. 'But I'm glad you're here.'

He didn't respond. He didn't want to read too much into what she'd just said.

'Tell me your name again.'

'It's Anders.'

She nodded, a smile growing on her face. 'Yes, I thought so. You don't forget a name like that.'

'Why do you ask?'

'Listen, I came down for my dinner and happened to spot you over here in the corner, so give me a few minutes to eat, but then come back upstairs, okay? But don't take too long. They've gone to dinner, too, but I don't know how much time we have.'

He knew without asking that 'they' were Olivia's family. He scanned the cafeteria but then realized she meant they'd left the hospital. He could feel his pulse increasing as the nap-induced fog began to clear and her meaning began to sink in.

He started to ask another question; he didn't think he could last the ten minutes it would take to finish her meal, but she just shook her head.

'Not now. We'll talk upstairs. I have something to show you.'

HE CHOSE one of the sacred escapes of his youth, a small, secluded spring on private but vacant land at the edge of the Ocala National Forest. He didn't divulge where they were going or what the spot meant to him; he told her only to bring a swim-suit, a towel and some dry clothes for later. They took off on the bike just after nine.

She fell in love with the place at first sight, just as he'd hoped. She told him it reminded her of Africa and pretended to pout when he laughed at the comparison. 'Well, we do have panthers out here, I guess,' he said.

'I meant the remoteness, the sense that you're a long way from anything or anyone. I like that.'

They left the bike at the trailhead and hiked the short dis-tance to the pool. After swimming naked in the icy water, they dried their bodies on a large rock in the hot sun and, afterwards, made love in the shade of the scrub oaks and water tupelos.

'How many other women have you brought here to your little piece of paradise?'

He grinned but didn't answer.

'Ah, quite a few, I gather.'

'No.'

'How many then?'

He reached up and pushed her hair away from her face. 'Why do you ask a question like that? You're not the jealous type.'

'No,' she agreed. She wore a small, almost bashful, smile. 'Not usually.'

He thought about how to answer. He'd been at this swimming hole many times over the years, with groups of friends of both persuasions, but he'd only ever brought one other woman here in the same way he'd brought Olivia. Yet even that he now dismissed as irrelevant, knowing his actions had been motivated more by lust than a need to share a slice of his life.

'Just one.' He ran a finger down her cheek and over her damp lips. 'But I didn't tell her I loved her.'

HE SAT in the now empty waiting room surrounded by the evidence left behind by her family. A paper cup with a few dregs of cold coffee in the bottom and lipstick prints on the rim; the morning's newspaper scattered on the small table in front of the sofa; a hospital issue pillow and blanket discarded on the chair in the corner.

The door to the room had been propped open, and Carrie peeked her head in, summoning him to follow her. He hadn't felt anything that remotely approached joy since before the accident, but if it was possible to feel joy at the prospect of visiting a comatose person in the intensive care unit of a hospital, then that's what he felt. His muscles tensed with eagerness.

Carrie gripped the handle to the entrance to the ICU, and just as she lifted her badge to swipe it across the access panel, she turned to Anders.

'Each patient has a devoted nurse. When I'm on duty, I'm it for Olivia.' He nodded and moved forward. 'Slow down,' she said, not unkindly. 'This is important for you to know before we go in there.' He nodded again, trying to check his impatience. 'The nurse covering for me knows the general rule about families, of course, but because she's just my relief, she doesn't really pay attention to who's been in and out. Nor could I necessarily identify those who are allowed in for the other patients. It's up to each of us to enforce the rule for our particular patient.

'I'm telling you this because it's important that you just follow my lead when we get in there. Act like you belong, not like I'm sneaking you in, because although I'm in charge of my patient, that doesn't mean there might not be another nurse who'd like to get me in trouble if she could. Got it?'

'I understand.'

'And it's going to have to be quick, Anders. If her family returns and we get caught, I'd be out of a job. No questions asked.'

She swiped her badge and pulled the heavy door open. 'Follow me.'

'Carrie? Why are you doing this for me?'

She smiled and winked. 'That's what I'm about to show you.'

ON THE other side of the doors, the silence of the hospital corridor was replaced by nurses quietly discussing their plans for the weekend, various beeps and buzzers, and the horrifying, artificial breathing sound of a ventilator. Anders recognized the last sound from sitting at his grandmother's side in her dying days, and it still haunted him. He trailed Carrie wordlessly around the curve of the half-moon nurse's station, where she let her relief nurse know she was back on duty with a simple nod. The other nurse eyed Anders, but he did as instructed and merely nodded a greeting, too. Carrie entered the last room, but Anders stopped in the doorway at the sight of Olivia in the hospital bed behind the wall of glass.

Like an uninvited guest, the images of the crash barged in. He saw the Mercedes coming up fast on them in the curve, the slide of the motorcycle's rear tyre, the sudden gripping of the pavement again and then, her body being tossed and tumbled as the bike high-sided, flipping over and over. The sounds of her short scream, and then the rev of the Mercedes' engine as it sped west, leaving a frightening silence in its wake. The interminable wait for the ambulances afterwards, as he hovered over her lifeless body on the side of the road and begged an invisible someone to make her okay. And though some part of him knew he'd really witnessed only snippets of the actual accident – he'd been flung, too – his imagination had no problem filling in the parts he hadn't seen.

He closed his eyes for a moment and gave a silent prayer of thanks that the ventilator noise hadn't come from this room.

'Come on in.' Carrie already faced a laptop computer placed on top of a rolling supply cart, her fingers flying across the keyboard as her eyes darted to the mass of machinery standing guard at Olivia's bedside. Anders moved forward only a few steps, but stopped again when he saw the catheter protruding from the far right side of her head.

Carrie waved him closer. 'Come on. You can touch her. You won't hurt her.' She faced Olivia now, pulling the sheet back to check wires, tubes, connections. Any concerns he had earlier about Carrie's youth were extinguished by her apparent competence. This was her territory and she knew it intimately.

She gently lifted Olivia's left arm and tucked the sheet under it so he could have access to her hand. He reached for it, and the moment he felt her warmth, he finally gave up a few of the tears he'd been holding in.

He glanced at Carrie. 'I'm sorry.' The words came out in a voice he didn't even recognize. He tried to wipe his face on his shoulder, because now that he held Olivia's hand between both of his, he wasn't letting go.

Carrie stopped her busy activities and stepped back; he could feel her watching him. 'Don't apologize.'

He leaned forward, one hand still holding Olivia's, and with the other he caressed her cheek as his lips covered her forehead, her nose, her lips, with lightweight kisses. 'I'm here, baby,' he whispered. 'I'm here.' Her skin felt dry, her slightly parted lips parched. He couldn't stop looking at the spot where the catheter entered her head. A patch of hair had been shaved off to accommodate the tube and the bandages.

'That's where she hit her head,' Carrie explained. 'She was bleeding under the skull and they had to relieve the pressure on her brain.'

He stared at Carrie and waited for more information.

She sighed. 'How much do you want to know?'

'As much as you can tell me.'

'The brain swells and accumulates extra fluid when it's injured. It increases in size, thus increasing the pressure. To prevent damage, the neurosurgeon drills a hole through the skull to relieve the pressure. It's called a craniotomy.'

He took a deep breath.

'It sounds worse than it is. She came through it beautifully. It's really now just a wait and see type thing.'

'Can she hear me? Does she know I'm here?'

Carrie met his questions with silence, and he glanced back at her to be sure she heard. With a tilt of the head, she stared at Olivia thoughtfully. 'The doctors say probably not, and maybe they're right. But you know what? I think it can only help to talk to her.'

She came closer. 'Here, I'll show you what made me change my mind.' She used a foot pedal to adjust the bed so that Olivia sat more upright. 'I can't believe I didn't notice it earlier, but she's got quite a head of hair, and this is pretty small.' She gently leaned Olivia forward, motioning for Anders to cradle her, and then she brushed her curls to the side, parting the hair down the back of her head. 'It's fairly new. The hair's still growing back.'

From Anders's angle, a small, black tattoo presented itself

upside down and threatened to blend in with the shorter curls of the same colour, but he knew what the tiny, scripted letters spelled as soon as he set eyes on them.

'It's my name.'

Carrie laughed at his statement of the obvious. 'Yeah, it is.' She suddenly realized he'd never seen it. 'You mean, you didn't even know it was there?'

'No.' So they'd each had their little secret, their little surprise they were going to spring on the other when the moment was right.

He pulled her closer and carefully cradled her head against his chest. He inhaled, but her hair's familiar sweet scent had been replaced with an antiseptic smell he associated with the bandage on her head. He closed his eyes and tried to memorize the feel of her limp body in his arms, because he knew this might be the only time he'd be allowed such unfettered access to her unless she came around – until she came around – and insisted upon it.

He kept thinking of how it felt when they were on the bike, heading back from the springs to the beach house, how the insides of her thighs pressed up against him and her arms wrapped tight around his waist. She usually rested her chin on his left shoulder so she could see the road ahead of them, but he'd noticed on this trip she kept lifting her head and looking behind them, something she only did when he was about to make a turn. And then her voice in his ear, just minutes before the crash. 'I think someone is following us.' The funny thing is, if they'd had their helmets on, he probably would have never heard her. And yet, if they'd had the helmets on ... He kept thinking what he should have done differently, what he *could* have done differently, when they'd reached the bike and realized their helmets were missing. He wasn't even sure why they hadn't carried them down to the spring; he hardly ever left them with the bike like they did that day, but the last place he thought he'd have to worry about theft was in the middle of the Florida forest. He'd been angry when he realized they'd been stolen, but not for a minute was he concerned for their safety. He'd ridden for years without incident, and out there on the rural roads he knew they'd have little traffic.

'I was going to ask her to marry me.' He lifted his head and met Carrie's eyes.

Carrie smiled at that information, but he wasn't done. The confession spilled out. 'I mean, the day of the accident. I was going to ask her when we were at the springs, but something startled us, we heard a noise in the woods. It was probably just an animal but for some reason she was so freaked out by it, and after that, she couldn't relax. So I decided to do it later, maybe that night at home.' He turned away and placed his cheek against Olivia's hair. 'But if I'd just done it, if I'd asked her, she would have forgotten the noise and we would have stayed longer . . .'

Carrie couldn't have known the events leading up to the accident, where they'd been and what they'd been doing, unless, perhaps, she'd seen a police report, but nevertheless she understood the import of his words. 'Oh, you can't possibly start thinking like that—'

'But it's true. If I'd asked her, we wouldn't have left when we did.'

'Anders.' Carrie's sigh weighted the room with sadness. 'Do you know how many people I hear say things like that? Please don't start second guessing yourself. Just focus on her getting better. That's what matters now, okay?'

He nodded. 'Yeah, yeah. I know.' He kissed Olivia's head, as if sealing a silent promise. 'I was such a fool.'

'No, you're no fool.' She started to say more, but instead she just closed her mouth and shook her head.

'What is it?'

'I just – well, I just knew the minute I saw the tattoo who her family was.'

# 2

HE'D CALLED his mom ahead of time to let her know he was coming, but he didn't want to upset her, so he didn't tell her why. When he walked into his childhood home, the smell of frying chorizo sausage and brewing coffee welcomed him, and he felt a twinge of nostalgia in his gut. She was making his favourite breakfast – scrambled eggs, jack cheese and the sausage rolled into a warm tortilla – but it didn't occur to her that the familiar smells conjured in his mind much more than early morning scenes from years before of her getting him off to school. Sometimes, though, he loved her even more for her ability to forget. Sometimes.

He greeted her with a lingering hug, and then he waited patiently as she touched his face, pushed back the hair from his forehead, and appraised him generally as she did at each visit.

'What's the matter, honey? You're upset about something.'

Despite the heat, he'd worn jeans and a long sleeve shirt to hide his injuries, but there were some things he couldn't conceal.

'I don't want you to freak,' he began, and she stepped back slightly in anticipation with her hands still holding his shoulders. 'We had an accident on the bike.'

'We?'

'Olivia and I.'

'Are you okay? Where's Olivia?'

'I'm fine, just a few scrapes. But Olivia ...' He hesitated. 'She's not doing too well, Mom. She's in the hospital.'

24

His mom stared at him with anguished eyes. 'Oh, baby, I'm so sorry. When did this happen? Why didn't you call me?' Without waiting for the answers, she started down the hall toward the kitchen.

He followed behind her, glancing surreptitiously, as he always did, at the framed photos on the foyer table. He always managed to avoid the ones with his dad in them: the ones from his and his siblings' graduations – high school for all of them, and college, too, for Karina and Stephen – and from Karina's wedding to Nathan. But without fail his eyes were drawn like a magnet to the picture of Levi, his mother's prized golden retriever. It'd been seventeen years since the dog had died, and still, she displayed the photo with all the others.

In the kitchen, she took his hand and led him to the breakfast table. 'Here, sit down.'

He complied, the morning sun in the window warming his face. A small bowl of salsa rested in front of him, and he dipped his finger into it. He waited while she poured him a glass of orange juice and a cup of coffee; he'd learned from past visits that despite his protests that he could help himself, she wouldn't allow it. Her activities didn't surprise him; he was used to her nervous energy and knew she coped best with bad news by remaining in motion.

She finally pulled out the seat next to him and reached for one of his hands. 'Tell me now.'

'It happened on Monday. She's in the hospital. She hit her head and she's in a coma.'

She gasped and covered her mouth with her free hand.

'I'm sorry I didn't call earlier, it's just that I didn't even see her until last night.' He hesitated. He hadn't planned to tell her he'd been admitted, too, if only for a night, but out it came. 'I'd been taken to the hospital in Deland. I called Lenny and he tracked her down for me – for some reason they took her all the way into Sanford Mercy – but he couldn't get any information on her condition. I didn't even know how bad it was.'

'*You* were in the hospital, too?' She left the remainder of her sentence – *and you didn't call me?* – unsaid.

'Just for observation, Mom. I'm fine. Really.'

'How did this happen?'

Anders's mother was a young fifty-seven years old – a woman who had spent a few years in the Peace Corps before meeting, marrying and eventually divorcing his father. She'd always supported her youngest son's wanderlust, even if it was more dreamed about than realized. But if there was one topic on which she remained steadfastly conservative, it was her opposition to his mode of travel.

'Some guy tried to run us off the road.' He shook his head in disgust. 'It was like he was gunning for us.'

She stared at him, thinking about what he'd said, and then rose from the table. 'Give me a minute, your sausage is going to burn if I'm not careful.'

. He watched her at the stove. She moved the sausage to a cool burner and began to cook scrambled eggs in a different pan. 'But how did she hit her head?' she said over her shoulder. 'I thought you'd promised me you always wear a helmet.'

'I do. They'd been stolen, and we were in the middle of nowhere. We didn't really have a choice.'

'Stolen? In the middle of nowhere?'

He closed his eyes and took a deep breath. *Be patient*, he told himself. 'I don't know, Mom. Your guess is as good as mine.'

When she returned to the table, she placed the plate of steaming food in front of him. She'd already assembled the large tortilla with layers of eggs, sausage and cheese, but she'd left it open because she knew he liked to add the salsa himself before rolling it up.

After pouring a cup of coffee for herself, she sat in the

same chair again and watched him begin to eat. It was the first meal he'd had since the accident.

'It's good,' he said after swallowing the first bite and following it with a chaser of juice. He gave her a smile. 'Thank you.'

'There's more waiting when you're ready for seconds.'

She remained silent then until he'd taken a few more bites and began to eat more slowly, busying herself with the cream and sugar for her coffee. Finally, 'Did you call her family?'

Anders gazed at his plate and pushed the egg droppings around with his fork. 'No.' Dismay grew on her face – she couldn't imagine the boy she'd raised would have neglected such a task – but he cut her off. 'They were already there when I arrived at the hospital. Like I said, the ambulance took me to a different facility, and by the time I'd been treated, released, and then detained by the cops, it was Tuesday.'

'Detained by the cops?'

'Well, there were no witnesses, other than the car that left the scene. So it's only natural they'd question me.' He shrugged, trying not to let her see how anxious he'd been about it. How anxious he continued to be, in light of his conversation with Olivia's father. 'It's nothing to worry about. They let me go without filing any charges, and when Olivia comes to, she'll back me up.'

'So they expect Olivia will be fine?'

'Yeah.' His voice rose an octave. He didn't sound convincing. 'The nurse thinks so.'

His mother sighed and leaned back in her chair. 'Well, thank God her family is there, too.'

Anders bit his lip and resisted the urge to roll his eyes. But in the same way she'd immediately sensed his mood when he'd walked in the door, she knew he had something to say.

'You don't agree?'

His mother believed family was everything. She didn't think

you had to like them, and you certainly didn't let them dictate your life, but she felt that being a member of a family bestowed certain benefits you couldn't get anywhere else, and certain obligations that were not to be breached except in exceptional circumstances. Despite her divorce, and despite everything his father had done to her, to them, she still thought Anders was wrong not to speak with him. He, on the other hand, thought she was crazy in that regard.

He sighed. 'It's just that she's sort of estranged from her family. I'm not sure having them there will be a good thing.'

'Sort of?'

He had the coffee cup to his lips and he took a slow sip before placing it back on the table. He used the delay to decide whether to tell her about his run-in with Mayfield the day before.

'Well, maybe "estranged" isn't the right word. But she's originally from up north, and she came down here to distance herself from them, you know?'

His mom just stared at him and waited for more. Without fail, her silence always caused him to keep talking, and he didn't disappoint this time.

'I just know from things she's told me that she doesn't get along with them too well, you know? She and her dad . . .' He paused. Olivia had told him only a little – her family was a topic she'd never wanted to talk much about – and he wondered now if he was forming conclusions about her relationship with her father based solely upon his own limited impressions of the man. 'She just comes from a lot of money, you know, and all the baggage that goes with it.'

He was acutely aware of how many times he'd said 'you know' and he knew his mom heard it, too.

'Anders, honey, you're not one usually given to clichés. Not that either of us in our steadfast middle-class ways would know,' she chuckled a bit, 'but what "baggage" would that be?'

He sighed, a little more loudly than he'd intended. 'I don't know,' he said. As if to bolster his argument, he said, 'Her dad just happens to be a jerk, okay?'

'Okaaaay.' His mom tilted her head as though she'd just gained a new understanding of something previously misunderstood. 'So I'm finally starting to understand the attraction between you two.'

He set his fork down and was silent. His leg began to shake under the table. She touched his arm. 'Honey, you're taking that comment the wrong way. I'm not saying it's a bad thing. It's just that the two of you didn't seem to have anything in common, and I'd wondered how you ended up together. That's all.'

He laughed sarcastically. 'Yeah, you and Dad had plenty in common, and look how that turned out.'

But after meeting Lawrence Mayfield, he was beginning to understand just how much he and Olivia *did* have in common. He wondered: had the two of them somehow known the other's history without ever having told each other about it? Was Mayfield violent, too?

His mother ignored his retort and leaned in closer to encourage him to look her in the eye. He did, reluctantly. 'Anders, I love Olivia. She makes you happy and that makes me happy.' She smiled then, and raised an eyebrow. 'I wouldn't have given you Grandma's ring if I didn't feel that way about her. You know that, don't you?'

The mention of the ring caused his eyes to well up. He wondered if he'd ever have the chance to give it to her now.

'So take it in the spirit I meant it, okay?' She unknowingly gave his arm a squeeze in the spot the skin had been ripped off, and he winced.

'It's okay,' he said quickly to reassure her. 'I'm okay.'

\*

HE MET Olivia at the Bentley Palms Golf Resort & Spa – or 'Palmetto' as the employees had nicknamed it, after the euphemistic term most Floridians used in place of the less poetic 'cockroach'. It was the same place he'd met many of the women with whom he ended up sharing a bed. And like the others, she'd been a guest. But in his opinion, all similarities stopped there.

He'd just come from the Lanai, the small restaurant overlooking the 18th green where weary golfers relaxed at the end of their rounds with a cold beer and a burger and fries. He'd violated the rule prohibiting the lawn maintenance crew from entering the restaurant while on duty, and with the help of his friend Shel, one of the waitresses, had snuck through the back to refill his cooler with ice. He'd escaped unseen, and now he and Lenny were in their cart on the way to the supply shed. The weed-whacker had snapped and they needed cable to repair it.

He first spotted her as they crossed behind the 10th tee to reach the shed. She was in the parking lot and had just climbed out of an old white pickup truck wearing a long, billowy skirt. Lenny had seen her, too. Both of them looked at the truck and then looked at each other. The truck was a beater. Most guests drove high-end rentals, and the few who drove their own cars rarely showed up in anything more than several years old unless they were part of the 'drive the Volvo or Saab till it drops dead' set. Anders's first thought was that she must be a new employee, but this idea was quickly dispelled when she walked around to the truck bed and lowered the tailgate to retrieve her luggage.

Lenny was on it.

'Ma'am,' he called out to her, 'would you like some help with that?'

She hesitated, obviously a bit surprised, maybe even made nervous, by the offer. Anders could see her appraising them.

30

'Well, okay,' she said slowly. She must have determined they were legitimate. 'Yes, I'd appreciate that.'

Lenny's face brightened. 'Our pleasure.'

They crossed the lot on foot to her truck. On the way, Anders attempted a furtive whiff of his underarms and then felt himself blush when he realized, by the slight smirk on her face when they reached her, she'd seen him do it.

He could already see Lenny conjuring ways to play the fortuitous meeting, though this woman wasn't his type. In the land of bleached blondes, dark tans (some real and some fake), and swollen breasts and lips (which he knew, more often than not, were both undeniably fake), she stood out with her dark, curly hair and pale skin.

She had three large suitcases in the back bed, and a small duffle with the handle of a tennis racquet sticking out on the passenger seat in the front.

'So you just arrived today,' Lenny said, stating the obvious in his most pleasant Eddie Haskell voice, 'uh, Mrs . . .' He fished for her name and marital status.

'*Miss* Mayfield,' she corrected. 'Yes, I just arrived.'

'Oh, *Miss* Mayfield.' Lenny smiled and nodded a little too emphatically. He could never understand when a softer touch was called for. 'What building are you in?'

She motioned to the building on the north side of the lot. 'I believe they call it Windswept.' She said it without a trace of sarcasm, but Anders had the distinct sense she found it amusing that the buildings had names.

Just as they began to lift the bags from the truck, the walkie-talkie at Lenny's waist buzzed. Though Lenny tried to hide it, Anders could see his resentment at the interruption. Lenny excused himself and stepped away to answer it.

When it became clear Lenny would be a few minutes, the woman turned to Anders and asked, 'So, do you have a name?'

'Yes, ma'am. Anders. Anders Erickson.'

'Ah, Anders Erickson.' She spoke the words with a fake Swedish accent. '*Ar du fran Sverige?*'

'Excuse me?'

'I asked if you were from Sweden.'

'No, ma'am. But my ancestors were.'

She smiled slightly. 'Yes, I figured that. But I must admit, you don't look the part, not with that dark hair of yours.'

'Well, there's Spanish on my mother's side.'

She nodded and continued to stare at him as if she was thinking about that.

Lenny called over to him. 'Hey, Andy, we're gonna have to make this quick. They need us over by the 16th tee. Seems the warthog's been causing trouble again.'

Her green eyes widened, but not with the fear he'd noticed in others when they heard mention of warthogs on the course. She was curious. 'Warthog? I didn't realize there were warthogs in Florida.'

'Yeah, I'm sorry, Miss Mayfield. Once they find a spot they like, it's hard to get rid of them. But Andy and I can—'

She casually interrupted Lenny. 'Tell you what. Why don't you head over there, and if it's not too much trouble Anders can stay behind and help me. I'll give him a lift over in a few minutes.'

Lenny stood motionless, his mouth hanging slightly open. He was unaccustomed to playing second fiddle to Anders and didn't know how to react. He probably wondered how she already knew Anders's name. Before he could protest or suggest an alternative plan, she turned her attention back to Anders.

'I'm in Unit 22, on the second floor.' Her thin arm motioned in the direction of the building.

He lifted her satchel over his right shoulder and picked up two of three suitcases, one in each hand. When Lenny stared at him with narrowed eyes and muttered, 'I'll catch ya later, Andy,' Anders merely gave him a shrug and called out, 'Don't hurt the little guy!' He refused to accept culpability in Lenny's reversal of fortune.

He made two trips, setting everything just inside the entrance to her unit. She followed behind and made a point of using the doorstop to keep the door open. He didn't blame her – she was a woman alone – but he couldn't help but wonder if something about him scared her.

'Don't *hurt* the little guy?' she asked as she passed by him toward the small kitchen.

'He wants to set out a trap, or poison. I've told him he's history if he does. I'll be putting poison in his beer.' He laughed. 'The warthog will move on eventually if we wait him out. We can repair the damage.' He shrugged. 'Anyway, he doesn't deserve to die for it.'

She studied him with probing eyes, and it made him uncomfortable.

He nodded to the suitcases. 'Looks like you plan to be here a while.'

'Hmm, yeah.' Her eyes swept the interior of the small condo with doubt. 'Hopefully, not here, exactly.' For just an instant, she didn't even seem to remember he was in the room with her.

'Is there anything else I can help you with, ma'am?'

She turned to him, returning from wherever her short reverie had taken her. 'Well, for starters, I'd appreciate it if you'd stop calling me ma'am. It makes me feel like you're addressing my mother.' She pulled out two water bottles – pre-stocked, as all the units were – from the refrigerator. He reached out to catch the one she tossed in his direction. 'Second, you can answer a question for me.'

'Yes, ma'am?'

When she frowned, he laughed. 'I'm sorry—'

She raised her hand to interrupt his apology. 'Listen, Anders, how old are you?'

'Twenty-nine, ma' – uh, Miss Mayfield.'

'And how old do you think I am?' She unscrewed the cap from her bottle, took a long drink, and waited for him to answer.

'I don't know, I . . .'

'Come on, just guess.'

He wondered if this was some sort of trick question. He wondered if she'd had plastic surgery, or maybe Botox injections, and wanted to see if they'd been a success. He couldn't imagine this was the case; she wore a minimal amount of make-up and except for the necklace around her neck, she wore no jewellery. She appeared completely oblivious to her windblown hair, and he noticed that her nails, though neat and polished, weren't the acrylic kind many women wore. He wouldn't have taken her for a plastic surgery patient, as so many of them roaming Palmetto were. Overall, she was quite natural-looking, and looked to be near his age. So he wondered, really, about the point of all this.

'I'd guess that you were about my age.'

'And you'd guess right. I'm thirty.'

He nodded, but he wasn't sure what she expected him to do with this information.

'So my question to you is this: if you're twenty-nine, and I'm thirty, then why do you insist on calling me "ma'am"? Or "Miss Mayfield"?'

He heard footsteps on the stairs and glanced out the open door. But it was only two elderly couples passing by on the way to another unit.

'It's just what I was taught, to be respectful.' He grinned. 'Plus, you haven't told me what else to call you, have you?'

'Ah, touché.' This time, the smile she gave him came easily.

'Well, I'd like you to call me Olivia, okay? I'll call you Anders, and you call me Olivia. Deal?'

He wondered how many occasions he'd have to call her anything. Especially if she didn't plan on being there long.

'Deal.'


HE FINISHED his coffee and declined his mother's offer of more. They spent the rest of his visit talking about Karina and her family in Chicago, and Stephen in Sweden. As if they were one big, happy family. As if Karina, Stephen and Anders were the closest of friends.

It wasn't until they stood at the front door, just as he was leaving, that she came back to Olivia.

'She'll be fine, baby. You just be there for her, okay?' *The way he hadn't been there for her, years ago?* 'Don't let her family get to you; just try to remember they're upset, too, and different people express their feelings in different ways.'

From over her shoulder, Levi looked up at him with his sad eyes.

It was her way of apologizing for what she'd said earlier, and he couldn't help but forgive her.

# 3

LENNY TOOK the news of Anders's encounter with Olivia's father the day before in typical Lenny fashion.

'You should have hauled off and hit him.'

That morning, after leaving his mom's house, Anders had stopped by the Mercedes dealership in Maitland to look for a model like the one that had run them off the road. His search was unsuccessful; to his eyes, one black Mercedes looked like all the others. Afterwards, he called the hospital to check on Olivia. He asked Carrie if he might be able to get in again at dinner time, but she seemed doubtful. She told him she'd call if she saw an opening.

He'd spent the rest of the afternoon alone at the house waiting for his cellphone to ring. When the day passed and no call came, he let Lenny persuade him to meet for a beer after Lenny finished work. Anders had taken the rest of the week off – he'd gotten off easily compared to Olivia, but still, he ached. He'd figured it'd be better to shoot the shit with Lenny than sit alone in the dark, quiet house, obsessing over Olivia's condition. They now sat in the bar at the Ocean Deck, eating chicken wings, downing cold Buds on draught and watching football on the overhead television screens.

Anders took a swig of beer and didn't bother to respond to Lenny's comment.

'Was he a big guy?' Lenny asked. 'You are a little scrawny.'

'I'm five eleven and weigh one ninety-five. I don't think most people would consider that scrawny.'

Lenny signalled the waitress for two more beers, and when

she arrived with the mugs, foam sloshing over the edges as she set them on the table, he said, 'Hey, hon, we need your opinion on something.'

'Oh, Christ,' Anders said, shaking his head. 'Let it go, already.'

'Take a look at this guy,' he said, motioning to Anders. 'How would you describe him? We need a lady's point of view.'

The waitress didn't quite understand what was being asked of her. 'Uh, I'm not sure ...'

'Physically, that is,' Lenny clarified. 'His body.'

She smiled at Anders and appraised him. He wondered how many times she'd been asked similar questions by drunken patrons. Though Lenny wasn't even drunk. 'Well, he's sitting down, so it's hard—'

'Stand up, Andy,' Lenny ordered.

Anders mouthed 'fuck off' to him and didn't move.

'– but he appears to be very nicely built.' She touched Anders's shoulder and he gave her a tight-lipped grin. 'I mean, he's obviously not a bodybuilder like you—'

'Uh huh,' Lenny agreed.

'– but he's—'

'Scrawny?'

She laughed. 'No, no, I wouldn't call him scrawny. No, not at all.'

Anders tossed Lenny a 'told you so' look.

'He's tight. Trim and tight.' She'd figured out what Lenny was doing and she carefully chose her words. Either one of them might be the one to leave the tip. 'He's lean. That's the word, I think. Lean. Like a runner.'

Lenny laughed out loud at that; Anders a bit less so, because although the light banter was probably what he needed, Olivia lurked in the back of his mind.

'But those wounds are looking a little nasty,' she added. Her voice was warm, and she touched his shoulder again, well above the spot where his skin had sheared off, to show her empathy.

'Well, let me ask you this, um . . .' Lenny looked at her nametag, pausing to also take in the sight of her breasts bulging from the low scoop of her tank top, 'Tina. What does a woman usually prefer? This,' he motioned to his own body, sitting up straighter, posing slightly, 'or that?' He pointed at Anders.

'Oh, I . . .'

Anders sighed. 'You'll have to excuse my friend, Tina. He's—'

'I think it depends on the woman, Lenny.' Anders turned at the sound of Shel's voice. She'd come up right behind the waitress, and now she winked at him.

Shel was Michele Sampson, Anders's friend, and before Olivia, his former neighbour and sometimes lover. She worked as a waitress at the resort. She was twenty-two years old, but her small, delicate features made her look much younger, and with the seven years between them, he sometimes felt he'd been fooling around with jailbait. The age gap seemed even more pronounced by her frequent insistence that they were just 'friends with benefits'. Though he knew it was just the term her generation gave to a certain attitude that had been around for years, he also knew it had been an attitude adopted primarily by guys. It bothered him a little that now younger women had been taken in by it under the guise of equality. It also bothered him that, despite this, he'd taken advantage of it.

'That's exactly what I was going to say,' Tina said in response to Shel's interruption. 'You're both gorgeous in your own way.'

Anders rolled his eyes, and the waitress used Shel's arrival to get back to work, promising that she'd bring Shel a beer, too. Anders was glad for Shel's intrusion but wondered why she was there. Ever since he'd started dating Olivia, Shel tended to avoid him. She'd called after the accident to see how he was – probably out of a sense of obligation, Anders thought – but he hadn't expected her tonight. Lenny must have run into her on his way from work and invited her along. 'Hey,' was all he said, though, when she took the seat next to him. She gave a tug on her tank top, a mischievous Tinkerbell emblazoned on the front.

'Why all the comparisons about your bodies?' she asked now. With a grunt, she added, 'Usually you're comparing women's bodies, not men's.'

Anders raised his hands in defence. 'Not me.' He pointed at Lenny. 'Him. He's the one hung up on the topic.'

Shel looked at Lenny for an explanation of the discussion she'd interrupted.

'Andy had a run-in with Olivia's dad at the hospital. He had to kiss up to a nurse to get in to see her.'

Anders shot Lenny a look over the top of his beer, pleading with him to tread carefully.

'Oh.' Shel scrunched her top lip in a funny way to indicate she didn't quite follow how that related to their bodies. 'But you saw her?' she asked Anders. 'How's she doing?' She tucked her short, boyish-cut hair behind her ears. Her small hand trembled slightly.

'She's in a coma.'

Shel gasped. To his surprise, her eyes teared up. 'Oh my God.' She looked at Lenny, as if he was to blame, and then back at Anders. 'I'm so sorry. When we talked yesterday, you said you weren't hurt too badly, so I just didn't realize it was so serious.'

When they'd talked the day before, he'd downplayed everything, partly because he'd been trying to convince himself and partly because he'd been talking to Shel. Olivia was not a topic the two of them discussed comfortably.

'She hit her head.' He shifted in his seat. He preferred the lighter conversation that Lenny offered. 'It'll be okay. She'll be okay. The nurse said we just have to give her time.'

'Sure, of course.' She turned briefly and gave Tina a fake smile as she dropped off Shel's beer. 'I'm sure she'll be fine.'

The three of them stared at the television screen then, each ignoring the awkwardness that settled on the table.

Shel finally turned her attention to Lenny. 'I was surprised when you mentioned the Ocean Deck. I thought you had Joey on Wednesday nights.'

'Yeah, I do. But Crystal pulled some shit on me again. She's having some family photographs taken and she claimed tonight was the only night the photographer could come to the house.' He snorted. 'I asked her why she didn't just go to Sears like the rest of America.'

Shel opened her small purse and pulled out a pack of Virginia Slims. 'Can we move to the deck so I can smoke?'

'Fine with me,' Lenny said. 'I could use a smoke myself.'

'Maybe you should just be glad her husband considers Joey family,' Anders said, focusing on Lenny's comment about his ex-wife. Shel knew Anders hated that she smoked, and by not making a move to the outside, he'd sent the message that he didn't want her to now. Like a child that has been publicly shamed by a parent, she silently complied with his unspoken request. She put the cigarettes back in her purse.

'Thanks, buddy, I'll remember that,' Lenny said.

'No, I'm serious.' Anders knew he was entering dangerous waters but he was still a little peeved that Lenny had mentioned Olivia in front of Shel, so he continued unchecked. 'I mean, would you want him living with some guy who doesn't really want him around? Despite what you think of Crystal, you should be happy the guy she married treats Joey like a son.'

'Where do you get off, Andy?'

'And maybe if you actually showed some appreciation,

instead of always responding to her with sarcasm, she wouldn't be so antagonistic.'

'Hey, you guys.' Shel tried to interrupt.

'You don't know what the hell you're talking about.' Lenny leaned forward when he spoke; his voice came out like a growl. 'Just because she sweet-talks you whenever she sees you, you think she's some sort of angel.' He pointed his finger at him. 'Well, let me tell you something. She's no angel. She's the devil incarnate. She's a two-faced bitch.'

Anders had known Lenny since high school, when Lenny's family arrived in Florida from New Jersey. Lenny went back to New Jersey for a few years, though, after the two of them graduated, and that's when he met and married Crystal. So Anders wasn't around to help his friend see beyond the big boobs and the contagious laugh; he wasn't there to subtly suggest that perhaps Lenny should give it more time, wait and see. In fact, when Lenny first arrived back in Florida, Anders suspected his friend had made a colossal mistake. He sensed immediately that Crystal was a climber, and Lenny and Florida were just two rungs near the bottom of her ladder.

Anders's instincts were confirmed when, early in her transformation from New Jersey brunette to Florida blonde, she came on to him at a party. He politely rebuffed her efforts, and kept his mouth shut about it when just weeks later Lenny came to him thrilled with the news of his impending fatherhood. He kept his mouth shut for the next five years, too, as he attended the various birthday parties and barbecues and Christmas parties thrown by Crystal, and overheard her growing complaints about Lenny's job, about the small house they lived in, about the old car she drove, about the schools Joey would attend if they didn't move to a better neighbourhood. He kept his mouth shut as he watched her body grow svelte from her mornings at the gym and her olive skin turn a beautiful shade of brown from her days in the sun. He even kept his mouth shut when

Lenny told him he suspected she'd been fooling around with her personal trainer, and then, shortly afterwards, when he announced their divorce. He was especially careful not to express his lingering paternity fears, but was relieved when Lenny had his own and insisted on testing, which confirmed that, yes, Joey was his. A year after the divorce, Crystal married her divorce lawyer.

So while it was true that Anders had remained on a friendly basis with Crystal, and had, for Joey's sake, often acted as a go-between between Lenny and Crystal, he had no delusions about her. She was drop-dead gorgeous, and yes, she sweet-talked him every time she saw him, but Lenny knew Anders well enough to know he saw right through her.

'It's not about Crystal,' Anders said now. 'It's about you, and your reaction to her.'

'He's got a point,' Shel ventured.

Lenny huffed. 'What? Now you, too?'

'I'm just saying . . .' Her voice trailed off and she picked up her beer.

'Fuck you both.' Lenny sat back in his chair with his arms crossed. After a moment of uncomfortable silence between them, he finally shoved his chair back and stood. 'I'm gonna go have that cigarette.' He looked at Shel. 'You coming?'

Her eyes moved to meet Lenny's, and then Anders's. She shook her head.

When Lenny left, Shel reached over and gingerly touched his forearm, just near the start of the wound. He winced from the mistaken anticipation of the sore itself being touched.

'Does it hurt as bad as it looks?'

'No.'

'Is there stuff I can't see?'

'My leg's a bit messed up, too, but nothing that won't heal.'

They remained silent for a moment. He kept his eyes trained

on the television above the bar while he sucked on his beer, and Shel drew invisible doodles on the table with her finger.

'Anders?'

He cut his eyes in her direction.

'I'm really sorry about Olivia.' He had the sense she referred to more than just Olivia's current predicament. 'I do really hope she gets better. I mean, I know how you feel about her and everything.'

He gave her a tight-lipped smile and nodded.

After a few more minutes, she said, 'Could I ask a favour of you? Do you think you'd be able to drop me by my house on your way home? I know it's out of your way, but I left my car in the shop this morning. Samuel dropped me off.' Samuel was an older, sixtyish waiter at the resort who treated Shel like a daughter. He liked Anders, too, and probably only agreed to give her a ride over because she told him Anders would be there.

He hesitated. He'd come on his Kawasaki sport bike since the Harley was wrecked, and he had only one helmet with him, which he'd have no choice but to let her wear. Even before the accident, he would have dreaded the idea of a long ride in the dark and the bugs without something covering his face. But now, riding naked struck him as pure madness.

But he couldn't deny her this small request.

'Sure, no problem.' He finished what was left of the beer in his mug and waved Tina away when she swung by to ask about another one.


HE BREATHED easier when they pulled onto the long dirt road that led to the small enclave of mobile homes on the edge of the mangrove. Though it'd been months since he'd moved out of the trailer he'd rented adjacent to Shel's, returning to this little outpost of what remained of Florida wilderness still felt like coming home. He was careful to ride in the car tracks, where the ground was more densely packed, and he kept his eye out for an opossum or a raccoon crossing the road, or worse, and far more dangerous, a deer. Shel had been silent for most of the ride home.

'Do you wanna come in for a bit, watch some tube or something?' she asked after she climbed off the bike, handing the helmet back to him.

'Shel—'

'Anders, it's okay. Really. Friends, remember?'

He weighed what to do. If he went straight home, she'd feel rejected and he'd have to face an empty house, a quiet phone, and the long night ahead. Hanging with Shel a while would stave off the inevitable for a few more hours, at least. But if he stayed, and later she wanted more than just someone to watch television with, he'd be forced to confront a much larger issue. But maybe not. Maybe it would never come to that.

And in typical Anders fashion, he followed the path of least resistance. 'Sure,' he said, and climbed off the bike. 'Why not?'

# 4

HE WOKE with his arm flung across Shel's waist and a morning hard-on in his jeans. It took a minute to get his bearings. In the still of dawn, in the brief moment when the night-time insects have stopped their song but before the chatter of the day has begun, he heard the traffic on I-95 and mistook it for the surf.

The small, sleeping figure pinned beneath his arm stirred, and only then did he realize it wasn't Olivia, and he wasn't in the beach house. He was still in Shel's trailer, fully clothed on top of the pull-out sofabed, where they'd watched TV together late into the night. Evidently they'd dozed off, though the TV had been turned off by someone, so he must have succumbed to sleep first.

He carefully lifted his arm so he wouldn't wake her and rose from the bed. After a quick stop in the john, he pulled on his boots and grabbed his helmet and keys off the end table – a hand-me-down, he knew, from Samuel. After fiddling with the knob of the flimsy door so it would lock properly, he stepped onto the concrete riser and quietly pulled the door shut behind him.

DAYS AFTER their first meeting, he'd run into Olivia playing tennis with Sergio Hernandez, the club's tennis pro and resident ladies' man. Sergio stood a lean six foot two, and with his dark eyes, sienna skin and Puerto Rican accent, he melted even the coldest of the women who played on his courts. He was a player in the purest sense of the word.

Anders was trimming some palms near the courts when he saw her. He heard her voice first. 'Love, fifteen,' she called out over the sound of a methodically bounced ball, and he looked up just as she tossed the ball into the air for a serve. He noticed immediately that she was a leftie, because he was, too. She brought the racquet around and over, making contact with the ball – *whump* – and sending it forcefully to the other side of the net. It landed just inside the service box, but Sergio returned it effortlessly, and a rally ensued.

She traversed the court, returning Sergio's long drives with ease and skill. She didn't sport the typical tennis outfit – white skirt and skin-tight tank or tee – worn by most of the women who played here. Instead, she had on what looked to be a pair of men's navy-blue gym shorts and a worn grey T-shirt with the sleeves rolled up to her shoulders. Anders wondered if Sergio had chastised her about it; he was a stickler for rules and saw it as one of his duties to make sure they were followed. Usually it was tennis whites or no tennis. The fact that he'd allowed her to play dressed like this surprised Anders; Sergio had taken a liking to her.

She finally missed a shot when she moved forward to play the net and Sergio sent the ball down alongside the alley, just beyond her reach. She emitted a small 'Oh!' before she turned to the back of the court to retrieve some balls for her next serve. She saw Anders in the same instant that Sergio, who must have noticed him earlier, called out to him.

'Don't you have work to do, Anders?' His tone reflected his unspoken opinion of where they each stood in the employee hierarchy.

'Anders!' Olivia said, greeting him at the back fence before he could respond to Sergio.

He tried to pretend that Sergio wasn't watching his every move as he met her at the fence.

'Hey, *mi chica bonita*,' Sergio called to her, 'are we going to play tennis or are we going to chat with the lawn guy?'

Olivia called over her shoulder to Sergio, 'I'm paying you either way, aren't I?' She winked at Anders and added, 'Anyway, I *asked* him to stop by. He's giving me a ride later on that Harley of his.'

Anders gave her a raise of his eyebrows and a slight smile to show his appreciation for her lie. He could hear Sergio mumbling to himself in Spanish as he grabbed a towel from his gym bag and wiped his brow.

'So, *Olivia*,' he put emphasis on her name so she would notice he hadn't called her ma'am or Miss Mayfield, 'how'd you know I have a Harley?'

'Oh.' She used the back of her hand to wipe her forehead. 'I saw you leave yesterday.'

He offered her the towel that hung out of his back pocket. 'It's clean,' he assured her as he pushed it through the fence. 'New day, new towel.'

She wiped the sweat from her face. Her hair was pulled back with a rubber band, but shorter dark tendrils had escaped and clung to her temples and neck.

'You don't look like a Harley guy.'

He laughed. 'And what's a Harley guy look like?'

'You know, a little heavier, older, lots of leather, lots of tattoos, hairier–'

'Hairier?'

'You know what I mean!' she said in a high, girlish voice.

'How do you know I don't have tattoos? Maybe you just can't see them.'

Her face, already flushed from tennis, turned a shade redder. 'Well, even if you do, you still wouldn't look like a Harley guy.'

'Is that good or bad?'

Sergio interrupted their conversation before she could

answer. 'O-li-vi-a!' He stretched out each syllable, emphasizing the long 'O'. 'Though I'm getting paid to spend time with you, Mr Erickson isn't. You really should let the muchacho get back to his job.'

She rolled her eyes. 'I'll be right there!' She started to back away from the fence, but her ankle twisted and she let out a small cry as she flung out an arm to break her fall. Her racquet bounced to the ground.

Anders called to her, asking if she was all right, but he darted to the opening in the fence without waiting for the answer and reached her at the same time as Sergio. She was sitting on the court rubbing her right ankle; her eyes held tears and he could tell she was working hard not to let them fall. Sergio stood above her and held out a hand for her to grab hold.

Anders squatted next to her and shot him a look. 'Give her a second, will ya?'

'I'm okay,' she insisted.

'Come on, you've gotta walk it off,' said Sergio.

She started to move but Anders saw her wince. He directed her attention away from Sergio's instructions by saying, 'Why don't we take a look first, just to be sure?'

Sergio shifted his weight impatiently behind her; Anders knew the action was meant for him. He untied her tennis shoe and gently removed it.

'I'll get it,' she said, and carefully peeled off her sock. Bubblegum-pink toenails popped out at him as she wriggled her foot.

'How's it feel? Is that better?'

'Yeah. I think I just bruised it.'

Sergio sighed. 'Anders, I'm sure she's fine. Why don't you let me take over from here *while you get back to your job*?'

Anders bristled at the comment. He could feel Olivia's gaze on him as she waited to see how he'd respond.

'I think we should let Olivia tell us if she's fine.' He offered her his hand as Sergio had earlier. 'Do you think you can stand on it?'

She grabbed on, nodding, and let him pull her up. 'Really, I'm okay, Anders. Thank you.' She glanced at Sergio. 'But I think I'm done for the day.'

Sergio glimpsed at his watch and shrugged. 'Okay, *mi hermosa*. Same time tomorrow, yes?'

She nodded again without looking at him, and he took off to start collecting balls in preparation for his next lesson.

Anders gathered Olivia's things from the ground and helped her over to her bag. As she sat on the bench and put her sock and shoe back on, he retrieved his towel.

'Is he always like that?' she asked when he returned and sat next to her.

He laughed. 'He doesn't like that you haven't fallen head over heels in love with him, like most of his female clients.'

She reached in her bag for a bottle of water, and after taking a drink, she offered him some. He shook his head.

'Well, he's probably right. I should get back to work.' He nodded at her foot. 'Are you sure it's okay?'

'Yeah, it's fine. Just sore.'

When he stood to leave, she asked, almost shyly, 'Anders? Am I going to get that ride?'

It took him a minute to realize she was serious, but once he did, he also realized she'd just answered his question about not looking like 'a Harley guy'.


WHEN HE got home from Shel's, he tried to reach Carrie, but the nurse who answered the phone in the ICU told him that she hadn't come on duty yet. He asked about Olivia, but she refused to give him any information. He considered whether to just go to the hospital and try to talk to her father again, but in the end, he didn't. He wasn't a pessimist, but he *was* a realist.

Later, he called again. He learned Carrie was on duty, but that she was too busy to come to the phone. Busy with what, he wondered, the idling nervous tension in his gut rising again. Carrie had told him Olivia was her sole patient, so if she was busy, something must be horribly wrong. Otherwise, why couldn't she step away for just a moment to put his mind at ease? He wavered between feeling like a needy pest to thinking he wasn't pushing hard enough. He left a polite message, asking her to call him, but when several hours passed and he still hadn't heard back, he tried a third time. Still no success.

On Friday morning he tried once more, and when he received the same, institutional response – 'We're sorry sir, Carrie is unavailable just now' – he slammed the phone down, grabbed his helmet, and raced toward the hospital on his bike.


HE PRESSED the buzzer at the entrance to the ICU and waited for someone to open the door. He'd checked the waiting room and had seen no signs of her family, so he thought perhaps he could talk Carrie into allowing him another brief visit. When an older nurse came to the door, he asked if Carrie was on duty. He didn't let on that he knew she was, that he was the same person who'd called that morning.

'Can I tell her your name, sir?'

She returned without the delay he'd expected and informed Anders in a short manner that Carrie was unavailable. As she turned her back on him, pulling the door behind her, he shoved his foot into the gap to prevent it from closing.

'Unavailable? What does that mean, exactly?'

The nurse looked up at him over the top of her bifocals,

her lips pursed in a sour circle. 'It means she is unavailable to see you right now.' She spoke to him as if he was an idiot for even asking.

'But it means she's here? She's in there?'

'Yes sir, but—'

'Then when *can* she see me? I'll wait.'

The woman placed one hand on a hip. 'Sir, this is a hospital. Carrie is here to work, not to have social visits.'

'I'm not here for a social visit. I'm here to discuss a patient.'

She sighed. 'Okay, what is the name of the patient? I'll relay that to her.'

*Finally.* 'Olivia Mayfield. Carrie will already know . . .'

He stopped mid-sentence when the nurse's face changed visibly from perturbed to nervous at the sound of Olivia's name.

'Sir, we have no one here by that name.' Her tone was brisk.

Panic clutched him. 'What do you mean?'

'Just what I said. If you want more information, I suggest you speak to the desk downstairs. Now, I need to get back to my patients.'

She tried to close the door again but he grabbed her arm. 'And I need to see Carrie.'

'You will remove your hand from me or I will call security and have you arrested.'

He released his grip. 'Ma'am, please . . .'

She pulled on the door again and it clicked loudly as the occupants of the ICU were once again securely sealed from the threats of the outside world.


HE SAT on the kerb with his helmet, numb to the scorching heat of the midday sun as it baked his skin. He'd already spent a good part of an hour trying to extract further information from the women at the information desk in the lobby, but they would only confirm that no one by the name of Olivia

Mayfield was a patient at the hospital. Had Anders not seen her lying in the hospital bed with his own eyes, he'd doubt whether she'd ever been there at all.

The only information he'd managed to obtain was that Carrie's shift ended at one, which was only another hour, so he decided to wait for her. He had no idea whether she would come out of the front entrance of the hospital, but he'd observed enough hospital personnel coming and going from this parking lot that he figured it was a possibility. And really, at this point, what other options did he have?

Carrie emerged at ten after one. He had moved to a shady spot under one of the many palm trees lining the parking lot, but he was weak from hunger and heat and had taken to closing his eyes in short intervals. He might have missed her if he hadn't opened them when he did.

He jumped up and called her name across the lot. She quickened her pace.

'Carrie!' he called out again and ran after her until he reached the driver's side of her car, an old, rusty Honda Civic. Her hands trembled as she jimmied with the key in the lock. She didn't look at him.

'Do you want some help with that?' Despite his escalating panic, he asked the question with an eerily steady voice.

She cried out at the absurdity of his question and whirled around with her back against the car. Her keychain still dangled from the door. She covered her face with her hands for a moment and then looked up at him. Tiny red lines marred the whites of her eyes; the thin skin under them was dark against her otherwise pale face.

'I just want you to leave me alone, okay?'

'What—'

'I can't tell you anything. I can't answer your questions. Bev already told you everything.'

'Everything? Are you out of your mind?'

'I just need you to stay away from me, okay?' She turned to her keys again and after unlocking the door, she yanked it open, forcing Anders back. But he held the door against her efforts to pull it shut. *What the hell was going on?*

Shaking, she struggled with the ignition in the same way she'd struggled with the lock.

'Carrie, look at me, will you?'

She gripped the steering wheel with her left hand but pulled back quickly from the heat with an 'Ow!' Her body went limp in the seat and she started to cry.

'Look at me, please,' he said quietly. His gut was wrenching but he knew he couldn't go berserk or she'd retreat.

She looked up at him reluctantly.

'Listen to what you're saying to me. Why are you acting so strange, so different from the other day? What about the tattoo?'

'Because I got in a lot of trouble for bringing you into the ICU.' Her voice was high-pitched and shrill. 'I almost got fired!'

Anders took a step back. 'I'm sorry. Did her dad find out?'

She shrugged and looked up at the roof of her car. 'I don't know what happened. I just know *someone* ratted on me, okay?' She started the engine. 'I've gotta go now.'

He moved closer again. 'Please, won't you just tell me if . . .'

She gave the car just enough gas so that the door cleared his body and she could pull it shut. To his surprise, she didn't drive off. Her window went down, and he stared at her in stunned silence for a moment and then finished his sentence. '. . . if she's alive?'

'I . . .' She tucked her hair behind her ears with a trembling hand. Her face shone with perspiration. 'I'm really sorry. I know it doesn't seem it, but I really am.' She nodded in a way that suggested she was trying to convince herself. She squinted her eyes at something behind him, then, and when he turned to see what it was, she drove away.

HE STILL remembered handing Olivia a helmet for the first time, helping her adjust the strap. She'd lifted her chin, exposing her neck to him, and the action of tugging the strap tighter, then tucking a few fingers underneath to make sure it wasn't too snug, had felt incredibly intimate.

They'd taken back roads – he hated the highway and he'd wanted to show her a Florida without amusement park billboards and strip malls and gated neighbourhoods. It wasn't until they approached the Dunlawton Bridge leading to beachside that she admitted she was searching for a particular house in Wilbur-by-the-Sea. At a stoplight she showed him a piece of paper with directions to an address on Atlantic Avenue, and he knew immediately it was either on the ocean or across the street from it.

He finally came upon the manatee-shaped mailbox that the directions claimed marked the house she was looking for.

'This must be it,' she hollered from behind him.

The small grey cottage sat at the top of a slight incline. Though the yard might have been landscaped at some point in the distant past, everything was now severely overgrown and the windows were boarded up. A screen door on the front hung precariously by one hinge; the screen was torn and flapped in the breeze. The roof was missing numerous shingles and appeared to have caved in at one corner.

He shut down the engine. After a moment of silence, he removed his helmet and looked over his shoulder at her. 'Is this what you were expecting?'

'Yeah, I think it was.'

'Shall we?'

She accepted the hand he offered to help her from the bike. They followed a coquina path that must have been a driveway at one time. She didn't turn to take the flagstone steps up to the front door, but instead kept walking toward the rear. Rotted wood steps at the side led to a deck at the back, and they both stopped on the top step to take in the magnificent view of the wide beach and the Atlantic Ocean in front of them.

'Wow.' Anders knew that no matter what they found on the inside, the value of the property rested completely on this sight. 'Who owns this place, anyway?'

He looked at Olivia; she stood still, mesmerized by the view. Her brow was furrowed, not from displeasure, or even concern, but simply from deep thought. He wondered if she'd even heard him.

But finally she turned, looked up at him, and said, 'I do.'

The news didn't surprise him, per se; she clearly came from money and he knew many of the vacant properties on the beach were owned by northerners who used them a few days out of the year, if that. But he felt something inside him then, a stirring of the possibilities.

'I guess I should find out just how bad it is,' she said. He followed her around to the front door as she dug in her small backpack for keys. 'I think the boarded-up windows might be a bad sign, huh?'

'No, actually they're a good sign. It means someone bothered to protect the place from hurricanes before leaving.'

He pulled the screen door to hold it open, and it came right off the remaining hinge.

'Whoops,' he said and let it fall to the ground beside him. She laughed, and he knew then that no matter what they found, it would be okay.

She gasped when they stepped inside and some sort of small tan furry creature scurried across the terrazzo floor and out the door. Anders had seen too many movies, he guessed, because he expected to walk into a room of old furniture covered in sheets and cobwebs. But the house, save a few two-by-fours leaning against one wall, some old wrought-iron lawn furniture in the kitchen, and a stained mattress in one of the two bedrooms, was empty. And though the bathroom happened to be in the same corner as the caved-in roof, most of the rotted wood, insulation, and other debris had landed in the tub. The small room was musty and the contents of the tub mouldy from constant exposure to the rain, but if this was the worst of it, she'd be lucky.

He found her standing in the doorway to the south-east bedroom, looking across the dark room to the double set of French doors that, once the plywood was removed, would open up to the sea. The south wall boasted a large picture window, though it too was covered. He knew she was considering the room's potential.

'Would you help me remove the wood?'

'You might want to wait until—'

'Just on this room. Please?'

He debated whether to try to talk her out of it. He didn't know her plans for the house, and he was ninety-nine per cent certain he wouldn't find any tools around the place that would enable him to replace the wood once they'd pulled it down. But the eagerness in her eyes didn't leave him the option of saying no.

They went back around to the rear deck, and when he couldn't remove the plywood with his bare hands, he took off down the road to one of the mansions under construction and returned with a piece of metal tie rod he found lying in the sand. He used it as a lever to pry the wood away from the house. Once exposed, the French doors opened from the outside with a simple tug and he made a mental note to add that to the list of things that needed fixing.

'Oh my God, it's beautiful.' She stepped into the room and turned on her heels to look back out at the ocean.

'Well, it could be, that's for sure. The whole place could be.'

'What do you think? How long would it take?'

He hesitated. 'Well, I'm not sure . . . That depends on–'

'I was hoping not to have to stay at the resort for more than a week or two. I hate it there.'

'You're thinking of *living* here?'

She nodded, smiling widely at him.

'Uh . . .' He was at a loss for words. 'I think a week or two is a little unrealistic.'

'Will you help me?'

'Olivia, you can't possibly tackle this yourself. There's a lot to be done here.'

'No, I mean help me figure out what needs to be done, find the right people to do it.'

Her enthusiasm was contagious and he found himself agreeing to whatever she asked. Within minutes, she had pulled a pen and small pad of paper from her backpack and was dragging him from room to room, making a list of everything that needed to be done to make the house liveable. He noticed that she also scribbled a list of the furniture she envisioned for each room. He wondered if he'd be asked to accompany her on a shopping trip, too. Anyone else and he would have laughed out loud at such a request; with Olivia, he knew already he'd follow her halfway around the world if that's what she wanted.

ANDERS LAY on the bed, curled up on his side and hugging Olivia's pillow. Despite the lingering heat of the day, the doors to the deck were wide open and he watched the pelicans dive for their evening meal over the calm ocean. He kept replaying in his head what had happened at the hospital: first the nurse's strange expression at the door to the ICU when he'd mentioned Olivia's name, and then Carrie's odd behaviour and her refusal to share the smallest bit of information so he'd have a fighting chance of figuring things out on his own. How could he be lying here in Olivia's house, on her bed, surrounded by her things, and yet have no idea where she was, whom she was with, *whether she was dead or alive*?

He grabbed his cellphone from the nightstand. Sitting on the edge of the mattress, he gazed at the ocean without seeing it and waited patiently through three rings.

'Hey, Anders, how are you?' asked Nathan only after Anders identified himself. They spoke so infrequently that his brother-in-law never recognized Anders's voice when he called. Anders didn't hold it against him; despite his strained relationship with Karina, he generally liked Nathan. And he wasn't so sure he would recognize Nathan's voice, either, if the tables were turned. 'How's Olivia?'

'I'm okay, but I can't say the same about her.'

'But Mom said you saw her, right?'

Anders knew that any updates he provided to his mother were promptly relayed to Karina in Chicago, and possibly, even, to his brother in Sweden. But neither had bothered to call him.

'Yeah, once.' Anders sighed. 'But she's sort of disappeared.'

Nathan remained silent at the other end. He was a criminal defence attorney and Anders figured he'd been trained in the art of extracting the most information from witnesses. Leave an open space and people can't help but fill it. Like he had at his mom's house, Anders complied.

'I went back to the hospital today, and it's like she never existed. No one will tell me if she's still there or if she left, or whether she's even alive. They don't even acknowledge she *was* there.'

'Man, I'm sorry. What can I do to help?'

'I'm just wondering ... is there a way ...' His voice broke and he stopped. 'Sorry.'

Again, Nathan waited.

'Is there a way to find out if she ...'

Anders sucked in, and to his relief, Nathan picked up on what he wanted to ask. 'Well, you know there'll be a death cert–'

'I know, but that'll take a while, won't it?'

'To show up in the public records, yeah. But what I mean is that the hospital would know. I would think they'd tell you that, at least.'

*Did he even hear what Anders had just said?*

'That's what I thought, too. But they won't tell me anything.'

He heard Nathan sigh. 'You want me to give them a call for you?'

Anders could feel every muscle in his body tighten. He remained still on the bed, but inside, he burned. He knew what Nathan was thinking. Nathan might like his wife's brother, but he didn't necessarily *respect* him. He wasn't necessarily *impressed* with Anders as a whole, despite how 'intelligent' he was supposed to be. Anders sometimes wondered if perhaps Karina had married a younger version of their father; a more agreeable, less oppressive, less *violent* version, he hoped, but a version nevertheless.

'Sure, if you think it might help. I'd appreciate that.'

LATER, AFTER she'd completed her tour of the inside of the house, he carried two wrought-iron chairs onto the deck and they dug into the Valencia oranges they'd purchased at a farm stand on the way to the beach, the sticky juice covering their fingers and their lips.

'It's really gorgeous here, isn't it?' She motioned to the ocean. 'Do you ever tire of it?'

'Never. I love it and I never take it for granted.' He regarded her carefully as, one by one, she put her fingers in her mouth and licked the juice from each. 'But I suspect you're used to magnificent views, too. Perhaps not this particular one, but I'd venture a guess you've seen quite a few.'

She looked away from him, squinted out over the water. He turned, expecting to see a ship in the distance, or a dolphin. But if she saw something, he wasn't privy to it. 'Have you ever wanted to leave everything behind?' she asked, turning back to him. 'Start over?'

The question surprised him, coming from a woman he barely knew. But he considered it. He knew he'd left plenty of opportunities behind; his father had made that abundantly clear. But he thought she was talking about more than that. She was talking about a whole life: people, places, memories.

'Not really. I love my life.'

'You're lucky.'

'You seem pretty lucky yourself.' He motioned at the house.

'I am . . . I know I am.'

'But?'

She sighed. 'Anders? Would it be okay if I told you something about myself?'

'I would be honoured.' And he meant it.

And that's when she told him the story of her African birth.

She explained how her pregnant mother had accompanied her father to Kenya for an important business meeting with his overseas sales force – 'Of course, all of my father's business meetings were important,' she said wryly – and that when her mother went into early labour, her father had insisted the cramps were nothing more than Braxton Hicks contractions. He'd ignored the doctor's advice and insisted they continue with the month-long safari they'd planned through Tanzania and Kenya.

'I was born in Kenya because my father was too stubborn and too proud to be told he was wrong,' she said, 'and my mother wasn't one to overrule him.'

As a result, Olivia was delivered in the middle of the African bush with the umbilical cord around her neck and only nurse-maids from a local Maasai tribe to assist her mother. 'As soon as my mother and I were stabilized enough to travel, we were both airlifted out of the camp near the edge of the Ngoron-goro Crater and taken to Nairobi, where my father's private corporate jet picked us up and flew us immediately to Paris.'

'What did your dad do that took him to Africa for busi-ness meetings?' Anders asked.

'Pharmaceuticals. His company does a lot of research and development of experimental drugs here in the States, but the manufacture and distribution of generics around the world has always been his bread and butter.'

'Well, it makes a good story,' he offered in an effort to make her smile.

'Yeah,' she said, laughing sarcastically. 'I suppose it served me well on college entrance essays and at the mandatory cock-tail parties with politicians and the CEOs of major corporations. I'm sure my father thought the risk to my life was worth it for that alone.'

'Was your father really that bad? He was probably just proud of you and showed it in a strange way.' He wasn't sure why he asked the question. He'd always hated it when others made excuses for his own father or downplayed the impact of his actions.

She didn't answer directly. 'You know, I spent most of my childhood bouncing between our house in Connecticut, a summer home on Nantucket, and Africa, yet he always talked about our travels as if spending months at a time in Africa was no different than a drive in the family station wagon down to Clearwater Beach. That's what infuriated me the most. Because I knew better. I knew my life was different from most, that I had every available privilege and then some. And yet ...'

She trailed off. He raised his eyebrows slightly, encouraging her to say it. Letting her know it was safe to say it. 'When I really needed him, he was never there.'

'How do you mean?'

She shrugged and averted her eyes. 'I don't know. Just everything.' She looked deflated, as though she'd told him more than she'd intended and now regretted it.

'Did you feel loved?' he asked quietly.

She studied him for a moment before answering. 'By my mom, yes,' she said. 'But not my father.'

Anders remained silent at the distinction; he wasn't quite sure how to respond, or even if he should. Had someone asked him the same question, his answer would have been identical.

'Is he still alive?' he finally asked.

'Yeah, but he sold his soul long ago in the name of the almighty dollar.'

'Well, I gotta be honest.' He laughed a little. 'If you're trying to get away from that, perhaps Florida isn't your best choice. At times it can seem the state is for sale to the highest bidder.'

She looked at the house. 'Then maybe I should just go back to that from whence I came, huh? It's where I really belong, I think.' She turned to him and smiled a bit, and he was glad he'd finally been able to lighten her mood. But he was already getting used to the idea of her living in this house, and he didn't like that she might be reconsidering.


THE PHONE made a noise and he jerked awake.

He flipped the phone open. 'Nathan?'

His question was met with silence and when he looked at the screen he saw why. The phone hadn't been ringing; it had been signalling the receipt of a text message. This was a feature of the phone Anders had never used, not once. In fact, he'd never used the phone for anything other than making and receiving calls, and he was at a loss as to how to retrieve the message. Where was Shel when he needed her?

'It's gotta be intuitive,' he said to himself as he began pressing what looked to be logical buttons. A few seconds later the words 'sorry call dad' appeared on the miniature screen, followed by a phone number. He stared at it, not comprehending what it meant or whom had sent it. Why wouldn't Nathan have just called him? And how could it help to call his dad, of all people? He considered whether to just dial the number on the screen, but he didn't think this was the best thing to do until he knew whom he'd be calling and why.

The phone rang, then, as he held it in his hand. He recognized the Chicago area code and knew this time it was Nathan. Good. Maybe he'd explain.

'Bad news,' Nathan said. 'It was like talking to Fort Knox. I couldn't get them to tell me anything.'

'Yeah, it figures.'

'Maybe you can file a missing person report. The cops would be able to find out real fast whether she left the hospital alive.'

Anders ignored the comment, though he stored the idea in the shadows of his brain in case he needed it later, if he became really desperate. 'Did you send me a text message?' he asked.

'What?'

'Just before you called me back, I got a text message. I thought it was from you.'

'No, wasn't me. What'd it say?'

'It said "sorry call dad" and then it had a phone number.'

'Dad? *Your* dad?'

'I don't know.'

'Well, look to see who sent it.'

Anders didn't respond immediately. 'I don't know how,' he finally admitted.

Nathan laughed and then walked him through the steps to determine who had left the message. Anders hung up and followed the instructions. All he found was a phone number he didn't recognize.

'Read it off to me,' Nathan said when he called him back, 'and I'll run a quick Internet search for you.'

The search revealed only that the number belonged to a cellphone originating from Winter Park, Florida, but the name of the phone's owner was unavailable.

'So someone who lives in the same state as you sent you a cryptic text message with a phone number,' Nathan mused. 'Have you dialled it?' Before Anders could answer, he added, 'Wait! Give me the number they sent you.'

Anders sighed. 'I'll call you back again.' He fumbled through the same steps he'd taken earlier to find the message and this time wrote down the number before calling his brother-in-law one more time.

He listened to Nathan's fingers tapping on the computer keyboard a thousand miles away.

'Well, same problem,' Nathan said with a sigh. 'But this number originates from Connecticut.'

Bingo. How could he have not realized it? The apology alone should have given it away. Carrie had come through after all, in the only way she felt she could without jeopardizing her job.

She'd sent him Lawrence Mayfield's phone number.


AFTER THE oranges had been eaten, she'd wanted to put her feet in the water. The stairs leading from the deck to the beach were in worse shape than the ones leading from the drive to the deck, so he jumped down first and lifted her like a child over the broken steps.

She rolled up the legs to her jeans and kicked about in the shallow part of the surf. 'It's warm!' she called over to him at his spot on the sand. He laughed, and she added, 'It's never this warm up north.'

Eventually she tired of her play and plopped down next to him. The sand clung to her wet cuffs but she didn't seem to notice or care. She pulled off her jean jacket, folded it up as a pillow, and lay back, knees in the air. He lay back, too, and closed his eyes. The sun was high now and he felt the heat on his face, but the sand was cool and the breeze coming off the water kept the temperature mild.

He must have dozed, because when he opened his eyes he saw that the tide had gone out and they were now much closer to the house than they were to the water line. He glanced over at her and was surprised to see not that she was sleeping – which she was – but that she had unzipped her jeans and pushed them lower on her hips, and had rolled up her top to just below her breasts. She showed less skin than if she wore a bikini, but he was a guy, and the sight of a partially disrobed woman turned him on just as easily as the sight of a practically naked one would have.

He closed his eyes again but he couldn't get the image of the open jeans and her exposed stomach out of his mind. He felt his own jeans get tighter. 'Damn,' he moaned under his breath.

He glanced over once more and another surprise greeted him. A four-inch line of white goop snaked down the middle of her stomach, just to the left of her belly button. He chuckled; nothing like well-placed seagull crap to kill the libido.

He considered what to do. He couldn't leave it there. He didn't want to wake her, but he didn't have anything he could use to wipe it off. She'd dropped her backpack in the sand a few feet behind them, so he retrieved it and spent a few moments pawing through the contents, looking for a tissue or a wet wipe, anything that could do the job. But of all he found – the pad of paper and pen, a hair pick, some keys, a small wallet, a bottle of sunscreen (that he realized now, he hadn't seen her apply), some lip gloss, and a prescription bottle – none of it served his needs.

He was about to toss the pack aside when out of sheer nosiness he picked up the prescription bottle. It had piqued his interest because it lacked a label; it lacked any kind of identifying information. He popped open the top and looked inside. He guessed there were maybe ten, twelve miniature blue pills at the bottom. He turned the bottle upside down and tapped a few into his palm, all the while feeling like some sort of cat burglar. He brought his hand closer and tried to make out the tiny writing on the pill. Cranitex MR. *Cranitex MR?* He'd never heard of it. He supposed that wasn't so odd; it wasn't like he was an expert on pharmaceuticals, but he'd expected it to be some sort of pain reliever, or maybe even a recognizable antidepressant, given the history she'd described. He finally wrote it off as another female mystery that was best left unsolved and tossed the bottle back in the pack.

He pondered the bird poop dilemma. Realizing he'd run out of alternatives, he unbuttoned his shirt and still wearing it, scooted close to her, gathered up the shirt-tail in his hand, and very gently began to wipe the small mess from her skin. He had almost finished when her eyes flung open and she shrieked. In an instant she was up on her elbows and edging her whole body up the sand away from him.

'What are you doing?' she cried. He'd already removed his hand at the sound of the shriek, but she pushed at it anyway and continued to scoot backwards.

'Whoa.' He raised his hand in the air in surrender. 'Olivia, Olivia! It's okay. It's okay.' The panic in her eyes lessened slightly and changed to confusion. 'A bird took a – went to the bathroom on your stomach.' He ventured a smile, to reassure her. 'I was just wiping it off for you.' He sat up and showed her the corner of his shirt.

A meek sound that could have been a laugh escaped her lips. A sound of relief.

'You okay?' he asked.

She nodded.

He looked her in the eye; he wasn't convinced. 'You sure?'

'Yeah, yeah. I'm okay. I'm sorry I freaked out.' She took a deep breath as if trying to calm herself.

He removed the shirt and went to the water's edge to rinse out the soiled shirt-tail. When he finished he put it back on, because even though the bottom half was wet, he sensed now was not the time to walk around shirtless in front of her.

When he returned, he saw that she'd pulled up her jeans and rolled down her shirt in his absence, though she still lay on her back in the sand. He sat a few feet away with his knees bent, arms across his knees, chin on his arms, watching the surf.

'Anders?'

He looked over his shoulder.

'I'm sorry if you think I overreacted.'

'I'm sorry I startled you. I should have just woken you up.'

He turned back to the surf. Closed his eyes and listened to the waves.

'Anders?'

He smiled and answered this time with his eyes still shut, his face to the sea. 'Hmm?'

'What do you think?'

'About what?'

'About the house. Should I stay?'

'Are you asking what I would do, or what you should do?'

'Both.'

'I would stay in a heartbeat.'

'And what about me?'

He'd only spent half a day with her, but he knew the intensity of his growing attraction prevented him from giving her an unbiased answer.

'I can't answer for you. I barely know you.'

'Would you like to? Even after everything I've told you?'

He still hadn't turned again to face her, but now he did. 'Yes.'

She smiled, held his eyes with hers. 'Come here.'

He lay down on his side next to her, his head propped up with his hand.

'Closer.'

He leaned in, the slightest grin growing on his face.

'Closer. I want to tell you something.' She was whispering now. He was right at her face, his ear to her lips. The wind blew her hair and it softly tickled his cheek.

'I want you to kiss me.' The words came out low and raspy. 'I've wanted you to kiss me all day.'

She hadn't even touched him and he was about to explode.


ALL HE knew about Lawrence Mayfield was what she'd told him that first day on the beach and what he'd experienced himself at the hospital. But it was enough. It was like being forced to call his own dad.

He paced through the house with the phone in one hand and the piece of paper with Mayfield's number on it in the other. He opened the refrigerator, reached for another beer, and then put it back. He'd lost count of how many he'd drunk over the past few hours, but he suspected it might have been enough to give him *too* much courage, and Lawrence Mayfield would pick up on that.

He stood out on the deck next, but decided the wind would make it difficult to hear. He returned to the house, to the bedroom first and then to the bathroom to relieve himself. As he stood in front of the toilet, he stared at her things on the little shelf above the tank: a bottle of White Linen cologne, a pink disposable razor, her birth control pills.

He returned to the bedroom. He opened the closet and eyed the taped shoebox on the top shelf. He fingered her hanging clothes, touching the jean jacket she'd worn on their first ride to the beach, so many months ago, it seemed. *Why hadn't she worn it that day to the springs?* he wondered now. But it wouldn't have mattered; it was her head that had needed protection, not her skin.

He thought back to the hospital room and pictured again how Carrie had lifted Olivia's dark curls to show him what she'd discovered. Olivia had marked herself for him.

He told himself to just get it over with. Taking a deep breath, he opened the phone and dialled the number.


HE WASN'T going to bother with hello. He planned to avoid all social niceties, even though it went against everything he'd been taught as a kid. His fear remained, but it had been sharpened by anger. That anger had pushed etiquette right out the door.

'Hello, Andy.' The cold greeting startled Anders, not because it was cold – he'd expected that – but because her father had identified him before he'd identified himself.

'Mr Mayfield, this is Anders Erickson. I spoke to the hospital and they told me that Olivia has been discharged.'

The hospital had told him no such thing; the hospital had refused to tell him anything, other than the fact that she wasn't a patient. He was well aware this didn't necessarily mean she'd been discharged. Let Mayfield think he knew more than he did.

He heard a small snicker. But Anders resolved not to let it bother him, because such behaviour had to mean she was okay, didn't it?

'Is that what they told you?'

'Yes.' He would not call him sir. It required a conscious effort, but he refused to grant him that one small concession. 'I'd like to know how she's doing, and where she is.'

'I'm surprised you care.' This time the man made a scoffing

noise. 'After all, it didn't take you long to spend the night with another woman.'

Anders's spine tingled at Mayfield's accusation. 'Are you *following* me?'

'Are you denying it?'

'She's my friend, for Christ's sake!' He knew his tone was too loud, too defensive, but he couldn't help it.

'Andy, who gave you this number?'

Anders remained silent; he'd caused Carrie enough trouble and he wouldn't betray her now.

'It seems we've lost reception . . .' Mayfield began.

'I'm not able to answer that question.'

'No?'

'Because I don't know,' he lied.

Mayfield broke into a full-fledged laugh. Anders could feel his contempt through the phone line. 'A little birdie dropped it in your lap?'

Anders began to understand the only way to deal with this man was to stay on the offensive. 'Where is Olivia?' he asked.

He wasn't sure what he expected him to say. Certainly there'd been no indication that her father would ever consider Anders worthy of information of any kind, much less the truth. He didn't know the reason for the man's intense disdain of him. Perhaps it was something as simple as thinking Anders was a bad influence on his daughter, a freeloader who'd somehow worked his way into her life, her house, and God forbid, even her heart. Maybe he thought Anders was after her money, *his* money. Or maybe it was simpler than that, even. Maybe he really did blame Anders for the accident, and believed he was someone she needed to be rescued from. End of story.

But Anders had always shied away from any effort to prove himself to others, especially when he sensed it would be futile. And with Lawrence Mayfield, he'd sensed it was futile from the minute he'd walked into the hospital waiting room.

So even though he'd asked the question in the most direct way possible, he fully expected her father to continue the game of cat and mouse. And he fully expected to play along for now, if only to glean the truth from any morsels Mayfield might inadvertently leave behind.

He didn't expect to be dropped on an entirely different playing field, without a warm-up, without the proper equipment, without a team.

'Olivia is no longer with us.' Before Anders could respond, to ask for clarification, he added, 'She succumbed to her injuries.'

He didn't move. It took a few moments to process the meaning of the words. Surprisingly, Mayfield didn't hang up.

'When?' he finally managed to ask. He knew it was a stupid question, but he was incapable of lucid thought just then.

'Does that really matter? You killed my daughter and all you can think to say is "when?"'

Anders collapsed onto the bed. 'I'm sorry.' His voice came out small. 'Will you please tell me what happened? Did she ever come out of the coma?' All he could think was that she might have woken up and wondered where he was, why he wasn't there. He didn't care anymore if he disclosed his knowledge of information that was supposed to have remained confidential. He just knew that if he didn't keep talking he would fall apart.

'Perhaps you should tell *me* what happened,' Mayfield said. 'Or would you rather wait and tell my lawyers?'

'What?' *What was he talking about?* He'd lost all ability to make sense of anything. The accident, the encounters at the hospital with both Mayfield and Carrie, this conversation, how the man knew he'd been at Shel's, the idea that Olivia was gone. Olivia. Gone. He glanced around the room as if he was already realizing he'd never share the space again with her.

'Mr Erickson,' it was the first time her father had called him anything but Andy, 'I intend to press charges against you. And

I might just pursue a civil action, also. As far as I'm concerned, you are responsible for Olivia's death, and I consider your apology a moment ago to be an admission of your culpability.'

'Are you fuckin' crazy?' he yelled into the phone, finally losing it. 'I already told the cops what happened. Since when does getting run off the road qualify as a crime?' His voice was loud but it quavered, and even though her father had no way of seeing his tears, Anders knew the man was aware he'd started to cry. Mayfield's sense of satisfaction was palpable through the phone.

'You seem to have a problem with hysteria.' His voice remained level despite Anders's outburst. 'I'd never known Olivia to be attracted to anyone like that.'

Anders clenched his jaw. 'Well, now you have,' he said, and through his growing grief he felt the smallest sliver of pride that he'd managed the quip, however slight the comeback had been. He had to end this conversation, but he needed one more piece of information.

'Could you please just tell me when and where the funeral will be? Or am I barred from that, also?'

'Ah, you're a quick study.' There was a long pause. 'Yes, Andy, the services are private.'

The line went dead before Anders had the chance to argue.

# 5

HE RAN out of beer. He didn't remember the ride over or know how late it was, but somehow he ended up on Lenny's doorstep, pressing repeatedly on the bell and then, when that didn't get a fast enough response, banging on the door. The open-air hallway was dark and smelled of old cigarettes. Despite the breezeway, there was no breeze and the air was stagnant and heavy with humidity. He still had his helmet on, but he could hear rap music and loud, boisterous voices from a second-floor unit above him.

Yellow light flooded the pavement when Lenny pulled the door open.

'What the hell is the matter with you?' he growled. He stood in the threshold wearing only boxers and rubbing at his sleepy eyes. 'You're gonna wake up Joey.'

Anders didn't speak, but something about the slight sway in his stance must have tipped Lenny off. He stepped closer, unfastened the helmet and lifted it from Anders's head. When he saw Anders's face, he simply said, 'Oh, Christ.'

'I ran out of beer.'

Lenny reached for his uninjured arm and pulled him inside. Anders spotted Joey standing in his pyjamas at the dark doorway to the apartment's only bedroom. 'Hey, buddy.' He tried to manage a smile for the boy.

Joey looked frightened. 'Hi, Andy.'

'Go back to bed,' Lenny insisted.

Joey didn't move, his eyes on Anders as if they'd been glued there.

'Did you hear me?' Lenny's voice was louder this time and the New Jersey accent grew thicker.

'Night,' Anders said, trying not to slur, and nodded to Joey as the boy retreated into the bedroom, closing the door behind him. He let Lenny push him into a seated position on the couch.

'She's dead. He said she's dead.'

Lenny jerked his head at the news. 'Fuck!'

'Yeah. Fuck. Fuck is right.' Anders closed his eyes and leaned his head against the cushion. He wouldn't cry, not in front of Lenny. His head was spinning. 'You got a beer for me, maybe?'

Despite his drunkenness, all his other senses seemed enhanced, and after a moment of silence from Lenny, he heard him sigh and move into the kitchen. Anders concentrated on the beat of the rap music, still slightly audible, until Lenny returned and placed the cold bottle in his hand. God, he hated rap music.

'He said I killed her.' He laughed maniacally. 'He thinks I fuckin' killed her.'

'You didn't kill her.'

He opened his eyes then and tried to focus on Lenny. 'Oh, I know that. Someone killed her, but it wasn't me.'

Lenny sat on the coffee table, facing Anders; it groaned under his weight. 'What happened?'

'I've fucked up before, but not this time, not this way. I know how to ride. I haven't dumped a bike since I was kid, and I've *never* high-sided in my life. Never.'

'I don't know that you've ever fucked up, my friend.' A small, self-deprecating laugh escaped Lenny's lips. 'Did he say what happened?'

'He wouldn't tell me anything. He wouldn't even tell me when the ...' His voice caught in his throat and he stopped talking.

'What? He wouldn't tell you when what?'

Anders shook his head again, wanting Lenny just to shut

up. He wanted him to know everything without having to actually tell him.

'Do you have that nurse's number with you?'

Anders pulled his phone from the back pocket of his jeans and found Carrie's number. He could have told Lenny that it was hopeless, that he'd already spoken to Carrie and she wasn't talking – that no one was talking – but he knew if he tried to say the words he'd break the promise to himself not to cry.

Lenny paced the room with Anders's phone at his ear as he waited for someone to answer.

'Whoa! Don't hang up – this isn't Andy – I mean, Anders.'

He hunched his shoulders as if the shape of his body could prevent Anders from overhearing what he said. 'No, no, wait,' he pleaded, pulling the slider open to his small porch and stepping outside. He forgot to close it behind him or maybe he just thought he was far enough away now not to be heard.

Anders strained to listen as Lenny tried to explain who he was and why he was calling. He heard the words 'messed up' several times, and once he heard 'hospital' and 'Olivia's dad'. And then when Lenny snapped the phone shut, he heard a hissing 'Bitch!'

'She's not a bitch,' he said from his haze when Lenny came back into the apartment. He could feel himself passing out and he couldn't be sure if his words made it to Lenny's ears. Maybe he'd only been thinking them.


HE HEARD Joey's voice and he opened his eyes to see the boy sitting in the small kitchen at the makeshift dining set – a card table and two folding chairs. He had a bowl of cereal in front of him and he was reading the back of the cereal box to his father. The apartment was still dark except for the kitchen light; Anders heard a steady rain falling outside. He shifted on the couch and felt a sheet draped over his body. He saw his helmet on the floor, and all at once he remembered his phone call with Olivia's father. He groaned and rolled over to face the back of the couch.

'Andy's up,' Joey announced.

The boy padded from the kitchen in his bare feet and climbed onto the couch with him.

'Hi, Andy.'

'Hi, Joey.'

Anders grunted when Buster, Joey's large Labrador given by Lenny as a guilt gift just after his divorce, leapt up to the couch with his small master and landed on Anders's gut. The dog panted its bad breath on his face, and he tried unsuccessfully to push it away. He'd wanted nothing to do with dogs since the day Levi died.

'Your bike got wet,' Joey informed him.

He groaned again and sat up to escape the dog, but the movement caused a pounding against the front of his skull. He noticed the full beer bottle from the night before still on the coffee table, and the sight of it made his stomach turn.

'I moved it to the breezeway for you,' Lenny called from the kitchen, picking up on Joey's comment. He came in with a mug of steaming coffee; his hair and T-shirt still showed the evidence of his trip into the rain.

Anders nodded thanks and took a sip. 'What time is it?'

'It's still early, about seven thirty.' Lenny motioned his head toward Joey by way of explanation. 'Sorry.'

Anders grabbed Joey and pulled him close for a hug. Joey squealed but let him do it.

'Did I wake you up last night, buddy?'

'Dad thinks so, but no. I was already awake.' He waited until Anders released him, and then he asked, 'Is it true that Olivia died?'

Anders looked in Joey's eyes and swallowed. How did such questions come so easily to little kids? Adults could dance around something for days. 'Yeah.' His forehead continued to throb; his nose felt congested and he wanted to be outside, on his bike and heading back to the house. He couldn't feel her presence here like he could at the beach. He tried to remember why he'd decided to come to Lenny's, but the night before was a blur.

Lenny turned on the TV in front of his beat-up recliner. He called it his football chair, and no one else was allowed to sit in it. So it surprised Anders when he motioned for Joey to move from the sofa. 'SpongeBob is on,' he said to entice him, and then he took the spot on the sofa left vacant by his son. Lowering his voice, he asked, 'Did you stop by Shel's last night before coming here?'

Anders just looked at him; he had no memory of being in his old neighbourhood.

'She called here earlier looking for you. When she got home last night, the door to her trailer was unlocked and she found a few empty beer bottles on the kitchen table. She said you're the only one who knows where she hides a key.'

The last statement, at least, he knew was true. Which meant it was entirely possible he'd been there. Which meant there was an even larger segment of the previous night he didn't remember. His stomach churned.

'Damn, Andy, you could have killed yourself, not to mention someone else.'

The irony of Lenny's accusation didn't escape him. He nodded, eyes lowered, acknowledging his idiocy.

'I hope you don't mind, but I told her about Olivia and, well . . . she was pretty upset.'

Something about Lenny's gentle tone caused Anders to look up. 'Really?' Though Shel had expressed her sympathy at the Ocean Deck, this news surprised him.

'Oh, come on. She might not have liked that you dated her, but she didn't wish the woman . . .' He stopped himself, as if realizing the word he was about to say was too crass, too soon, to say out loud. But Anders didn't really mind. He'd never been one for euphemisms.

'Did you talk to Carrie?' he asked Lenny. That part of the night, at least, he remembered.

Lenny sighed. 'Well, I tried. She was very cagey. She didn't like the idea of me talking to her from your cellphone. It was weird.'

'How am I going to find out what happened?' Anders said quietly.

'For all you know, she's not even really dead.'

Anders hadn't even considered the possibility that Mayfield had lied to him.

Lenny shrugged. 'You never know. Maybe he's hiding something,' he said, 'and *she* knows what it is.'

'She's scared.' Anders surprised himself with the statement. After Mayfield broke the news about Olivia, he'd attributed Carrie's strange behaviour in the parking lot to distress. Only now did he realize it might have been fear.

Suddenly Lenny smacked his palm on the arm of the sofa. 'You need to talk to Crystal.'

Anders said, 'Crystal?' at the same time Joey said, 'Mom?'

Lenny rose and returned to the kitchen. Anders followed, trying to ignore the pounding behind his eyes when he stood. He found Lenny at the sink scrubbing a little too hard at a bowl that had most recently held only Captain Crunch and milk.

'Why Crystal?' he asked carefully.

Lenny returned the jug of milk to the top shelf of the refrigerator and the cereal box to the pantry.

'Lenny, why Crystal?'

His friend finally stopped his activity and leaned against the counter, arms crossed in front. 'She works part-time in billing. She's been there about a year now. She got bored being just a trophy wife, I guess. I think Casanova knows someone and got her the job.'

Anders knew 'Casanova' was Lenny's nickname for his ex-wife's new husband.

'At the hospital? The same hospital where Olivia was admitted?'

Lenny nodded and looked down.

Anders continued to stare at him. Only when Lenny finally met his eye again did he say, simply, 'Oh.'

'You were trashed last night. There was no sense mentioning it to you then. And it was one in the morning. We couldn't do anything.'

Lenny reached for a pack of cigarettes and a lighter near the phone. With his cut-up, grass-stained hands he knocked a cigarette into his palm and lit up. Anders wasn't a smoker, but the cigarette looked good to him just then. Lenny noticed and tossed the pack to him.

'Look, she could probably get some answers, if she wanted. And that's a big "if", you know?' Lenny glanced into the family room at Joey and lowered his voice. 'Crystal doesn't do a damn thing out of the goodness of her heart. She always wants to know what's in it for her.'

He thought about what Lenny was saying, whether Crystal might be able to find out what had happened to Olivia. He didn't even consider that Lenny might be right about Mayfield lying – it would be false hope to allow himself to think so – but still, he couldn't fully accept her death without seeing it for himself, or at least some *proof* of it. But Mayfield was like a sentry at the gate, refusing to let him have even a glimpse.

He suddenly wondered if Olivia would be buried in the rain, and just thinking about it, just picturing a casket being lowered into the wet ground with her bruised body inside it, almost caused him to lose it.

'You okay?' Lenny asked.

'No, not really.'

'Andy—'

'What do you want me to say? That's my answer, okay?' The pressure was becoming unbearable. He rubbed at his eyes.

Lenny looked nervously in Joey's direction and Anders realized he'd yelled.

'That's my answer,' he said, softer this time. 'I'm not okay.'

'You want me to talk to her?'

Anders stared at the dingy linoleum floor and the dated kitchen cabinets. All the sparse furnishings in the sad Deltona apartment were well-worn; even the sheet Lenny had covered him with had been scratchy and thin. When Lenny and Crystal had been married, they'd lived in a small pink house in a newer neighbourhood; it had white shutters and little lanterns that lit the walk to the front door, and ibises that visited the backyard after each rain. Lenny had been a proud homeowner, tending his postage-stamp yard with the same care he tended the golf course. Anders had teased him about being domesticated; Lenny had teased Anders about living in the backwoods squalor of the mobile home park. During the divorce proceedings, he'd offered Crystal anything she wanted just to get more time with Joey, and she'd taken it all.

So Anders well understood the price of the gift his friend was offering.

He finally nodded. 'Yeah, I want you to talk to her.'

# 6

HE DOWNSHIFTED as soon as he saw the squad car in the drive. He was on A1A, still a good quarter-mile away from the house when he spotted it. He eased the bike into the grass and took his time dismounting and removing his helmet. He told himself they might be there with some good news.

'Hey,' he said, nodding to the two officers who emerged from the car. Neither had been involved in his interview on Tuesday.

They nodded a greeting in return, and the younger one of the two gave the sport bike the once-over.

'You have a moment, Mr Erickson?' said the older man.

Anders led them into the house and winced when he saw the mess he'd left from the night before. He didn't even try to count the empty beer bottles.

'You have a party here last night?'

Anders jerked his head toward the voice; the younger one had spoken. Anders guessed he was about his age, though his perfect posture, close-cropped haircut and thick but well-trimmed moustache suggested he had a stick up his ass a mile long. What could compel him to be so cruel? *Yeah, a fuckin' pity party*, he wanted to say, but he kept quiet and started gathering the longnecks and carrying them into the kitchen.

'Mr Erickson, I'm sure you've heard about Ms Mayfield.' The older officer looked like he could have been somebody's dad, or maybe even a grandpa.

At the confirmation of Mayfield's claim, Anders closed his eyes and struggled to maintain composure. When he opened them, he mumbled, 'Yeah.' Then, 'Could you tell me what happened? I'm having some trouble ... getting information.'

'Ms Mayfield passed away yesterday morning, sir,' he said. His voice wasn't unkind, but it wasn't particularly comforting either.

'Yesterday?'

'Yes, sir.'

Anders continued to nod his head slowly. If he could somehow manage to absorb everything at a snail's pace, then maybe he could control his emotions. Carrie's behaviour outside the hospital began to make more sense, though he still couldn't believe she hadn't told him herself. 'Do you know if she ever came out of the coma?' He wanted to add 'Did she ask for me?' – but he didn't.

The older man hesitated, and Officer Tight-Ass jumped in. 'Sir, I'm not sure we fully understand what happened from a medical point of view, but even if we did, I don't know that we could legally disclose such information to you.'

'And why's that, Officer ...?' He paused, inviting the man to give his name. Wasn't it protocol to introduce himself at the beginning, anyway?

'Hewes. This here is Officer Reardon.'

Anders stared at the man and waited for an answer to his question.

'As I'm sure you know, the privacy laws have become much stricter regarding whom we can release medical information to.'

'We lived here together!' he snapped. 'She was with *me* on the bike!'

Their calm in the face of his outburst only infuriated him more.

'Yes, sir,' said Hewes, taking a step closer, 'that's why we're here.'

Anders now knew the purpose of their visit. He leaned

against the counter with his arms crossed tightly and wondered whether to call Nathan right then. But he had nothing to hide.

'Okay. What can I help you with, then, officers?'

'We need to ask you a few more questions,' said Hewes.

'Ask away.'

'Would you like to sit down?'

'It's my home. If I wanted to sit, I would.'

'Yes, sir, I only meant–'

'Can you get on with it, please?'

The officers exchanged a glance. Hewes pulled out a notepad as Reardon asked, 'You told the other officer about the black Mercedes. We need for you to rack your brain a bit more, see if you can remember any other details that might help us locate it. Because otherwise ...'

Anders took a deep breath. Maybe they were only trying to help. Maybe he was projecting his anger and fear on the wrong people.

'Like I told the other cop on Tuesday, when it came up alongside me, I only saw it from the corner of my eye. It was a big black hulking mass of metal, as far as I was concerned. My first thought was to try to avoid contact, not to identify the make and model. That was my last glimpse until after I'd been thrown. By the time I turned to look, it was burning rubber trying to get out of there. The only reason I knew it was a Mercedes is because I saw the emblem on the trunk.'

'*Did* it make contact with your motorcycle?'

'I think so, because I can't imagine I would have reacted the way I did unless I had no choice. But I honestly don't remember. It all happened so fast. Would that matter?'

The two officers exchanged another look.

'What?' Anders persisted. 'Why do you ask?'

Hewes answered. 'Well, you said the Mercedes tried to run you off the road, yet we found no transfer of black paint to your vehicle. What you've told us would make more sense if we had that evidence.'

Anders grunted with frustration, and then Reardon took over again, 'Did you see the driver? Or anyone else in the car?'

'The windows were tinted.' Like every other cage in Florida, it seemed.

'And you couldn't identify the model? Or have any memory of the licence plate? Even one or two characters would help narrow it.'

'No. No. I'm sorry.'

He opened the fridge to grab a water bottle. He saw the left-over strawberries they'd used to make fruit salad that morning at breakfast. They now looked soggy in the bowl and a few mould spores had sprouted under the cling wrap.

'I'm a bike guy, you know? I'm not a car guy. I don't pay much attention to cars.' He laughed, sadly. 'My friend's little boy is only eight years old, but you can point to any car on the road, and he can tell you what it is. I even went by the Mercedes dealership on Wednesday, thinking maybe if I looked on the lot, I'd recognize the model. But ...' His voice trailed off.

'What about Ms Mayfield? Do you remember if she said anything about what the car looked like?'

'No.' He looked hard at Reardon, wanting him to under-stand just how hard this conversation was for him. He knew Hewes didn't care. 'She was too busy dying, apparently, to look.'

'Mr Erickson, I'm sorry, I—'

'I told your guy on Tuesday, her *last* words to me were "I think someone is following us."' He spoke the next words slowly, putting emphasis on each individual word. '*That was the last time I ever heard her voice.*' Narrowing his eyes at the younger officer, he added, 'Unless you count her screams.'

The two men shifted uncomfortably and this surprised

Anders, because he knew they'd dealt with much, much worse in their careers.

'So what happens if you never find the car?'

Reardon looked him in the eye. 'Well, sir, that's what we wanted to talk to you about.'

Anders just stared at him, waiting.

'There's a possibility you could be charged with vehicular homicide.'

'You're out of your frickin' mind.'

'You must understand that we've found no evidence to support your version of the accident.'

His *version*? He said it as if they believed Anders was lying.

'We're not here to arrest you. We're trying to be courteous. But—'

'Did you ever get to talk to her?' His tone grew desperate. As distraught as he was, though, he knew their answer might give him at least a sliver of the information he'd been seeking and everyone refused to surrender.

Reardon began to answer, 'Ms Mayfield was unable to—' but he stopped suddenly when Hewes spoke over him, 'No. Unfortunately, we didn't.'

'Ms Mayfield was unable to what?' Anders asked Reardon, pointedly ignoring that Tight-Ass was still in the room. But Hewes answered anyway.

'She was unable to help us. We were unable to talk to her before she passed away.'

'So she never came to?'

The men in front of him were silent.

'That's what you're saying, isn't it? That you weren't able to talk to her because she never regained consciousness? Isn't that right?'

He knew there were other possible explanations for what Reardon had said. Maybe she had awakened, but they didn't get there in time. Maybe that's what they meant. But as much as he was trying to take advantage of their slips of the tongue, they weren't falling for it.

'We can't divulge that, sir.'

Anders threw up his hands. 'So that's it? You just charge me, then? How the hell do you make that determination? Did Lawrence Mayfield insist upon it?'

'We didn't say charges were imminent. We haven't concluded our investigation. We just want you to understand it's a possibility, now that Ms Mayfield—'

He slammed the water bottle down on the counter behind him and moved forward. 'That's it. I'm done talking to you. Get out of my house now.'

'*Your* house?' Hewes said it as if Anders had just made an admission against his interest which would only bolster their case against him. He would have given anything to know what her father had told these guys about him.

He motioned to shoo them toward the front door. 'Yes, my house. I still live here for now, so I call it my house. Do you have a problem with that, Officer?'

He followed them outside and watched from the front stoop as they climbed into the squad car. The powerful engine turned over. Suddenly, remembering something Reardon had said when they'd first arrived, he bolted from the top step and ran down the drive to stop them before they backed out.

He leaned with his face at the open driver's side window and his forearms on the frame. Despite the air pushing through the vents, the interior of the car was still hot and both officers had already started perspiring. As the driver, Hewes was closest, but Anders focused his stare on Reardon in the passenger seat.

'Officer Reardon, you said something to me when you first arrived.' The man nodded, waiting. 'You said, "Mr Erickson, I'm sure you've heard about Ms Mayfield."'

'Yes?'

Anders cocked his head. 'Why were you sure?'

'Excuse me?'

'Why were you sure?' he asked insistently. 'I mean, why were you *sure* I'd heard that news? Given all those privacy laws everyone keeps referring to, who did you think would have told me?'

Anders gazed into the man's ageing eyes, searching for his conscience. As they stared at each other, the police radio crackled and a despatcher squawked a report of a break-in at a vacant beach motel in Daytona. Reardon turned his head and mumbled something to his partner, and Hewes put the car into reverse.

'Good day, Mr Erickson,' he called dryly as the car edged out the drive, forcing Anders to back away or risk being trampled.

# 7

AFTER HER divorce from Lenny and quick remarriage to the man who helped her do it, Crystal moved with her new husband into an equally new home in one of the perfectly manicured, gated neighbourhoods so ubiquitous to Florida. Anders pulled onto the drive leading to the subdivision entrance and stopped at the gatehouse to give his name. After quickly appraising him and checking a list, the guard lifted the gate and waved him through.

Anders cruised slowly toward the back of the neighbourhood, taking in the view. Each house looked the same with its neutral stucco exterior and barrel-tile roof. St Augustine grass grew in each half-acre lot with the help of automatic sprinkler systems and copious amounts of fertilizers and weedkillers. Azaleas, crape myrtles and sago palms decorated the yards, and Spanish moss hung in whispery veils from the limbs of live oaks. Canary Island date palms held court over a few of the largest homes, a clear sign of additional wealth, and ducks splashed in the small lake near the front of the neighbourhood. He couldn't deny the beauty of the setting, yet it was all a little too perfect for his taste.

Just as he'd promised, Lenny had gotten past his hatred for Crystal long enough to intervene on Anders's behalf and ask her to help him out. Anders knew that Crystal liked him well enough; his influence with Lenny often helped smooth over visitation disputes, and she'd mentioned in the past how much Joey liked him, too. He'd been surprised, though, when she'd called and suggested he come by her house on Monday to talk about what he needed. He'd assumed they'd talk over lunch at the local Panera Bread, which seemed to be the meeting place for many of the suburban moms. Though he was supposed to have returned to work that day, he'd called in sick to make the meeting with Crystal.

She answered the door in black leggings and a hot pink hoodie which was open at the front to show a pink floral sports bra and her tanned, toned stomach. Though she was a New Jersey native like Lenny, she'd adopted a certain Florida look and had her bleached blonde hair with its dark roots pulled high into a ponytail. She had a phone at her ear, but she gave Anders a big smile and motioned him in.

He smelled coffee brewing as soon as he stepped into the foyer. As he followed Crystal to her kitchen, he surveyed the tall Cherry cabinets and the gleaming granite countertops which opened up onto the large family room. She'd decorated the family room in shades of white: eggshell walls, a thick-piled snowy rug over shiny hardwood, two plush alabaster sofas. He couldn't imagine that an eight-year-old boy lived in this home.

One entire wall consisted of five glass doors that slid open telescopically to allow the family room to become one with the outdoor lanai and pool. At one end of the pool, water trickled down carefully placed boulders and the peaceful sound floated into the house. A roaring fireplace on the opposite wall surprised him until he realized it wasn't wood-burning. Crystal must have seen him looking at it, because when she snapped her phone shut, the first words out of her mouth were, 'Ambience, I turn it on for the ambience.'

She took his arm at the elbow and led him to a double-wide lounger outside on the lanai.

'Sorry about the phone call. Make yourself comfortable. Can I get you some coffee?'

'Uh, sure. Black's fine.'

She returned and gave him a straight shot of her cleavage when she placed two cups, one black and one with cream, on the small table next to him. Lenny claimed her breasts were real, but Anders wasn't so sure.

She touched his shoulder. 'I'm so sorry about Olivia, honey.'

He mumbled 'Thanks.' He didn't want her fake sympathy; he just wanted to cut through her crap. 'Can I ask you a personal question?' He couldn't believe he was about to ask what was on his mind, but something about her rubbed him the wrong way.

'Anders, hon, even though you hang around my ex, I still adore you. So you can ask me whatever your little heart desires.'

'Do you always walk around the house dressed like that?' He grinned slightly to take the edge off the question.

Crystal smiled and posed with her hands on her hips. 'Well, I'm going to the gym after our visit, but I won't say that I didn't hope you'd notice how good I looked and then relay the information to Lenny.'

'For what purpose?'

'Oh, stop acting so naive.' She pulled the rubber band from her hair and let the thick mane cascade onto her shoulders. 'So that he realizes what he lost, of course.'

She sat on the end of the lounger facing him, and with the ease of someone manipulating pretzel dough, tucked one long leg underneath the other Indian-style. She held her back straight, posture-perfect. He marvelled at her flexibility.

'Why would you care? You're happily married now.'

Crystal laughed and placed one hand on his leg. 'There are no happy marriages, hon.'

'I don't believe that.'

She winked. 'That's because you've never been married.'

His stone-faced response to her comment must have reminded her of the purpose of his visit. 'I'm sorry, hon. I know you and

Olivia had something special, and it was tragically short-lived.' She shrugged. 'But some day you'll see. Time may heal all wounds, but it also kills most loves.'

'Have,' he said.

'What?'

'Have. Olivia and I *have* something special. It didn't die with her.'

She leaned back a bit as if what he'd said spooked her. 'Yes, I'm sorry,' she said. 'Lenny said you needed some help. What can I do for you?'

'I need to take a look at Olivia's hospital records.'

She began to shake her head. 'That's protected infor–'

'Crystal, I know. That's why I need you. I need to know what happened to her.' He took both her hands in his. 'Listen, for all I know, she's still alive.'

For the first time since Anders entered her home, Crystal's expression showed real emotion. It could have been concern, it could have been fear, or maybe a mixture of the two, but Anders finally felt the possibility of having a genuine conversation.

'What are you talking about?'

'Just what I said. Maybe her family just *wants* me to believe she's dead.' He told himself he didn't really believe this, not after the visit from the cops. But he thought it was the only way to convince her. To make her believe it was truly a matter of life and death, not just death.

She let out a nervous giggle. 'That's ridiculous. Do you realize what you're saying? Why would they want that?' When he just stared at her, she added, 'Plus, even if you were right, the hospital would have to be in on something like that to make it work – and believe me, hon, there's just no way.' She pursed her lips. 'Uh uh. No way.'

'Stranger things have happened. And her parents have more money than God.'

'I don't know. It's just too far-fetched. The controls are so strict. It would require quite a pay-off.'

He scoffed. 'Well, if anyone's capable of such a pay-off, it'd be Lawrence Mayfield. And I mean both financially and ethically.'

She reached out and touched his cheek, but he didn't think the view she gave him this time was contrived. 'Hon, I know it must be a nightmare for you, what happened to Olivia. Especially since you were driving . . .' he grunted and turned his face away, but she gently moved it back so he faced her '. . . but Anders, you've got to accept it. You must understand you're coming up with all these wild ideas because you don't want to accept she's gone.'

He grabbed her patronizing hand and removed it from his cheek. 'It *is* a nightmare, you're right. But I'm not crazy.'

'I didn't say that.'

'In so many words.'

She shrugged and the smug Crystal returned. 'I just don't think your behaviour is very healthy.'

Anders laughed at that. The perfect Barbie doll with her perfect body and perfect house and not so perfect second marriage believed Anders's behaviour to be unhealthy. 'Look, Crystal, I didn't come here to be psychoanalysed. I just want to know if you'll help me. Okay? Just tell me if you'll help me.'

She held her hands out in front of her, surveying her acrylic nails, and sighed a bit too dramatically. 'What exactly do you want me to do?'

'I told you, I want to see her records. You could get them for me, couldn't you?'

'Yeah, and lose my job and go to jail in the process.'

He'd pissed her off, and as a result the tone of the conversation had changed. He sensed they'd now begun some sort of negotiation, and because he had nothing to offer, he'd already lost. Lenny had warned him, 'Just be careful. Crystal always wants to know what's in it for her.' Anders had attributed the comment to the cynicism of an ex-husband, but now he wondered. He had to retrieve the more sympathetic woman he'd been talking to a minute ago.

'Look, maybe you're right. Maybe this is crazy. But put yourself in my shoes. You'd want to know for sure, wouldn't you?'

She shrugged noncommittally.

'If I see the records, and they're all in order, then I'll know you're right. I'll know it's time to let go, and it will be easier because then, at least, I'll know what happened to her. Right now I'm completely in the dark.'

'It's just a really, really big risk for me.'

Maybe flattery was the route to take. 'I know. I know. But you're smart enough to do this without getting caught. I wouldn't ask you if I didn't think so. And I wouldn't ask you if it wasn't a matter of life or death.' He begged with his eyes. 'If she's alive, I need to know that. I need to help her.' She sat still, but he could see her thinking. He hoped she was thinking about the logistics of getting the records. 'Please. I would be so indebted to you.'

She smiled then. She reached for his coffee cup, and as she handed it to him, she said, 'Yes, you would be, wouldn't you?'

He took a sip but kept his eyes on her from over the rim of the cup. She stood and began to wander the lanai, touching the soil of her potted plants, picking dead blooms from the row of African violets she had lined up on a shelf. He thought again of Lenny's warning. But maybe there was a way to use her greed to his advantage.

'Yes, I would. You name it. If there's anything I can do for you, I will.'

She moved to the summer kitchen, filled a small watering

can with water, and returned with it to the flowers. With her back to him, she gave each container a drink.

He rose and stood next to her near the shelf. 'Crystal? Did you hear me?'

'Yes, I heard you.' She reached for one of the plant's furry leaves with her free hand and rubbed it gently between her thumb and forefinger. 'Do you know what an African violet symbolizes?' she asked without looking up from the flower.

'No.'

'It symbolizes devotion.'

He wasn't sure where she was going with this, but he hoped it would somehow lead to her agreeing to get the records for him.

She placed the watering can on the shelf and turned to him.

'You know, I'm very impressed by how devoted you are to Olivia. I'm envious.'

She took a step toward him and now stood mere inches away. The top of her head came just above his chin, and when he breathed in he inhaled the herbal scent of her shampoo.

She looked up at him. 'So what are you going to tell Lenny?'

'What do you mean?'

'What are you going to tell him? He'll ask, you know. He'll ask you how I looked.'

They'd come full circle. If all she wanted was to get at Lenny, well, he could do that. 'If you really want to make Lenny jealous, that's easy enough.' He grinned. 'I'll tell him what a fine piece of ass he's missing, okay?' *And that she was a messed-up broad he should be happy to be rid of . . .*

'Anders, I don't think I'm making myself too clear.' She placed a finger on his chest and drew a line down the middle to his stomach. 'Do you find me attractive? Do *you* think I'm a fine piece of ass?'

He stared at her face, at the full head of silky blonde hair surrounding it, at her dark-brown eyes and her damp lips that he knew had been artificially plumped to their present fullness. If she took one more step in his direction, her large breasts would press into him and he'd be able to grab a tight, firm ass. By any guy's standards, she was good-looking. She wasn't his type, but he couldn't deny her physical appeal.

'You're a beautiful woman. You know that.'

'I'm glad you think so.' The finger reached the bottom of his T-shirt and she slipped her hand underneath.

He took a step back. 'Crystal—'

'I'm not going to bite you.'

'Your husband might—'

'Oh, don't give me that. That's my concern, not yours.' Before he could protest, she was kissing him, and he was kissing her back, tasting the sweet coffee taste mingled with whatever gave her lips their look of perpetual wetness. He thought of Olivia and tried to imagine the tongue circling slowly in his mouth belonged to her, tried to think of anything that would let him do this if that's what it took to get the information he needed. But it wasn't working. When he felt Crystal's hands move to the button of his jeans, he pulled away wordlessly, shaking his head.

'Come on, Anders.' She quickly filled the space he'd created between them and he found himself backed into the counter of the summer kitchen. 'What happened to "if there's anything I can do for you, I will"?'

'You know what I meant. Not this.'

'I *thought* I knew.' She smiled and raised one eyebrow. 'Did I misunderstand?'

'Yeah, you misunderstood.' He heard the contempt in his voice, and he reminded himself to check it or he'd never get what he wanted.

'What? You'd rather I ask you to do my lawn in ex-change for helping you?' The laugh that accompanied her question was laced with sarcasm. 'Now, what kind of man would you be if you'd rather break your back in my yard than in my bed?'

He had so many answers to the question, but he knew none of them would advance his cause. So he merely said, 'I just can't.'

'Oh, I bet you can,' she murmured. She reached up and wove her fingers through his hair. 'I'll bet you can do any-thing you need to if it means finding out what happened to Olivia.'

He closed his eyes. She thought her touch would help con-vince him, but the sensation of her fingertips on his scalp just made him ache for Olivia more. What if Lenny was right? What if she hadn't died? Would it be okay as long as it led him back to her?

As if Crystal knew what he was thinking, she said, 'You just need to decide how far you'll go for her.' After a caress of his cheek, she shrugged and stepped away. 'Maybe I was wrong about the depth of your devotion.'

She collected the cups and carried them into the house. He felt like he'd just been stripped and left standing in the cold. When he realized she wasn't coming back out, he followed her in and picked up his helmet from the sofa table. She busied herself in the kitchen, ignoring him.

'You're Lenny's ex.'

'So?' She still refused to look at him as she poured the remaining coffee down the sink and rinsed the pot in the faucet.

'I can't do that to him.'

'You've got a lot of rules.'

She carried the old grinds to the trash and dumped them, and then put the sugar in the cabinet and the cream in the fridge. Frustrated, he shifted his stance. He kept thinking he'd find another way, but at that moment he didn't know what, exactly, it would be.

'Crystal, *please*. Can't you just do this for me?'

'Ball's in your court.'

'Fuck you,' he mumbled under his breath and headed to the front door. *Ball's in your court.* He wished at that moment he had a ball to shove down her throat. In the driveway, he climbed onto the bike, and as he placed the helmet on his head, he saw her leaning against the doorway, arms crossed, watching him.

'Ah, Anders.' She made a clucking sound. 'I never guessed you'd be a shrinking violet.'

'You're a whore.'

'Well, that might just be to your benefit. Let me know if you change your mind.'

'I won't.' Balancing on his right foot, he held the clutch and jammed his left leg down onto the gearshift. He pressed the ignition and the bike came to life.

'We'll see.'

He didn't hear her final words, though, because he'd gunned the engine and was halfway down her driveway by the time she'd spoken them.


LENNY DROVE out to the beach after work to check on Anders and, presumably, to find out about the meeting with Crystal. They had just started on their second six-pack of Budweiser when Lenny finally asked the question Anders had been hoping would never be asked.

'So did you talk to Crystal?'

They sat in Adirondack chairs on the deck overlooking the sand and the ocean; the sun was setting at their backs and it cast a pink glow to the sky. Every few moments, dolphin fins cut a slice through the calm waters as the animals headed north.

The sight usually thrilled Anders, but now he barely registered their existence.

He raised the bottle and drank half of it in one long gulp. 'Yeah.'

'And?'

Anders turned to Lenny and saluted him. 'Permission to speak, Captain?'

Lenny flung his head back and laughed loudly. 'You can say whatever the hell you want about her. Don't hold back.'

'She's a bitch.'

Lenny grunted. 'Tell me something I don't know.'

'She's a whore.'

Lenny had his beer at his lips, but he cut his eyes over to Anders. His smile lingered, but he must have suspected there was a story behind Anders's invective. No matter what Anders might think about a woman, they both knew he usually kept his opinions to himself out of a polite respect, drilled into his head by his mother since birth, for the fairer sex.

'Is she going to help you?'

'Yeah, for a price.'

'Well, of course. She wouldn't be Crystal, otherwise. What'd she want?'

Anders just looked at Lenny. He had no idea how Lenny was going to take the news.

'What'd she want?' Lenny persisted.

'Me.' He mumbled it from behind the mouth of his bottle.

'What?'

'Me!'

Lenny started laughing, but when he saw that Anders wasn't laughing with him – to the contrary, Anders glared at him – he settled down. 'You're serious?'

Anders nodded.

'What the fuck! First I'm not good enough, now pretty boy lawyer's not good enough either?'

Anders rolled his eyes. 'She doesn't want to marry me. I guess I'd be a little side dish to her beefcake.'

Lenny stood and began to pace the deck. His Mediterranean skin was dark from so many hours in the sun, but now his face had a distinctly red tinge to it, and it wasn't sunburn, and it wasn't the beer. Anders had known Lenny for years now, and he knew that nothing could set off his already hot temper like Crystal. For some reason that Anders couldn't even begin to understand, Lenny still loved her, and hated himself for it.

'Hey, I'm sorry, man,' Anders said.

Lenny registered a meagre nod and reached for the pack of Marlboros on the table next to Anders. He leaned against the railing of the deck as he lit a cigarette, cupping his hand around the flame to protect it from the slight breeze. 'What'd you tell her?' he mouthed, the cigarette still dangling from his lips.

'Whattaya mean, what did I tell her? Whattaya think I told her? She's your ex. I told her to go to hell.'

'What about the medical records?' Lenny's eyes bore into Anders and it made him uncomfortable. He realized that Lenny doubted him.

'I'll figure out another way to find out what happened.'

Lenny took long drags on the cigarette and blew the smoke in Anders's direction. The wind carried it away, but Anders could feel his own anger growing.

'Okay, let me get this straight. She'll get the records for you, but what?'

Anders just looked at him. It seemed pretty obvious.

'Did she come on to you at the house, when you were there?'

'Yeah.'

'And you just said no, and left?'

'Basically, yeah.'

'Basically, yeah?'

'Yeah.' Lenny's eyes narrowed, and Anders added, 'I mean, there was more of a conversation than that, but yeah, that was the gist of it.'

'Okay, let me get this straight. Crystal *hit* on you.'

'What part of "Yeah" don't you understand?'

Anders had lost his patience with Lenny. For all the grief he was getting, he was beginning to think he should have just gotten it over with and screwed her. If he had, he might have the records by now, and he'd be one step closer to knowing what had happened to Olivia. To hell with both of them.

He went into the house for another beer. He returned with two and set one on the railing next to Lenny with a slam. 'You don't deserve it, but here.' He pictured it exploding with foam when Lenny opened it. He sat on the steps leading to the beach, his back to Lenny.

'How'd she look?' Lenny asked.

Anders looked up behind him, surprised by the change in Lenny's demeanour. He couldn't help but laugh at him. 'You know, she said you'd ask that.'

Lenny's face had the look of a sad dog waiting for a treat.

'God, Lenny, forget about her. She's not good enough for you.' He added with another laugh, more to himself than to Lenny, 'Never thought I'd say that.'

'Why would she want you?' Lenny asked then, as if he was truly perplexed. 'Do you think she's trying to make me jealous?'

Anders just shook his head. 'Who knows? She's a head case. Let it go. Be glad she left you.'

Lenny nodded and looked in the other direction down the long expanse of coastline. He flicked his cigarette ash and then took another drag. This time he was careful to blow the smoke away from Anders. 'What are you gonna do?'

'I told you. I'll find out some other way. You don't have to worry about me.' He looked at Lenny and waited for him to meet his gaze. He wasn't sure his next statement was completely accurate – after all, he didn't quite understand Crystal's motivation himself – but he felt that Lenny needed to hear it just then. 'She just wants to get between us, man. Don't let her do it. You hear me? Don't let her do it.'

# 8

ANDERS SPENT the next couple of days placing calls to anyone he thought might give him information. During his breaks at work, he called every funeral home in the area, asking if services were scheduled for anyone named Mayfield, even though he suspected her family would bring her back to Connecticut for that purpose. But wouldn't someone have to prepare her for the trip? He called the medical examiner's office, only to be given the same line he'd received from the hospital about privacy laws. He called the county morgue, but they told him that if someone died in a hospital, she would be processed through that hospital's on-site morgue. He even called the driver's licence bureau before remembering that she'd never obtained a Florida licence; she'd driven on her Connecticut one.

By late Thursday afternoon his despair had gotten the better of him. He'd exhausted all ideas for getting information. It had been eleven days since the accident and almost a week since she'd died. He began to accept that he wouldn't even see her buried; she was probably already lying in the cold, hard ground. He sat on the couch in a stupor.

He was surprised to hear a truck pull into the drive. He didn't rise, though, not until he heard a knock on the screen door and a female voice call, 'Anybody home?'

As he walked to the door, he spied a FedEx truck through the front window. A large but muscular middle-aged woman smiled at him through the screen.

'I have a letter for a Mr Erickson. Is that you?'

'That's me,' he said, and opened the screen door to sign for the package before taking it. His gut tightened as it had when he first saw Reardon and Hewes in the driveway. Had Mayfield made good on his threat to sue him? He looked up at the woman as she handed him the large cardboard envelope, and her smile faded upon seeing the sadness in his eyes. He asked, only half-jokingly, 'You guys don't work as process servers, do you?'

The smile returned but this time it was a sympathetic one. 'No, sir.'

'Have a good evening,' he managed, and watched at the door until she'd climbed back into her truck and driven away.

He found a smaller, business-sized envelope inside the larger FedEx mailer with the name and address of some New York City law firm in the upper-left corner. His hands trembled as his fingers ripped it open, and the letter fluttered as he read it. Once. Twice.

He was being evicted.


'IT'S JUST a warning letter,' Nathan assured him. Anders was relieved but not really surprised when he called and found his brother-in-law still at his office so late. 'To really get you out of there, he'll need to hire local counsel. You don't need to start worrying until you start getting notices from Florida. And even then, you'll have some time. Trust me.'

'It says *he* owns the house. She told me she owned it.'

'Well, Anders ...' His brother-in-law hesitated, and the unspoken insinuation hung loudly in the silence between them.

'Can you find out for me? You know, who really owns it?'

Nathan sighed. 'Does it matter? Even it she owned it, he's probably the representative of her estate. So same difference, from your standpoint.'

*No it's not*, he wanted to say. But instead, he said, 'I'd just like to know. I'd appreciate it if you'd find out for me, or tell me how to find out.'

'Yeah, okay. No problem.' His tone had softened. He'd dropped his attorney voice for one of a sibling. 'By the way, Karina said to tell you "hello" if you called again, that she's really sorry about Olivia. She's worried about you.'

*But she still hadn't bothered to call, had she?*

He hesitated. 'Tell her thanks. Tell her I'm okay. I'll be fine.'

BUT HE wasn't okay, and he wasn't fine. When he hung up the phone after asking Nathan again about the records and explaining everything he'd done to get at the truth, he sank back onto the couch and buried his face in his palms. Though he might have some time on the house, his brother-in-law had basically told him to give it up with the hospital records unless he was prepared to break the law or have someone break it for him. Anders didn't tell Nathan that, yeah, he was prepared, but the price had been too high.

HE WOKE late the next morning after a fitful sleep, not even remembering he was supposed to be at work by seven. His anguish over Olivia was partly to blame for the long night, but he knew, too, it was something else.

He rose from the bed and showered, his body numb to the temperature despite how hot he ran the water. When he returned to the bedroom, he pulled open the top drawer of the dresser. In one swift movement he scooped up a pile of her things – a few panties, a tank, and some camisoles – and held them to his face. He closed his eyes and breathed deep, trying to inhale the scent of her.

He rifled through the drawer some more, searching for the perfect item. Once he'd chosen something, he shoved it in his pocket before he changed his mind, and within minutes was on the bike heading towards what he'd come to think of as the land of desperate housewives.

CRYSTAL STOOD at the door waiting for him, since the front gate had called to announce his arrival and get permission to allow him in. She didn't speak as he climbed off the bike and unfastened the helmet, pulling it from his head and raking his hair with his fingers, though the smirk on her face told him she knew why he was there. Even with only a few minutes' notice, she again looked as if she'd just stepped from the pages of a Victoria's Secret catalogue. She wore a black bikini top that pushed her breasts up and out, and her taut, tanned stomach led to a sheer pink sarong tied low on her hip. The sarong covered the black string that served as the suit's bottom half.

'You look good, Crystal,' he said, trying to butter her up in case she decided to renege on her offer.

'You think so? I was sunbathing when the gate called.' She didn't move from the doorway as her eyes took in the length of his body. 'You're looking good yourself, though a little tired. You seem to be holding your own without Olivia.'

He stared at her, the anger starting to build like a smouldering furnace freshly stoked. 'Barely,' he muttered.

If she knew she'd pissed him off, she didn't show it. 'Did you reconsider my offer?' she asked. She fiddled with the tie of her sarong, using the movement as an excuse to poke her thigh through the break in the fabric.

He shifted his stance a bit, stood straighter. 'I need your help. I'm desperate, okay?'

'Desperate times call for desperate measures.' When he just looked at her, she backed up and waved him in. He followed her in to what he'd come to think of as the 'white room'.

'Make yourself comfortable.' She motioned to the couch. 'Can I get you anything? Some iced tea, or a coffee?'

He lowered himself onto the couch, fearful of the slightest bit of bike grease on his jeans. 'Ice water would be fine.'

When she returned with the water, he said, 'It's "Desperate affairs require desperate measures." Horatio Nelson.' He lifted the glass and downed two-thirds of it.

It took her a moment to understand what he referred to, and then she smiled. ' "Desperate affairs", huh?' She winked. 'I like that even better, given our particular situation.' She sat on the other end of the couch and reclined back with one arm resting on the back cushion. 'I don't get you. How do you know things like that?'

He merely shrugged and finished the rest of the water. The ice clinked when he set it on the glass-top coffee table.

'You're a lot smarter than you let on, aren't you?'

'Are you gonna be able to get the files?'

She leaned toward him, her breasts threatening to break loose from their restraint. He tried to look her in the eye. 'Anders, if you're going to do this, why don't you just relax and let yourself enjoy it? I don't think I've ever met a man so uptight about getting laid.'

'Maybe that's because usually you're not bribing the man.'

She lifted his chin with two fingers. 'Yes, hon, my point exactly.'

He turned his head to escape her grasp.

She leaned back with a dramatic sigh, as if he was a hopeless cause. 'Well, if it makes you feel any better, I already have them.'

For the first time since Carrie had led him to Olivia's hospital room, Anders was overcome with elation. All his seething anger at Crystal dissipated. With her help, he'd finally taken that first step to finding out what had happened. Like a child on the eve of his birthday, he couldn't hide his excitement. 'You do?'

'Of course I do. I knew you'd be back.'

He didn't even care about her continued jabs. 'How'd you get them?' Without waiting for an answer to the first question, because he really didn't care about that now, either, he added, 'Can I see them?'

She stretched, tilting her face to the ceiling and showing him her neck as she used her hands to pull her long hair into a faux ponytail. She draped the thick strand around the front, where she let it fall across her right shoulder. 'Payment first, hon.'

'You'll get your payment. Just let me see them.'

She came across the couch onto his lap, languid as a cat, and faced him, straddling her legs on either side of him. He could smell the coconut suntan lotion on her brown skin; he could see a bit of the white lotion near her cleavage where she hadn't rubbed it in completely. Despite himself, he could feel his body responding to the onslaught of sensations. She began to unfasten the buttons of his shirt. Keeping her eyes focused on her work, she said, 'I don't trust you for a minute. You love her too much.'

Though this was all about Olivia – she was the point of his visit, of course – these last words caused his throat to tighten. At that moment he almost admired Crystal for her ability to distil everything down to something so simple, so honest. Almost, but not quite.

'Okay, you win,' he lied. He grabbed her wrists and stopped her activity. 'But not here. I don't want to be where Joey plays, or in the bed you share with your husband, either.'

'Would a guest bed meet your strict ethical requirements?'

He nodded. She climbed off him ever so slowly and grabbed his hand to lead him down the hall toward the bedrooms. He scanned his surroundings, knowing what he wanted to do but not quite sure how to do it. He didn't spot anything that gave him any ideas or would help him with the execution of his plan.

JULIE COMPTON

The guest bedroom was decorated no less luxuriously than any other room of the house he'd seen. If he were a different kind of guest, he would look forward to time spent on the down comforter-topped bed. If he were a different kind of guest, and if she were a different kind of hostess.

As she untied her sarong, he sat on the edge of the bed and tried to think. He watched it drop to the floor, and it was all he needed. He looked up at her and smiled.

'Why don't you get your lotion? I'll rub it on you.'

He realized after he'd spoken that he had no idea if her lotion was outside; for all he knew, she'd applied it in her bathroom before ever going into the sun.

But for once Lady Luck was in his favour, because she whispered 'I'll be right back' and left the room. He jumped up and followed her, and even though she noticed him behind her, she didn't seem to understand that he was going to betray her, as she'd suspected earlier he would. Maybe she thought he planned to apply the lotion while she lay in the sun.

As soon as she stepped onto the lanai, he slammed the slider shut behind her and locked it. She turned at the sound of the door gliding along the tracks, and her mouth opened in surprise. Before she could speak, he hurried through the house and checked the other exterior doors – the front door he'd come in through, and the door to the garage. All were securely locked, and he could only hope he hadn't missed one and that she didn't have a key hidden somewhere outside. When he returned to the slider, he found her sitting on the double-wide lounger applying lotion to her legs. Furious at her nonchalance, he wasted no time making his demands.

'Are you gonna tell me where the files are,' he called through the glass, 'or am I gonna have to turn your house upside down to find them?'

Without looking up, she shook her head. An answer to the first question, he guessed.

'Bitch,' he mumbled to himself, and turned from the door to begin his search. He made a half-hearted pass through the family room, figuring that'd be the last place she'd keep them, and then he opened every cabinet and drawer in the kitchen. It wasn't a logical spot for files, but he thought maybe that's why she might have hidden them there. When that proved fruitless, he peeked into several rooms until he found their office, and then he went to town. He opened every file drawer and pulled out every file, leaving the rejects discarded in a mess on the floor – more out of revenge than necessity or even carelessness. He pawed over the bookshelves, looking for any evidence, but he found nothing. Nothing. He fell into the leather desk chair and groaned, but then immediately sprung back up and headed for the master bedroom, where he tossed pillows from the bed, lifted the mattress, opened every closet, every drawer in both nightstands and the long dresser, rifling through their contents and tossing items onto the floor in his wake.

His search continued throughout the house in this manner, growing more desperate and destructive as both his failure and his anger grew. In the guest bedroom, he grabbed her sarong from the floor and marched back to the slider, ready to strangle her with it if that's what it took to get her to talk. The sight of her lying topless now on the lounger, sunning herself as if she was completely unaware that an angry madman was ransacking her house, enraged him. He'd never felt so wild from his powerlessness, and his desire to physically hurt her scared him.

He banged on the door to get her attention before pulling it open. 'Crystal! Tell me where they are, damn it!'

She didn't flinch, didn't even open her eyes. 'You'll never find them. And if you made a mess, please clean up after yourself, will you?'

He crossed the lanai and grabbed her wrist, yanked it up. Her perfect breasts shook and he realized in that instant that

Lenny had been truthful; they were real. He grew even more furious that he'd let the sight distract him, and he squeezed her wrist hard, finally getting a look of concern, and a wince from the pain he inflicted. 'Don't be stupid,' he said, his voice an unrecognizable growl. 'Tell me.'

'No, don't *you* be stupid,' she hissed. She raised her left arm, displayed a phone in her hand. 'How're you going to explain the mess to the cops? And that little red mark that's forming on my arm as we speak?' He loosened his grip on her slightly, unaware that he'd done so. 'Not to mention, you'll never get your precious files this way.'

He squeezed tight again and shoved her arm above her head, twisting it slightly, and she let out a squeal. 'Tell me, Crystal,' he said again. 'I'm not really in control of myself right now.'

She narrowed her eyes; the slightest grin on her face dared him to hurt her. 'Fuck it out of me, then,' she said, her voice low and hoarse, her back arching. He realized that she was afraid of him but she was also turned on by the fear. 'Either fuck me or let me go, because I'm about to hit the speed dial for the cops.'

Out of the corner of his eye he saw her thumb move on the phone. He dropped the sarong and lunged over her, trying to grasp it with his free hand. He caught her other wrist but the action knocked the phone to the ground; it bounced once and slid a few feet from the lounger. He hovered above her, both of her arms held firm now, but he could see the LCD was lit on the phone, though he couldn't be sure whether this meant a call had been initiated.

'Come on, Anders,' she whispered. She raised her knee and rubbed her leg against him, and he knew she'd just confirmed for herself what he'd been trying to deny. 'It's now or never. Do what you have to do.'

In his confusion between anger and desire, all thoughts of what he might be doing to Olivia and Lenny momentarily vanished. All he could think was *fuck her, get the files. Fuck her, get the files.* It was so simple; one thing would follow the other. There was no longer any wrong associated with it in his mind. It was the only thing to do, the necessary thing, and thus the right thing.

In one swift motion he released her arms, and his hands went to the waist of his jeans. He struggled with the button and yanked the zipper down as her hands worked to tug them from his hips. With a pull of a string he got her bikini bottom out of the way as she unbuttoned the last button on his shirt and pushed it open to expose his stomach.

She let out a cross between a moan and a deep laugh when he slid into her. Before long her moans grew louder, and in a low, cooing voice she began to talk him through it. And though she sounded just like the women in the porn films he'd watched over the years, and he knew it was all an act, he was still a man, and her vocal performance had the desired effect on him. He moved inside her faster, his own throat emitting sounds more of despair than pleasure at what he was doing. Her strong legs wrapped around him, and with her nails digging into his backside and her lips at his ears, she egged him on, 'Come on, Anders, harder ... harder. Fuck me harder.' She stopped talking only when he felt her muscles involuntarily gripping and tightening around him. She grunted, and began to shudder, and she finally lost all control as she let loose a lengthy, unrehearsed cry of pleasure. Her body's intense response caused him to lose it, too, and he buried his face between her neck and shoulder to muffle his own cries as he came.

The sense of shame that had taken a brief leave came rushing back. He quickly rolled off her to the other side of the lounger and pulled his jeans back up to their rightful place.

In an effort to remove himself mentally from what he'd just done, he concentrated on the sounds of Florida suburbia: the intermittent call of a mockingbird, the rustle of the palm fronds in the breeze, the water gently bubbling down the fountain into the pool. He stared at the screen enclosure above him, but from the corner of his eye he saw her face turn in his direction, a satisfied smile on her face. Self-satisfied, he thought. She ran her hand up the length of her stomach and over her right breast. Their mingled sweat coated her skin.

'Now that wasn't so bad, was it?' she said, the smile lingering.

'Get the files,' he said without looking at her.

'My, you sure keep your eyes on the target, don't you?' She sat up, reaching for her sarong on the ground. She tied it around her chest like a towel.

'Just get the files.' He glanced at her with contempt and noticed the slightest flicker on her face as she raked her eyes over his body. Instinctively he looked down in the direction of her gaze. He spotted it at the exact moment her hand shot out to grab it – the patch of deep-purple fabric peeking out from the front pocket of his jeans.

'What's this?' she said, pulling the item from its temporary home. He tried to grab it from her but she twisted, held it out of his reach. 'Someone's panties.' He stared at her wordlessly. 'A thong. Olivia's thong?' she asked, and looked at him curiously. It took only a moment before the realization crossed her face, and he knew then that she understood exactly why he'd brought it. To confirm this, she dragged it over his face. 'Hmm, is this the scent of her perfume? Or a cache in her dresser?' she asked. He turned away but she dropped the thong on his cheek. He yanked it off as she leaned in close. 'Turns out you didn't even need an aphrodisiac, did you?'

He glared at her, but she just shook her head and laughed a bit. 'Oh, Anders,' she said, clicking her tongue in mock pity.

She retrieved the phone from his side of the lounger and then went inside, leaving him to stew in his embarrassment.

When he could finally summon the nerve, he went in after her. He found her in the kitchen, dressed now in shorts and a tight T-shirt, pulling items from the refrigerator and pantry as if beginning to prepare that night's dinner. The kitchen had been straightened, but the other evidence of his rampage remained, and, for now, she just ignored it. He imagined her at the dinner table later, lying to her husband and son about her day.

'The files,' was all he said.

She grabbed a brown wallet pouch from the edge of the kitchen's computer alcove – he was certain it hadn't been there earlier in his search – and tossed it onto the counter in front of him. He saw Olivia's name on a white label, along with the hospital's other identifying information, and his pulse began to race. If he found the answers he needed inside the folder, even some of them, it would have all been worth it.

The pouch was frighteningly lightweight when he lifted it. He pulled the black tie and raised the flap. His breath caught when he saw the dark interior. It was empty.

'What is this?' He took a step toward her, jabbing the folder in her direction, and before she could answer, he said, 'Is this your idea of a joke?'

'Not at all.' She squirted dish soap into her hands and began to wash them in the faucet. 'That's exactly how I found it.'

'What do you mean?' The rage was building again. When he moved even closer to her, his footsteps determined and heavy, she stepped back and for the first time looked alarmed.

'Just what I said. I think you were right. I think someone's been bought off.' When her explanation didn't appear to be appeasing him, she added, 'I even asked around. Even the computer stuff is gone. It's as if it never existed. Even the records clerk was stumped.'

He flung the folder away and came at her, pushed her up

against a tall cabinet and wrapped his hand around her neck. He imagined squeezing the life out of her, watching her tanned face go white as her blood stopped pumping under his fingers.

'You bitch,' he said through gritted teeth. 'If you were a man, I'd kill you.'

He felt her swallow under his palm. Between the two of them, he wasn't sure who was shaking harder.

'Stop it,' she begged. 'I gave you what you wanted. It's not my fault it all disappeared.'

'You messed with my head. You should have told me right off.' He applied more pressure, and her wet hands came up, trying to pull his arm away.

'Anders! Stop it! You're hurting me!'

'From your performance outside, I thought you liked that.' He was up in her face, his eyes drilling into hers, only inches away. Tears filled the rims, and her lips began to quiver.

'Please—'

'Please what, Crystal? Huh? Please fuck you harder?'

She tried to wriggle to freedom but he was having none of it. All the fury that had been boiling in small tremors was now erupting in full force. From the moment he saw Olivia's lifeless body on the ground, to just minutes before when he looked into the harrowing depths of an empty file folder, he'd tried to contain it. It kept escaping, but he'd always managed to chase it down and rein it in. But now the force of it was just too strong for him to control. All colour began to drain from her face. He knew he'd kill her if something didn't stop him first.

'Something' turned out to be Joey. Or rather, a picture of Joey, tucked into the cabinet moulding behind Crystal's head. In their struggles, she had moved sideways, and Anders found himself staring at a picture of her son in a blue and white baseball uniform, posing with a bat held in the air, ready to take a swing.

He stared at it a moment as his mind connected the boy

in the picture to the woman in his grip. Whatever else she might be, she was Joey's mother. The mother of Lenny's son.

He loosened his grip on her neck and she scrambled away from him.

In the calmest voice he could muster, he said, 'If Lenny *ever* finds out about this, *ever*, I will come back and finish the job. You understand?'

'Get out.' Her voice through her tears had none of the moxie from earlier.

'*Do you understand?*'

She nodded.

He strolled past her out of the kitchen, grabbing his helmet and kicking a throw pillow out of his path in the family room on his way to the front door. Once he was out of her sight and what she must have believed to be a safe distance, her crying turned into a full-fledged bawl. He listened a moment, taking pleasure in the sound, and then slammed the door shut behind him.

# 9

HE PROMPTLY opened a beer when he returned to the house and sat on the back deck to drink it. By midday he'd drunk enough to numb his brain if not his heart, but this time he had no desire to head to Lenny's apartment. Instead, he sat on the bed and stared at a strip of four small pictures tucked into the dresser mirror frame. They'd posed and hammed for the camera in a booth on the Daytona Beach boardwalk, and the last thing he remembered thinking before sleep claimed him was that the pictures had been taken the weekend before the bulldozers razed one of the last remaining arcades.

HE OPENED his eyes and saw her standing in front of the mirror. At first he thought she was looking at the pictures, too, but then she lifted something from the dresser and he realized she was picking up her necklace, the one with the crane he'd rescued at the scene of the accident. She grasped the opposite ends of it with her fingers and brought her hands around the back of her neck. Her hair was piled high in a clip and he could see the tattoo. She struggled to connect the clasp.

'Do you want me to get it?' he whispered.

She didn't respond.

He rose from the bed and stood behind her. 'Do you want me to get it?' he asked again.

She still didn't answer – didn't even look at him – and it occurred to him she must be upset about what had happened with Crystal.

'Olivia, I'm sorry, please don't be . . .' When he reached up to take the necklace and hook it for her, she was gone.

HE RETURNED to work at Palmetto the following Monday. No one ever said anything about his repeated absences, and he knew that Lenny had probably run interference. Each day the two of them worked alongside one another, as always. At first Anders tried to answer Lenny's questions: had he learned any more about Olivia? Was Mayfield going forward with the eviction? Had the cops concluded their investigation of the accident? How was he holding up? Though Lenny had offered no further solutions – he was just as ignorant as Anders when it came to working a system – he'd offered his ear, and Anders had gratefully, if reluctantly, accepted it. But as Anders's efforts dwindled, so had their conversations; he simply found it too uncomfortable to be around his old friend. Once they'd punched out at the time clock, he made a concerted effort to avoid him, declining his offers to get a beer after work or shoot some pool. Anders knew Lenny attributed the increasing distance to his grief over Olivia, and though these assumptions were, in a sense, accurate, they didn't come close to explaining the full story behind his despair. He'd never had a secret from Lenny, not to mention one of this magnitude.

On Friday after work, Lenny walked out to the parking lot with him. Anders didn't see Lenny's Dodge Ram near his motorcycle, so he knew they weren't merely heading in the same direction.

'What are you gonna do?' Lenny asked. 'What's your next step?'

Anders climbed onto the bike and busied himself with strapping on his helmet. The face shield was tinted and he left it down.

Lenny tried again. 'You're not just gonna lie down and take

this shit from her dad, are you?' When he still failed to get any response, he reached over and angrily flipped up the shield.

'Hey, what the hell's the matter with you? I'm asking you a question.'

'I just don't want to talk about it now, okay?'

'Come on, man, you don't really believe she's dead, do you?' Lenny asked. 'I mean, think about it, what proof do you have? Nothing. Not a damn thing.'

Anders just stared at him, thinking about the empty file. The file he couldn't tell him about.

'Am I right?' Lenny persisted. 'Do you *really* think she's dead?'

'I don't know.'

'Sounds like a "no" to me.' He sighed. 'You've said it yourself, things just don't add up. Her old man screwed you.'

'Yeah, but what can I do about that? He's a multi-millionaire.'

'I don't know, but who gives a shit how much money he has? Olivia didn't seem to care.'

That much was true.

He gazed out over the lot and thought about the day she'd first arrived in the old pickup. Had he known the future, would he have been so eager to help her? He usually avoided any challenge like it was a terminal disease, but in this case, yeah, he believed he would have stuck around. But he also would have tried to alter the events to come.

'Anders?'

Anders jerked his head to meet Lenny's gaze. In all the years they'd known each other, Lenny had never called him by his proper name.

'Can I say something without you getting royally pissed at me?'

He thought of saying something smart like *don't you always?* But instead he simply nodded.

'You're an incredibly intelligent person. But for reasons I've never understood and maybe are none of my business, you've skated through life trying to hide it and hanging out with people like me, working the grounds, picking up a few bucks here and there. It's like your life has been one big attempt to give your old man the finger.'

'You don't know what—'

'Hey!' Lenny raised his hand. 'Let me finish, okay?'

Anders leaned back and gave a little wave as if to say *Have at it*.

'You're smart. Above average smart. You don't think she knew that? You don't think that's part of what attracted her to you?'

He remembered how she'd studied him that first day and quickly dispatched Lenny. He wasn't sure what she'd seen in him, but he didn't for a minute think it had anything to do with his brains.

'Look,' Lenny continued. 'I know you're not lazy. I've seen you bust your ass many times. And until all this, you seemed pretty happy, so I guess I can't fault you for your choices, though it pisses me off a bit—'

'Why? Why the hell do you care what I do?'

Lenny shook his head in disgust. 'Look around you. If I had your brains, you think I'd be working here?'

Anders grunted and looked away.

'You're a lucky son of a bitch, and you don't even seem to realize it. You've always taken it easy, and till now I guess it worked for you. It pissed your dad off and it was a way for you to never fail at anything.'

'Lay off me. You don't know as much as you think you do. You don't know what he did.'

'I know a little bit. And it doesn't matter what he did. My point is, you're still letting him do it.' Their voices had become louder as they'd argued, but now Lenny lowered his and he spoke the next words gently. 'She's not gonna just walk through the door one day, Andy. You're gonna have to go out and get her.'

'I've tried, man. I've tried.' He couldn't help but think of Crystal again. 'I don't know what else to do!'

'And you know something else?' Lenny said as if Anders hadn't even spoken. 'If she's alive, I think she's counting on you. I think she's counting on you to come and get her.'

THE NEXT morning he walked the beach all the way up to the Sunglow Pier, his fishing rod in one hand and his tackle box in the other. The seagulls followed at his shoulder. He and Shel used to come out here all the time; they'd rise early and make the short drive from their neighbourhood, and later, share a meal of whatever they'd caught at one or the other's trailer. He'd almost considered calling her, but Lenny's lecture was still on his mind and he knew he'd make lousy company.

For some reason he'd never come with Olivia and now he regretted it. He wondered what had stopped him. Had he questioned whether she'd enjoy watching the grizzle-faced, leather-skinned old fishermen who frequented the spot? Had he thought she wouldn't want to fish, or have the patience to sit idly by for hours as he did? Lenny's words became more urgent in his head as everything he did reminded him of lost opportunities.

He bought bait at the small shop behind Crabby Joe's and settled into a spot about halfway down the pier, away from the regulars. They'd want to engage him in conversation and today he'd come out more to think than to fish.

He'd barely thrown his line in when his cellphone rang in his back pocket. All heads turned in his direction – usually this early in the morning only the tourists dared to spoil the atmosphere with their technology – and he sheepishly mumbled his apologies as he scrambled to silence it. When he saw the caller ID, he left his spot and stood against the exterior wall of the bait shop for privacy, all the while hoping his unattended rod didn't get pulled over the rail and into the ocean by a fish.

'Hope I didn't wake you,' said Nathan. 'I'm meeting some colleagues for racquetball at seven but wanted to talk to you before I headed to the gym.'

Nathan's simple sentence illuminated every difference between the two men: Nathan played racquetball with 'colleagues' on a Saturday while Anders fished, either alone or with a friend, and Nathan actually thought he'd be waking his ne'er-do-well brother-in-law, as if he didn't realize or it didn't matter that the clock in Florida read an hour later than Chicago.

'No, I've been up for a while. I'm at the pier fishing, actually.'

'Oh.' Nathan's voice registered surprise. 'I'm envious. How's the weather?' He chuckled. 'On second thought, maybe you shouldn't tell me. It'd be too painful to hear as I look out my kitchen window at the frozen tundra we call our backyard.'

The tightness in Anders's shoulders eased. He needed to cut Nathan a break. Despite Karina's strained relationship with her younger brother, her husband had done nothing but help Anders. He glanced up at the blue sky and was conscious of the rising sun warming his back. 'Don't feel bad. It looks like rain. What's up?'

'I found out who owns the house.'

The tightness returned, but for a different reason.

'Someone named Makena Mbatia. Do you know who that is?'

*Did he know who that was?*

The woman Mayfield claimed had known Olivia since birth. The woman who 'might possibly know her better' than her parents. The woman who'd whispered to him that day as he left the hospital waiting room.

*Don't give up.*

'Yeah, I know who she is.'

And if he wasn't entirely truthful, if he didn't know who she was, exactly – well, at that moment, he planned to make it his business to find out.

# 10

THE SHOEBOX had been on the top shelf of the bedroom closet for as long as he'd lived in the house with her. Which, at the time of the accident, had been about five months. He'd known from the first time he'd seen the box that it probably didn't contain shoes; she wasn't that organized and, anyway, the lid was taped to the bottom. She'd never shown him what was inside. When he asked about the contents, she'd shrugged and told him, 'Just some old mementos from Africa.' He'd accepted that answer and not given it much further thought.

In their few months together, he'd come to understand her affinity for the continent. He knew the necklace she wore had been given to her by one of the Maasai women who attended her delivery, and he'd noticed right off the small African touches she added to the beach house: the mahogany fruit bowl on the counter, the blanket in the traditional red and blue Maasai colours she kept at the end of their bed. In contrast to the first story she'd told about her father's behaviour surrounding her birth, later stories about her travels to Kenya and Tanzania, though she told them infrequently, were happy ones. He believed she felt about Africa the way he felt about Florida, and when he suggested that someday they visit together, she seemed pleased with the offer. 'I'd really like that,' she'd said. 'I'd like you to see it.' But like so many other things, he'd assumed they had all the time in the world to do it.

He'd never considered opening the box without her permission, even right after the accident. To do so, he'd thought, would be a blatant violation of her privacy. But so much had changed in the past two weeks. He still believed looking inside the box was wrong, but it didn't seem to matter anymore, given the stakes. Just like his betrayal of Lenny, he told himself that whatever was in the box might provide the answers to his growing list of questions. Why he hadn't thought of it *before* succumbing to Crystal, he didn't know.

He wasted no time returning from the pier and pulling the shoebox down from the shelf. He had no idea what he was looking for, or what he might find, but, clearly, this Makena woman had played a large role in Olivia's life and he hoped the contents of the box might have some clues.

He peeled the yellowed tape and it gave easily, cracking and falling apart in some spots. He slowly raised the lid. At first all he saw was a few pieces of folded notebook paper. The top piece rested at an angle, with something solid underneath that prevented it from lying flat. He lifted the papers – he noticed now some overseas airmail envelopes mixed in with the notebook paper – and pulled out a small black velvet box from underneath. He knew there could be a million different explanations for its existence, but only one of those explanations mattered and his stomach had already determined to assume the worst. His mouth suddenly felt dry.

*Don't open it.* His thoughts battled between reason and desire. Could the contents of this box really matter now? She hadn't seen fit to care what was inside, why should he? Whatever it was, it belonged to some past life in which he was nonexistent – would always be nonexistent – and nothing could change that.

*Yet she'd kept it.* For some reason, she'd kept it. Maybe it was simply the box her necklace had come in. Maybe the explanation was that simple.

The phone rang and called to him from the quicksand of

his reverie. He looked over to the nightstand and watched the red light on the handset blink with every ring. He remembered how she never really heard the phone, how she taught him to ignore it, too, if it rang in the middle of their love-making. 'You don't *have* to answer it, Anders,' she'd say. 'If someone really wants you, they'll call back.' She hadn't owned an answering machine for the house phone, and he'd discovered he appreciated the amplified sense of freedom its absence provided, the inability for someone to impose an additional obligation.

But now, a missed phone call could mean missing information about Olivia. That realization finally bubbled to the surface of his consciousness and he lunged across the bed and grabbed the phone in the middle of the fifth ring. The word 'Hello' had barely left his lips when he heard the click at the other end signalling that the other person had already given up.

'Damn!'

He flung the jewellery box across the room. It bounced against the wall and left a small dent before falling to the floor with a thud. He'd wanted to crack it open like an egg and watch its secrets spill onto the terrazzo, but it remained impenetrable, mocking him with closed mouth.

He sprung from the bed, reached for the box, and yanked it open. A moan slipped from his throat when his speculation about the contents became fact. He stared at the brilliant diamond ring tucked into a red satin bed. He didn't know anything about diamonds other than what he'd learned second hand from overhearing women talk, but he had no doubt that on a scale of one to ten, this one was off the chart. It was emerald cut, big as a raspberry and perched in a platinum setting.

He grabbed the shoebox and dumped the papers on the floor. He sifted through everything and plucked the corner of a small newspaper article peeking out from the letters.

CLIFTON, CONNECTICUT – What appeared at first to be another heartbreaking tale to come out of the war in Iraq seems to have concluded with a fairy tale ending.

Earlier this month, Clifton resident Olivia Louise Mayfield received a package in the mail with an engagement ring – just hours before mistakenly being told that her betrothed, Cpt. Brent Campbell, had been killed in Iraq, her father, pharmaceutical magnate Lawrence Mayfield, said Saturday. 'Brent had purchased the ring when he returned from his first tour in Iraq late last year, but had planned to wait until the war was over to propose,' said the soldier's father, George Campbell. 'He returned to Iraq earlier this month with his unit and while he was there, changed his mind about waiting.' According to his father, Cpt. Campbell's waning optimism about the war convinced him to instruct a friend to gift wrap the ring and have it sent to Ms. Mayfield. Mr. Mayfield confirmed that his daughter received the ring just hours before soldiers appeared at their door with the devastating news. 'Understandably, she was crushed and beside herself,' he said. 'They were childhood sweethearts.'

The flag flew at half-staff at the gates to the Mayfield estate until the families discovered the mistake a few days later, when Cpt. Campbell phoned Ms. Mayfield from overseas to make the proposal official. 'Olivia was shocked to hear his voice, and he was shocked to hear of his passing,' said Mr. Mayfield. 'Of course, those emotions soon turned to relief and joy.' The Army was promptly alerted to the botched information – a result of a computer glitch, apparently – and now both families are celebrating the upcoming nuptials.

Though the printed words gave him no comfort, someone had used black marker to scrawl one word – LIARS!! – across the middle of the article.

The first question to come to mind was 'Who was Captain Brent Campbell?' He thought he knew the answer, in a general sort of way. But the answer to the second question was less obvious. Who had written 'LIARS!!' across the article? It had to have been Olivia, didn't it? He couldn't really tell if it was her handwriting; it might have been, but he couldn't say for sure. And what did it refer to? What, exactly, had been lied about? Did Campbell never actually propose? Or maybe this Campbell guy did in fact propose, but she had never accepted. Or maybe he and Olivia were never childhood sweethearts as the story claimed. Maybe the ring represented something more than an offer of marriage. Maybe, even, the ring he'd thrown across the room wasn't the same ring referred to. The largest question of all loomed over all of these riddles, though. *Why had she never shared any of this with him?*

He dug around in the box some more and fingered the letters. All seemed to come from an APO address in Iraq, or from Kenya. He opened one and began to read:

> *My loving Olivia,*
> *There are no words to express my longing for you*
> *from the other side of the world. You know, don't*
> *you, that you are always in my thoughts? I retire*
> *each night with the sound of your voice in my head*
> *and I wake with your name on my lips. But the dis-*
> *tance between us, as always, makes it difficult. I'm*
> *counting the days until—*

He quickly turned over the letter and closed his eyes. It was too private. He told himself it had nothing to do with her disappearance and he had no right to read it. But even as he negotiated with himself, he knew there was another reason he'd stopped reading: He didn't want to know about her relationships with other men.

It was simply too painful.

OLIVIA HADN'T yet moved into the house. The repairs had begun six weeks back, but because of some delays with the plumbing, it would be at least another week or two before the house would be habitable. They'd spent the day painting the interior walls, using colours with names like Ocean Spray, Caribbean Mist, and Early Sunrise. Somehow, when their work for the day was done but before they'd begun to clean up, they'd ended up horizontal on her new bed, on top of the large paint cloth that covered both the frame and the mattress, which itself was still covered in the plastic it had been delivered in. If it was less comfortable than they'd envisioned for their first time, neither had seemed to notice or care. That it happened at all surprised him, because since the first day on the beach, he'd known he couldn't rush anything. She was generous in her affection, yet often tensed up if he returned the attention too eagerly. The prolonged chase had been thrilling, unlike anything he'd experienced with other women, but confusing, too.

Afterwards, they lay perpendicular to one another on the bed, his cheek on her belly, as the late day sun cast shadows in the room and the tropical breeze blew across their bare skin. A portable radio on the third step of the ladder played older jazz. The station's scratchy reception had almost lulled him to sleep when the news at the top of the hour interrupted the music:

*Today the parents of Kylie Woods, the young Deland elementary teacher beaten to death last week by her ex-husband, publicly spoke out against the local police*

*and justice system, saying both failed to protect their
daughter.*

Anders felt goose bumps rise in a wave along Olivia's skin
as the reporter recited the story in an urgent, sensationalistic
tone:

*Mr and Mrs Woods claim Kylie had been in fear for her
life for some time, and had placed numerous calls to the
police over the past few months after receiving escalating
threats from ex-husband Gerry Haines. They blame the
denial of her recent request for a restraining order on
a personal connection between Haines and an unnamed
person within the Volusia County judicial system. They
plan to file suit against the city and county on Thursday
seeking retribution and, Mrs Woods says, 'to prevent
another young woman from suffering the same fate.'*

'Fat chance,' Olivia said as the reporter took a breath before
moving on to the next story. The hairs on her arm stood at
attention.

Anders propped himself up and lifted his head so he could
see her eyes. She met his gaze and, seeing the question on his
face, gave a little shrug. 'It wouldn't have mattered if she'd
gotten her restraining order. Guys like that are single-minded.
They do what they want, and they get away with it.' She closed
her eyes then as if to escape his stare.

'Olivia?'

'Hmm?' She gave him the smallest of smiles as she ran her
fingers through his hair.

'Do you have first-hand knowledge or something?'

The Mona Lisa smile lingered on her lips. 'No.' She looked
out the window. 'No, I can honestly say I've never been hit by
a man.'

He believed her, he had no reason not to, but he knew there had to be more. He almost told her about his mom, then, and his dad, but then what would she think of him? Would she believe the apple didn't fall far from the tree?

Instead he just lay his head back down, his body parallel to hers this time, and nuzzled his nose into her hair. He listened to the distant noise through the open window of a hammer and an electric saw, another beach mansion replacing a weathered bungalow. They both fell asleep soon after, after the tools fell silent and dusk stole the day's last light from the room. He slept deeply until a plaintive cry woke him near midnight.

And for the first time, he witnessed one of Olivia's nightmares.

HIS MEMORIES were interrupted by the sound of crushing shells as a car pulled in the drive. He remained still as he heard the engine grow silent, the car door creak open and then slam shut, the occupant's light footsteps as he or she came up the walk.

'Anders?' Shel's quiet voice called through the open windows. 'Hey, Anders, it's me.' A succession of raps on the front door followed her words.

He quickly gathered the papers and placed them back into the box. As he did so, he noticed a small matchbox with a picture of a beer stein and the name and address of a bar printed on the front. *Jimmy's*, it read. Why would she keep a matchbox from a bar in Connecticut? What was the significance?

'Anders?' Shel called out again. 'You in there?'

He found Shel standing on the doorstep in cut-off jean shorts and a Mickey Mouse T-shirt, though he could see the strings of a bathing-suit top tied around her neck underneath the tee. She had a beach bag slung over her right shoulder and flip-flops on her feet. She smelled like Coppertone sunscreen, and for just an instant the scent brought him back to Crystal's house.

'Hey, Shel.' He didn't move to let her in. He realized that perhaps it wasn't wise to let anyone see what had become of the house in Olivia's absence.

'Hi, Anders.'

Her eyes travelled the length of his body before settling on his face. Only then did he think about the sight he himself presented. The soiled and probably smelly jeans, the bare chest, the unshaved face, the uncombed hair. Her expression registered concern, though he could tell she was trying to hide it. Still, he merely looked back at her.

'How are you?' she asked when he didn't invite her in. 'I haven't seen you in a while, and I was a little worried. Lenny's been filling me in.'

He didn't bother to mention that Lenny didn't know the half of it. 'I'm surviving.'

'Could I come in?'

'Yeah, sure.' He mumbled something about ignoring the mess and moved away from the door.

'I was heading to the beach, and I thought you might want to come, too.' She took in the surroundings, the concern growing to alarm. He saw her eyeing a pack of cigarettes on the coffee table, a look of pure confusion on her face. 'I thought maybe you needed to get out a bit.'

'Thanks, but I got out this morning, actually. I almost called you, in fact, to see if you'd want to meet me at the pier.' His words garnered a small smile from her, despite the melancholy tone of their delivery. 'Anyway, as you can see,' he motioned at the room behind him, 'I'm a little behind in my housework.'

She laughed, but stopped as soon as she saw he wasn't laughing with her, not even a little. She stepped in front of the open doors leading to the deck – he always left them open unless it was just too cold – and breathed deep. 'Come on, it's a beautiful day. Look at the ocean. It would do you good.'

'Look, I know what you're doing, and I appreciate it. I really do. But I'm just not up to it.'

'Would you let me help you clean up, then?' She looked at him with her big eyes, and he knew then that she needed to help him as much as she thought he might require it.

So he acquiesced, taking the beach bag from her and hanging it over the back of one of the kitchen chairs while she moved to the stereo and turned on the CD player. The growl of Stevie Ray Vaughan's guitar and voice filled the small house.

They began in the kitchen. He circled through the house, collecting the remains of almost three weeks' worth of scrappy meals while she attacked the stack in the sink. In the bedroom he stopped to shove Olivia's box back onto the closet shelf so Shel wouldn't see it.

'What else?' he asked, returning to the kitchen after starting a load of laundry. He had to hand it to her; the activity and the music had improved his mood slightly. It felt like a start, like he'd made some movement, at least, in the right direction. Like preparing the nest for the fledgling.

By the time they finished two hours later, the third load of laundry was in the wash, the second was in the dryer, and Shel stood in front of the couch folding the first for him. He ducked into the bathroom and took a quick shower.

When he returned she was sitting on the couch, her legs outstretched with her bare feet on the old wooden-plank coffee table, a piece Olivia had found at the flea market and repainted a creamy white. She held the television remote in her right hand and a wine cooler in her left. The volume on the television was down – images flashed by on the screen as she surfed mindlessly through the channels – and the same CD played on its third go-around. A brisk breeze blew in from the ocean, and Anders inhaled the clean smell of the house and air.

She switched off the television and tossed the remote onto the table as Anders plopped down on the couch next to her. They sat in the silence for a moment until Shel spoke again, her voice tentative. 'So, how are you really, Anders?'

He glanced at her sideways, gave her a tight-lipped smile. 'I'm okay.'

'You miss her.'

'Yeah. Terribly.'

She repositioned herself, coming to a sitting position with her feet tucked sideways under her, and cuddled up next to him with her head leaning against his shoulder. One arm wrapped around his waist, and he set his hand on it.

'Shel?' She looked up at him. 'Thanks. For everything, I mean. For helping me with the house, and you know, just checkin' in.'

She smiled sadly. 'Anders, you're like my best friend,' she said, laughing a bit. 'My best guy friend, at least. I know you usually have Lenny and all ...' She hesitated and for just an instant looked as if she'd said something wrong. '... but I don't know, sometimes a girl just understands better, you know?'

He closed his eyes and concentrated on the music, absorbing the slow rhythms in a way he hadn't when they busied themselves with the house cleaning. Shel was lightly rubbing his forearm, and for a moment he let himself imagine it was Olivia. Her touch was like a magnet drawing the longing to the surface, and it grew unbearable. He wasn't sure, but a short moan might have slipped from his lips.

'Oh, man, I'm so sorry,' she whispered.

He didn't say anything. He was just glad she was there. It seemed to him that Shel might have been the only person who hadn't told him, at some point since the accident, that he was crazy. He bent and touched his lips to her fine hair, giving the top of her head a single kiss.

'What was that for?'

133

'I don't know.' After a bit, he said, 'So what about you? What have you been up to since I saw you last?'

'I'm almost done with my first semester of classes.'

He knew she referred to classes she'd signed up for at the community college. She'd been working at Palmetto since high school, and four and a half years of waitressing had convinced her that she needed to go to college.

'Meet any cute guys yet?' he teased. He'd been thrilled when she first told him about enrolling because he thought she might finally start hanging with friends nearer to her age. When she didn't say anything, he added, 'Is that a yes?'

She shrugged. 'Boy meets girl. Boy seduces girl. Boy dumps girl.'

He remained silent, partly from guilt because he'd brought it up, and partly because he just didn't know what to say.

'It was a professor,' she said then, as if confessing.

He leaned to the side, trying to see her face, and she squinted up at him. She had the braced look of a child who thinks she's about to be swatted for some transgression. They both knew her pattern, the continued attraction to older men – Anders knew he'd been a piece of the pattern – but somehow this admission about a teacher took it to a new level.

'It was stupid, I know,' she said, answering his look. 'I just ... I don't know. He made me feel special.'

'What happened?'

'He's my English professor. He'd stand up there in front of the class getting all excited about poetry and literature and words and I got excited just listening to him. I've never met a guy like that, you know? I wrote some paper on *The Great Gatsby* and he called me into his office to discuss it. He made me feel like I was a genius, like I understood things that no one else in the class understood.'

'Maybe you really did,' Anders offered.

'No. He was playing me big time. You know, he'd say these corny things to me, about how I had this inner light, and how he was a moth attracted to my light ...' She laughed sarcastically. 'I ate it up. I ate it up and went back for more.'

'And then what? He decided after a few crashes into the light that he was done?'

'No ...' Her body tightened; the change was so slight but he felt it against his stomach where her arm still rested. 'One day I stopped by his office, just to say hi, really, and there was another student there. I overheard him giving the same exact line to this girl. You know, about the light and all that.' She lifted her arm for a moment, moved as if to get something from the corner of her eye. 'Yeah, he'd been playing me, all right. You know what the worst part of all is? I knew it in my gut all along, I think, but I just couldn't resist it. When he talked to me like that, it felt so good, you know?'

'He's a jerk. You're lucky to be rid of him.'

'I know that.'

'You should report him.' When she didn't respond, didn't even acknowledge she'd heard him, he said, 'Did you hear me? You need to report him. He shouldn't be teaching.'

'I can't.' She sighed. 'You don't understand. I just can't.'

'You can.'

'No. It's not like I'm blameless. I was willing.'

He grunted. 'Shel, will you listen to yourself? *He was your teacher.* Report him.'

She sighed again and didn't say more.

'Hey.'

She glanced up at him, expecting more reprimands.

'You do have light, you know. He was right about that, so don't let the fact that he's a jerk make you think otherwise.'

She rolled her eyes and laid her head back on his shoulder, laughing a little.

The music lulled them into silence. His eyelids grew heavy and he began to doze. He opened his eyes when he sensed what felt like a small patch of warmth on his sleeve. No sooner did he notice it than he recognized it was *wet* warmth, coming right through his T-shirt, and it was in the exact spot where the side of Shel's face rested against him. In the instant he realized she was crying, she tilted her head up and gently touched her lips to his. Her small hand felt his cheek then, and made its way through his hair to the back of his head. She made a sound in her throat as her lips opened and her tongue invited him in. Without thought he returned the kiss; it'd been a long time since they'd done this, since before the day he'd met Olivia, but it immediately felt familiar to him, both physically and emotionally. Though he wouldn't ever be able to articulate it, a part of him understood that it had always happened when one of them was hurting. And now, of course, they were both hurting.

They moved effortlessly to a reclining position. The long length of his body hovered over her smaller one; he was intuitively careful not to crush her as the kiss resumed virtually uninterrupted. She still held one hand to his head while the other worked its way under his shirt to his back.

The music paused between songs, and their small noises mingled with the whistle of the breeze to fill the silence. In the moment before the next song began, he heard the tern. Olivia's tern. It must have been sitting on the deck railing; he couldn't miss the characteristic *ker-wik* of its call.

He tried to pull away but she lifted her head to stay with him. She reluctantly dropped her head to the couch only when he turned his head to the side and began to rise to his knees.

'Anders.' She grabbed his upper arm and he let her pull him down closer again. 'It's okay to do this,' she whispered. 'We both need this.'

The sides of her face still showed damp traces of her tears and her lips were swollen from their kissing.

'Shel—'

She covered his lips with her index finger. 'Come on, it's okay. It'll be a good release for both of us.' As if she could read his mind, she added, 'Nothing more, just a release.'

'Look, I can't. It just doesn't feel right.' He managed to climb off her without resistance this time and sat on the edge of the couch with his head in his hands.

'Why won't you let me help you feel a little better? Friends, remember? This is what friends do for each other.'

He laughed at the absurdity of her last sentence, and before he could stop himself, he said, 'I don't need a sympathy fuck, Shel.' It came out sounding haughty and contemptuous, and he knew it was the wrong thing to say the minute it escaped his lips. He looked over at her to gauge her reaction. If he didn't know better he would have thought someone had just slapped her across the face.

'Well, did you ever think that maybe I do?' she said finally.

They stared at each other as her words sunk in, and then she rose from the couch and started for the kitchen.

'Aw, come on,' he said, rising quickly to follow her. He touched her arm, but she shrugged him off. In the kitchen she grabbed her bag from the chair but he blocked her exit. 'Look, I didn't word that right but—'

She put her hands on her tiny hips. 'No, you sure didn't.'

She lifted her chin, raised her eyebrows. She was going to give him the opportunity to apologize, to put a spin on his words in an effort to smooth everything over and maybe even give her what she claimed she wanted, needed. But the frustration with her that had caused him to make the comment in the first place, however unartfully spoken, only blossomed with her easy willingness to let him reconsider.

'Look, it's more than just *an act*, okay? It's more than something two people do to help each other get off.'

He could see her swallow and somehow he knew she'd misunderstood. She shifted her stance. 'Are you saying we . . . it's something more to you?'

'No!' He lashed the word at her, causing her to flinch. He shook his head in disgust, at himself for raising his voice and not explaining well, and at her for misunderstanding. He tried to speak more softly. 'No. I'm saying it *should* be. When two people . . .' He sighed and his shoulders fell as he watched her shrink in front of him. 'It's supposed to be, okay? You know it, and I know it.'

She crossed her arms, hugging herself as if she was cold, and stared in the direction of the kitchen window. He touched her arm to get her to look at him.

'What we did . . . no, *what I did* . . . I was wrong, and I'm sorry.'

He forced himself to look her in the eye as he attempted his apology, but all he saw was the return of her scepticism. 'You're full of shit,' she said, glaring at him.

'Look, all I'm saying is, what you said, about what friends do for each other, it's . . .' He didn't know how to say that he just thought she was selling herself short, and he regretted being a willing accomplice. 'It's *not* what friends do for each other, you know?'

'No, I don't know. You wanna explain that statement, Anders?' Her voice was level, though her lip quivered and she looked like she was about to burst into tears.

'Friends *look out* for each other, friends don't fuck each other, okay?' He knew he sounded like a father lecturing his teenage daughter but he didn't care. 'A friend would tell you to have a little respect for yourself, don't give yourself to every guy that—'

'Are you calling me a slut now?' Venom dripped from each word.

'Oh, for Christ's sake—'

'Oh, but it couldn't be that, could it?' The tears began to flow in rivulets but she didn't even seem to notice. 'Because if I was a slut you'd have no problem with it, would you? If I was a big-boobed blonde slut from New Jersey who had something you really, really wanted, you'd have no problem with it, would you?'

His body became so rigid he felt like he'd just received a jolt of shock therapy.

'*What did you just say?*'

'Like you're one to be talking about respect.' She pushed her way past him out of the kitchen. 'Like you're one to be talking about *friendships*, for that matter!' she called over her shoulder.

Somehow he compelled his leaden body to turn and go after her. He found her bawling at the front door, one hand on the knob. He knew his worst assumptions about what she'd said were true. But still he said, 'Tell me what you're talking about.'

She turned her back to him; whether she couldn't bear to look at him or she didn't want him to look at her, he didn't know. 'Oh God, stop it! I know. Lenny knows.'

'Shel—'

'What? You didn't really think you could do something like that and she'd keep her mouth shut, did you? It's like you handed her a gun to shoot him with.'

He stood mute; nothing he could say would adequately respond to the truth of what she'd just said. At his silence she reached for the door again. 'I've gotta go,' she muttered through her sobs.

'It didn't happen like you think.'

She halted on the front stoop, her ears tuned to every word, wanting him to redeem himself somehow.

'It was more like an act of violence.'

'You raped her?' Her wet, bloodshot eyes locked on his; they reflected an odd mixture of doubt and hope that startled him, and without even realizing it, he stepped back.

'No, of course not.'

'Well, maybe you should have. He might have had a chance of understanding that.'

A soft grunt of incredulity broke from his throat; his mouth hung slightly open. Shel took off, head down, toward her car.

As she opened the driver's side door she shot him one last hateful look. 'I mean it when I say this, Anders: good luck finding out what really happened to Olivia. It may be the only thing that'll make losing his friendship worth it for you.'

# 11

HE WALKED into the police station on Monday morning wondering what had taken him so long. Nathan had told him he had a right to see the report of the investigation, but he'd thought by showing his face at the station, he would somehow be inviting them to arrest him on the spot. He'd assumed he would find out at some point whether they intended to charge him; they'd either show up at the beach house to arrest him, or they'd contact him somehow to let him know he was off the hook. The passage of time since the visit from Reardon and Hewes hadn't dispelled this belief; it just made him think that the wheels of justice moved even slower than originally thought.

But the impact of Shel's parting words on Saturday had provoked him to action in a way that Nathan's information, Lenny's speech, or even the contents of Olivia's box, hadn't.

It wasn't until he walked through the double glass doors and saw the buzz of activity that he realized how irrelevant their accident must be in the total scheme of police business. A long counter spanned the width of the room and behind it sat several clerks. All stared without expression at the computer screens in front of them, even the ones who appeared to be helping someone at the counter or on the phone at their ear. A set of thigh-high swinging doors, similar to the kind seen in courtrooms, flapped back and forth noisily as station employees went back and forth, back and forth, looking busy as they talked on their cellphones or fingered through files of papers. Some were in uniform and had pistols displayed at their waists. In the back, behind the counter and the clerks, was a glass partition, and behind it, rows of desks, every one of them cluttered with files. Doors lined the hallway to the side of the open area, opening into more private offices, he guessed. The sound of ringing phones was incessant.

He took a number and sat down to wait, wondering if his sense of anonymity was a good thing or a bad thing, given the circumstances.

He rose as soon as his number was called and approached the woman waiting at the far end of the counter. Her greeting consisted of nothing more than meeting his eye.

'Uh, yes, ma'am, I was trying to find out how to get a copy of a police report.' He hesitated before continuing. He wasn't sure how much detail to give. He suspected this lady wasn't long on patience, yet she just stared at him as if waiting for more. 'There was a motorcycle accident—'

'You got a number?'

'Excuse me?' Suddenly he remembered the little piece of pink paper in his hand. 'Oh, yes.' He set it on the counter in front of her.

Her eyes landed for an instant on the paper and slowly looked back up at him. If her expression changed, it wasn't for the better. 'A case number.' She didn't say it, but he could hear it: *Idiot*. When he didn't immediately produce anything, she sighed. 'Did the officers at the scene give you a case number?'

'Oh. Oh, yes,' he said again. He dug in the front pocket of his jeans and pulled out the crumpled yellow form. He laid it on the counter as he had the other, but he spent a few seconds smoothing it down before pushing it in her direction.

She slid it off the counter and ignored him as her eyes first found the information she needed on the paper and then returned to her computer screen. She began to punch at the buttons of her keyboard. He tried to appear patient and undemanding as he scanned the items on her counter space: a pack of cigarettes and a lighter waiting for her next smoke break, two ragged photos tucked into the corner of her desk pad – one displaying a curly-haired toddler, the other a mangy beagle – and a coffee-stained mug with 'Java Bitch' written on the side. The absence of a man in the pictures caused him to look at her left hand. A lone copper band graced her pinky finger. As if she sensed him studying her, she looked up, and he gave her a closed-lip smile.

'The investigation has been closed. It's fifty cents a page if you want a copy of the report. You'll have to go to the records division to get it.'

'What?' *What did she mean by 'closed'?*

'Like I said, you can get a copy, but it's not free.'

'You said the investigation has been closed. When? Why?' He didn't know whether to be relieved that he was off the hook, or perturbed that they'd given up searching for the black Mercedes.

She let out another sigh, this one more dramatic than the last, and turned back to the screen. 'Two weeks ago today, actually. The officer on the case filed a supplemental report.' She squinted as one finger pressed repeatedly on a key to scroll down the page. 'No fatalities, insufficient evidence of criminal intent, it says.' She leaned back in her chair and looked up at him, as if to say 'You want any more information, fork over the money.'

He felt dizzy on his feet, and he gripped the counter to steady himself. Her voice came to him from a watery depth somewhere. 'Sir?'

He looked at her, but before he could force any words out, she said again, 'Sir, are you okay?'

'Can you just tell me, who filed the report? Which officer closed the case?'

She glanced at the screen again, sneaking a cautious peek at him as she did. 'Officer Bryson, it looks like.'

'What about Officers Reardon or Hewes? Did either one of them sign off on it, too?'

Without even looking at her computer again, she shook her head. 'Sir, you must be mistaken. There's no one on our force with the name of Reardon or Hewes.'

HE BURNED rubber on the way out of the police station lot. He didn't even realize he intended to go to the hospital until he found himself on the road that ran along Lake Monroe. He sped past the fishermen on the banks, passing the day in their folding lawn chairs with small coolers at their feet, and barely registered their existence.

The front desk informed him that Carrie's shift didn't begin until one, so he rode down the road a few more miles to pass the time at a biker bar. It was approaching lunchtime; the gravel lot bulged with expensive bikes wearing studded leather saddlebags and sporting a lot of chrome. The display informed him of the crowd he'd find inside. Sure enough, the small dark room buzzed with a smattering of professional types – lawyers, bankers, some doctors from the hospital. He sat at a table near the back, ordered a pulled-pork sandwich and a cold Bud, and finished the first Bud even before the sandwich arrived. Two hours and several beers later, he stepped from the almost empty room into the glaring sun. He hadn't touched the sandwich.

Back at the hospital, he bypassed the desk in the lobby and took the elevator directly to Carrie's floor. By now well-versed in the ways of the ICU, he pressed the button outside the entrance and waited for someone to answer. A nurse he didn't recognize came to the door, and before she could even greet him, he blurted, 'I need to see Carrie.'

Her hands went to her hips in a stance of authority. 'Can I tell her your name, sir?'

He thought she looked at him hatefully. It didn't occur to

him that the sweaty sight he presented and the beer on his breath might have something to do with it. 'Anders. Tell her Anders is here.'

'Give me a minute, sir.'

He stood against the wall and fiddled with the helmet in his hands as he waited. In a matter of minutes the door opened again, and he didn't even give the nurse a chance to make excuses. He leaned toward the opening and yelled, 'Carrie! I need to talk to you!'

The nurse was on him, grasping his arm roughly and attempting to push him back. She called for someone to help her.

Suddenly Carrie appeared, muttering, 'It's okay, I'll take care of it.' The other nurse looked sceptical but Carrie waved her away. 'I'll get rid of him.'

The door closed and the two of them stood alone in the barren hallway.

'You'll *get rid* of me?'

'I asked you to leave me alone.'

He couldn't believe such a stern voice came from such a delicate person.

She looked down angrily at the helmet in his hands. 'You didn't ride a motorcycle here, did you?'

'Why didn't you tell me? Why didn't you tell me she was alive?'

She gave a quick, nervous glance down the halls in each direction. 'We need to go somewhere private,' she said, even though the halls were empty. She grabbed his hand and led him to a door, and after she'd unlocked and opened it to wave him in, he saw it was a small supply room with a grey metal desk and chair against one wall. She flicked on the light and closed the door behind them.

She sat on the desk, one foot on the chair. 'This is it. This has got to be the last time you do this to me, understand?'

'Why didn't you tell me?' he asked again.

She just shook her head and looked away, her lips sealed tight.

'Carrie, why didn't you tell me?' he persisted. 'You *lied* to me.'

'I didn't lie to you.'

He grunted. 'Don't split hairs with me. It was a lie of omission.' She didn't respond to that accusation and he deemed her silence an admission of guilt. 'You knew she was alive and yet you didn't bother to tell me.' He could see her swallow, her small jaw remained set. 'Where is she?' She shook her head again and lowered her eyes. 'He didn't just tell me she'd died,' he kept on, trying to crack her. 'He accused me of *killing* her.'

She shifted on the desk. 'I'm sorry. But what do you want from me, Anders? What do you expect me to do? I made the mistake of taking you into her room *one time*, and now you act like I'm your confidante or something. I barely know you! I was just her nurse!'

Her words stunned him at first, and then the anger returned.

'What do you mean, what do I want from you? I just want to know what happened to her. I want to know where she is. My God, is that asking so much?'

'No, but . . .' She grabbed at the sides of her head as if shaking her brain cells back into their rightful place. 'I mean, yes! It's confi–'

'Nothing adds up. You know I'm right. Why the secrecy? What didn't he want me to find out? Why couldn't I see her in the hospital?'

'Because he's her father and he *said* you couldn't.'

She spouted the party line, but he knew from her refusal to look at him she didn't agree with it. He had to go at her from a different angle. He pulled a plastic chair from a stack of extras in the corner and plopped onto it backwards right in front of her, his legs straddling the seatback. In a low, conspiratorial voice, he said, 'Did you know her records are gone?'

Her face blanched. 'What are you talking about?'

'Olivia's hospital records are gone. They've disappeared. There's nothing but an empty file.' They stared at each other as if in a contest. He won when she finally looked away again, shaking her head in denial. 'Did you hear me? *Somebody took her records.*'

'That's crazy,' she said nervously. 'Maybe they're just lost—'

'Everyone keeps telling me I'm crazy. I'm not crazy!'

'You're drunk. And you're yelling at me.'

'I'm sorry.' He closed his eyes, tried to calm himself and keep his volume down. 'Yes, I might be just a little buzzed. I will cop to that. I've had a hell of a day and the cold beer was calling my name. But I just found out my girlfriend is alive and I have no fuckin' idea where she is. You know, the girlfriend I thought was dead and whose death I was being blamed for? And I also just found out he sicced fake cops on me. Or cops using fake names. So *forgive me* for having a beer or two.' He knew his sarcasm was making matters worse but he couldn't control it.

'What are you talking about? Fake cops?' She attempted scepticism, but in her eyes he could see his words starting to have an effect. 'And how do you know this about the files? You can't see them, you know that. They're confidential.'

He thought of Crystal. Even though she'd double-crossed him, he believed her claim about the files. In that, at least, he didn't think she'd screwed with him.

'I have sources.'

She let out an uneasy laugh, though the frightened look on her face told him she didn't think it was remotely funny. 'Now you sound like him.' She looked at the floor then and said, almost to herself, 'This is so messed up.'

Her change in demeanour scared him. He knew for certain now she was hiding something. If anyone might have answers, it was Carrie, but he would have to persuade her to talk.

'What's messed up? Tell me what's going on. Tell me where she is.'

'I don't know.'

He reached for her hands and she let him hold them. 'Listen to me, Carrie. You know as well as I do that whole files don't disappear. Sure, maybe paper might get lost, but there are computer files, right?' She looked at him, but she wouldn't give him a nod to confirm or deny what he'd said. 'It's all gone. There's nothing left but an empty folder with her name on it. I saw it myself.'

'But why would there be an empty folder even, if someone was trying to erase all evidence of her being here? I just can't believe—'

He squeezed her hands. 'Just tell me one thing, just one thing. Did she regain consciousness?'

The gulf of silence that followed his question convinced him that Olivia might be alive, but she hadn't recovered. So Carrie surprised him when she finally answered with a hesitant nod of her head.

'But?'

'Listen, I shouldn't be talking to you. I'm going to—'

'Carrie, stop it already!' She recoiled from him instantly, pulling her hands away. 'I'm sorry,' he said, softening his voice, 'but don't insult me. Stop making me beg you for every little tidbit of information. Either give it to me, or don't. But I'm tired of the games. I'm tired of everyone's games. And I honestly believed you'd be the last one to play them.'

'I'm not playing games.'

'Okay, then, so trust me, will you?'

'And what have you done so far to make me trust you, huh?' Now she was mad, too. 'You come in here drunk—'

'I'm not *drunk.*'

'– and thank God you didn't kill anyone getting here. From the phone call I had from your friend the other day, it sounds like this isn't the first time you've taken to the road when you shouldn't have. And yet you want me to trust you! I've already been written up once because I let you in that day. He was furious. And now, this.' She waved her thin arm at him as if he was rubbish. 'What am I going to tell my supervisor when she gets wind that you stopped by to see me today, especially in the state you're in? I'm starting to think he was right about you.'

'What do you mean?' he asked quietly, sinking with shame at her indictment, '*right about me?*'

'You're on this mission,' she continued, ignoring his question, 'and you're dragging me into it. Maybe you have the cojones to tangle with her dad, but I don't.' She sighed loudly. 'Look, I don't know what he has against you or what's going on, but he made it quite clear that I was not to share any information with you, or anyone else without his permission. Maybe it's time to just let it go, you know?'

At these words he leaned away and laughed disbelievingly. 'Oh, sure: "Anders, I know you loved this woman, and she loved you, but someone has kidnapped her, so just forget about it."'

'Kidnap is a strong word. We're talking about her father.'

'We're talking about a father she despised, Carrie. I guess I just find it hard to accept that she went with him willingly. Didn't look back. Didn't bother to collect her things. Didn't say, "Hey, what about Anders, you know, the guy who lived in my house? I should let him know I'm leaving."'

Carrie looked away then and Anders knew he'd hit on something.

'What? Did he force her to leave against her will?'

She opened her mouth to speak, but words didn't come.

149

'Please, what do you know? What are you too afraid to tell me?'

She turned back to face him, her lips pursed in frustration, her eyes wet with suppressed tears.

'Please, Carrie,' he said. 'Remember why you brought me to her room in the first place? Remember the tattoo? Maybe she got it for a reason, you know? Maybe she had a feeling about something, so she'd marked herself with my name for a reason—'

'That's not what I thought.'

'But think about it now. It could be the reason, couldn't it?'

She breathed in deeply, for courage, he thought, as if she knew once she confided in him, there would be no going back.

'Look, I believe you. About the files missing and everything. I know this is bigger than a father trying to keep a boyfriend away from his daughter. That happens more than you'd imagine. But there's something else going on here. I want to tell you what I know, I really do.' She shrugged her shoulders as if conceding defeat in some unknown battle. 'Maybe because I want someone else to know all this in case something happens to me—'

'What do you mean, in case something happens to you?'

'– but I'm afraid. So you have to promise me he'll never find out where you learned what I'm going to tell you.'

'Okay.' He nodded a little too emphatically. He just wanted her to get on with it.

'Promise me,' she said, repeating her demand. 'And promise me you'll be very, very careful.'

'I promise. Please, just tell me.'

'After I let you in that day, I received more than a simple dressing down by my boss. In fact, anyone who was involved in Olivia's care got talked to by the head honchos here. I mean, they always make sure we all understand HIPAA, and we're told in no uncertain terms that our jobs are on the line if we don't adhere to the requirements of the law, but this was different. The top brass was involved. I don't know, maybe he paid them off, or maybe because he's a drug company bigwig, he's got connections or he has something else to hang over their heads. But it was almost like *they* were scared, too, you know?'

Anders waited, not quite believing that the situation could be worse than it already was.

'And then he paid me a personal visit. He caught me getting out of my car one night in the parking lot at my apartment.'

*At her apartment?* 'What did he do?'

'He threatened me.'

'What exactly do you mean, he threatened you? To get you fired? Or are you *physically* afraid of him?'

Her eyes welled up again; she nodded slowly. 'Yes, I think I am. He's scary. There's something about him. I wouldn't be surprised if he knew we were in here talking right now.' He thought of how Mayfield had known he'd been at Shel's. Carrie leaned in closer. 'He made it quite clear to me that if I told you anything, if I told anyone anything, I would pay the price, and I would pay dearly.'

'What do you mean?' he asked again. His tone was becoming increasingly desperate.

'I don't know. I think he meant to leave it to my imagination. And maybe I'm just paranoid, and he's just a bully and he knows my imagination would be more threatening than reality. But I don't think so. I think you need to be very, very careful. I think we both do, really.'

Anders felt light-headed, but he couldn't tell if it was a result of being enclosed in this little, stuffy room, or whether it was the growing sense that he was in way over his head. Maybe it was both.

'And what about Olivia? What haven't you told me about Olivia?'

She shook her head as a warning to him, but he persisted. 'I need to know. Even if it's bad, I need to know.'

'I just don't want you to be more upset—'

'Just tell me, Carrie.'

'She regained consciousness before her discharge, but ... she didn't remember much.' She eyed him to see if he understood her meaning, but he just waited. He knew what she was about to say – his leg began its jittery shaking – but he needed to hear it out loud. 'She ... she didn't remember you.'

He rose fast from the chair and paced the tiny room. Despite the air blowing from a small vent in the ceiling, his lungs couldn't seem to fill with enough air. He leaned against the door and crossed his arms. She regarded him warily, as if he was an animal wanting out of a cage.

'She didn't remember anything, really, about the accident, about her life here even—'

'Did she know who *she* was?'

Carrie scrunched her face. 'Yeah ... yeah, she seemed to remember who she was, who her family was, her life back in Connecticut, but ... I don't know, it was just really weird.'

'What?'

'She had a sort of selective memory, you know? She had vague memories of her life in Florida, but they all seemed very general. They weren't nearly as detailed as the memories she could give about her life before she moved here, though I have no way of knowing if even those were accurate. Her family said they were. When she was asked about specifics, like where she lived in Florida, or who her friends were, she became very frustrated because she couldn't remember anything. Eventually, her father insisted we stopped questioning her. When I was alone with her, I tried to ask her about you, and ...' Her voice trailed off, and she shrugged. 'Nothing.' She studied him, then, as if she thought perhaps he could have lied about them living together. 'The only boyfriend she mentioned at all was someone named Brent, and—'

'Was it Brent Campbell?'

'I don't know. Just "Brent". But her family seemed to know him.'

'Do you expect that she'll eventually regain her full memory?'

She breathed in, weighing her words. 'Well, in most cases, patients do. It's not uncommon for someone to lose their memory after a concussion, and usually when the memory begins to return, it returns quickly, and fairly completely.'

'Where did he take her?'

'That I don't know.' He must have looked sceptical because she added, 'I really don't. I'm not keeping anything from you anymore.'

He believed her. His mind started to integrate this new information with what he already knew. 'Can I ask you something? Have you ever heard of Cranium – no, no, I mean Cranitex MR?'

'No.'

'It's some sort of drug.'

'No. No, there's no drug by that name.'

'Yes. Yes, there is.'

'Anders, I think I would know—'

'I saw it, in her backpack.'

Carrie looked at him. He knew she wanted to argue with him, to insist again that he was drunk, crazy, because wasn't all of this crazy?

'It was a little blue pill. The bottle was unmarked, but the pills weren't. I remember, Carrie. I remember because it just seemed odd at the time.'

'How long ago was this? Maybe it's new.'

'No, it's been about seven months.'

'What was it again? Cranitex MR? I'll look it up and see.

But I'm telling you, I don't think so. And, anyway, what's your point? I mean, you saw this so long ago, long before your accident.'

'I don't know. I just thought if you knew what it was . . . or maybe her dad mentioned it. I don't know. I don't know, really, what I'm thinking.' He sighed. He was tired and drained, and his ability to think straight seemed to worsen instead of improve as the effects of the beer waned. 'I just don't know. All I know is that *someone* ran us off the road, and it was intentional, I'm sure of it. Now she's gone and, according to you, doesn't seem to have a clue that I even exist.'

They both fell silent, lost in their own thoughts, their own concerns. He glanced up at her; she'd finally begun to cry. Her tears fell quietly, and she pulled a tissue from the front pocket of her uniform to wipe at them. He'd been so absorbed in his quest for answers that despite everything she'd told him, he really hadn't accepted the full impact of this on her. He'd been afraid for Olivia's life, but he began to understand that Carrie might be afraid for her own.

'Carrie.'

She looked up at him with red-rimmed eyes. She laughed slightly. 'Sorry. It's just a little overwhelming. I mean, I'm a *nurse.*'

He smiled. 'And I'm a lawn guy.'

This provoked a heartier, genuine laugh from her.

'Maybe you should go to the cops,' he offered. As soon as he said it, though, he knew it wasn't an option. Not after what had happened with Reardon and Hewes.

'No, no. I think that would make things worse. They wouldn't do anything, anyway. It's all too vague, you know? I just want to forget about it.'

Anders did know. The whole sense that something bad had ⁓ned, something much worse than the motorcycle acci- vague and intangible. If Lawrence Mayfield could

154

silence an entire hospital, manipulate cops to harass him, and somehow control his daughter's memory, who knew what other entities he might control. For now, it was beyond the province of the authorities.

'I'll stay away from you. He won't know I talked to you, I promise. But I need you to promise me that you'll let me know if he tries anything.'

She nodded, but he wasn't convinced that she would follow through.

'What are you going to do?' she asked quietly.

He thought about it. That was the question, of course, wasn't it? He knew now Olivia was alive, and he knew her father had wanted to make damn sure he didn't know it. He knew a woman named Makena Mbatia owned the house he lived in – the same woman he thought had told him not to give up, and he knew Olivia had been engaged to a man named Brent Campbell. On second thought, he knew only that a newspaper article *claimed* they'd been engaged; he didn't really know if, in fact, it was true. And finally, he knew that, for some reason, Olivia had kept a matchbox from a bar in Connecticut, her home state.

'I guess I'm going to Connecticut.'

# Connecticut

# 12

JIMMY'S BAR was at the end of a gravel road, exactly where the cashier at the gas station had told Anders he'd find it, and it matched the description she'd given him. A cross between a cabin and an ageing mobile home, it reminded him more of a building he'd find in the backwoods of Florida than deep in the middle of a Connecticut pine forest. An industrial lamp post at the edge of the parking lot cast a weak glow, but the structure's dark brown cedar shingles and black roof still made it difficult to see until he was right up on it. The gold light spilling from the small windows and a crooked neon Budweiser sign near the door provided the only other beacons. He wondered what in the hell Olivia had been doing in this type of place.

As soon as he shut down the engine to his rental car, loud voices and throbbing bass from inside the shack replaced the tinny sound of the car's radio. He counted six other cars in the lot. One was a Ford F-150 pickup, but the others – two Saabs, a BMW convertible, a high-end SUV, and some other pricey model he couldn't identify – didn't fit the setting.

The cashier had given him a funny look when he'd first asked for directions to the place.

'Is there something wrong?' he'd asked.

She'd laughed a bit – it had almost been a cackle – and said, 'Let's just say Jimmy's caters to regulars, and you don't look like a regular.'

Now, looking at the cars in the lot, he understood. He had no doubt that he would be exposed as an outsider the minute he walked through the door of the joint. Had it been some sort of roadside bar, he could have said he was passing by and decided to stop for a drink. But out here in the deep woods at the end of the road, there would be no claiming that his visit was an accident, not a destination. He wondered how he would pull this off.

He stepped from the car and tugged his thin coat tighter against the bitter cold.

As he pulled the heavy door open, the sound of Lynyrd Skynyrd's 'Sweet Home Alabama' filled his ears. He rolled his eyes at the music; it was the Yankee frat boy's idea of gettin' down. He paused on the worn, unfinished wood floor and took in his smoky surroundings. To the left, he spotted the long bar, a simple Formica slab. Behind it, bottles of assorted spirits lined the wall, perching precariously on dusty glass shelving. There was no mirror to reflect the glass as was common in most bars, though there were a few more beer signs hanging by chains from the ceiling. Five or six vinyl-cushioned barstools sat empty against the front of the bar, which was illuminated by just three pendant lights. A fifty-something man in a Harley T-shirt – Anders felt sure this guy belonged to the Ford – worked at a sink behind the bar, rinsing a few beer steins. The T-shirt gave Anders the sense that he might have an ally if things got ugly.

In the middle of the room were a few small tables, some wood, some Formica like the bar, each surrounded by an assortment of mismatched chairs. These, too, were empty.

All the noise and action came from the right half of the room, near two pool tables that took up most of the space in the small building. The music blared from a jukebox in the corner, and at least ten men surrounded the tables, cue sticks in the hands of some, beers and other drinks in the hands of others, cigarettes dangling in mouths or smouldering in small aluminum ashtrays on a beer shelf. Anders guessed they were all around his age, maybe a bit younger, and all were obviously – no doubt about it – shit-faced drunk. They were busy trying to talk over one another, laughing at each other, and not one of them seemed to notice his entrance. Maybe if he played it right, this would turn out to be a lot easier than he'd originally thought.

He approached the bar, nodded to the bartender and asked for whatever beer was on tap. The bartender's eyes lingered on Anders a bit longer than made him comfortable, but Anders pretended not to notice and busied himself with pulling out his pack of cigarettes. What had started as a small crutch was quickly becoming a bad habit.

The bartender noticed and tossed him a box of matches identical to the one Olivia had kept. He placed the beer in front of Anders, its foam spilling over onto the bar, and said, 'You wanna run a tab?'

Anders just shook his head and laid a bill on the counter. He took a long drink, trying to quench the thirst he didn't realize he had until the amber liquid touched his lips. When the bartender returned with his change, Anders nodded in the direction of his shirt.

'You ride a Harley?'

'Yeah, got a '04 Road King and a vintage Chopper. You?'

'Had a Dyna till I was run off the road . . .' The moment he said it, he realized he shouldn't have. He needed to stay away from anything that might blow his cover. Not that he'd given much thought to what his cover might be. 'Now I just ride an old Kawasaki crotch rocket.' He hated the term and wouldn't usually use it, but he knew that's how the older Harley guys thought of the fast sport bikes and their younger riders. He figured he would play into the perception. A little self-deprecation could go a long way.

The bartender lifted Anders's glass and swiped the bar with a rag. 'Tough break; at least you're alive.'

'Been down to Daytona?' he asked to change the subject.

The man leaned one elbow on the counter, and Anders knew he'd made some headway, however minor. 'Oh yeah, more than once. Haven't been since 2004, though.' He laughed. 'That's when I picked up the touring bike. Figured I needed a more comfortable ride home.' He was a big guy. Despite the beer belly that came with his age, he'd managed to maintain an impressive set of biceps, and his hands looked strong enough to strangle any of the guys at the pool tables, if he needed to. 'You get there often?'

Anders nodded. 'Yeah, I live . . .' He caught himself. 'I live up north, but I head down each year for Bike Week. Wouldn't miss it.'

'Whereabouts you from? Haven't seen you before in these parts.'

He picked up his beer again and guzzled, buying time. He'd been an idiot, thinking he could come in here and wing it.

'Chicago,' he said, thinking of where Karina and Nathan lived with their kids. At least he'd been there a couple times, before Karina's cool treatment of Anders had turned downright glacial.

'Chicago, huh? What brings you out here?'

'I'm a reporter chasing a story.' *Where the hell did that come from?* He liked the sound of it, though, even if every visible muscle on the bartender's body tensed when he said it. Maybe he didn't like reporters.

But he likes women, Anders thought. The *Sports Illustrated Swimsuit Calendar* pinned to the wall near the cash register confirmed that much. So maybe it was time to work a bit of the truth into his story. He took another drink to quell his nerves and emptied the glass.

'Some time back I heard about that gal from around here whose boyfriend was in Iraq, something about her receiving an engagement ring in the mail on the same day she'd mistakenly been told he died.'

The bartender drew him another beer without asking. 'The Mayfield girl.'

Anders's gut tightened at the mention of Olivia's name. 'You know of her?'

'Everyone knows the Mayfields.' His focus darted briefly in the direction of the raucous group on the other side of the room. Anders waited, but the man didn't offer more.

'Yeah, well, it seemed to me like there might be a larger story.'

The bartender snorted. 'The story is what they're doing to our boys over there, and then everyone wonders why the shit hits the fan when they get back home.'

Anders swallowed hard. He had the distinct sense that this man had unknowingly just given him a load of information, though it would be up to Anders to figure it out. 'What do you mean?'

The man shook his head and glared at him. 'Uh-uh. I ain't talking. Next thing I know you'll have my face on the Nancy Grace show.' Anders didn't know who the hell Nancy Grace was, but he got the message. He was right, this guy *didn't* like reporters. He cursed himself again for not planning a bit better. The bartender leaned over the bar and pointed an angry finger at him. 'And let me give you a little piece of advice. I'd think twice before you go around telling everyone you're a reporter. Especially these boys.' He motioned toward the pool tables. 'You might find yourself lying out back with a busted face and a cue stick shoved up your ass.'

The bartender regarded Anders coldly as he set the drink in front of him. Anders knocked it back, his Adam's apple bobbing as the liquid made its way down his throat.

'What'd you say your name was?'

Anders glared back at the man. He placed the drained glass

on the bar, a little harder than necessary. 'I didn't.' He stood, pushing the change from the first beer towards the man, and added another bill to the pile. 'And between us, I just quit my job at the paper.'

HE RECLINED back against the wall, sitting sideways in the booth, one of his lanky legs propped up on the bench, the other with its foot on the floor, fidgeting as usual. He took a long drag of his cigarette, wishing that it was a joint, and then blew the smoke out slowly toward the ceiling and watched it float away and dissipate. His head was swimming in beer and whiskey; he shouldn't have mixed the two.

He'd been surprised when, several hours earlier, he'd approached the group and asked if he could get in on the next game, and they'd accepted his presence without question. He would have liked to believe it had something to do with the alcohol-instilled confidence he'd projected, but he knew the likelier explanation had to do with *their* condition, not his. Despite his protests that he'd had enough, they began buying him shots of Jack Daniel's Single Barrel after he'd won the first game of pool. It went down easily, and sure enough, his skills diminished as the night wore on.

It didn't take long to discover that several of the men were soldiers in the Army Reserve. Officers, not enlisted men. Many of them clearly came from money like Olivia, but unlike Olivia, they revelled in the privileges it afforded them. Though Anders put up a friendly, non-threatening front, he formed his conclusions about them quickly. As far as he was concerned, they were spoiled rich boys who'd grown up attending private military or prep schools and spending their summers in the Hamptons or on the islands off Cape Cod. Maybe it made sense that this would be their local hang-out, a spot away from the masses, a place they could call their own and do whatever they wanted without interference from others who might not recognize their status and authority.

He'd finally settled into one of the booths with a few others who'd given up at pool: some guy in a blue oxford named Grant, a brainy looking guy with glasses named Marshall, and a red-faced, red-haired dude whose name he didn't catch. A large, muscular guy they all called Duke – though Anders thought it had to be a nickname – hovered at the end of the booth whenever it wasn't his turn to shoot. He appeared to be the ringleader.

Anders listened to their drunken conversations and joined in when he could, hoping for an opening to ask about the Mayfields without being too conspicuous. Yet as the hands on the crooked clock near the john passed midnight, his focus slipped and it was all he could do to keep his eyes open.

He thought about how nice it would be to crawl into bed and fall asleep, and this thought caused him to remember that he hadn't found a motel for the night. *Shit.* More poor planning on his part. Back in Florida, he'd gone from the hospital to the Orlando airport, stopping at the beach house just long enough to pack and call a cab. A few hours later, he'd landed in Hartford, Connecticut, intent on finding a place called Jimmy's on the outskirts of a little town called Clifton. He hadn't worried about the rest.

'I need a woman,' he found himself saying out loud, thinking about how, before Olivia, it'd always been easy to find a place to rest his head, whether he'd been horny, too drunk or simply too tired to make it back to the trailer. Lenny liked to say that women thought of him like a puppy, always wanting to bring him home.

The two guys across from him misunderstood his meaning, though, and they howled with laughter. He smiled, enjoying their reaction.

'We all need a woman,' said Grant. He raised his glass into

the air and the others followed suit. 'To the fairer sex!' he shouted. They mocked a toast and slammed back whatever remained of their drinks. 'Another round, Jimmy!' he called to the bartender, and it finally dawned on Anders that the guy behind the bar was the same guy whose name was on the dark sign out front. He wondered if Jimmy would eventually cut them off, although the time for that had long since passed.

'Even better, we need a whore.' The voice rising above the rest belonged to the apparent bodybuilder, Duke. He stood at the end of the booth with a cue stick in one hand and a shot glass in the other. 'One who'll shut her mouth and open her legs.' His words slurred.

The comment came out angry and foreboding, but Anders felt like he was the only one who noticed. It brought even louder hoots and howls from the rest of the group.

'Yeah, where's Campbell when we need him?' said another guy from the far side of the nearest pool table.

Anders's head spun and his eyelids were heavy, but every drunken sense came alive when he heard the name 'Campbell'. Were they talking about Brent Campbell? Nervous laughter followed the question; each man in the room waited to see how the others would respond.

'No, man, the question is, where's *Olivia* when we need her?'

Anders jerked his head up at Duke's voice just as the room exploded. Whatever trepidation any of them felt a moment earlier had been released now that Olivia's name had been mentioned. Anders had no way of knowing the reason for the original reticence, but, clearly, they'd all reached a tacit decision that the mysterious topic was no longer verboten.

'Woo baby!' one of them yelled, and from another, 'Give – it – to – me – now!'

Anders shot a glance at the bar. Jimmy had a clipboard in

his hand as if he'd been taking inventory, but he now stood still, his jaw set, staring at the uproarious group. Staring at Anders.

*The story is what they're doing to our boys over there, and then everyone wonders why the shit hits the fan when they get back home.*

Anders looked away, back to the wildness in front of him. He wished desperately to be sober. 'Who's Olivia?' he asked, hearing the strangeness in his own voice. He had to keep it under control; he couldn't let them see that this conversation was anything more to him than a late-night, drunken discussion of pussy in a bar. He forced a smile.

His question caused Marshall to bang his fist on the table in delight. 'Who's Olivia?' he said, repeating Anders's question. 'Who's Olivia, you ask?' He threw his head back, laughing. 'Hey, boys! Should we tell him about Olivia?'

A chorus of animal noises filled the shrinking room. The contents of Anders's stomach, which consisted of nothing except beer, whiskey, pretzels and the beef jerky he'd inhaled about an hour ago, threatened to reverse its course. He could think of several different things they might 'tell him' about Olivia, and none of them were comforting. He could only imagine how many other things he hadn't even thought of. His eyes darted from monstrous face to monstrous face; it took every bit of resolve he possessed to stay seated, a fake grin on his face, while he tried to present a curiosity borne of pure lust instead of pure fear. He could feel Jimmy's stare but he refused to meet it for fear of tipping off the men in front of him.

'Aw, I don't know,' a guy in a yellow polo shirt crooned, 'hate to get him all worked up when there's not a broad in sight.' More guffaws.

The red-faced man across the booth from Anders reached for his cigarettes and lighter. 'She's a living legend to some of these guys,' he said, tapping a cigarette from the pack. Grant picked up on the comment and called out in a louder voice, 'At least to the ones who were lucky enough to be present that night, eh?'

'Still pissed about taking grandma to Bingo, huh, Ramsey?' came a voice from near the first pool table, where a few of them continued to take practice shots.

Another voice. 'Olivia took supportin' the troops to a whole new level.'

The comments came at him non-stop from all sides.

*They're talking about before she knew you.* But were they? And even if they were, he felt the sting of betrayal from her failure to tell him about her past. But if she had, he doubted the indignation growing inside him would have been any less. Despite his own history at Palmetto, he couldn't resist the male urge to hold her to a double standard.

Anders gave them a look: *Come on, I'm waiting, spill it.*

'Let's just say several of us have shared a few intimate moments with her,' said Marshall, and he laughed.

'Yeah, all on the same night!' called another unseen voice from behind Duke.

Anders shook his head. 'You're all full of shit.' He brought the cigarette to his lips, saw his hand shaking.

His comment pissed off the bodybuilder. 'Oh yeah?' He motioned for the red-faced guy to give up his seat, and then slid into the booth and leaned in close across the table. He nodded for Anders to lean in, too, but Anders resisted. The guy held Anders with his eyes. 'You see that table over there?' Anders glanced at the far pool table but his eyes returned quickly to the face in front of him. 'We took turns fucking her right on that table. If you look close, you can probably still see the stains.' He laughed at himself, like he'd made a joke. 'We nailed her good.'

Anders looked to see the others' reaction to this, but they

all just stared at Duke, some of them nodding, as if admiring him for his storytelling skills.

'Her tight little pussy wasn't so tight by the end of the night,' he added, and it was all Anders could do not to reach across the booth and smash his face into the tabletop.

Instead, he continued to shake his head in denial, his eyes narrowed and scanning the group. Except for the guy sitting in the booth with him, most of the others had gathered near the end of the table, and he felt trapped. He was just as drunk as the rest of them, and even if the alcohol hadn't dulled his flight instinct, he had no easy escape.

'I'm supposed to believe some chick let all of you fuck her on that pool table?'

Had they all been sober, Duke probably would have never responded the way he did, and Anders's night might have ended much differently. But just then, the guy was engaged in a verbal testosterone battle with Anders and all he could think about, apparently, was winning.

'Who said anything about it being voluntary?' he said, raising one eyebrow as a visual touch of sarcasm, for good measure.

The question hit Anders like a sucker punch. The unimaginable images he'd been conjuring in his mind of Olivia flirting with these guys, coming on to them and then letting them have her, one at a time, fell away instantly, but in their place emerged a much more horrific picture. He had to catch himself from lunging for the guy's neck. He didn't stand a chance against the gang of them, and he doubted Jimmy would come to his aid.

His entire body quaking, he pushed his way out of the booth. 'Get outta my way. You're a bunch of fuckin' animals.'

One of the guys standing at the end of the booth caught his arm as he stood. 'Hey.'

'Get your fuckin' paws off me!' Anders shouted, shaking

him off. It took every bit of restraint not to take a swing at the guy. His stomach churned and the whiskey felt like it was boiling at the base of his throat.

He stumbled across the floor, praying that his legs would make it at least to the john. They did, and he slammed his palm into the door to push it open. The stench of old beer and urine smacked him in the face and he staggered to the closest urinal, just in time for most of the contents of his stomach to reach its target. He cursed and his voice echoed against the cold tiles as he sunk to the floor in despair, his back against the wall. He squeezed his eyes shut, trying to block out the image of her that wouldn't go away. Her thin body splayed across the table, struggling without a hope of breaking free as they took turns raping her. Violating her. He bit his lip until it drew blood, though he wasn't even aware of it until he tasted the iron on his tongue.

He shook violently from his rage. He could search the ends of the earth for her, but he couldn't change the fact of what he'd just learned. He'd always wondered if he'd be capable of taking another's life, but he knew now he could. He would.

Desecrate. That was the word. They had desecrated her.

He needed desperately to see her picture. Just as he reached for his wallet and found his back pocket empty, the lights to the john switched off. Duke's sinister voice pierced the dark.

'I think we have what you're looking for, *Anders*.'

He groaned from his spot against the wall, both from the agony of hearing the bastard say his real name and from the knowledge of what was coming next. He heard the figure take a few steps closer. Even in the dark, though, he knew the rest of them were there, too.

'I'm guessing from the contents of your wallet that you've also had the pleasure of Olivia's company, haven't you?'

Anders remained silent, waiting, hoping he came out of this alive.

'Answer me!' the guy demanded, and a boot landed hard in the side of his ribs. 'Haven't you?'

'Fuck you.'

'You know, you really shouldn't carry a wallet if you're trying to maintain a cover.' The boots were right next to him now. 'Of course, can't expect too much brain power from a lawn jockey.'

*Go to hell*, Anders thought. He tried to remember if there was a window, though he doubted he could attempt an escape with the ensuing chaos that would surely erupt merely from trying.

'Your photo of Olivia's not too bad, but you'd be able to jerk off a lot faster if you had the picture of her spreadeagled on that pool table. I'll be sure to make you a copy.'

Succumbing to the taunts, Anders wheeled around for Duke's legs and tried to pull him to the floor. Duke grabbed a handful of Anders's hair on his way down, causing his head to beam against the side of the urinal before landing in the loose splatters of his stomach. Despite the dark, he saw flashes of light, and in the instant it took him to recover, the ape had already climbed on top of him and was pummelling his face with his fists. Anders fought back, and felt he was doing an okay job of it given the difference in their size, but then someone grabbed his arms and twisted each one into an unnatural position. He screamed in pain. He heard Duke say, 'Don't break 'em, I promised Jimmy we'd only rough him up,' and then, although his arms weren't free, at least they weren't being broken. But now blows to the gut came with punches to his face and he lost count of how many men were attacking him. The smell and taste of blood surrounded him, and even in his drunkenness he was acutely aware of it filling his mouth and dripping down the side of his face. He tried to cough; the blood sputtered out. He'd lost all strength to fight back and even as he struggled to maintain consciousness, he knew it was only a matter of time and he welcomed the peace.

Someone at his back raised him from the tiles and then lifted him from his underarms so that he hung, semi-standing, like a rag doll.

'Stand up!' Duke stood right in front of him, his face mere inches away. Anders tried to stand on his own but his legs buckled. The guy holding him hoisted him upright again. 'Why don't you tell us who you are and what you're doing here?'

Even in his agony, all Anders could think was: *Thought you had all the answers already.* He let out an unintelligible laugh at his ability to be a smart ass even when being beat to hell.

The guy didn't like that Anders still experienced even the slightest pleasure, and he landed a swift kick to his crotch. Anders moaned and instinctively tried to double over to relieve the pain, but was held in place by the goon behind him.

'If you want this to end, you'll tell me what you're doing here.' Duke's voice was quieter now, colder. 'Otherwise, it's going to get worse.'

Anders felt around the inside of his mouth with his tongue, tried to spit some blood out the side to clear it. A hard knock to the side of his head, another moan. He struggled not to vomit again.

'I'm just trying to find her,' he said finally. He *did* want it to end. Desperately.

'Why?'

'Isn't that obvious?' He mumbled the words through split lips.

'Why'd you come here?'

Anders knew he meant the bar, their hang-out. He realized they were afraid he was after them. And he was, now.

'I didn't know about . . .' He stopped. He couldn't say it out loud. '. . . about what you told me.' His entire body throbbed with pain, and he groaned from the effort of speech. 'I just knew she was from around here, I knew she'd been here at this bar.' He closed his eyes, tired from the effort of speaking, and hoped it was enough.

Duke was right up in Anders's face now, and his hot, whiskey smelling breath threatened to make him sick again. 'We told Jimmy we wouldn't kill you, and we won't, not here. But don't think I'm joking when I tell you: we know how to kill, we've done it before, and if we find out you do anything with the information you've learned tonight, we'll hunt you down. You got it?' Anders managed a nod. 'And we'll make damn sure you get the treatment we usually reserve for the enemy. Understand?'

Another nod, almost imperceptible. He didn't think he could hold on much longer.

'Oh, and one more thing.' The sinister, jeering voice was back. 'I wouldn't feel too bad for Olivia if I was you.' He laughed. 'Her cries sounded like squeals of pleasure to me.'

He saved the hardest blow for his final one, straight into Anders's gut, and with a cry Anders collapsed into unconsciousness on the cold, hard floor.

# 13

HE WASN'T sure whether it was the bone-chilling cold or the sound of his own moaning that woke him, but when he opened his eyes he was level with the ground, his cheek pressed into a mixture of gravel, dead leaves, and dirt. Lots of dirt. He didn't even really feel the gravel digging into his face – the other aches that permeated the rest of his body were too great to notice a few rocks in his cheek – but in the dim light of the parking lot's one street lamp, he saw the gravel inches from his eyes, his coat a few feet farther, splayed like the drawing of a body at a crime scene, and then farther away, but blurry, the trunks of the towering pines that surrounded the little bar. He started to turn his head to confirm his location, but cried out when a sharp pain inside his brain shot right into his forehead, between his eyes. His breath floated in the air, but he didn't need to see it to know the temperature had dipped even further below freezing; whatever the thermometer read, it was much too cold for this Florida boy to survive for long.

He attempted to sit up, and though he succeeded on his first try, the motion caused a jab in his side and once again he lost what was left of the evening's spirits. Another short cry escaped his lips when he saw that his stomach contained more blood than beverage. The sight of it stirred his memory of what had happened in the bathroom, and even worse, of what he'd learned in the bar. He let his body fall back against the ground and didn't even try to stop the flood of despair that gripped him again.

Now that he was conscious, he started to shake from the

cold. His teeth chattered, and he noted it as something entirely new to him. He heard heavy footsteps in the gravel, and he closed his eyes as if that could somehow inoculate him against the approaching threat. And even though he knew the sound was coming closer, he still started when a hand touched his tender shoulder.

'Take it easy.' The voice rang familiar. Jimmy.

'Get your friggin' hands off me.'

'You gotta get up, you'll freeze to death. It happens around here, you know.'

'Your concern is flattering, as late as it might be.'

'Come on.' Jimmy took him by the arm and he let himself be brought to a sitting position again. 'Do you think you can stand?'

Anders nodded, but didn't move. The inside of his head throbbed, and on the outside his face was tender and bruised from where they'd landed repeated blows. He started to catalogue in his mind the extent of his injuries. From the pain in his side, he suspected he'd suffered a broken rib. The right side of his top lip was split open like an overcooked sausage, and he sucked in cold air from the surprise of the resulting sting when he touched his tongue to it. Lifting a finger to brush the gravel from his cheek, he winced when he realized some of it was embedded in his wounds. At least he didn't have a cue stick stuck up his ass, as Jimmy had predicted.

Jimmy came around to his front and retrieved his coat from the ground.

'At least try to get this on,' he said, holding it open for Anders to fill the armholes. Silently, Anders complied, squeezing his eyes tight to ward off the next onslaught of pain and the expletives that clung to the tip of his tongue, fighting to escape.

With Jimmy's help, Anders rose unsteadily to his feet. He patted his back pocket for his wallet and then that memory came back, too. He groaned, causing Jimmy again to say 'Take it easy' because he mistook the sound as another expression of physical pain.

'My wallet.'

'I put it on your passenger seat. They left it behind in the bathroom.'

Anders nodded his appreciation and began to take tentative steps in the direction of the car. 'By the way, thanks for the warning,' he mumbled as he gained distance from Jimmy, his anger growing anew now that he knew he'd survived with his walking ability still intact. He tried to ignore the soreness between his legs.

'Hey!' Jimmy yelled across the lot. 'I *did* warn you, prick. But you wouldn't listen. You asked for it.'

Anders whirled around, and the movement made him dizzy on his feet and caused the knife inside his brain to plunge one more time against his forehead. He gagged, but there was nothing left to throw up. 'What? What did you just say to me?'

'I said, you asked for it. I told you to watch out for them. They're bad news.'

Anders let out a disgusted laugh. 'You people around here are fucked up, you know that?' He turned again and pulled open the driver's side door of the car. 'First I get run off the road, and her piece of shit father tries to tell me I killed her. And now when I get beat all to hell by some guys who raped her – in your lovely establishment, I might add – you try to tell me I asked for it.' He gingerly placed his body in the seat. 'What the fuck's that all about?' He gripped the steering wheel and rested his head on his hands. 'And where the hell are my keys?'

Jimmy stood just outside the car now. 'So you've *met* the esteemed Mr Mayfield, have you?'

At the change of tone in Jimmy's voice, Anders sat back and looked up to him. 'Met him? Yes, that. And accused by him, ignored by him, lied to by him, threatened by him.' He grunted. 'I'm starting to think he might have had a hand in what happened to me a few hours ago, too. Am I right?'

Jimmy sighed loudly. 'Maybe in a roundabout way, but I doubt it.' He waved his hands in the direction of the parking lot exit. Anders saw only dark woods. 'Why don't you let me take you to a motel not far from here? You're in no condition to drive, and you need to get out of the cold and get yourself cleaned up.'

'What I need are some answers. And some keys.' He reclined the seat to avoid having to use his own strength to stretch his body, and patted his front pocket. The keys, to his relief, were still there. He started the engine and turned the heater to full force. 'I can drive myself. Where is it?'

'It's not obvious,' said Jimmy. Without waiting for an invitation, he walked around the front of the car to the passenger side, tossed the wallet to Anders, and sat down. The car sank from his weight. 'Go on. I'll get my truck later.'

Anders eyed him cautiously and put the car in gear. Despite Jimmy's failure to save him earlier, he sensed the man wanted to spill his guts to someone, and Anders was ready to listen.

ANDERS OPENED one eye when he heard the pounding on the door. He opened only one eye – the right one – because the left one had swollen shut. Once again, the memories of the night before rushed at him as if someone had turned on a faucet in his brain.

The pounding continued and his body responded with a slow but growing throb in all the places he'd suffered blows.

He assumed that Jimmy stood on the other side of the door. The night before, he'd taken care of getting Anders into a room, but he'd refused to talk. The motel clerk had given him a ride back to his truck. No one else would have known to find him here, unless Jimmy had betrayed him. Which was entirely possible. Even probable.

He inched back the motel room's heavy drapes and scanned the lot. He saw the same two cars from the night before – his and the motel clerk's – and a third one, but it wasn't Jimmy's. Or at least it wasn't the Ford pickup Anders had assumed belonged to him.

'Come on, I know you're in there,' the male voice called from the other side of the door. The voice didn't belong to Jimmy either, and Anders couldn't identify it. But it didn't sound especially menacing.

'Who is it?' he asked. He leaned against the door because standing without support seemed a little too strenuous just then.

Even through metal he thought he heard the voice sigh.

'My name's Matt. I was there last night. I need to talk to you.'

Yeah, right, Anders thought to himself. Come right in and have a few more goes at me, why don't you? But all he said out loud as he walked away from the door toward the bathroom was, 'Go fuck yourself.'

One more single pound on the door – obviously a pound of frustration – and then, loudly, 'I have information about Olivia!'

Anders stopped and turned his head. The voice must have sensed his reaction, because he added, 'Jimmy told me you were here.'

He opened the door and immediately recognized the guy in front of him. When he saw the perpetually pink cheeks and the carrot-coloured hair, and the guilty eyes that seemed to take a step backwards in anticipation that Anders might throw his own blows, he felt for the first time since arriving in

Connecticut that maybe, just maybe, he was finally headed in the right direction.


THEY TRUDGED in silence into the diner and to a booth in the corner. Anders sat with his back to the wall so he could see through the filmy windows. It'd been only a day, but he already felt he'd lost his anonymity in this small New England town. If anyone else came looking for him, he wanted to see them first.

They each ordered a cup of black coffee to start. Anders endured the wary stare he received from the waitress at his messed up face, and when she'd left, he leaned back, waiting.

'Look, I'm not sure who you are—' Matt began.

'Why don't you tell me who *you* are?' Anders said, his voice spitting acid. The anger from the night before had returned once he'd shaken the sleep from his brain, and it had only swelled in the time it took to shower off the blood and stink, pull some clothes on his fragile body and drive the fifteen minutes to the diner.

The guy shifted in his seat, and Anders noticed he had difficulty looking him in the eye. No surprise there.

'I'm not who you think. I'm not one of the guys who ...' He stopped.

Anders leaned in and narrowed his eyes. 'Go ahead, say it.'

When Matt just lowered his eyes, Anders asked, 'What's the matter? You can do it, but you can't say it?' He didn't try to hide his contempt.

'That's what I'm trying to tell you. I didn't do it. I was there, but I wasn't one of them, I swear.'

The waitress reappeared and set two steaming mugs in front of them. Anders lowered his voice and said, 'Didn't do *what*?'

Matt didn't move, barely even breathed, even after she'd left them alone again.

'Huh? *What*, exactly, didn't you do?' he persisted. His voice remained calm but it belied the eruption building inside of him. It almost disturbed him more knowing that someone with at least a glimmer of conscience had been present, and yet he still hadn't done anything to help her. 'You didn't stick your dick in her, is that what you're saying?' Matt rolled his eyes but there was no real bluster behind the gesture. 'You didn't even touch her, is that it? Are you saying you stood on the sidelines and merely watched? Or were you an even better guy than that? You sat in a booth and sucked on your beer, all alone, and what the hell, because you didn't watch, you didn't even get off. Is that what you mean, when you say you were there, but you didn't *do* it?'

'Shut up,' Matt said under his breath.

'What's the matter, Mattie? Something about this conversation making you uncomfortable?'

'I didn't help them,' he insisted.

'What's that mean, exactly? Are you saying you didn't hold her down so the *others* could stick their dicks in her? Is that it? How many *didn't* you help?'

Matt just glared at Anders.

'*How many?*' he demanded so loudly and so sharply that Matt flinched and nearby diners glanced over to their table.

As if he was afraid to move, Matt barely registered a shrug and mumbled, 'I don't know, five, I think.'

Anders let out a short gasp. Whether it was the sheer number, or the specificity that made it all the more real in his mind, he didn't know. Maybe it was both.

'Listen to me,' Matt said, his voice quiet and tentative as if he expected Anders to lose it at any moment. 'That's why I came. I'm trying to help you.'

It might have been his attempt at an admission of guilt, or at least some responsibility, but Anders wasn't having any. 'You're a liar.'

'You know, you're a piece of work. Did you even hear me? I'm trying to help you.'

Anders let out a scoffing noise and pointed at his own face. 'Look at me, asshole. You and your friends did this to me, in case you don't remember. Oh, but let me guess –' he made the wild face of a mad scientist with a brilliant idea '– you were there, but you didn't do it. Right?'

Anders could see the guy's jaw tense. 'I helped last night, yeah.' He paused. 'But *not* with her. I didn't do it and I didn't help them.'

'Yeah, you did. You helped them *by not* helping her.'

Matt looked down for just an instant. 'Okay. You're right. But now I'm *gonna* help her by helping you, okay?'

All he wanted was to drag this guy outside and re-enact the battle from last night, except this time he wouldn't be on the receiving end. But what his brain wanted and what his body wanted were two different things, and, anyway, he needed what this Matt claimed to have.

He took a deep breath and immediately regretted it. He winced from the pain of what had to be a cracked rib. With one elbow on the table, he carefully brought a hand to his brow and tried to absorb again what had happened to Olivia without this guy studying his every facial movement.

'You got a cigarette?' he asked after he'd collected himself.

'Yeah,' Matt reached for the inside pocket of his coat, 'but I don't think they'll let you smoke in here.'

He grabbed a cigarette from the pack Matt offered. Matt slid a lighter across the table when he realized Anders intended to ignore his warning and light up right there.

The first drag calmed him, and warmed him in a way the first sip of coffee, moments before, hadn't. Matt remained quiet and watched, Anders knew, for some sign that it was okay to talk.

He dumped a small dish of creamers onto the table to use

the bowl as an ashtray. He waited until he'd smoked the thing down to the filter before finally meeting Matt's bloodshot eyes.

Matt began by asking, 'Do you *know* Brent Campbell?'

Anders shook his head, and Matt sighed, repositioning himself in a way that suggested this would not be a brief conversation.

'He's a crazy son of a bitch, a *smart* crazy son of a bitch, that's the first thing you need to know. And it's the one thing you'd better remember above everything else I'm about to tell you.'

Matt paused, giving him a chance to comment, but Anders just waited.

'The guys last night, some of them go way back with him, to boarding school, and some served with him in the war.'

'And which group are you a member of?' he asked, unable to drop the sarcasm, to let the anger go completely.

'I served with him.' With a grunt he added, 'I'm public school through and through.'

The waitress appeared and Matt placed an order. She noticed the ashes and the lone butt in the small bowl but only scolded Anders with a look.

'Okay. So Brent Campbell is crazy,' he said when she'd left them alone again. 'That's what you knocked on my door to tell me?'

'I knocked on your door because I think Olivia's in more danger.'

*No shit, Sherlock.* Anyone who'd met Lawrence Mayfield would have to reach the same conclusion.

As if he'd read Anders's mind, Matt added, 'Mortal danger.'

Anders swallowed. There hadn't been the slightest hint of exaggeration or fooling in the statement. 'I'm listening.'

'What happened at the bar to Olivia,' he lowered his eyes, 'was orchestrated in advance. By Campbell.'

'What?' He didn't know what shocked him more. The fact

that her supposed fiancé had something to do with the assault, or that Matt knew about it *ahead of time* and *still* didn't take action.

Matt lifted a hand, sensing his thoughts. 'Hear me out. I only found this out after the fact, from Adam.'

'Who's Adam?'

'The big guy. Duke.'

Ah, the bodybuilder.

'Brent and Olivia go way back, too. Their families are close. Their fathers had some business connection, though I'm not sure what it is. Her dad owns a major stake in a pharmaceutical company, and her family used to spend a lot of time in Africa with Brent's family.'

'Africa?'

Matt nodded. 'Yeah, apparently Brent grew up primarily in Kenya, in Nairobi. Anyway, Brent and Olivia knocked around a lot together when they were little, and from what I've been told, both families had the cute notion that the two of them would end up a couple. Supposedly they did, for a while, at least, until Olivia got older and wiser.'

'But he'd asked her to marry him, didn't he? Not too long ago?' he asked.

'Yeah. You've fast-forwarded a bit, but yeah.' Matt narrowed his eyes. 'How do you know that?'

Anders hesitated. He didn't want to mention the article, not until he'd heard the whole story this guy had to tell. So he lied. 'She told me.'

Matt nodded. 'And she basically told him, in so many words, to go fuck himself. She'd grown to despise him. Their relationship had always been a little lopsided; Adam says he was a bit obsessed with her even when they were younger. He says Brent treated her like he owned her, you know? And apparently neither her parents nor his dispelled that belief.' He laughed a bit. 'I don't understand why she would have put up with him as long as she did, but they all say it was because her father put so much pressure on her.' He shrugged. 'I don't know, maybe the dad had something hanging over her head.'

Anders was sceptical. 'Like what?'

'I don't know. But the way Adam tells it, her dad controlled her for a long time. Don't know how else he would have managed to do that. Maybe it was just a money thing.'

'His money doesn't matter to her.'

Matt laughed at him. 'Don't fool yourself. Money matters to everyone.'

'So how does this relate to Campbell asking his friends to rape her in a bar? And more importantly, to her being in mortal danger.'

'I'm getting to that,' Matt said.

Anders thought Matt seemed to enjoy the telling of his story just a little too much. He relished being the one with all the information and controlling just how it came out.

'Well, can you get to *that* a bit faster? Because after your expressed concern that Olivia is in mortal danger, I've got the sense that time is of the essence.'

Matt breathed a disgusted sigh. 'Okay. The shorthand is that he orchestrated the attack in retaliation for her snubbing his marriage proposal. That's what I mean, man. He's controlling. He's crazy. He's not the type to take rejection well.' He leaned over the table and lowered his voice. 'But here's the thing. I don't think she knows he was involved. Her dad whisked her away before news of the attack went beyond the circle of those involved. I don't even know if *he* knows Brent was involved.'

'You're telling me *her father* protected those guys?'

'I don't know. It seems strange to me, too, because from what I've seen, the man protects himself and no one else. But he's very rich, and very well known in these parts, so if protecting his own reputation meant having to protect them, too ...' Matt shrugged. 'Maybe he convinced himself it was best for her to avoid the publicity surrounding a charge like that, and a trial.'

'This is unbelievable.'

Matt stared across the table at him. 'Like I said, he's one crazy bastard. His idea of a good time always involves cruelty of some sort.'

As the last words sunk in, the waitress appeared with Matt's breakfast of ham and eggs. She looked to Anders to see if he'd changed his mind about eating, but he motioned her away. His empty stomach churned and the acidic coffee only made it worse, but food held no interest for him just then.

'What do you mean, *always*? He's done shit like this before?'

Matt shrugged. 'To chicks? I don't know. But I've seen first-hand what he does to animals.'

Anders swallowed and didn't say anything. The guy across from him couldn't have known the nerve he'd touched.

'You don't believe me?'

'I'm just waiting for evidence.'

'He used to grab stray dogs off the streets in Baghdad, and he'd tie them up in this field behind an abandoned school. He'd leave them there and let them starve to death. *I'm doing an experiment,* he'd say. He claimed he wanted to find out which one was the strongest. *Survival of the fittest, don't you know?*' Matt chose a menacing tone to imitate Campbell.

'And you didn't help them, either, huh?' Anders's voice was deadpan, but his eyes spoke the sarcasm for him.

'Who? The dogs?' He made a dismissive sound. 'You don't have a fuckin' clue, do you? You ever served?'

Anders shook his head.

'Then fuck off. You go risk your ass and then you come back and say that to me.'

For just a moment, Anders wondered if perhaps Campbell had turned his cruelty directly on Matt at some point.

'What about Jimmy?'

'Jimmy?' Matt laughed, and the look on his face told him that, yes, he'd concluded Anders was indeed naive. 'No one's told me this, but I'd venture that Jimmy was bought off. Or perhaps Campbell has threatened him.'

'And you all just hang out at the bar and pretend it never happened?' Anders grunted. 'Or better yet, you brag about it to guys like me without any fear of recrimination.'

Matt looked out over the restaurant without responding. Anders could feel the vibration from the guy's foot thumping quickly, subconsciously, under the table, a habitual tic he noticed because he shared it. He stared at Matt until he finally turned and looked him in the eye. And then he asked the question he'd come a thousand miles to have answered.

'So where is she now?'

'I'm not sure, but—'

Anders groaned. 'You said—'

'— that's why I wanted to talk to you. I think she might be in Africa—'

'*What? Right now?*' It was the last thing he expected to hear.

'— with Campbell.'

'Oh, God.' Anders dropped his face into his hands, ignoring the pain of it being touched.

'She showed up back here in Connecticut not long ago after having been gone for a while. I heard talk about her having been in an accident in Florida or something, that she was really messed up and it affected her memory. Next thing I know, the two of them are back together, as if nothing ever happened.'

'The accident, I was with her.'

'Yeah, after we saw your wallet, I gathered you were the guy from Florida she was involved with.'

Anders reached for the pack on the table and knocked another cigarette into his palm. His hands shook as he tried to light it. He spied the waitress approaching with more coffee, and she tossed him another look of reproach. He'd obviously tested her tolerance too much.

'Sir . . .' she began as she topped off their cups.

'Please,' he pleaded, and before he could add 'there's no one nearby' she'd appraised his fragile condition and gave her acquiescence.

'As long as the customers don't start complaining,' she warned.

He nodded his thanks and inhaled a long drag.

'I found out from Adam last night that he took off with her to Africa last week.'

'*Goddammit*,' Anders said slowly through clenched teeth. Last week. While he was sitting in the beach house, moping about her absence and his inability to do anything, she was here, in this town, probably just a short drive from where he sat at that moment. And now an entire ocean separated them. An ocean and his complete ignorance about how to bridge it.

'And despite what Adam said about it being an innocuous "pre-wedding" honeymoon, I have a hunch it might be something else. Because he's gotta be afraid she'll find out—'

'What do you mean, you have a hunch it might be something else?' His voice was weak and he had to push the question out, because he already had his own hunch.

'He used to talk about Africa, the African bush in particular – which, remember, he knows well – as the perfect place to commit murder. He said that you could murder someone there and never get caught, because after the animals have finished with the remains, they leave no trace. If the prey is healthy, the predator will even eat the bones.'

Anders's body trembled uncontrollably as if it believed he still stood outside in the bitter cold, though just then, he was sweating. Everything that had happened from the moment of the accident, and everything that he had learned, all of it seemed horrific enough in its own right; but now, as this man on the other side of the table wove the information together like some sort of grotesque tapestry, Anders found it difficult to breathe. His chest grew tighter, and he thought he was about to collapse under the weight of it all. He needed air.

'I gotta get outside,' he mumbled, and tried to escape from the booth. But Matt was up, and standing there to catch him.

'Hold on. You don't look so good.'

He didn't resist as Matt eased him back down into his seat. He crossed his arms and rested his head on the table, eyes closed. The words *I don't feel so good either* went through his mind but when he spoke the words, they came out as, 'Where? Where in Africa did he take her?'

Matt ignored him, and he heard him asking the waitress for some ice water and a cold, wet rag. She must have been fast because the next thing he remembered a cold cloth draped the back of his neck. He still shook, but now it felt like more of a shiver. He heard her ask Matt if he was all right, and Matt suggested she bring some food.

He tried to lift his head, but was overcome with dizziness and nausea.

'Just take it easy a minute,' Matt insisted. 'I'm not going anywhere.'

So he waited, and when the waitress brought dry toast, he ate it, and he drank the hot tea she placed in front of him, and gradually he began to feel, if not better, at least manageable.

'Where are they?' he asked again when he was able to raise his head without feeling like it was about to roll off.

Matt shook his head. 'I can't say for sure. He grew up in the Nairobi suburbs, so I'm guessing they're there, or maybe at a bush camp in Kenya somewhere. That's his old stomping ground.'

'Do you know how long they're supposed to be there?'

Matt lowered his eyes. Anders knew they were thinking the same thing: was he already too late?

'I don't really know, but these aren't people who go someplace like that for a one or two week vacation, if you get my drift.'

Yes, he got the drift. People like the Mayfields and the Campbells had the money to go anywhere in the world for as long as they wished. Unlike Anders, who at that moment was trying to figure out where in the hell he was going to come up with the airfare to Africa, not to mention the money he'd need to survive once he landed.

After a moment, Anders asked, 'Why are you helping me?'

Matt squirmed in his seat, repositioning himself and looking around the restaurant before meeting Anders's stare again. 'Look, maybe I was a coward that night, okay? But—'

'There's no maybe involved.'

'Yeah, okay, you're absolutely right. I was a coward. But I'm not a rapist. And I have no intention of being an accomplice to a murder.'

'But you didn't have a problem being an accomplice to a rape.' Anders couldn't help himself; despite all the information the guy had given him, despite how he'd helped him in more ways than one, he still couldn't let his anger go. Matt just pressed his lips together and let it pass.

'Why tell me?' Anders asked. 'Why not go to the cops?'

Matt grunted. 'You really have no idea how things work in their world, do you?'

MATT INSISTED on driving Anders to the emergency room at the local hospital so someone could look him over. He thought it ironic that one of the participants in his beating was now acting as his guardian, but after his near collapse in the diner, he didn't think he could argue.

Seven hours later Matt deposited him back in the motel's parking lot. His ribs had been taped, his hand bandaged, and he'd endured the discomfort of having a nurse pluck bits of gravel from the wounds on his face. They'd run labs and taken abdominal and chest X-rays and a CT scan to check for internal bleeding and concussion, and ultimately concluded that although some of his organs might be badly bruised, he'd suffered no long-term injuries. After examining his genitals a little too roughly and causing him to almost lurch off the table from pain, the young male doctor had informed him dryly, 'Well, you should still be able to father children.'

'You know anything about Makena Mbatia?' Anders asked Matt as he slowly climbed from the car.

'You can't live around here and *not* know about Makena. She's lived with the Mayfields for what seems like forever. Why?'

'I saw her only briefly in Florida, but I got the sense ... I don't know ... she might just help me, if I asked. I'd like to talk to her.'

Matt snorted. 'Good luck. Whattaya gonna do, ring Lawrence Mayfield's doorbell?'

He thought about that. He tried to imagine Mayfield's reaction if he found Anders on his doorstep.

'Look,' Matt's expression softened, 'I'll tell you how to get to the Mayfield estate, but you'll never get to her by just showing up over there unannounced.'

'I realize that.'

'The house is in the middle of several acres and it's heavily forested. Plus, they've got cameras around the perimeter of the property to rival the Bush compound at Kennebunkport.'

'So what do you suggest?'

'Well,' Matt said, 'if you can wait till Saturday, you can probably find her at the farmers' market. It's the last one of the year, and unless the weather really sucks, they'll still hold it, even in the cold.'

Given what Matt had told him about Campbell, Anders thought waiting until Saturday was akin to waiting a year. But he couldn't just board a plane for Africa that afternoon, anyway; he didn't even have a passport. And the issue of money still taunted him. The only two people he would have felt comfortable asking to borrow from – Lenny and Shel – were now out of the question, and even if they'd miraculously forgiven him, he doubted either of them had a slush fund. So waiting for Saturday seemed the least of his problems just then.

'Where is this farmers' market?' he asked.

'Smack dab in the middle of town, in the town square. It's a popular spot on Saturday mornings,' Matt paused to laugh, 'but she'll stand out like a sore thumb, you'll see.'

# 14

ANDERS WOKE early Wednesday morning, his stomach rumbling from hunger. The day before, not long after Matt had dropped him off, he'd fallen asleep on top of the bedspread and had slept through the night. Now, white light seeped through the cracks in the drapes and he heard scraping against the walkway outside his door. He dragged his aching body from the bed and pulled the drapes back, but quickly squinted and turned away from the blinding brightness. Overnight, the world outside his window had become shrouded in a thin layer of snow.

He let his eyes adjust and then opened the door and sucked in the fresh air. The snow that had blown up against his door collapsed at his feet.

'Sorry about that, buddy. Hadn't reached your door yet.'

Anders looked up quickly at the sound of the voice. His spirits fell when he saw the man pushing a shovel wasn't whom he'd hoped it might be. The accent had been familiar, and the way he'd called him 'buddy' had momentarily confused him into thinking the improbable, but this man was small and skinny. He was nothing like Lenny.

THE RINGING had already begun at the other end of the phone by the time Anders realized he should have blocked the caller ID, if that was even possible on a cellphone. He hadn't spoken to Lenny since before the day Shel had shown up at the beach house, and he knew the lapse wasn't unintentional, for either of them. If Lenny recognized Anders's number, he might not answer.

He heard the sound of an idling mower in the background first, just after the third ring, and then Lenny's voice. 'Yeah?'

Lenny answered the way he answered all his calls, but Anders was sure, from the subtle undertone of anger surrounding the word, that Lenny knew exactly who was calling.

He hunched forward to block the biting wind and, without realizing it, began to twirl on his spot in the middle of the parking lot to get better reception. He held the phone against his ear with his palm because his fingers were too cold and too sore to maintain a good grip.

'Lenny? It's Anders.'

Silence. But he could still hear the mower, and he became painfully aware of the different climates they were each experiencing at that very moment.

'Lenny, you there?'

'I'm here.'

He might as well get to the point; he sensed he might lose his reluctant audience at any second. 'I need your help.'

Silence, except for the mower. Why the hell didn't he just shut down the damn mower so they could have a normal conversation?

'Lenny?'

'You got a pen handy?' His voice faded in and out as the reception waned.

Anders stood straighter, a bit surprised at the change in Lenny's tone. 'Yeah, yeah, hold on a sec.' He followed his tracks in the snow to his room and grabbed a pen and pad of paper off the nightstand. Once outside, he brushed clean a spot on the hood of his car and used it as a desk. 'Okay, I'm ready.' Anders scribbled the number Lenny recited two times. 'Okay, got it. You want me to call you back at this number?'

Once more, Lenny clammed up at the other end.

'Lenny?' Anders could still hear the whir of the equipment so he knew the call hadn't been dropped. 'You still there?'

'I'm here. You said you needed help, didn't you?'

'Yeah.'

'Well, you've got the number now, so call it.' He layered his voice thick with sarcasm. 'Call Crystal. I'm sure she'll be more than happy to help you again.'

Now it was Anders's turn to be silent. He kicked at the gravel underneath the snow and began turning again. His eyes scanned the woods around him as if he thought there might be someone witnessing his shame. No words came and he finally hit the hood with his fist in frustration.

'What's the matter? She take your tongue when she took whatever else you had to offer?'

'Christ, she had me by the balls. What do you want me to say?'

Lenny laughed loudly, but he didn't sound amused. 'Yeah, I'll bet she did.'

'Come on, man, don't let her do this.'

Another haughty laugh. 'Seems I've heard that once before.' Suddenly the noise behind Lenny evaporated and Anders heard only footsteps, then quiet. When Lenny spoke next his voice came through loud and clear. 'Let's get one thing straight, Andy. *She* didn't do this. *You* did this.'

Anders grunted. 'She was playing me! I'd run out of options and she knew it.' The door to the office opened and the desk clerk emerged holding a large trash bag. He didn't wear a coat and Anders shivered just looking at him. He gave Anders the once-over on his way to the trash bins at the edge of the lot. Anders turned his back to the man and lowered his voice to a whisper. 'And she tricked me. Did she tell you that?'

'Did Shel tell you how I found out?' Lenny asked, ignoring Anders's question. 'You know, buddy, I wouldn't have even believed it. That's the funny part. You could have told me she was a lying bitch and I would have believed *you*. I trusted *you*.'

'Look, I'm—'

'But I heard it with my own ears.'

Anders sighed. 'What are you talking about?'

'It was like listening to the soundtrack of a porn movie with the picture blacked out.'

'I don't know what the hell you're talking about.'

'She *recorded* it, dumbfuck!'

'What?'

'Seems the two of you left a little message in her voicemail.'

Only at the mention of voicemail did Anders suddenly understand what Lenny was talking about. He remembered the phone in Crystal's hand, and how it had dropped to the lanai when he'd tried to grab it from her. He squeezed his eyes shut. God, she *had* played him. She had played him so well.

'Lenny, listen to me, please. I'm sorry. I really am. She tricked me. I know it's no excuse, but I was desperate, and she led me to believe she had the files right there in her house. I tore up the place, but I couldn't find them. I was so desperate. I wasn't thinking straight. I just did what I thought I had to do to get them.'

'And to hell with anybody else, was that it?'

Anders leaned against the side of the car, a silent resignation, not even noticing now the wet, cold metal through his jeans. He couldn't say anything that would appease Lenny, because the words didn't exist. Lenny was right. Lenny was one hundred per cent right.

HE STOPPED in the motel office and bought a pack of cigarettes from the machine. The clerk tossed a matchbook onto the counter, and Anders nodded his thanks as he scooped it up and braced himself for the cold again.

'Just keep the smoking outside the room,' the clerk called from behind the closing door.

He opened the driver's side door to his rental car and gingerly lowered himself into the seat. He felt stiffer than the day before, and despite the tape, the slightest wrong move caused a sharp pain in his ribs. His hands trembled as he tried to unwrap the cellophane; he was cold but he also needed this cigarette, badly. Once it was lit and he'd taken the first drag, he lifted one leg and then the other into the car and rested back against the headrest. He closed his eyes, blew out the smoke and tried to remove his mind from the aches that permeated his body. He suddenly thought about Shel and surprised himself by laughing out loud. What would she say if she saw him now, chain-smoking like an addict?

He pulled his cellphone from his coat pocket and dialled the number from his childhood. His mother answered on the second ring.

'Anders?' He frowned when he heard the concern in her voice. 'Thank God, I've been worried about you. You never answer the phone at the beach anymore.' *You could've tried my cellphone, Mom.* 'Where are you?'

'I'm in Connecticut.'

'Connecticut?'

'Yeah, Connecticut.' He closed his eyes again, already tired just thinking about how he would explain himself to her. God, she was so patient; she'd always been so patient with him. He owed her the same.

'Okay.' She didn't ask him why he didn't tell her before leaving, she didn't demand information. She just asked, quietly, 'What are you doing in Connecticut?'

'I came here looking for Olivia.'

His mother's stunned silence reached him through the phone. 'I thought—'

'No, she's not. She's alive.'

'Oh, baby, that's wonderful news!'

'Yeah.'

But she heard the obvious despair in his voice. 'Did you find her?'

He took a deep breath and wiped at his eyes. 'No. No, I didn't.'

'Oh, I see.' She spoke slowly, cautiously. 'Anders, hon—'

'Mom, could you overnight my birth certificate to me?'

'Sure, honey, whatever you need. But can you tell me a little bit of what's going on? I'm so worried about you.'

'I think she's in Africa. I need to get a passport.'

'Africa?' For the first time, he heard alarm, though she tried to disguise it. 'Shouldn't you *make sure* she's there first?' She paused, then gently: 'Anders, baby, please don't be upset by this, but are you sure she's alive?'

'She's alive, Mom, okay? I'm sure of that.'

'I'm just really—'

'Mom, please. I think it's just better if I don't go into too much detail. I just need you to do this for me, okay? I need you to trust me. I'm fine, and I just need this. Okay?' His voice shook and he coughed to clear his throat. He brought the cigarette to his lips and took another long, strong drag.

She responded with silence. He knew it wasn't a mad silence, or a hurt silence even, only that she was thinking of how to get the information she wanted while still honouring his request.

He turned at the sound of a car kicking up the gravel. A beat-up station wagon pulled up in front of the office – Christ, how long had it been since he'd seen a station wagon, with wood panels, no less – and five children of assorted ages tumbled out from the back. Their shrieking voices pierced the sharp air as they began to run wild through the snow in the desolate parking lot. The man Anders assumed was their father emerged from the driver's side and strolled into the office without a glance back at the kids.

'What's that noise, honey? Where are you?'

A woman emerged from the passenger side, and like a mother hen, she gathered them close to her with just one loud rebuke.

Anders realized his mother had spoken. 'Oh, just some kids. A family. I'm in the parking lot of my mo-, my hotel, and they just arrived.'

'Do you want me to send some money, too?'

The father returned and the mother turned her attention to him. He spoke to her but Anders couldn't hear the words. They were both smiling, and then laughing at something he said. Here they were, getting ready to stay in this shitty motel with their shitty station wagon and their gaggle of screaming kids, and they were happy. A lump formed in his throat.

'No, I'm fine. Really, Mom, I am.' He gave her the address and reminded her to send it overnight. He was anxious to end the call. 'I gotta go, Mom. Okay? Please don't worry about me. I'm fine, I promise.'

He closed the cellphone before she could respond, because he knew that whatever she said next, it would cause him to start bawling as if he was a kid again and she was the only one who could make it better. Except she never could.

# 15

HE ARRIVED at the Clifton town square early on Saturday, just as the vendors were setting up their stalls, and parked his rental car at the kerb. The sky had just begun to lighten, and a few of the antique-style street lamps lining the sidewalks around the square flickered as they tried to decide whether day-light had arrived for good. The air was frigid. Most of the snow had melted, but frost clung to the blades of grass beneath his feet. He leaned against the hood of the car, clutching a Styro-foam cup of hot coffee and mindlessly blowing at the steam rising from the top while he waited for it to cool.

He scanned the quaint shops and homes that lined the square. Most of the homes were colonial, with flat fronts and black shut-ters framing every window, or Victorian, with elevated front porches and railings. The shops were small and useful – a news-stand, a bookstore, a clothing store and, right next to it, a shoe store called 'The Cobbler'. His favourite was the coffee shop where he'd bought the cup in his hand; it had smelled of fresh dough-nuts and maple bacon and didn't say Starbucks out front. In fact, what appealed to him the most about the little town was the absence of what he'd grown to despise in Florida: the homo-geneous proliferation of chain stores. Part of him couldn't imagine how, having grown up in such a place, things had gone so horribly wrong for Olivia. The other part of him knew.

The crowds began to arrive as the sun burned away the frost. To his surprise, many people approached on foot, like pilgrims coming from all directions to a holy shrine. Some pushed strollers; others carried empty canvas bags which he assumed would go home full. Most were bundled up against the cold, but a few joggers appeared wearing nothing but nylon running shorts and sweatshirts or thin jackets, their exposed thighs looking numbingly pink.

Though he felt he'd kept a pretty good lookout, he hadn't seen anyone resembling Makena. Indeed, he hadn't seen anyone, even, who shared her skin colour.

Tossing his empty cup into one of the wire trash baskets placed sporadically around the square, he started for the middle, where the market was now in full swing. He weaved his way through neighbours stopping to chat and patrons haggling over prices with the vendors. After traipsing past almost every stall, he was about to give up and ask someone when he heard the voice. The same low voice he'd heard that first day in the waiting room of the hospital. Except now it was speaking in a language completely foreign to him.

He wheeled around and spotted her. She sat on a stool behind a stall table, her head down as she concentrated on carving an intricate design into some sort of gourd. She wore a flowing gypsy-style skirt of brilliant gold, green and copper colours, and a thick-knitted, deep-red sweater reached below her slim hips. A matching hat covered her ears, but her long beaded braids emerged like a kaleidoscopic waterfall from underneath it. Of course he hadn't seen her; he'd been searching the crowd of customers, not the vendors in the stalls, and earlier, before the crowds arrived, the vendors had been but shadows in the dim light of dawn.

As Makena spoke, he could see that the woman standing next to her in the stall understood the foreign words. This woman, dressed in the conservative style of the rest of the town, laughed and responded in the same language, but effortlessly switched to English – though with a British accent – when addressing customers.

He took a step toward the table. 'Makena.'

The British woman looked first, but she returned to her discussion with a customer when she didn't recognize him. Makena's head rose slowly, her eyes following a bit behind, as if she didn't want to lose her carving spot. She looked at him for the briefest moment, glanced back at the gourd, and then quickly jerked her head back up. She said something in the language he couldn't understand, causing the other woman to look again, too.

They stared at each other for what seemed to Anders like an eternity, and then Makena stood, placing the gourd and her tool on the stool behind her. She came around to the front of the table and took his hand. Her own hand was surprisingly warm.

Without a word she led him away from the stall, away from the crowds, away from the market. He didn't even consider talking; somehow he knew he didn't need to.

She led him down a small side street and up a few short steps to the entrance of a Congregational church. Its white clapboard facade and tall steeple stood starkly against the winter blue sky. She stopped, finally, when they entered the empty nave, and whispered her first words to him: 'We will have privacy here.' The room lacked the sweet smell of incense he associated with the Lutheran church of his youth, and he was glad of its absence.

She turned to face him and took his other hand, too. Looking him in the eye, she said, 'You have come for Olivia.' She whispered the words in a thick accent, and even though there'd been no lilt at the end indicating a question, he nodded.

She nodded, too, quite slowly, and her lips curved slightly in satisfaction. Suddenly she dropped his hands and engulfed him in a tight hug, and even though his body still ached, he found himself smiling for the first time in weeks. He'd never even met this woman, not formally, at least, and she was treating him like a long lost son returned to the womb. When she released him, she touched a gentle thumb to his cheek.

'Who did this?'

He shrugged. 'Some guys who didn't like my asking about her.'

Her eyes narrowed in thought as if considering the possible identity of his assailants.

'But you are strong?'

This time she didn't draw a conclusion. He understood she'd asked because there were some things she knew, and other things she needed *him* to know, to believe about himself.

He thought about everything that had happened since the accident: how he'd let Olivia's father take her away, how he'd allowed himself to be tricked by Crystal and, in doing so, betrayed Lenny, how he'd been beaten after blowing his cover in the bar. How he'd done nothing but drink and smoke to cope with it all.

But he was here, wasn't he? He was still here. He might be taking baby steps, but he was taking them. He'd take them all the way to Africa if that's what he needed to do to bring her home.

'Yes, ma'am. I am.'

She nodded, satisfied. 'Good.'

'Ma'am—'

'I want you to call me Makena.'

'Makena.' He tried it out, making an effort to pronounce it the way she did, with a short 'e' sound. 'Do you know where she is? Is she in Africa?'

She tilted her head, as if assessing him, and pleased with what she'd seen so far. 'Yes. But how do you know this?'

'One of the guys who did this,' he motioned to his face, 'told me. He also told me he thinks she's in danger, that Brent Campbell might hurt her.'

'Brent? Hurt her?' She scoffed. 'Olivia's soul is not happy but I do not believe she is in physical danger.'

'I think she is. I think he's already hurt her once and he'll do it again.'

'You know of Brent?'

'Yes, a little.'

A door creaked open from the side, at the other end near the pulpit. They both glanced up at the man who emerged. He waved and Makena called out, 'Good morning, Pastor.'

Anders felt his pulse speed up, fearful he was about to lose his audience. He lowered his voice so as not to be overheard. 'I think even Olivia might have understood she was in danger.'

Makena studied him. He could see she trusted his words – though he didn't know the origins of that trust – but he could also see the pleasure she'd exhibited at his arrival had been replaced with deep worry. She reached for his hand again. 'We must talk at length, but not now.'

'But—'

'I know you have many questions for me, and I have many for you, but this is not the place. I want you to come see me later today at the house. Do you know where it is?' She raised an eyebrow; every question was meant to elicit more than an answer to what had been asked. Every question was part of an ongoing appraisal.

For the first time in his life he willingly submitted.

'Yes, I know exactly where it is. But what about her dad?'

'The Mayfields will be away. Do not be concerned with them. It is important that you come to the house if you hope to win Olivia. Do you understand?'

*Win* Olivia? 'Ma'am, I—'

'Do you understand?'

He sighed, looked at the floor. Of course he didn't understand; he didn't understand anything that had happened since the day at the springs. And he was leery of showing up at the Mayfield estate, especially after Matt's description of the security. He dug his hands into the pockets of his inadequate coat and glanced up at the pastor. The man busied himself with changing a bulb on the small lamp that lit his sermons and seemed not to be paying attention to them. Tomorrow morning this room would be filled with worshippers, each with their own troubles and needs and aching for answers.

He turned back to Makena; she was a tall woman, at least his height if not an inch or two taller. Other than the brief passing in the hospital and this cryptic conversation, he really knew nothing about her or her relationship to the Mayfields. What if he was their prey, and she was the bait, wittingly or not? There'd been ten men at his beating at the bar, so at least that many knew of his presence in town and his motivation for being there. It wasn't that unreasonable to believe Lawrence Mayfield might have caught wind of it, too.

But what choice did he have? He needed information, and this woman seemed to be the only one who might have it.

HE ALMOST missed the entrance. After Matt's description, he was expecting something straight out of some horror film, with iron gates and heavy stone pillars and possibly even barking pit bulls baring their fangs at him from the other side. The white post and rail fence surrounding the property and the matching gate that opened as soon as he pulled up close to it offered a surprisingly friendly welcome.

He'd already braked and begun to turn in when he spotted a black limousine coming down the drive like an apparition emerging from the woods. Sweat broke at the back of his neck as he yanked the steering wheel to veer back onto the road. He quickly scanned his surroundings, looking for another drive to duck into and out of sight, but saw nothing but rail fences and dense woods lining each side of the road. He drove on at a steady speed and hoped the occupants of the limo would assume he was nothing more than a confused traveller.

In his rearview mirror he watched the limo turn onto the road in his direction. He increased his speed slightly – enough to gain distance but not so much to arouse suspicion – but the limo matched it and then closed the gap.

He told himself it was all coincidence. And even if it wasn't, so what? Even if Mayfield knew Anders had arrived in Clifton, what could he do about it? He might be well known in this town, but he didn't own it. Yet even as Anders tried to bat away his fears, he wished desperately that his rental car had the tinted windows so prevalent in Florida.

He finally came to a small intersection with a gas station and a Dunkin' Donuts. He considered his options: he could stop and hope the limo continued on, or he could keep driving until the limo made its own turn. He glanced at his fuel gauge and realized he was running low on gas. What if he kept going and the limo never turned? He decided it'd be better to stop by choice in a populated spot than run out of gas God knows where.

Giving a turn signal to see if the limo would do the same, he pulled in. In the mirror he saw it brake, and he prepared himself for a confrontation with Lawrence Mayfield.

He stared, perfectly still, into the mirror. Still on the road, the limo slowed to a crawl, and a rear window went down. *You can see him, but he can't see you*, Anders told himself. *He sees only the rear of a car, at best, and the back of a head, at worst.* He waited as seconds stretched before him.

He didn't realize he'd been holding his breath until, after the limo's window finally rose and the long car pulled away, he exhaled.

*

AFTER WAITING to ensure Mayfield wouldn't return, he filled his tank and returned in the direction he'd come. At least now he knew for certain the man wouldn't be home.

Once again, the gate opened just after he stopped in front of it, but this time his was the only car in the vicinity. With every nerve standing at attention, he drove another half-mile through the woods to reach the house. The dwelling that greeted him in the clearing was another pleasant surprise. The whole thing – a compound, really, with two barn-like structures connected to the main house at either end – was immense, as he'd expected, but the classic New England colonial style of the large main house was similar to many other homes he'd seen in the area, with its white siding and multiple black shutters. He could already envision the place at Christmas with a candle in every window and a wreath on the door.

He approached the front door on a long, wide walkway of red brick pavers. Only then, as his eyes took in the large dormant oak gracing the front lawn, did he notice the first of what must have been numerous cameras on the property. The lens was small and rested in one of the tight valleys created where the thick trunk separated into several limbs. Surely it was the existence of a similar device that had signalled someone to open the gate for him.

He stood at the door and took a deep breath.

HE WAS greeted by a man he assumed to be a butler of some sort. He was an older man, his tall frame dressed in khakis, a white long-sleeved polo-style shirt and a sweater vest. Without identifying himself by name, Anders announced he was there to see Makena, to which the man simply replied, 'She is expecting you, sir.' He welcomed him into the large foyer, and though he pretended not to notice Anders's obvious discomfort at the opulence of his surroundings, his eyes couldn't help but linger on Anders's bruised and swollen face.

He was left alone in a room with a wide stone fireplace, deep leather couches, and enough books to fill a public library. The little wall space that lacked bookshelves was covered with framed photos of Lawrence Mayfield, and sometimes his wife, standing with various politicians and dignitaries. Anders's sense of outrage at the absence of Olivia in these photos was extinguished as quickly as it had ignited when he moved to the fireplace and saw the mantel was devoted to her.

Though he carried her picture with him and had slipped it from his wallet many times over the past weeks, the onslaught of so many images of her, from so many stages of her life, staggered him. Here was Olivia as a little girl, perhaps four or five years old, dressed for safari and holding a rifle as comfortably as most children held dolls. There was the teenager Olivia, next to a horse, this time clothed in English-style riding gear, mugging for the camera. In another photo she sat on a camel, and despite her young age, the vast desert behind her told him she hadn't been on a simple outing to the local zoo. Many of the pictures he thought must have been taken on the continent of her birth; some had acacia and baobab trees in the background, in others she leaned against a Land Rover, or shared the frame with wildlife – elephants or lions in the distance, or monkeys at her feet. The photos that overwhelmed him the most, though – the ones that made him want to bolt from the house – were the photos with Brent Campbell. Sometimes Campbell was a boy, other times a grown man, but Anders recognized him easily from the newspaper clipping he'd found in her shoebox. His fair hair and square face stayed constant as he aged, and stood in stark contrast to the Mayfield clan's dark locks. In every picture, at every age, his stance asserted some sort of proprietary hold on Olivia. In a number of the earlier pictures, a woman Anders didn't recognize shared the frame with them; he wondered if it was Campbell's mother.

Anders had known all along, intellectually, that he was but a blip on the radar screen of her life, but the collection on the mantelpiece drove the point home like a stake in his heart. He remembered Makena's question about his strength and began to doubt whether he'd given her the correct answer. He'd had many questions since the accident, but now he began to wonder if he even belonged here, chasing after Olivia like a dog's head chases after the tail. Maybe they were never intended to be together.

'Anders, thank you for coming.'

He turned at Makena's voice and only then, when he no longer faced the flames, was he aware of the intense heat of the fire. It licked at the back of his jeans and made the rest of the room feel cold.

'I'm beginning to think I shouldn't have.'

'Nonsense.' She moved to a couch and motioned for him to sit with her.

'You told me the Mayfields would be away.' His tone was too defensive, too accusatory; he remained standing. 'But I almost ran into him at the entrance.'

'I'm sorry about that. Their trip was delayed and I had no way to contact you.' She winked then. 'I trusted you to figure it out and work around it.'

'What about the guy who answered the door?'

'He knows only that you are my guest. What did you give him as your name?'

'I didn't.'

She smiled, pleased with his answer. 'And you saw the pictures?' He glanced at the mantel and nodded. 'What do you think?'

He began to understand that everything about Makena was intentional. He tried to tell himself her manipulations were meant to benefit him, but he still chafed at her efforts. 'What did you mean for me to think about them?'

She again motioned for him to sit, and this time, he did. She reached for his hand and held it lightly between both of hers. 'I'm sorry if they were difficult to see. I wanted you to understand where Olivia comes from, what she—'

'What I'm up against?'

'Perhaps that, too.'

'Then why not just tell me?'

'Some things have to be seen to be understood.'

He grunted. 'Well, I don't think Olivia thought her life was as perfect as your little photos make it out to be.'

He started to pull his hand away but she held tight, leaned in to meet his eyes.

'They are not my photos, Anders. They are her father's photos, and *that* is what you must understand. This is *his* idea of her perfect life, as you say.'

'One in which I don't belong?'

'In his eyes, that's correct. And if he is the king of his castle, she is the princess, with all of its burdens.'

'This is no fairy tale.' He laughed sarcastically. 'She's an adult, and has been for some time.'

'I agree. But for someone accustomed to controlling people of all ages, that fact, unfortunately, doesn't mean much to him.'

'He told me she'd died. He *blamed* me.'

Makena sighed. 'I'm sorry about that.'

'You knew, didn't you?'

'Yes, but—'

'How can you justify that?' he snapped, and this time she released him when he pulled his hand away. 'How can you just let someone remain in the dark like that?'

'There's a lot you don't know. That's why I asked you to come to the house.'

He returned to the mantel and lifted a small silver frame

to study the picture. Olivia dressed in an emerald-green ball gown, Brent Campbell in a black tux. They were young, perhaps seniors in high school or freshmen in college, but her dress was much too elegant for any prom dress. He wondered what the event had been.

'Did she ever tell you about him?' she asked quietly.

Anders just shook his head without taking his eyes off the picture.

'Did she tell you about me?'

'No, in fact she told me her grandmother gave her the beach house. She said it was hers. I only learned that you owned it after . . . after the accident, when he was threatening to have me evicted.' *He underestimated me*, he thought. He searched the photo for some sign, some evidence of what resided inside her heart back then. 'That's when I decided I needed to pay you a visit. Who *are* you, exactly?'

'She told me about you, you know.'

He looked up then. He didn't even notice she'd ignored his question. 'She was in touch with you, from Florida?'

'Yes, quite often.'

He softened. 'What did she say?'

Makena laughed gently. 'She said much when she talked about you, but it all meant the same thing. She wanted to spend the rest of her life with you, and hoped you felt the same way.'

*She knew I felt the same way.* 'But now?'

The reflective smile left Makena's face and she stared into the fire.

'She doesn't remember me, does she?'

She rose from the couch and came close to him, touched his arm. For the first time she seemed surprised by the information he'd obtained on his own. 'You know about the medicine?'

'What medicine?'

210

Her face was a mosaic of confusion and concern. 'How do you know about her amnesia then?'

'*What medicine, Makena?*' She mumbled to herself in another language, the language he'd heard her speak at the market. 'Are you talking about Cranitex MR?'

At his mention of the drug's name, she switched tongues. 'Yes. You are aware of this drug?'

'I don't know what it is. I only know that she had it in her possession. I saw it in her backpack when I first met her.' He remembered her reaction that day, when she'd woken to find him rubbing the bird crap from her belly. It now made sense, in light of what he'd learned in the bar. Had she stopped taking a drug that was supposed to help her forget?

But Makena looked puzzled by this information. 'She had this with her in Florida? I knew he'd given it to her after the accident, but ...' Her voice faded into her thoughts. 'Did she tell you what it was for?'

'No, she didn't know I'd seen it.' She stared at him with a glimmer of distrust in her dark eyes, and he felt she might be wondering whether she'd misjudged him. 'I was only looking in her backpack for something else, a tissue.' When she nodded, accepting his explanation, he asked, 'Is this drug what's affecting her memory now?'

Makena nodded solemnly. 'Yes, I'm afraid so.'

'I don't get it. The nurse at the hospital had never heard of it. She insisted there was no drug by that name.'

'Yes, she is correct, in a sense. There is no drug by that name on the market. Not yet, anyway. There are still a lot of ... uncertainties associated with it, I guess you'd say.'

Anders studied Makena's face, trying to make sense of her words. Was she saying someone had used Olivia as a guinea pig? 'Does her father's company make this drug?' He knew the answer even before she nodded to confirm his assumptions. 'What kind of uncertainties are you talking about?'

'Its effects are still not entirely reliable. The goal is to block certain memories, but so far treatment has been most effective only when administered in conjunction with shock treatments. They've also been trying hypnosis, which is what they did with Olivia, but with some patients there have been issues.'

'What do you mean?'

'Well, some respond better than others to hypnosis, as you can imagine. But the biggest hurdle has been that a few have had problems with spotty memories coming back without warning after missing just a dose or two and exacerbating their emotional state.'

'What do you mean, "their emotional state"? What is the point of this drug? Whom is it meant for?'

'It's intended to help victims of trauma, but . . .' She stopped when he turned and gazed, trance-like, at the menagerie on the mantel. 'What?' she asked, and when he didn't answer, she asked again. '*What?*'

'He gave it to her so she'd forget what happened at the bar.' He muttered the sentence to himself.

'What are you talking about? What bar?' She grabbed his arm and broke his stupor.

'You don't know?' This woman who seemed to be intimately connected to Olivia, who seemed to know every detail of her life before Florida, didn't know the most horrific fact of all?

''Don't know what, Anders?' Her usually slow, deliberate voice quickened. 'Please, what are you withholding?'

'I'm not withholding anything. I just assumed you knew . . .' Their eyes met. The fear staring back at him would be nothing compared to her anguish when he told her. He didn't even know *how* to tell her. 'Makena . . .' He wanted to lie to spare her, but of course he wouldn't. He couldn't. He now understood her reluctance to believe Olivia's life was in danger. 'She . . .'

Makena stood straight, steeling herself. 'Tell me.'

'She was raped.' He whispered the words, as if there were others in the room he didn't want to hear, and Makena gasped. 'She was gang-raped, in a bar over off those back roads west of town.'

Now it was Makena's turn to shake her head, disbelieving what he'd said.

'Here, in Clifton?' she demanded, lowering her strong body back down onto the sofa, her anger already rising to mask the pain. She was a woman who didn't waste any time; she was ready to tuck the pain away, gather the information she required and then act on it. 'When did this happen? Who did this to her? How do you know this?'

Anders didn't even know where to begin. 'The guys who beat me, the guys who *did* it – I don't know who they are, really, just that they're friends of Brent Campbell. They told me about it.' Her face hardened with doubt; she was looking for any excuse not to believe him. 'You have to understand, they didn't realize at first who I was, they were drunk and they told me in a bout of male bravado, I guess you could call it.' He paused. 'But they weren't making it up, I'm certain of that. My beating was their way of warning me to keep my mouth shut.' He shrugged. 'And I don't know when it happened, exactly – sometime before she came to Florida, but after Brent proposed and she turned him down.'

'You know this, too?'

He nodded. 'The guy I mentioned to you at the church, the one who told me she's in danger? He filled me in about a lot of things. About Brent.'

She'd been staring at the floor, but she looked up at the ominous tone in his final words. She waited, wary, understanding she hadn't heard the worst of what he had to tell.

'Brent's the one who orchestrated the attack.'

'No, you are lied to. No. It is not possible.' But the tears building in her eyes belied her words.

'I have no proof for you. Only what I feel in my gut. And my gut tells me it's true.'

She wrapped her arms around herself as though she was cold. He knew he should hug her the way she'd hugged him in the church – to offer some sort of comfort – because he knew she blamed herself, but part of him inexplicably blamed her, too, and he couldn't bring himself to sit down next to her and do it.

'Explain something to me. Why did Olivia come to Florida?'

'She was very unhappy,' she said through slow tears. 'Her relationship with her father was never a good one, but it deteriorated rapidly after she turned down Brent's offer of marriage. She wanted to return to Africa. Though she had every available luxury here, she'd always preferred life in the bush.'

As Makena spoke, Anders had the sense that she, too, preferred life in the bush, or at least somewhere in Africa, and he wanted so badly to know how she'd ended up here, in the Mayfield prison, and why she didn't leave.

'She has many friends there, and she often spent months at a time working at their camps. The more primitive, the better, as far as she was concerned.' She glanced up at the mantel sadly. 'No luxury safari camps for Olivia.'

'So why didn't she go?'

She looked hard at Anders, as if imploring him to understand what she was about to say. 'I talked her out of it, at her father's request.'

His jaw fell. He couldn't believe it. Did everyone do this man's bidding?

'She wasn't well,' she insisted, seeing his reaction. 'She'd fallen into a deep depression—'

'Yeah, rape could do that,' he mumbled.

'Anders, please understand, I didn't know. I saw a profound change in her, but I didn't know the source of it, and she didn't tell me. She'd been admitted to the hospital, for observation, he told me; I thought it had to do with the depression. Mr Mayfield wouldn't give me details, and he asked me not to discuss it with her. He thought it would upset her. I knew she'd been put on antidepressants, and he convinced me she needed to be close. So I suggested staying at my property in Florida as an alternative. It needed work, and I felt the project would keep her busy.'

Finally, out of weariness, Anders sat next to her again. 'She probably didn't tell you because she didn't know.'

'What do you mean?'

'She had the pills in Florida, remember? I saw them.' He made a scoffing noise. 'I'd bet she never took antidepressants. She was probably taking Cranitex.' He guessed she'd probably stopped taking them as soon as she arrived in Florida, because after he'd moved in with her, the bottle he'd seen in her backpack remained untouched in the bathroom medicine cabinet. As a result, he'd treated the meds like any other old, forgotten prescription and had never questioned her about them. He began to form his conclusions out loud. 'So he agreed to let her go because he'd drugged her first. For some reason, he needed to cover up the rape, and he could only do that if she didn't remember it.'

*And then, when he'd realized she was starting to remember, he'd whisked her out of Florida?*

She grabbed his hands. 'Oh, Anders, I don't know. I know he seems like a horrible man to you, but I don't believe he'd—'

'He *is* a horrible man, Makena. You saw how he treated me. He told me I'd killed her!'

'Yes, but he—'

'Stop it!'

She pulled away abruptly at his harsh tone.

'Why do you continue to make excuses for him? Why do

215

women make excuses for the men who treat them like shit?' He closed his eyes as soon as he'd said it. It'd slipped out and her stunned stare told him she understood his last comment was directed at someone outside the room. 'I'm sorry.'

She remained silent.

The fire popped and he turned his head to look into it, away from her penetrating gaze. She wanted more but he wasn't willing to give it. 'Just tell me something. You said she was in touch with you from Florida. Did she ever mention she'd stopped taking her antidepressants?'

When she didn't answer, he turned. The horror of realization blossomed on her face as he watched. She nodded faintly and began to sob again.

'And you told her father, didn't you?'

'Because I thought it was a good thing!' she cried out. 'She was so happy in Florida, and I thought he'd be happy for her, to know she was recovering.'

'Yeah, he was happy for her, all right. Happy enough to kidnap her from her home and send her off to Africa with the man who destroyed her in the first place.' He stood, wanting to lash out at something.

'No! It's crazy. I don't believe Mr Mayfield would do that, not if he knew Brent hurt her. And I don't believe Brent would hurt her like that. What you're saying is crazy!'

Her sobs grew, and she covered her mouth with her hand as if she could contain them. He touched her shoulder awkwardly, trying to offer what he could in spite of his anger at her reluctance to believe him, and when she felt his touch, she grasped his hand and pulled him back onto the sofa next to her. She wrapped her strong arms around him and began to rock, keening loudly. The haunting sound broke something in him, and he finally gave in and returned the embrace.

*

MAKENA FED him a dinner of beef stew and fresh bread warm from the oven. They ate at a small cafe table in the large kitchen, and though the two settings couldn't be more different, something about it almost reminded him of the simple meals he'd eaten at the card table in Lenny's kitchen. He told Makena of his plan to travel to Africa.

'I support that,' she said. 'I do. I'm not sure how reliable some of the information you've received is, and I think you've jumped to conclusions about Mr Mayfield, but, regardless, Olivia should get off the drugs and then make her own decisions. I firmly believe that.'

He stared at Makena a long time. From the beginning, he'd sensed he could trust her, and yet she'd known Mayfield was giving his daughter a drug to forget him. An unreliable drug meant for trauma victims. He thought of the old adage: Keep your friends close and your enemies closer. But which was she?

He had an idea. 'Come with me.'

She laughed a deep laugh. 'To Africa?'

'Yes. How long has it been?'

'Too long.'

'You could help me.'

She reached across the small table and touched his hand. 'Oh, I plan to help you, Anders. I can't come with you, but you won't be alone. I promise you that.'

'What about Brent?' he asked. Makena sipped her red wine and regarded him from above the glass. 'If my information *is* reliable, he's not going to give her up without a fight.'

She set her wine glass on the table and gazed into it as she considered what he'd said.

Finally, she met his eye. 'Then we will have to plan for both eventualities.'

*

LATER, AFTER she'd convinced him to stay over for the night, she insisted they take a walk. He liked the idea of being out-doors. It would be a welcome relief from his dank motel room, where he had nothing to do but worry about money and wait for his passport to arrive. Makena excused herself to retrieve her coat and returned with two.

'This belongs to you now,' she said, handing him a thick down coat while critically eyeing the old, thin one he wore. He accepted it silently.

The sky had grown dark during dinner, but a clear night and a half moon lit the way as he followed her across the yard and into the verdant woods. Pine cones and leaves crunched beneath the weight of their feet as they picked up the trail at the edge of the road; he could see his breath in the dry night air. He shoved his hands into the warm pockets of the coat and wondered how many years it had taken her to grow accus-tomed to the cold here.

'When will you leave?' she asked as they walked.

'As soon as my passport arrives. I drove up to Boston on Thursday to apply, after I received my birth certificate. I had to go there to get it expedited.' He didn't mention he was still trying to figure out how to pay for everything.

She merely nodded and kept her eyes on the hard ground at her feet.

'Can I ask you something personal?'

She laughed sadly. 'I think we've been quite personal with each other, so I can't imagine what you might ask that would be overstepping boundaries.'

'Why are you here?'

She looked at him sideways.

'I mean, how did you end up here with the Mayfields?'

'Oh, the answer to that question will require a bit of ex-plaining. I'm not sure, given your feelings about Mr Mayfield, if you'll understand.'

He shrugged, as if to say, 'Try me.'

'I was there when Olivia was born.' She smiled at him. 'I delivered her.'

She began to explain in more detail the story Olivia had told him that first day at the beach about her birth. 'Mrs Mayfield went into premature labour while staying at a bush camp in Kenya, near my village. The camp manager didn't think he had time to airlift her out of the bush, so he asked us to help.' She winked at Anders as if letting him in on a secret. 'Unlike some from more developed parts of the world, he knew our ways well; he trusted our methods.' Anders thought of how easily *he'd* trusted her, without even knowing her. 'Mrs Mayfield was convinced I saved both of their lives, and she insisted I come back to America with her, to work for them and look after Olivia.'

'Did you?'

'Well, I'm here.'

'No, I mean, did you save their lives?'

She waved the idea away. 'Oh, I don't think so! If I hadn't untangled the cord, someone else would have.'

'But you came.' He studied her. 'And you stayed.'

She kept her gaze focused on the trail in front of them. 'Yes.'

'Why? Olivia's grown now, and I get the sense you'd rather be back in Kenya.'

She sighed and waited a long time before answering. 'I would. But I am able to help my people much better from here.'

'In what way?'

'Olivia's father pays me well. And he is a smart man; he knows where the money goes.' Anders was silent and she mistook his meaning. 'Please, Anders, do not judge me.'

'I'm not.'

'And truly, Olivia is like a daughter to me, no matter how old she gets. Staying has allowed me to protect her as best as

I could.' Her voice took on a melancholy tone. 'Though if everything you say is true, I seem to have failed at that.'

Anders felt a pang of guilt from his earlier outburst.

'And I made a promise to Mrs Mayfield before she died.'

Anders stopped. 'Before she *died*? What are you talking about? Who was that woman I saw in the hospital waiting room?'

She took his hand and pulled him to start walking again. 'That was her stepmother.'

They continued to walk in silence while Anders absorbed another bit of Olivia's life that she'd chosen to keep from him. Makena must have sensed his wounded spirits.

'Let me explain something to you that might help you understand Mr Mayfield a bit more.' Anders kept his eyes on the hard ground. He didn't expect to be convinced. 'Olivia was extremely close to her mother. So was Brent.'

'Brent?'

'Yes. Brent's mother died in childbirth, so Olivia's mother filled the maternal role for him. She loved him like a son.'

'Wonderful.'

Makena ignored his editorial. 'Olivia was sixteen when her mother died, and it devastated her. And it devastated Brent, too. Luckily, they had each other.'

Anders rolled his eyes at that statement. 'How did she die?' he asked.

'Well, she died of kidney failure, but that in itself was a complication of MS.'

'MS? Olivia's mom had multiple sclerosis?'

Makena nodded. 'It was irrational, but she blamed her father.'

'Why?'

'His company had been researching and working to develop a drug at the time that might have helped her. Needless to say, she passed away before the drug was even ready for trials.'

'Oh, come on,' Anders said. 'I doubt Olivia would blame her father for *that*.'

'She was young and in pain. Like I said, it wasn't rational.' She paused as they each climbed over a fallen tree trunk that blocked the trail. 'Anyway, her mother asked me to stay on here, to take care of Olivia. She feared Olivia would be lost, given her already strained relationship with her father. I promised her I would.'

'But I don't get how that helps me understand her father.'

'Yes. Well, Mr Mayfield made his own promise to Olivia's mother.'

Anders looked at Makena then, examined her face for clues. 'What kind of promise?'

'You should be happy to know that Mr Mayfield never really liked Brent too much.' She shrugged. 'I think he was jealous of the boy, you know? The two women in his life adored Brent—'

'Wait, but Olivia didn't adore him.'

'No, not as she grew older. But when they were young, she did. He was her best friend.'

He thought of the pictures on the mantel. 'Go on . . . about her dad's promise.'

'Mrs Mayfield knew that Brent loved Olivia, would always love her. She believed he would take care of her, as long as Mr Mayfield didn't chase him away. And she knew her death would be as devastating to Brent as it would be for Olivia, and that having Olivia in his life would help him recover from that. So she made her husband promise to make every effort to keep them together, to not let his dislike of Brent destroy his and Olivia's relationship.'

'Was Olivia aware of this?'

'No, her mother was smarter than that.'

Anders grunted. 'So you're trying to convince me that her father wanted me out of the picture because of some deathbed promise to Olivia's mom? Back when Olivia was a *kid*?'

'I believe that's part of his motivation. He felt immense guilt himself over her death.'

'Bullshit. That's just bullshit.'

Makena didn't answer Anders's objection. By their mutual silence, he guessed they'd reached a fragile détente over their respective opinions about Olivia's father.

But his mind wouldn't stop churning. As they neared the end of their walk, he could see the landscape lights through the trees illuminating the front of the house. He needed to ask her outright the question that had been nagging at him ever since their discussion in the library. 'So if you didn't know about what happened in the bar, then you thought her father was giving her that drug because ... why? To forget me? To forget Florida? Because you obviously knew she was taking it after the accident.'

'Yes.'

'And you thought this was okay? That using any means to keep his promise was acceptable?'

His tone grew angrier, but she didn't back down. 'No, Anders, I *didn't* think it was okay. But I also didn't think it was my place to object. He is her father.'

He grunted with disgust. 'Then why am I here?'

This time Makena stopped, turned to look him in the eye. 'Because I was wrong. As you said, she is a grown woman. She should make her own decisions about these matters. And because ...'

He waited. The resulting stillness surrounded them like a cloak. It was something he'd noticed since being there – how *quiet* it seemed, especially at night. Perhaps it had something to do with it being winter; perhaps summer was different.

'. . . because she never sounded as happy as when she called from Florida.'

# 16

THE NEXT morning Anders returned to the motel and stopped in the front office to buy another pack of cigarettes from the machine. The desk clerk was nowhere to be seen. Standing in the parking lot, patting at the pocket of his new coat every once in a while to make sure the various envelopes of instructions and contact information Makena had given him were still there, he smoked his way through two cigarettes and then headed for his room. He stopped short just as he was about to put the key in the lock, jerking his hand away from the knob as if it'd been hot to the touch. The door wasn't completely closed.

He put his ear up to the door and could just make out the low noise of voices and laugh tracks coming from the television set. He checked the window but the drapes were shut, just as he'd left them. Suddenly the clerk's absence from the front desk seemed ominous. But maybe it was just the cleaning lady, though how much could she have to do? He hadn't even slept in the bed the night before.

He heard a laugh then, louder and more real than the ones coming from the TV. His tension melted and he kicked the door open to give the intruder a taste of his own medicine.

It didn't work. Lenny lay calmly on the bed, his head propped up on two pillows, his feet crossed at the ankles, and the remote in his right hand. He glanced up at Anders as if he'd seen him just yesterday.

'Hey, Andy.' He shut off the TV and sat up. 'Where the hell you been? Already spending your nights in someone else's bed?'

Anders simply stared at Lenny. He wasn't quite sure how to respond, given the tone of their last conversation. Finally, he asked, 'How'd you find me?'

'Your mom. She called me after you called her.' He let out an acerbic laugh. 'I think she was a little surprised that she knew more about your whereabouts than I did.'

'Why'd she call *you*?'

'She said you were taking off to Africa, and she was a bit worried about you, to say the least. She thought I'd know more of what was going on. She also called Shel, who freaked.' Lenny stood and took a step toward Anders. 'Of course, I couldn't tell your mom anything, since it was just one more thing I was in the dark about.'

Anders moved back slightly, maintaining the space between them. 'So why'd you come?'

'You know, I'd planned to take a swing at you when I saw you, but it looks like someone else already beat me to the punch, so to speak.' He laughed again, and instinctively Anders reached up and touched his face. 'Your mom didn't mention that.'

'She doesn't know.'

'You know, buddy, when you start lying to the people closest to you, you've got a big problem.'

'I didn't see any point in worrying her. I'm healing.'

The smug smile left his face. His eyes went cold. 'I wasn't talking about your mother.'

Anders looked down, shoved his hands into the pockets of the down coat. 'Look, Lenny, I'm sorry, I tried to tell you on the phone—'

'Shut up, Andy. I don't want to hear your shit-eating apologies.'

He nodded; he was tired of making them, anyway. Though he was still leery of provoking Lenny in any way, he took a chance and crossed right in front of him to the small table and chairs near the window. He tossed the coat onto the bed, and then pulled his shoes off and began rubbing at his cold feet.

Lenny returned to the bed with a little bounce. With his hands behind his head and his elbows sticking out like wings, he eyed Anders. 'Anyway, I've forgiven you,' he announced.

His tone suggested it was Anders's turn to speak. Instead, Anders pulled another cigarette from the pack and then offered the pack to Lenny.

Lenny sucked on his cigarette and then held it in front of his face as if studying it. Finally, he rose from the bed and joined Anders at the window.

'You look like shit.' The smoke blew from his mouth as he spoke.

'Yeah, well, I feel like it, too.' He lifted his shirt and showed him the tape on his ribs. 'I'll spare you the X-rated injuries.'

'What happened?'

Now Anders let out a sarcastic laugh. 'How long you got?'

Lenny waited until he met his gaze. 'I'm with you till we bring her home, buddy.'


WHEN HE finished recounting everything that had happened since he'd last seen Lenny, Anders saw that his friend's eyes were closed. But he knew he was awake when his right hand reached down and he scratched himself in the crotch.

'Lenny?'

Lenny opened his eyes and looked over at him without moving his head.

'I almost killed her.'

Lenny knew whom he meant. He stared at him as if trying to decide if he was joking. He finally shrugged and grinned, just a bit. 'Yeah, so have I a few times.'

'No, I mean, literally.' He swallowed. He needed Lenny to know just how serious he was, and how he'd scared himself with his rage. 'I had my hand at her neck, and she couldn't breathe. Her lips were turning blue.'

Lenny remained so still that Anders could see the rise and fall of his chest. Finally he let out a sigh. He scooted straighter in the chair, rubbed at his face and raked his hair with his fingers. 'Andy . . . you're not your dad.'

'I'm not so sure.'

'I am.' Lenny sighed. 'Look, man, I lived with her. I know what she can do.' He grunted. 'Why do you think I'm here? I realized I was playing right into her hands, being pissed at you. I'm not sure what happened with you two, but you're telling me you almost killed the bitch, so I gotta believe that whatever happened, you were only reacting.'

Anders shook his head. 'Or overreacting.'

'Maybe.' Lenny shrugged. 'But give yourself a break. That still doesn't put you in the same league as your dad. Nobody provoked your dad. He was just a crazy sonofabitch taking his shit out on everyone else.'

'Yeah.' But he wasn't really convinced. Lenny's opinions about his dad were based entirely on what Anders had told him, and he'd never told him everything. He hadn't told him about the incident that finally convinced his mom to leave his dad.

'So what stopped you?'

He glanced at Lenny, who wore the tiniest grin. Anders had the sense that Lenny would have enjoyed witnessing Crystal's momentary terror.

'Joey.' A shadow of the old anger crossed Lenny's face, so he quickly added, 'There was a picture of him on the wall, behind her head.'

Lenny nodded slowly, as if thinking about it, and his gaze lingered. 'Joey, huh?'

He nodded. He couldn't read how Lenny felt about the information. Maybe he should have kept it to himself.

'Joey, huh?' Lenny asked again, but this time he'd spoken

to the air. Suddenly he stood, a big grin growing on his face, and gave Anders a friendly slap on the back. 'Well, there's your proof, buddy. There's your proof.'

Before Anders could ask what he meant, Lenny clapped his hands together once. 'You hungry? Let's go get some chow.'

Anders was taken aback by the sudden change in Lenny's mood. He wasn't hungry – Makena had fed him well both last night and this morning – but he was so grateful for Lenny's presence that he was willing to agree to anything. He began to pull on his shoes and coat.

'Oh, I almost forgot.' Lenny turned around just as they were about to walk out the door and dug a sealed envelope from his carry-on bag. He handed it to Anders. 'Your mom asked me to give this to you.'

He took it tentatively, unable to think of anything else his mom might have had to send him. He carefully ripped the envelope, and a folded cheque fell to the ground. He picked it up but read the note before unfolding it.

*Dearest Anders,*
*I trust you already received your birth certificate*
*(what a special day that paper represents for me!).*
*After some thought, I've decided to send another little*
*something, too. When you decided to forgo college,*
*your father insisted we hold on to it in case you*
*changed your mind. Well, to hell with your father!*
*I say, you're almost thirty now – I doubt you'll*
*change your mind! Anyway, I spent some time in*
*Africa myself, years ago, and I can't think of a*
*better education. So good luck and Godspeed.*
*    Love, Mom*

He laughed out loud. He'd never loved her more than at that moment, and it had nothing to do with the mad money she'd sent. Slowly, unsure at what he'd find, he unfolded the cheque. It was a cashier's cheque. He held it away from his body, then brought it close to his face, and finally opened his eyes wider, as if all these things would help him see it more clearly.

'Holy shit.'

It was written for fifty thousand dollars.

# Africa

# 17

THOUGH THEY took off from New York in late morning with the sun high in the sky, the Boeing 767 barrelled quickly over the ocean into a night sky, and before long the miniature windows went black and passengers' faces glowed from the blue reflection of the screens on the seatbacks in front of them. Some dozed in the relative quiet that settled over the cabin; others turned on their overhead lamp to read. From his window seat Anders stared at the darkness and thought of those satellite images he'd seen of the earth from above, the line between night and day strikingly vivid when viewed from thousands of miles away.

He spent the first few hours of the flight trying to find a comfortable position for his sore body while Lenny chatted easily with the older man in the aisle seat. Lenny quieted down only after the man fell into a quick slumber, and finally Anders broached the question that had been nagging at him since Lenny first mentioned the phone call from his mom.

'So, is Shel still mad at me?'

Lenny looked up from his magazine. He waited a minute, as if trying to measure his words – so uncharacteristic of him – and then he said, 'She's worried about you.'

As if he'd just realized the chair could recline, Lenny focused his attention on the small button and fiddled with the various angles of repose until he found the most comfortable setting. They both heard a sigh from the passenger behind him.

'She tell you what happened at the house?'

'A little bit.' When Anders just waited without reply, Lenny added, 'I talked to her only briefly before I left town. She was all caught up in something with some professor at her school. We didn't talk about *you* too much.'

'What do you mean, she's all caught up in something? She's not back with him, is she?'

'No. Actually, from what I understand, she reported him.'

Anders's jaw dropped, but as the news sank in, one corner of his mouth slowly pulled up in the start of a smile. 'You're shittin' me, right? She reported him? She went to the administration?'

'Yeah, so she says.' Lenny laughed a little. 'She showed up at work a day or so before I left, walked into the restaurant with her shoulders back, big grin on her face, like she owned the place. Everybody noticed the difference. Samuel said, "Michele, you win the lottery or something?" and that's when she told us what she'd done. You would have thought she'd literally kicked the guy's butt, she was so proud of herself.'

Anders laughed, too, and just shook his head. He still couldn't believe it. He felt his own pride for her swell.

Little Shel.


AFTER A layover in Dubai, they landed in Nairobi just after four in the afternoon. They emerged from the baggage claim and customs into a crowd of bus and taxi drivers jockeying for fares, but they quickly spotted a driver holding up a torn piece of cardboard with Anders's full name written crudely across the front. Makena had kept the first of her many promises.

Anders wished they could head straight for the camp where he'd finally find Olivia; the closer he got to her, the farther away she felt. But Makena had explained it would be too late, that they'd need to stay overnight in Nairobi, where the driver would help them collect supplies. They could head out to the bush early the next morning. As far as Anders was concerned, morning couldn't come soon enough.

IT WAS well after lunchtime the next day before they arrived at the camp. For someone who'd hardly left Florida, much less the United States, the long drive on this new continent should have been a source of endless wonder, but Anders was so anxious to see Olivia he'd barely noticed the wildlife their driver pointed out along the way.

At the entrance, they were greeted by the camp's assistant manager, a young South African woman named Nikki. She had to have noticed Anders's damaged face – though it was healing, only an idiot wouldn't realize he'd taken a beating in the recent past – but she didn't ask about it or even let her eyes linger. After checking them in, she led them to their tent and invited them to rest until later that afternoon, when all the camp's guests would meet in the lounge for sundowners. At Anders's blank stare, she laughed and said, 'I believe the Americans call it happy hour.'

Anders sat on the large, king-size bed as Lenny regarded their surroundings with awe.

'Who'd have thought, huh?' Lenny said, walking through the large tent and shaking his head in amazement at the toilet, sink and shower. 'It's better than the Ritz.'

'When have you ever stayed at the Ritz?' Anders mumbled. Makena had told him that Olivia preferred to rough it. *No luxury safari camps for Olivia.* So why, then, were they here?

Lenny would have been content to take Nikki's advice and nap for an hour or two, but Anders tersely reminded him of their reason for being there and insisted they leave the tent as soon as they'd both taken their showers.

'Don't forget, I'm Joe and you're Craig,' he said, reminding Lenny of their aliases as they ducked through the flaps to leave the tent. He hoped Nikki and her bosses remembered too. Makena had known they'd have to show their passports at check-in, and she had wisely anticipated the issue by instructing them to tell the managers they were there to investigate possible poaching in the area, and thus preferred to use assumed names around the guests. 'They'll see right through the lie, but they'll honour your wishes.'

THE 'LOUNGE' was a large rectangular room constructed of wood beams and canvas walls, with one long side completely open to the air. At one end was a small cabinet that served as the bar, and a few chairs and a bookcase with books and games. At the other end, three large sofas formed a U-shape around the centrepiece of the room, a large stone fireplace in which logs had been laid but not yet lit. Except for two members of the camp staff, the bartender and Nikki, Anders and Lenny were the only ones there.

They passed the next few hours playing poker and leafing through large, glossy books with sweeping photos of Africa. Anders couldn't concentrate; he kept glancing at the yard outside for signs of Olivia and Brent. Though the afternoon had been hot, the air cooled quickly as the sun began to settle in for its nightly slumber. Nikki came by and lit the fire, and soon dancing orange flames illuminated the room. The fire provided not only warmth but a much-needed focal point for Anders's racing thoughts.

The respite was short-lived, though, as camp guests slowly trickled in, most with hair still wet from their post-game drive showers. Anders's agitation increased when he realized that camp protocol required him to mingle with the other guests. Unlike the camp staff, the other guests showed no reticence over asking him about his face.

Lenny, meanwhile, had snagged Nikki, and from all appearances, he was enjoying the social hour much more than Anders. Whatever appeal Lenny held for American women must have translated well, because Nikki reciprocated his interest and focused all of her warm hospitality on him. She sat at the end of the sofa closest to theirs, diagonally to Lenny, and leaned forward with her knees almost touching his. Her frequent laughs sounded genuine, and Anders found himself growing resentful that Lenny still found it possible to enjoy life. He kept his eyes peeled on the path from the tents as he pretended to listen to tales from the other guests of their day on the savannah.

'You expect friend, Joe?' asked a young Polish woman, Brigette, in her broken, heavily accented English.

'Oh, no—'

'You keep look to the door,' she said. It was an odd choice of words, he thought, since the lounge, with its open wall, didn't possess a door.

'No, it's just my first day in the bush, so I'm a bit nervous.' She accepted it as the truth, and on some level, perhaps it was.

But then the moment he'd been waiting for arrived, and any concern for Brigette's feelings faded when he spotted Olivia's figure in the distance approaching through the trees. He didn't feel Lenny touch his arm to give the much delayed signal and to calm his reaction. The world had gone silent except for the sound of his blood throbbing at his temples.

Even if he'd never met her, his eyes would have locked on the woman coming towards them. She appeared to him as a goddess among mortals. She walked with her back straight and her head held high on her long neck, yet she somehow imbued her otherwise regal stride with a sensual fluidity. She seemed to float across the yard.

All the other guests wore sage and khaki clothes and appeared to have shopped at the same safari outfitter, but she'd ignored tradition and was wearing a white, gauzy sundress that reached mid-calf. As she came closer, he could see that she'd also disregarded the warnings about covering her feet; they were minimally protected by flat leather sandals. Her only accommodation to the threats of the bush was a small grey sweater covering her otherwise bare shoulders. Maybe she knew she had more to worry about than mosquitoes and malaria.

The man Anders recognized from the pictures as Brent Campbell walked at her side, one arm at her waist with his hand, Anders imagined, touching the small of her back to guide her. He was a substantial man of medium height – slightly shorter than Anders – but sturdy and strong, and self-possessed. Thick, dirty blond hair framed his chiselled face and with his free hand he casually combed it across his forehead with his fingers. He was dressed in full safari regalia, but unlike the other guests, he wore the get-up with ease.

Anders should have spent more time assessing the man with Olivia – he knew it was important to know the enemy – yet he couldn't take his eyes off her. Despite everything he'd been told, he simply refused to believe she wouldn't recognize him once she looked in his direction. They entered on the far side of the room and stopped near the small bar to chat with Niles, the camp manager, and his wife, Ginny. From his spot on the sofa Anders could see she'd pulled some long hair from the front to a clip at the base of her neck, presumably to cover the gap left from her surgery. He wondered how Brent had explained the wound, and whether either of them had noticed the tattoo.

'Andy!'

Lenny's voice at his ear was quiet but insistent, and it broke his reverie. He shot a look of warning at Lenny but Lenny only admonished him. 'I tried three times to get your attention with "Joe" but you didn't register it. Stop staring at her,' he hissed under his breath. 'You're being too obvious.'

Anders nodded quickly and with a small apologetic smile to Brigette for his lapsed attention, tried to turn his focus back to her. Finally, with Niles and Ginny at their side and cocktails in their hands, Olivia and Brent approached the group on the sofas and Niles dutifully began the round of introductions. Anders knew he had to stand, but he froze at the thought of it. How could he look her in the eye, how could he shake her hand, *touch her*, without revealing everything? And then what? What if Brent Campbell knew? What if he could just tell? What if he'd seen a picture of Anders at some point? He suddenly realized how poor their planning had been, how truly out of their league they were.

Lenny took charge. He rose to greet Olivia and Brent, distracting them from Anders's odd, dazed behaviour with his loud voice and firm handshake. With his free arm, he unobtrusively gave Anders a boost up from the sofa.

Anders stood and met eyes with Olivia. She *didn't* recognize him, he could see that, but for just an instant both Olivia and Brent gazed curiously at the jaundiced bruise surrounding his left eye. Their reaction unnerved him further, and he stumbled through the introduction with barely a 'Hello' or 'Nice to meet you' while Lenny carried the brief conversation. A few times she glanced in his direction, and he believed she recognized how he felt just then, and he sensed she felt the same way: detached from the events happening around him.

Olivia and Brent's meet-and-greet with everyone in the room lasted only a few minutes. He never got the opportunity to touch her, not even shake her hand; she'd never offered it and he'd been too stupefied to offer his. The whole situation grew unbearable. It just didn't seem possible, or fair, that after so much time apart, he could be sharing the same space with the woman he used to share a home with, *a bed with*, and yet all he could do was watch her from across the room while he attempted, quite unsuccessfully, to carry on meaningless conversation with others.

The sky grew dark quickly and the group was called to

dinner at a long table set up in the grass under the trees and the stars. Hurricane lamps hung from branches above them and votive candles lit the length of the white tablecloth. The beauty of the scene pained him.

He approached the table slowly and waited to choose his seat until after Olivia had chosen hers. It was only when she stepped back slightly so Brent could pull out her chair, and then turned to the side to slip in, that Anders caught a glimpse of the slight swell of her abdomen.

'Oh, Jesus,' he managed.

Lenny was already taking his seat and he glanced up. 'What is it?'

Anders looked down at Lenny but didn't say anything.

'What is it? Sit down.'

Numbly, he pulled out his own chair and took a seat next to Lenny and directly across from Olivia. As the table filled, the group quickly resumed the conversations interrupted in the lounge, and the wine steward, a large African in the traditional dress of the Maasai tribe, circled the table and offered each guest a choice of white or red.

Niles and Ginny took their seats last, one at each end of the long table, and Niles gently tapped on his water glass with a fork. The small crowd quieted down and gave him their attention. A high-pitched squeal rose from the dark bush just as he was about to speak, causing everyone to laugh nervously.

'Ah, I guess one of our resident vervet monkeys wishes to have the floor first,' he said cheerily in his distinctive British accent. He waited a moment and then continued.

'Since most of you just arrived today – everyone, that is, except my good friend Brent and his beautiful companion Olivia, who have been with us for several weeks now,' he paused and acknowledged them with a nod, and Anders felt his gut wrench as Brent basked in the brief attention, 'I'd like to take this opportunity to welcome all of you to our lovely home here in the bush. Ginny and I have run this camp for many years now, and we're blessed and thrilled to share it with all of you. You will soon experience the magic that draws us to this place, and makes us fall in love with it, over and over again.'

He grew silent for a moment, and the only sounds to be heard were insects singing from spots unseen. He smiled at the diners. 'I think I can safely say that each of you, in your own special way, will fall in love during your stay in the African bush.' He winked at Ginny down the long expanse of table and then raised his wine goblet in toast.

In the sepia glow of the warm candlelight, every lit face waited with anticipation, glasses at attention.

'To falling in love,' Niles said.

Brent whispered something into Olivia's ear, his arm resting on the back of her chair. She smiled slightly and lifted her eyes as she lifted her glass, and for just a moment, and merely because he happened to be the one sitting across from her, those big green eyes landed on Anders. He willed her to hold his gaze, to do as instructed and fall in love with him all over again, but she turned back to Brent, oblivious.

THE DREAMY mood that had settled on the table during Niles's short speech grew larger and more festive as the noise of clinking crystal was followed by exclamations over the feast placed before them. Olivia talked and laughed throughout dinner, and even if she was a different, more reserved person around Brent, Anders could see she loved being in Africa. The other guests peppered Olivia and Brent with questions about their shared history, and before long she began reminiscing wistfully about the time she'd spent there, with and without Brent. She was no longer merely polite, she was engaged.

It was all too terribly merry for Anders, and he was grateful when at the end of the five-course meal, Brent announced that he and Olivia were retiring early and asked for the escort back to their tent. Anders hated the idea of the two of them alone in their tent for various reasons, not all having to do with her safety, but he and Lenny had already agreed to take turns standing guard through the night, on the off chance that Brent had it in mind to sneak away with her. He told himself this was unlikely, that whatever the man had planned, it wouldn't happen here at the camp, surrounded by witnesses and far from any easy escape. Plus, their efforts would be backed up by the two large Maasai who guarded the tents round the clock from predators of a different sort.

They returned to their tent to find the sheets turned down and two hot water bottles warming each side of the bed. A hurricane lamp on the nightstand illuminated the room.

'Makena was right. I think Niles and Ginny know our story is a farce,' Lenny said, snickering. 'I think they suspect we're a gay couple.' He sat on the end of the bed and began to pull off his boots.

Anders understood the enormous effort it must take for the ultra-masculine Lenny to accept lightly the thought that others might think he was gay, and so he tried to respond with humour. 'You may be my only option when this is over.'

He failed; Lenny looked up at his broken tone. 'Andy—'

'I think she's pregnant.'

Lenny sat motionless on the bed. 'Oh.'

'Either that or she's been eating incredibly well since the accident.' He sighed. 'I could see it when she sat down for dinner tonight.'

'Well,' Lenny offered, 'maybe it is the food. Look at how we ate tonight.' But Anders knew Lenny didn't believe his own words any more than Anders did.

He sat on the bed and then immediately stood again when

he realized how easy it would be to collapse into it from exhaustion. 'Why don't you get some sleep first?' he said. 'I'll sit outside for a while.'

'Andy? Are you worried it's not yours?'

He shook his head. 'No. It's gotta be mine. I'm worried that *she* thinks it's *his*.'

# 18

ANDERS PLANTED himself in the papasan chair on the deck and covered up with the extra blanket he'd found on a shelf in the tent. Within minutes he heard Lenny snoring.

The camp's ten guest quarters were situated close to the river in a modified semicircle with their openings facing the water. Each tent rested on elevated bamboo platforms, with three steps leading from the small deck to the ground. Two tents separated theirs from Olivia and Brent's, which was at the end, but the interior light caused the far tent to glow against the black night and he could vaguely make out their figures moving about the room as they prepared for bed. He dreaded the moment they extinguished the lamp, even though whatever might happen between them in the dark had without a doubt already occurred long before Anders's arrival to witness it from afar.

As he watched their muted silhouettes behind the canvas walls, he began to question what he was doing. If he was honest, he really had no idea whether the things Matt had told him about Brent were true, yet here he was preparing to somehow snatch her away from the man. Brent might not be someone he'd choose to have as a friend, but he'd given no indication of wanting to hurt Olivia, and she certainly hadn't displayed even a hint of fear of him.

Matt had led Anders to believe Brent was crazy, if not evil, but from his own experience so far, her father was the greater threat. The Olivia he'd known certainly had no fondness or respect for Lawrence Mayfield, and Anders himself had experienced his manipulations first-hand. Makena claimed that Mayfield's actions were misguided yet ultimately motivated by good intentions, but Anders felt her judgement could easily be clouded by the need to keep the money flowing to her extended family in Kenya.

If Brent truly had no intent to hurt Olivia – and really, but for Matt's hearsay, this appeared to be the case – then what was Anders even doing there? Who was he to decide that she'd be better off remembering? Was his desire to see her head cleared of the mind-altering drugs simply the justification for a selfish crusade on his part to get her back? He knew, at least in part, it was. Yet, if she was carrying his child . . . There were so many unanswered questions that he mistrusted either option: conceding her to Brent, or stealing her back.

Both left him feeling he could do nothing but cause her further harm.

DAMP AND COLD, he started awake and saw that it was morning already. He was still on the deck, and Lenny still snored inside the tent. He jerked his head in the direction of Olivia's tent but was unable to determine anything without getting closer. He threw off the blanket and crossed the grass quietly until he could see the bottom of the tent's zipper and the closed padlock.

'Damn!' From the instructions they'd received the day before about how to protect the interior of their tent from the inquisitive monkeys, he knew the padlock meant Olivia and Brent were no longer inside.

He returned to his own tent and shook a reluctant Lenny awake. 'They've gone already!'

Lenny sat up and rubbed his eyes. 'Damn, it's cold in here. I thought Africa was supposed to be hot.'

'Did you hear me? They're gone!'

'Christ, Andy, will you calm down? They're probably at breakfast, you know?'

'Then get up, let's go.'


BUT THEY weren't at breakfast either. This fact became clear from listening to the banter about everyone's plans for the day. Nikki reported that Brent and Olivia had taken off before dawn for an all-day game drive.

After the meal, Anders approached her at the long buffet table set up in the grass. She stood in front of it, pouring hot water into her mug while the kitchen staff began clearing dishes.

'Excuse me, Nikki? Do you know which guide went with Mr Campbell?' He hoped the answer wasn't Leng, the guide Makena had instructed them to request.

She chuckled as she dipped a tea bag into the hot water. 'Mr Campbell doesn't use a guide, Mr Erickson. They went alone.' She leaned against the table, crossing her feet at the ankles. Steam rose from her mug and she blew at the liquid to cool it.

'What do you mean?'

'Mr Campbell knows the bush just as well as our guides. Better than some. When he was younger, he even guided tours himself.'

Anders struggled not to let her see his rising panic. He almost asked if she knew when they were expected to return, but stopped himself when he realized he had no legitimate reason to ask for such information.

'Is it possible to request a particular guide?'

'Why? Are you wanting Mr Campbell to be your guide?' She laughed again. 'Not sure he's for hire anymore.'

He thought about her idea; tucked it away for later. He forced a laugh for her benefit. 'No, I was wondering about Leng.'

'Oh, Leng is a delightful guide. He's a member of the Maasai tribe, very knowledgeable and, even better, he never gets stuck in the mud.' She winked at him. 'I'll see that your request is honoured.' She moved away from the table, indicating she had other tasks to attend to. 'Are you and Lenny ready for your buckets to be filled, or do you prefer your showers after your drive?'

Only then did he notice that she hadn't used the aliases for their private conversation. Even stranger, she'd used *his* surname, but Lenny's given name. He hoped her budding relationship with Lenny had something to do with it.

LENNY REMINDED Anders that Brent had been alone with Olivia for several weeks now, and she was still alive, so their absence was probably as represented: a game drive.

'They'll be back by dinner,' he said. 'He's not going to do anything here where he knows people, unless, of course, *you* manage to spook him. Let's just follow the script Makena gave you and get her away from him.'

So Anders acquiesced, though he really had no choice, and now they bounced along in the back of a Land Rover with Leng at the wheel. Nikki had kept her promise.

Leng narrated their journey as they crossed the Maasai Mara, and Anders quickly understood why Makena trusted him to help them. He navigated the expansive landscape with ease, relying on, it seemed, nothing more than certain trees and watering holes as landmarks and an awe-inspiring sense of direction. He was as knowledgeable as Nikki claimed, about the place and its people but also about the abundant wildlife that roamed the land. For each animal spotted, he drove them closer for a better look and explained about its habits – what it ate, whether it was nocturnal, how often it mated, the female's gestation period, and on and on it went. He was a wealth of information, and there didn't seem to be a question he couldn't answer.

Anders knew this because Lenny kept asking them, over and over, one enquiry after another, as if they were two modern-day explorers on a research trip. And it drove Anders insane.

They finally stopped for an early lunch around eleven. Leng arranged serving dishes and drinks on the hood of the vehicle and prepared a plate for each of them. Anders stared at the food, a little amazed by the small feast. It wasn't cheese and fruit; it wasn't even a simple sandwich. No, Leng had served them hot lasagna, warm bread, and a fresh tomato salad. In the middle of the Maasai Mara, far away from civilization.

Despite his eagerness, he waited until their guide had finished his meal before finally broaching the subject he'd come so far to discuss. Makena had advised him not to try to explain anything on his own, just to give Leng her letter.

'We have a common acquaintance, Leng,' he said.

'Acquaintance?'

Anders realized it was an English word he didn't know. 'Friend. I know an old friend of yours. Makena Mbatia? She told us to ask for you.'

Leng nodded and smiled wide. 'Ah, bibi Makena. Yes. She is much loved. You know her?'

'Yes. She has been very kind to me.' He reached into the back pocket of his jeans and pulled out the thick envelope containing her letter. 'Craig and I aren't really here on vacation. In fact, our names aren't Craig and Joe. We're here to help Ms Mayfield, and we need your help.'

At the man's confused look, he handed over the envelope. 'This is a letter to you from Makena. It will explain everything.'

Anders glanced at Lenny, who leaned against the front grille of the Land Rover as he scarfed down his third helping of lasagna. Lenny lifted his eyebrows like Groucho Marx as if to say, 'Here goes.'

Leng opened the envelope with obvious pleasure at being the recipient of a letter from Makena. When Anders saw the length of the note she'd written – it was at least several pages of single-spaced, college-ruled notebook paper with writing on both sides, all of it in Swahili, he assumed – the depth of the trust he'd placed in Makena finally hit him. He knew the success of this trip was in her hands. He looked at Lenny again, who was also staring at the letter in amazed silence. It would be a while before Leng had a response for them to its contents.

'We'll just wait in the truck,' he said, thinking it'd be easier for Leng to concentrate without them waiting impatiently at his side. Leng's expression had grown serious as he read, and if he heard Anders, he didn't acknowledge him.

'What are we going to do if he doesn't get it?' he whispered to Lenny. 'Or if he doesn't want to help? Or if she's just a shill for Mayfield and this is all a trap?'

Lenny shot him a look that said 'Just shut up' and so he did.

THEY WAITED in silence after that and watched three elephants – two adults and a baby – standing at the far edge of a nearby watering hole. One of the larger elephants dipped its trunk into the water and then curled the end of it to his mouth. Behind the small family, a large herd of zebra crossed the land with no obvious sense of urgency. Some paused their slow progress to regard the Land Rover and its occupants curiously, but otherwise ignored them.

Anders imagined Olivia as a girl, the things she must have seen. According to Makena, she'd spent months at a time in the bush, and the stories Olivia told at dinner the night before confirmed this. Like growing up in a zoo, he thought, except here the animals roamed free while the humans were confined to the cages of their vehicles.

Suddenly Leng was standing at the side of the truck. He looked Anders in the eye.

'I understand what is needed, Mr Erickson. I think it is best if we do not delay. Do you wish to retrieve her tonight?'

The question brought to mind the first and only time he'd ever dived off a cliff, during his trip to California. As his stomach tightened with fear, he knew then, as now, that hesitation was the devil's folly. He glanced over at Lenny and Lenny nodded imperceptibly.

'Yes, I think so.'

The guide began to pack up the lunch things from the hood of the Land Rover. 'Then we should return to camp immediately, so I can begin to make necessary contacts before nightfall.'

He lifted the cooler. Lenny reached for it and placed it on the floor in the back.

Leng climbed into the driver's seat and looked over his right shoulder before starting the engine. 'Do not worry, Mr Erickson. Everything will be in place by nightfall. We will keep her safe.'

'Leng?' As he spoke, he glimpsed a small zebra limping far behind the rest of the herd. The animal was young, with the brown stripes of a foal. 'I'd rather you call me Anders.'

Leng saw him watching the animal. 'His leg makes him vulnerable,' he said, shaking his head, though there was no remorse in his voice. The zebra's fate was merely a fact of life on the savannah. 'He won't survive the night.'


THEY ARRIVED back at camp just after one. Lenny returned to the tent for a nap, but Anders, determined not to lose sight of Olivia again, waited in the lounge until Brent returned with her a few hours later, just before high tea. As he noticed their vehicle approach, he moved to the small grove where the staff had set out the tea and biscuits, and watched as one of the tribesmen greeted them and offered his hand to help her climb down from the truck. She was laughing as she carefully lifted her skirt to step down onto the running board. The skirt ballooned when she leaped from the running board to the ground.

She was especially animated when she joined the other guests in the grove, and he soon learned why. As she stirred her tea and lowered herself into the open seat next to him, she began to tell the gathering group about the manyatta they'd visited. Brent stood behind her with his hands placed propri-etorially on her shoulders, and Anders wondered again if he'd noticed the tattoo.

'Excuse me.' A young French girl staying at the camp with her parents raised her hand. 'What is a manyatta?' She asked the question as if the grove was a classroom and Olivia was her teacher.

'It's a Maasai village,' Olivia said, and went on to explain to the girl in more detail about how the huts were made from cattle dung over a framework of sticks and almost always arran-ged in a circle to protect their herds from predators. She spoke to the girl in simple language, anticipating that her English might not be strong, and for a few moments, the two carried on what felt like a private conversation. Olivia gave the child her undivided attention, even switching to French a few times, until her parents gently admonished their daughter for pester-ing her. For the first time, Anders realized, he'd glimpsed what she might be like as a mother.

'We met a group of volunteers who were just breaking ground on a new primary school near the village,' she announced to her fellow guests, including Anders, though he felt invisible to her. 'I'm trying to talk Brent into staying on longer so we can help.' She patted Brent's hand affectionately, but she tossed him a look over her shoulder that Anders thought contradicted the physical action. Anders read it to mean, 'Now that I've announced it to all these people, you can't very well say no, can you?'

'Oh, were you planning to leave us soon, Brent?' Ginny asked, sounding genuinely surprised.

Anders waited with bated breath for the answer, grateful that she'd asked the question so he wouldn't have to. He shifted in his chair, then, feeling someone's stare, and he turned to see Brent looking directly at him. The man's eyes were like cold steel, and despite the warmth of the day, goose bumps crawled like a scorpion up Anders's spine. Brent slowly turned his gaze to Ginny and gave her a tight-lipped smile. 'No, life's become much too interesting here.' He rubbed Olivia's shoulder, working his hands up under her hair to massage the back of her neck. 'If Olivia wants to stay, we'll stay.'

# 19

WHEN THE guests gathered in the lounge a few hours later for sundowners, Brent announced they'd be taking dinner in their tent. Anders became frantic. He was convinced it had something to do with the death stare Brent had given him during tea.

'He knows,' he insisted to Lenny as he pulled him nearer the bar, away from the guests.

'He knows *what*?'

'Who I am. Someone's tipped him off. Do you think it was Nikki? How much did you tell her? You're trusting her too much.'

'I haven't told her anything. He's probably just fed up with you ogling his girlfriend. Did you ever think of that?'

'You weren't there. You didn't see the look he gave me.'

Anders decided to skip dinner, too, so he could keep watch over their tent. Lenny didn't like that idea; he thought it important that Anders eat, because once they were on the run, there was no telling how long they'd have to go without a meal. 'Bring me some food, then, will you?' was Anders's answer to that objection, though he knew he'd be too nervous to eat.

He sat on the deck of their tent and watched Olivia on hers. She sat in a canvas chair and held binoculars to her face. He turned to see what she'd spotted, but whatever had caught her attention was too far away for his naked eye.

As long as it remained light, he had a clear view for his surveillance. He knew from the night before that the sun set fast here near the equator, and he wondered how they would accomplish their mission once it dipped completely out of sight and the camp went black. They'd brought the Maglite flashlights as Makena had advised, but even a match flame no larger than a tick would be much too noticeable in the cover of the approaching dark, which she'd warned was overwhelming and sometimes almost suffocating to those not accustomed to it. He had a sense that the impending night could be their friend, but only if they could figure out how to navigate it without the benefit of sight.

Olivia stood, and Anders could see that she wore the same gauzy skirt she'd had on at tea. The skirt draped long on her legs, like her dress the night before, but the fabric was sheer enough and the light just right for him to see the outline of her legs underneath. It fluttered now in the faint dying breeze.

Brent came out of the tent and wrapped his arms around her waist from behind; Olivia shrugged him away. He disappeared back inside then, and Anders fantasized about walking over, taking her hand – 'Let me save you,' he'd say – and together they would escape without looking back. It wouldn't matter that she wouldn't recognize him; it wouldn't matter if she never regained her memory. Whatever she'd seen in him before, she'd see again, wouldn't she?

Brent reappeared, carrying a bottle of some sort – wine, or champagne – and two glasses. Olivia glanced at him but directed her attention back to her binoculars. Brent made a show of opening the bottle, and just as he'd finished filling the glasses, he looked in Anders's direction. Anders stubbornly held his gaze, and to his surprise, his rival raised his glass and nodded a toast.

He could see Brent's mouth moving. Olivia lowered the binoculars and turned in Anders's direction. She shrugged just before Brent's commanding voice filled the thickening air.

'Would you like to join us?' he called over. The invitation contained no trace of sarcasm.

Anders swallowed. He'd been invited directly into the lion's lair. He had no choice but to accept, but he didn't know if he could bear to stand so close to Olivia in such an intimate setting and yet maintain his distance. And what if Lenny returned in his absence?

He called out a 'Thanks' as he started for the stairs of his deck. He made every effort to walk the short distance with a calm, natural gait, but he felt that merely having the intention to do so made his tightening stomach and thrashing heart all the more apparent. He dug his hands deep into the pocket of his jeans to stop them from trembling.

Brent offered his hand as soon as Anders stepped onto their deck, reintroducing himself and Olivia as if they hadn't spent the past two days in the same small camp. Olivia merely tipped her head and gave him an unengaged smile. Anders tried to read whether she saw his arrival as an unwelcome intrusion or whether her coldness was a reflection of her feelings for the man she was with. Brent ducked into the tent one more time, announcing that he would retrieve another glass. Anders saw that the bottle was indeed champagne. He glanced at her stomach, and she saw him do it. Her eyes flickered the beginnings of a question but it stopped on her lips when Brent emerged through the flaps.

He filled Anders's glass and handed it to him.

'To new friends.' He raised his glass, and Anders and Olivia followed suit. When each had taken the obligatory sip, he motioned for Anders to take a seat. 'So, Joe, was it?' he said, holding the back of Olivia's vacant chair as an offering to her, 'tell us about yourself.'

Olivia made herself comfortable next to Anders. Her legs crossed at the knees so that her right calf and ankle bobbed slowly before him; her left wrist and hand draped on the armrest inches from his. It was all Anders could do not to touch her arm. Though logically he understood the drugs had robbed her memory, he had trouble accepting that in such close proximity she wouldn't sense the pull between them and know that he exercised monumental restraint by not giving in to his desire.

With some difficulty brought on by this added distraction, and after ingesting half of his champagne, he launched into the story he and Lenny had concocted. Once again, he found himself claiming to be from Chicago, the only place outside of Florida he had the slightest knowledge of, though slight it was. He told them that he and 'Craig' were old friends spending a few weeks travelling before Craig tied the knot later that year, sort of an overseas bachelor party. In his nervousness, he said something stupid like, 'His fiancée didn't like the idea of him being gone so long, but between a trip to Africa or the more typical bachelor party at the local strip joint, she preferred this idea.' He thought the whole thing sounded ridiculous, but Brent laughed appreciatively and seemed to accept the story without question. If he'd been warned that Olivia's Florida beau might be on his trail, as Anders had feared, he showed no suspicion that the man he'd invited onto his deck might, in fact, be that beau.

'What happened to your face?' Brent asked.

Anders wasn't sure why he didn't simply offer the same explanation he'd given the other guests – that he'd been an unwilling participant in a bar fight after beating the wrong guys at poker – but instead he responded vaguely, 'I was defending a girl's honour.'

Olivia sprouted a small smile, but Brent was unfazed. 'Looks like you lost.'

When Anders just stared at him without comment, Brent said, 'Chicago, huh? So, what do you think about what Daley did to Meigs Field?'

Anders's heart beat faster. He searched his brain, willing the information to come. He knew it was there; it had to be there somewhere. He recognized Daley's name, of course. The

Daley name was to Chicago what the Kennedy name was to Massachusetts. But Meigs Field? Was he talking about baseball? No, no, of course not. That was Wrigley Field. Any idiot knew that. Jesus, he was losing it. Meigs Field, Meigs Field. Nothing registered.

He shrugged finally, and said, 'Haven't given it much thought, really.'

Brent leaned against the rail of the deck with his feet crossed at the ankles and studied him closely, one eye narrowed and his head cocked to the side. 'Never met a Chicagoan who didn't have an opinion about it.'

'I'm not a native.' He shrugged again, trying to shut down this line of questioning.

'What part of Chicago did you say you're from?'

'Buffalo Grove.' Where Karina lived.

'Hmm. You don't strike me as the suburban type.'

'Well, neither of you strike me as the type to rough it in the bush, yet here you are.' He smiled and winked at Olivia.

He'd wanted to change the direction of the conversation, and it worked. Brent laughed, as if Anders had complimented him and he got immense enjoyment from the praise. He drained his glass before responding. To Anders's relief, Olivia hadn't touched her drink beyond the initial toast.

'Well, Joe, we're flattered, but you must know you're in one of the more luxurious camps in Kenya.' Anders nodded. 'But I can assure you, we are both equipped to *rough it*, as you say. I grew up on the savannah, and Olivia spent much of her youth here with me.'

The statement confirmed what he'd already learned from Matt and Makena, and what Olivia had talked about at dinner, but it caused again the growing sense that he was the outsider in Olivia's life and always would be. And even though he reminded himself that Brent believed he was just another guest at the camp, he still felt, somehow, the comment had been made for exactly that purpose.

'This is a special occasion for us,' Brent added, and leaned down to give Olivia a peck on the cheek.

'Really? And what occasion would that be?' Anders looked to Olivia, hoping to hear the answer from her. Would she announce her pregnancy? Or, as Duke had claimed to Matt, the impending marriage? It suddenly occurred to him that they might have already tied the knot.

Her lips parted to speak, but Brent beat her to it. 'We've reunited after some time apart, haven't we, babe?' He squatted next to her and wrapped his arm around her shoulders, giving Anders a big, self-satisfied grin. His perfect teeth evidenced years of orthodontia. 'We were sweethearts at one time, but the war intervened.' He kissed Olivia on the lips this time, lingering long enough to cause Anders to look away.

'That's rude, Brent,' Olivia said, turning her head. 'We've got a guest.' She'd sensed Anders's discomfort, though she couldn't know its true origins. Could she?

Brent chuckled. 'I'm sure he understands,' he said, standing again. He looked to Anders for affirmation but all Anders could muster was a tight half-smile.

Brent ignored Anders's lukewarm response and began to divulge a bit of his own history. As he talked in the rapidly fading light, Anders thought he understood the reason for the invitation to join them at their tent: Brent wanted someone to impress. He'd tagged Anders as someone beneath him, and now he could awe him with his West Point education, his service to country as an officer in the United States Army, and his brief apprenticeship in the pharmaceutical industry with Olivia's father. Anders had learned back in Connecticut the importance of suppressing his emotions – he might never have suffered the brutal beating if he hadn't taken off for the bathroom in anger

– so now he bridled all clues to his sentiments about Lawrence Mayfield.

But what surprised him the most was Brent's candour as he attempted to regale Anders with stories of his adventures in Iraq. Perhaps the champagne brought it on, or perhaps his need to brag outweighed his usual reserve, but he became emotional, and sometimes bitter, in the telling.

'This is a war like no other,' he said, pointing in Anders's direction with his glass. 'Everyone sits on their asses in the States and they have no idea, *no idea*, what's going on over here.' He spoke as if the tent was in the middle of Baghdad. 'Life has not changed for Americans, as it did in other wars. There's no sacrifice to speak of, because everyone sits on their asses watching *American Idol* and surfing the web for celebrity gossip.'

Anders found it ironic that he spoke of sacrifice from his luxury tent in the middle of the Maasai Mara, in a country in which he'd probably arrived, Anders suspected, by private jet.

'After 9/11, you'd think it'd be different. But people have forgotten the threat. No one seems to realize our entire way of life is at stake.' He lifted the sweaty bottle from the small table and with a look he offered Anders more champagne, but Anders just shook his head. Brent refilled his own glass.

'I wish everyone could spend just one day doing what we do over there, you know? Then they'd understand.' He began to describe the raw danger of just driving down an empty street, or entering a building where they had no idea what waited for them on the inside.

Anders could see that some of Brent's tales made Olivia uncomfortable; at first she pretended not to be listening with her face turned away, her eyes on something in the distance. But the distance evaporated when night arrived and Brent lit a citron candle at the corner of the deck.

'He doesn't want to hear this,' she said finally, trying to cut him off. She smoothed the lap of her skirt and began to shift in her chair.

Instinct took over and Anders forgot his earlier restraint; he touched her forearm. 'No, it's okay.' Though she didn't find it odd, or appear offended by his casual intimacy, he pulled his hand back quickly when he realized what he'd done. Brent had noticed the quick exchange and he met his eye. 'I think I *should* hear it,' Anders added quickly, giving Brent exactly what he wanted. He knew Brent thought he was just another unappreciative civilian who took for granted the risks Brent and his fellow soldiers had faced every day. And he also knew, on some level, Brent was right.

His encouragement had the desired result. As Anders struggled to banish from his thoughts the first skin to skin contact with Olivia in well over a month, Brent returned to his monologue and seemingly forgot that this stranger on his deck had just caressed his girlfriend.

'We get these enlisted guys – boys, they're all just boys – and they arrive all pumped and ready to mow down the first thing that moves. They think because they've played Call of Duty on their Xbox, they know what it's like to fight in a war.' He made a scoffing noise. 'They learn real fast that they don't know shite.' He looked straight at Anders and narrowed his eyes. 'You ever see a man with a bullet hole right between the eyes?'

'Brent!' Olivia said.

'Or how about a man without a face, because it's been blown off?'

Anders stared back at him without answering.

'But he's still screaming for you to help him because he hasn't died yet?'

'Stop it!' Olivia demanded. 'What is *wrong* with you?'

Brent glanced at her as she rose from her chair, but quickly directed his attention back to Anders. 'Well?'

Anders held his gaze and shook his head. He felt grateful for the low light now; it disguised the heat blazing on his cheeks.

'Let me ask you this, Joe.' He'd lowered his voice to a whisper. Olivia stood at the edge of the deck with her back to them, but she whipped her head around to hear the question. 'Have you ever killed a man?'

Every muscle and tendon in Anders's body grew tight and his eyes remained locked on Brent's. Olivia's loathing of this man was palpable. He wasn't quite sure what part of the performance made him the angriest: the fact that he believed he was being subtly threatened or that it took place in front of Olivia and clearly upset her. He levelled his voice when he spoke.

'Not yet.'

In the light cast by the small flame, Brent tilted his chin and evaluated the response. One side of his mouth began to lift into a small grin.

Olivia made a grunting noise. 'I've had enough. I think I'll leave you boys to your chest-thumping and the mosquitoes.'

Anders wanted to point out that it was Brent who'd done all the chest-thumping, but he decided it was unnecessary when she gave him a polite smile and said, 'Good night, Joe. You may want to get back to your tent while you can still find your way.'

At her words Anders glanced in the direction of his own tent, but all he could see was blackness beyond the deck's illuminated bubble. He wondered if Lenny had returned, whether he'd found their tent empty and wondered what had happened to him. But he'd look over and see Anders here, wouldn't he? Hopefully, Lenny would understand that Anders still maintained his cover.

He returned Olivia's smile and wished her good night. 'I think I'll take your advice.' *But I'll see you later tonight*, he wanted to add.

Olivia's departure had silenced Brent, and Anders took the opportunity to stand and begin to make his leave. He placed his glass on the small table, but paused when the hurricane lamp was lit in the tent. He listened to the sound of trickling water followed by gentle splashing sounds, and he knew that Olivia had poured hot water from a jug into the bowl to wash her face. He knew her routines, however modified for the bush.

'I see you've taken quite an interest in my companion, mate.'

The sound of Brent's voice, with its British affectations, brought his attention back to the man standing before him. He wore the slightest smile.

'Excuse me?'

'You've been watching Olivia since your arrival at this camp.' Anders began to protest but Brent raised his hand. 'Please don't deny the obvious. You're attuned to her every movement. Even she noticed.' He paused as if to give Anders the opening to make further denials. 'Frankly, I'm flattered. I must have good taste, eh?'

Anders swallowed, his brain unable to determine the correct response. He remained silent, waiting to see if he'd somehow already triggered a trap. Brent poured more champagne for each of them and lowered himself into the chair Olivia had vacated. Anders ignored the glass being offered to him.

'I'm returning to my tent now. Thank you for your hospitality.'

'No need to run off. Anyway, it's dark. We'll need to signal an escort for you.' He lifted his brow. 'Camp rules, you know.' But he didn't move to make the 'signal' and Anders knew he didn't intend to, not yet. He lowered his voice. 'I'm not offended by your interest in her, Joe. I'm intrigued.'

Anders's flight instinct had reached full throttle but his feet clung to the deck like it was quicksand.

'What is it about her that interests you so?' He spoke quietly, Anders knew, so Olivia wouldn't hear.

'Look, you've misunderstood. I'm just going to—'

'Would you like to join her in there?'

'*What?*'

'Did I stumble over my words?'

'I don't even know what you're saying.'

'I think you do.'

At that moment, he believed everything Matt had explained to him about the attack, and the fury he'd felt in the bar returned. The need to remove her from the situation became overwhelming. He considered what might happen if he tried to take down Brent right then and there. He knew the guy must have had some training in hand-to-hand combat, but just then Anders held the unrealistic belief that the adrenalin charging through his body could overcome this disadvantage.

But he also remembered again how he'd allowed his emotions to get the best of him back in Connecticut, and he'd vowed not to let it happen twice. Maybe he needed to use this turn of events to his advantage. It could be a way to gain easier entry into the tent later. But he couldn't appear overanxious.

He sneered at Brent. 'Is this some sort of *offering*?'

'Possibly. I don't think she'd object too much, given the obvious connection between the two of you. She says you seem familiar to her.' He gave Anders a half-smile. 'I think she really likes you.'

The words should have signalled Anders that he was being played, but his mind was too wrapped up in the memory of what he'd learned in Connecticut that he couldn't hear the hints hidden below the surface. He simply thought he was being offered what Brent had already given his friends.

'She's *pregnant*, for Christ's sake!' He regretted the outburst immediately; he was certain he'd blown any chance of getting inside the tent the easy way.

Yet Brent just grinned again; he might have been amused by Anders, but he certainly didn't appear to feel threatened. His eyes blinked mischievously as if he was giving serious thought to the allegation. The silence hung in the air and Anders tried to interpret the reason for the man's lack of response.

'But that shouldn't matter,' Brent said finally. His next words staggered Anders. 'I mean, that is . . . since it belongs to you, *Mr Erickson*.'

The reality of what had just happened slowly reached Anders's brain. For just an instant, he blacked out, and as the pinpricks of light cleared and he could focus again on the man in the chair before him, his mind raced through the possibilities: Makena, Matt, Leng, Nikki, *any of the guys in the bar*. He didn't know any of these people and yet he'd trusted too many of them.

He stood frozen, unable to determine the next course of action. Even if his earlier belief that he could take the man was accurate, which he realized now, at the moment of decision, had been a ridiculous belief, what then? Everything they needed to rescue Olivia was back in the tent, waiting for to-night's execution of their scheme.

He'd gotten impatient. He should have turned down the invitation to join them on the deck. He should have gone to dinner with Lenny. Even now, with every sense awakened, he could hear in the distance the dinner sounds of clinking glasses and easy laughter floating over in the night air, mocking him.

He simply needed to play this guy the way he'd been played. If not a physical battle, then a mental one. He needed to buy himself time, at least until Lenny returned to the tent and realized something was wrong.

He walked purposefully to the other chair, pulled it a bit

closer to Brent, and sat down. He leaned forward, his elbows on his knees, and looked him in the eye.

'Well, since it belongs to me, perhaps you should do the honourable thing and tell her the truth.'

Anders sensed a slight release of tension in Brent's body, as if he, too, had been bracing for a physical altercation. His head went back and his eyes widened like an actor on a stage. 'The truth?'

'Tell her about me, and the pills, and let her make her own choice.'

'Ah, so you know about her medicine.'

He scoffed at the use of the word 'medicine' to describe the drugs they'd plied Olivia with. As if the pills were meant to treat some unfortunate condition. 'Yes, I know about the *medicine.*'

'And you know what it does.'

He saw something behind the man's eyes, something that suggested he had knowledge about the drug that Anders himself hadn't yet discovered. And it gave Brent an edge that cut deep into Anders's fluctuating confidence.

'Isn't it obvious? She looks right through me.'

Brent chuckled and took a drink of his champagne. 'And you believe that without the medicine, she'd *see the light* –' he spoke the last three words as an evangelist speaks the gospel '– and choose a Florida Cracker over someone worthy of her upbringing and stature.'

*Florida Cracker.* The term his father hated to be called, thinking it derogatory of the earliest settlers of the state, including his own Swedish ancestors. He believed it was akin to calling him a hick. Anders, on the other hand, accepted the label with a source of pride he reserved for all the things still 'real' about his home state. If Brent had intended to insult Anders, he hadn't succeeded.

'If worthiness is her only concern then, yes, I do think she'd choose me.'

Brent laughed again but Anders didn't think it sounded quite so self-assured this time. 'What other concerns might she possibly have?'

He shrugged. 'I don't know, but that should be for her to decide.' Let Brent wonder what else he knew.

When Brent didn't respond, just took another sip and stared into the flames of the candle, Anders asked, 'What are you so afraid of, Brent?' Though he knew. Of course he knew. Why else would Matt have feared for Olivia's life? If Matt's fear had been warranted, that is. Anders still wasn't sure.

'Certainly not you.'

Anders smirked. 'No, obviously not me.'

Brent stood and Anders followed. He wasn't about to leave himself physically vulnerable, though he thought the sudden repositioning was more a reflection of the man's nerves than a lead up to combat. Brent didn't appear to believe Anders knew of the rape and subsequent cover-up. So Anders played dumb and asked, 'Her father, perhaps?'

Brent had just begun to peek into the tent, to check on Olivia presumably, but at Anders's question he spun around. The wild look in his eyes startled Anders and he took a step back.

For the first time, he saw the cold-blooded killer that Matt feared. *He's a crazy son of a bitch, a smart crazy son of a bitch, that's the first thing you need to know*. In fact, everything Matt had said about the man seemed, finally, to be displayed naked before him. He became convinced that Matt hadn't been the nark.

'*Her father?*' Brent spit his words at him, unable to disguise the seething disgust. 'You've got that backwards,' he added under his breath, but Anders had caught it.

He just had no idea what it meant.

266

'Why's that?'

Brent fell into his chair and looked up. 'Why's what?'

*He's getting drunk*, Anders thought. 'Why do I have that backwards?'

A maniacal laugh filled the quiet air surrounding the deck, and Anders suddenly wondered if Olivia could hear their conversation. 'Let me tell you something, Mr Erickson. Her father is a weasel, though not a very smart one. He's got money, and power, but he's not half as clever as he believes himself to be. You wouldn't be here right now if he was.'

'No, you don't think so?'

'I know so. He's been manipulating you from the start, but he's not done a very good job of it.' He poured himself another glass of champagne and offered the almost empty bottle to Anders. When Anders shook his head, he said, 'Oh, come on, we're in this together now. Be a man.'

Nothing was making sense to him, but he decided to humour Brent. Taking the seat next to him, Anders reached for the bottle and emptied what was left into his glass on the table. 'What, exactly, are we in together?'

'I'm not the one who initially gave Olivia the medicine, you know.' He laughed and added, 'Though that's not to say I haven't benefited from its effects.'

'What are we in together, Brent?' Anders repeated.

Brent turned and stared at him. 'Saving Olivia from her father, of course. But you've placed us in a very difficult position. You've placed Olivia in danger.'

'Why's that?'

'Well, let's think about it together.' Brent winked, and something about the gesture made Anders think the situation was disintegrating before his eyes. Brent was too self-assured. He had knowledge of *something* that gave him a distinct advantage, so much so that he didn't even worry about getting drunk. 'If

I do what you request, then Olivia regains her memory and, arguably, she could accuse me of kidnapping her.'

'Or worse.'

Brent regarded him curiously. 'Or worse?'

Anders decided to throw out some bait and see if he'd bite. 'It's my understanding that you're responsible for much more than kidnapping her.'

'Is that so?' Brent tipped the champagne glass for another drink but found it empty. Anders just stared at him and waited. He'd finally learned to let someone else fill the silence. But when Brent turned his attention back, the look on his face was totally clueless. 'I simply have no idea what you're referring to.' Anders almost believed him.

'I ran into a few of your buddies while I was in Connecticut.'

Suddenly Brent laughed out loud, his head tilted back dramatically. 'Oh, let me guess. Matt Murphy.' He shrugged. 'His word is worthless. He's a lackey of her father and he's never gotten over his, how shall I say, *financial disadvantages*. If Matt Murphy told you something, it's because Lawrence Mayfield wanted the information fed to you.'

If what he said was correct, did that mean Mayfield knew about his visit with Makena? Had his trust in her been misplaced, or had she unwittingly been a leak? Anders was determined not to let Brent see his growing confusion. 'So far everything he told me has proved reliable.'

'Well,' Brent leaned forward as if letting him in on a secret, 'what better way to get rid of both of us than to sic us on each other, right?'

'Why would he want to get rid of you?'

'Because I know too much. I know things that could put him away for years.'

'What kind of things?' He thought back to everything that had happened in Florida, not only how Mayfield had manipulated him, but how he'd manipulated Carrie, the hospital, the cops. He remembered Carrie's intense fear of the man.

But Brent merely lifted one side of his mouth to indicate there were some secrets he planned to keep.

'Now, if I decline your request,' he said, returning to his earlier train of thought, 'if I believe Olivia is better off not remembering her time in Florida, one point on which her father and I agree, by the way, then what becomes of you? You've travelled a long way for her. I can't imagine you came for the sole purpose of asking me to – what'd you call it? – do the honourable thing, and if I say no, you'll just put down your weapons and walk away.'

'I don't have any weapons, Brent. Do you?'

The man smirked. 'You're clearly a man with a mission, though, aren't you?' He stood and rubbed at his lower back with one hand. The action made Anders nervous, especially since he hadn't answered his last question.

'Yes, I am.'

'So do you see my dilemma?'

'I suppose I do.'

'You can't expect me to just *put up* with your presence in our lives.'

'No, of course not. And I certainly wouldn't want to be you right now, not with such a difficult decision.' This time it was Anders who smirked.

But Brent surprised him by laughing out loud. '*Au contraire*. If you're as smart as I think you are, you shouldn't want to be *you*.'

As he spoke the words, his hand moved to his back again.

Suddenly the candle on the deck went out and an explosion of animal noise broke out from behind Brent. And then, simultaneously it seemed, Brent was going down, tackled by Lenny who had come up, growling, over the railing from behind, pulling Brent's feet out from under him. Lenny tossed something across the deck to Anders. 'Go get her!' he hollered, 'he's waiting for you on the other side!' and somehow Anders understood that 'he' meant Leng and 'the other side' meant the opposite end of the camp, near the entrance.

He pushed through his shock to look at whatever Lenny had thrown, and immediately saw it was the metal canister of chloroform the Nairobi driver had procured for them, at Makena's instruction, on their first day. But the small antique inhaler Anders had bought while still in the States was back in their tent. He grabbed the canister and bolted for the entrance of the tent. To hell with the inhaler; he'd just have to be careful to use less, not more, of the chloroform.

But Olivia was already there on the other side, earbuds hanging from her neck. Only at the sight of her did he realize that he couldn't possibly use the chloroform to knock her out, especially if he couldn't measure it.

She desperately tried to tug at the large inner zipper to keep him out. In a flash of inspiration, he remembered what they'd explained about the tents during their orientation. He heaved his whole body against the seam, and the Velcro gave, just as it was engineered to do in the event of a fire and the zippers melted, sealing the occupants to a certain death. He fell through to the other side, knocking Olivia to the floor and landing partially on top of her.

She screamed and tried to scramble away, but he held her and tried to talk at her – 'I'm not going to hurt you! ... I'm trying to save you! ... Listen to me!' – just tried to convince her that he was the good guy, and the bad guy was the one she shared a tent with, but the sounds of the violent struggle taking place on the deck didn't help his cause. Nor did the stabs shooting across his midsection; his fragile ribs couldn't take much more.

*They used to administer chloroform to knock out women during labour*, he told himself. *It can't be that bad.* Without thinking of the consequences, just acting as fast as he could to get the job done before the commotion brought the others, he scrunched a handful of her skirt in his hand and poured chloroform onto it, and then, begging her to forgive him, forcefully held it over her nose and mouth as she struggled in his grasp.

The effect came swiftly, and she collapsed into him.

With a groan he hoisted her over his shoulders and escaped the tent. Lenny was on the ground at the bottom of the deck, still wrestling with Brent but clearly holding his own. 'Just go!' he yelled. Anders ignored the directive. Trying to disregard his searing pain, he lay Olivia down carefully and then returned to the tent to retrieve the chloroform and a sock he found on the floor. On his way out, he spied her backpack on the desk and snatched it up in the hope her passport was inside.

After dumping chloroform onto the sock, he cast it in Lenny's direction. Brent laboured under Lenny's weight to grab it before he did. He failed.

'*Just go!*' Lenny ordered one more time as he fought Brent's attempts to push the sock away from his face, 'I'll be there in a minute!'

This time, Anders complied. With the backpack on one shoulder, and Olivia weighing him down on the other, he took off to find Leng.

# 20

WHEN LENNY reached the Land Rover with their bags hoisted on his shoulders, he was already scolding Anders with a breathless rant.

'What the hell happened? Why the *fuck* did you go over to their tent? If I hadn't decided to take my shower before dinner, I wouldn't have been there when it happened, and you would have been screwed! Are you out of your mind? What were you—'

'I had it under control till you showed up.' He'd already wrapped Olivia's limp body in a blanket, and now he shifted in his seat to readjust her weight against him.

'You *are* out of your friggin' mind if you think you had it under control. I heard part of your conversation.'

Lenny practically threw Anders's bag at him, but Anders merely took it and began digging for the water bottle, the smaller bottle of GHB, and the funnel. His hands shook as tried to mix a few droplets of the GHB into the water. Her head lolled about as he positioned it to accept the funnel and liquid without gagging. He hesitated.

'What are you waiting for?' Lenny asked, still standing at the side of the vehicle.

'She's pregnant!' he spat at him. 'Remember?'

'She's gonna be dead if you don't get your ass in gear. That chloroform won't last long, for her *or* for him.'

Anders glanced at Leng, but he sat quietly in the driver's seat and waited.

'Andy,' Lenny calmed his voice, 'we gotta do this. Better

she loses that baby than we lose her. And you're assuming the worst. She'll be fine. You measured it out earlier, right?'

'Can't we just tie her up and gag her?'

'And have her struggling and screaming from here to wherever the hell we end up? We need to buy some distance before we deal with that.'

Leng's radio crackled and they all listened as Niles's voice asked one of the guards to check on a possible disturbance near the far tent.

'Andy, *come on*.'

Anders reluctantly gave her the drink. He hoped it was the last drug she'd be forced to take.

When he'd finished, Lenny pulled himself over the side and into the seat row behind Anders and Olivia. 'I'm in,' he called up to Leng, and as the vehicle began its rough ride into the dark wilderness, he returned his attention to Anders. 'He was going for a gun.'

Anders leaned his cheek against Olivia's head and with one hand pushed her hair away from her face. He hated doing it this way – it scared him, and he felt sick giving her what was essentially a date-rape drug – but Lenny was right; she wouldn't have come willingly. He wanted to tell Lenny what had happened, how he'd ended up on their deck, that he hadn't had a choice, not really. He wanted to explain that from the moment Brent had spoken his real name and he'd realized his cover was blown, his actions had been purely instinctive. His sole goal had become survival. But Lenny didn't want to hear excuses. He just needed to blow off steam, so Anders stayed silent and let him.

Lenny grunted at his non-response, but Anders didn't care. He had her back.

DESPITE THE urgency of the drive and the skill required to navigate the primitive roads, Leng drove with one arm casually resting on the top of the steering wheel as if they were out for a midnight game drive. Even with the chill in the air, he still wore the red and blue tribal blanket in the toga style Anders had grown used to seeing, one naked, muscular shoulder providing a glimpse of his full strength. Leng's weapon of choice was a spear, and though Anders now knew Brent travelled with at least one gun, he told himself that with Leng as their guide, they possessed the more superior arsenal.

As they drove, it occurred to Anders that they were no different than the animals in the bush; they just wanted to make it through the night alive. He knew that many of the nocturnal ones were probably watching them now as they bumped along through the darkness.

Lenny cursed from the elevated back seat whenever they hit a bad patch of road, which was quite often. He was obviously hurting from his brawl with Brent, but Anders still felt the two of them, Leng and Lenny, were like two bookends, protectively insulating him and Olivia from the surrounding threats.

'Try to sleep,' Leng called over his shoulder. 'I must go slow in the night.'

Anders scanned the dark horizon for signs of other vehicles. 'How far to your village?' he asked.

'My village is five kilometres, but it is too close. Mr Campbell will look there first when he knows I have left camp, too. I will take you to the city, much farther, but better to hide.' He suddenly pointed to the right and shone his strong flashlight, startling Anders and causing all of his senses to stand at attention again. 'Look! Simba!' he said, his mouth open in a wide smile.

Anders jerked his head to look, and in the beam of light he saw the glowing white pin pricks of a male lion's pupils reflect back at them. His muzzle was matted and wet with blood. At his feet lay the corpse of a small zebra, its chest cavity ripped open.

'He's taken the heart,' Leng stated matter-of-factly. 'Simba always takes the heart first.'

THEY ARRIVED in Karen, at the edge of Nairobi, in the early morning hours. Anders wondered if Leng had radioed ahead, because when they pulled up to the gates of the wall surrounding the hotel compound, guards waited for them. They shone their flashlights under the car before granting them entrance. As if he sensed Anders's question, Leng said, 'They check for bomb.' Anders wasn't sure whether to feel comforted by this.

They drove through the lush grounds of what was obviously a luxury hotel until they reached reception. Again, Leng explained without being asked that they would be safer at such a property. 'Mr Campbell will not look for you here,' he said. Anders understood without being told: Brent would assume they travelled on a budget.

As Leng arranged for their rooms in a combination of whispered English and Swahili, Anders realized their guide planned to sleep in the Land Rover. He insisted on buying him a room, and after some resistance, Leng gave in. Anders's assertion that he'd feel safer with him close by was the tipping point, though when they trudged down the open air hall to the rooms, each of which faced a centre courtyard overflowing with bougainvillea, he realized Leng *wouldn't* be close by. Instead, he'd sleep in a small room at the back of the property near the staff quarters.

He'd also had to fight about sleeping arrangements with Lenny, who wanted to share a room with Anders and Olivia. Lenny claimed it was better to stay together, but Anders knew Lenny just wanted to keep an eye on him after what had happened back at camp. He told Lenny that he needed to be alone with Olivia when she came around, that she'd be scared enough without waking to find two strange men guarding her. Like Leng, Lenny also gave in, though more reluctantly.

He helped Anders carry her to the suite. They laid her on the couch and stood over her limp body, gazing with exhaustion and disbelief at the task they'd accomplished. Anders didn't know whether to laugh or cry.

'I feel like a criminal.'

Lenny collapsed into a chair. 'You *are* a criminal. So am I. It's called kidnapping, and it's a felony, at least at home. First degree, I think. God only knows what they'd do to us here if we're caught.'

Anders stared at Lenny, who had closed his eyes and was breathing heavily. 'You're serious, aren't you?'

'You bet your ass, I'm serious. Let's hope what they gave her wears off quickly so she can back us up.'

Anders turned his attention to Olivia. 'Let's hope what *I* gave her wears off quickly. The rest I can deal with.'

He sat on the edge of the couch next to her and readjusted her shoulders and arms so she appeared more comfortable. He ran his fingers through her hair, once again attempting to calm the curls and push them off her face. He felt Lenny watching him, so he suppressed the urge to caress her cheek, to talk to her.

'Why don't you let me stay here with you tonight?' Lenny asked, trying again.

'No.'

'Andy . . .'

'I can handle it.'

'She's not going to recognize you. Nothing will have changed. Not yet.'

'I know.'

'You're going to have to keep her tied.'

Anders touched the tie that bound her wrists together and

then slipped his fingers under it; back and forth, back and forth, trying to loosen the grip. He'd refused the rope they'd planned to use and had insisted instead on something soft, so Leng had cut a strip of cloth from his blanket.

'You hear me?'

'Yeah.'

'You untie her and you're gonna have a huge problem on your hands.'

'I won't untie her.'

'And you can't be all over her when she wakes up. You'll freak her out.'

'I know. I won't.'

Lenny nodded, giving up. He rose from the chair with a large stretch. 'Christ, what a day.' He grabbed his coat from the bed and at the door, turned. 'You sure? I can stay.'

'I'm sure.' He answered without looking at him.

Lenny sighed loudly. 'Room twelve. Right? Just call and it'll take me all of thirty seconds to get down the hall.'

'Right.'

Lenny pulled the door behind him, and just before it closed, Anders called out his name. Lenny's head appeared around the edge.

'Do you think he'll find us here?'

'Yeah,' Lenny said, 'I think if we don't get out of here tomorrow he will. But not tonight. I think we're safe for tonight.'


ANDERS DOUBLE bolted the door and carried Olivia to the bed. He'd carried her before, of course, playfully scooping her up when they'd walked on the beach and then baptizing her, squealing, into the ocean; or the time when he'd first moved into the beach house, he'd insisted on lifting her and walking with her in his arms over the threshold of the front door as if they were newlyweds. But now, without the earlier adrenalin, she felt like a dead weight in his arms. Pain sliced his middle as he slowly lowered her onto the bed.

He worked the bedspread, blanket and top sheet from underneath her, tugging at them until they finally pulled free. Her skirt had twisted around her thighs, so he slipped his fingers under the elastic waist and inched it down her legs until he could remove it. His hand brushed against her calves, and he was struck by their smoothness. He stopped, unable to do anything else after this unexpected touch except picture her on the side of the tub at the house, one leg elegantly raised and the razor gliding methodically over her skin. He could see the soap trailing wet down her shin, dripping from her calf, bubbles between her toes. He remembered how she hardly ever painted her fingernails, but her toes always glowed with some shocking colour: candy apple red, bubblegum pink, an orange the colour of a construction cone on the side of the highway. Even now, her toes were well manicured and painted, at least that much hadn't changed, though the pale pink made him nostalgic for something bolder.

He touched the top of her foot and then lightly ran one finger along her arch. Her big toe twitched once, but otherwise she gave him no response. No smile of pleasure. No frown of annoyance.

He remained at the end of the bed and watched her sleep. He wanted to touch her more, to feel the silkiness of her legs again and the tautness of her stomach under her shirt. He wanted to lie next to her and bury his face in the heat of her neck, inhale the organic scents of their earlier struggle, the sweat and the dirt of the bush. He placed a palm on her ankle and slowly rubbed her leg, moving upwards, stopping finally, his hand at her hip. A sound broke from him, like a whimper. If he was honest, he wanted to ravish her, force her somehow to wake up and remember. He took a deep breath, tried to stave off the hunger. Though he knew his desire grew from a different seed, it was still too close to what had happened to her already and it frightened him.

He reached up and began to pick at the knot that bound her wrists. He pushed Lenny's warnings from his mind; he didn't care anymore. It was simply unacceptable to him to leave her tied up. He might as well have tethered her to the bed like an animal. He thought it would be worse for her to wake up bound than to wake up to freedom, regardless of whether or not she knew where she was or whom she was with.

He tossed the tie to the floor and lay down next to her, nuzzling up close on his side, one arm around her, one leg over both of hers. It was a mistake. He knew it as soon as he felt the full length of her body against his, reminding him of how they used to enter the first stages of sleep together. He placed his lips against her cheek, closed his eyes and tried to hide against her, but the contact with her skin only made it worse. He let out a moan, arguing with himself.

'Olivia.' The word came out as a plea.

He forced himself to roll away from her. His chest tightened and he fought back the racking sobs buried deep inside him since the day of the accident. As his hand found its way to the zipper of his jeans, he stared at the bathroom door across the room and told himself to take his business in there. Instead, paralysed, he simply tried to forget she was next to him.

But as desperately as he craved the release, as badly as he needed to escape, even if for just a minute, he couldn't let himself do it. Because in the moment he'd slipped the tie from her wrist, he'd finally grasped the utter extent of her vulnerability.

She had nothing. No one.

No one, but him.

And that knowledge rendered all his selfish needs obscene.

*

HE FELL asleep and woke later to feel her absence next to him. His fear dissipated as quickly as it had arrived when he saw that she had just rolled over and now faced the other side of the bed. He guessed this meant the GHB had worn off and she was now merely asleep, not unconscious. The long-awaited reunion was imminent. The clock read 4 a.m., but the room was still brightly lit. He sat up on the edge of the bed and rubbed his face. He needed more sleep, but he also needed to be alert and prepared for her awakening. He spied the cloth tie on the floor from when he'd tossed it away earlier. Lenny's voice sounded in his head: *You untie her and you're gonna have a huge problem on your hands.* But he couldn't do it; he couldn't let her wake to find herself bound with him as her captor.

He rose to turn off the lights, first the free-standing lamp near the couch, then the one on the nightstand. God, he was so tired. He convinced himself that a few more hours of sleep could only help, but he knew part of his desire to lie down again stemmed from his need to be near her.

He crept gently back into the bed. He could see the outline of her body in the dark just inches away, but he didn't touch her. He knew she'd wake with no memory – Makena had told him it might take some time for the Cranitex to wear off and that the return of certain memories could be spotty – and he didn't want to give her an additional reason to fear him. He wondered if Brent had been honest; had he seemed familiar to her? He stared into the back of her head. *Come back to me. I can't fight them alone anymore.* He'd expected to feel relief once he had her away from Brent, but relief had proved elusive. He tried to ignore the new fear growing inside him, the fear that the largest obstacle to getting her back wasn't Brent, or her father, but the mere inches between them now that somehow, some way, he had to find a way to bridge.

*

THE SOUND of heavy footsteps startled him awake, and he opened his eyes to see the first shades of dawn creeping between the seams of the room's heavy brocade drapes. His heart beat fast inside his chest, a tight fist trying to sound the alarm, but he remained still, listening. Olivia was on her back again, and he watched her eyes open and move around in her head, taking in the strange surroundings, trying to get her bearings, trying to determine if she was dreaming. He heard men's voices in the courtyard outside their room, a discussion of strategy before the hunt. A scream erupted from Olivia's throat when, out of the corner of her eye, she saw him. He knew everything was occurring simultaneously in a matter of seconds, but he felt as if he was watching the scene unfold in slow motion. He'd expected each dilemma separately, but he'd never anticipated all hell breaking loose at the same time.

Olivia scrambled from the bed, pulling part of the covers with her as a shield. 'Where am I? Who are you?' She clearly recognized him from the camp, but not from Florida. 'What did you do to Brent?'

He sat up. 'Please, just—'

'Stay away from me!' She backed up until she ran into the drapes. Her voice was high and unfamiliar to him. 'Who *are* you?' she demanded.

The voices were getting louder, closer. He stood on the opposite side of the bed and put his hands out in a sort of surrender, to show he meant no harm. The action brought back a different memory of their first day at the beach, when she'd freaked out on him.

'Please, listen to me.'

'*Who are you!?*' She screamed it at him this time.

'My name is Anders. Anders Erickson.' He spoke the words in a measured tone, slowly, hoping to see a glimmer of recognition. Again, nothing.

Her eyes darted around the room; he knew she was looking for her skirt. He spotted it tangled in the bedclothes and
reached for it, then tossed it across the bed to her. She caught
it in mid-air but just held it with the covers, too frightened to
go further.

'I'm not going to hurt you. Please just let me . . .' He stopped
mid-sentence because her frightened gaze moved downward
from his face. She was looking at the crotch of his jeans, with
its zipper still partially open from the night before.

'Oh, no, no, no.' He yanked the zipper shut and fastened
the button. 'I didn't do anything to you, I swear. I would never
hurt you, Olivia *Louise*.'

'You know my middle name.' Her voice trembled.

'Yes, I know your middle name. I know you very well.'

This scared her and she began to sob. 'Please just let me
go.'

'I will, I promise. But please, first just listen—'

'Olivia!' A voice outside shouted her name; she jerked her
head in the direction of the window. Anders didn't recognize
the voice; he wondered if she did. Time was of the essence and
he began to move to her side of the bed. The voice came again,
calling from below. 'Are you there? Which room are you in?'

Her hands moved to the curtains and without further thought
or hesitation, Anders dove at her, tackling her onto the bed.
She cried out and fought against him, kicking her feet and
flailing her arms, using her nails to scratch him. He could take
her, she was no match for his strength, but he didn't want to
hurt her and he was more concerned with shutting her up.

When the phone rang, he knew it was Lenny.

'Damn it!' He grabbed the skirt, which in their struggle had
come to rest once more on the bed, and shoved a corner of it
into her mouth until her cries became muffled squeals. 'I'm
sorry, Olivia, I'm so sorry,' he said as he straddled her hips,

avoiding her stomach but letting his full weight pin her. He held her arms by the wrists above her head with one hand and with the other he stretched for the phone. Her legs continued to kick; they were useless to her for now but he didn't think he could maintain control for long with just one hand.

He didn't say anything before Lenny started talking at him. 'They're here.' *No shit*, Anders thought. 'I'll deal with them, you just find Leng and get out of here with her, you hear me?'

He was staring into Olivia's frightened eyes as he spoke. 'We can't leave you here alone, they'll kill you.' Her eyes grew even larger at his words, and she increased the pitch of her squeals, writhing more desperately beneath him.

Lenny must have heard her. 'You untied her, didn't you?' Anders almost laughed, he'd said it so matter-of-factly. 'Damn you, Andy!'

Their skin was sweaty and becoming slick; he felt her wrists slipping and he tightened his grip. Too hard, she let out a yelp of pain. 'The shit hit the fan at the same time,' he said, panting into the phone. 'I haven't been able to explain to her.' Their eyes were locked and he could tell she was listening intently to every word.

'Just get the hell out of there in any way you can and don't worry about me. I'll catch up with you somehow.'

One wrist began to slip free; he let the phone drop as soon as he heard the click of the phone being replaced on the receiver, and he grabbed the escaping arm. He knew it wasn't rational, but he was starting to get angry at her for resisting so much, for not trusting him. He heard Lenny's voice outside then, calling to the approaching cadre, tossing them a red herring. It signalled the start of the clock running for Anders. He pressed her arms hard into the bed, on either side of her head.

'Olivia! Listen to me!' He leaned down close, his lips touching the side of her face and his breath loud in her ear. 'I'm here because I love you. Your life is at stake, my life is at stake. The people outside want to hurt you. I know this is a lot to take in at once, but I need you to trust me. Do you understand?' She didn't nod, and her eyes still burned with terror, but she listened raptly, noiselessly. 'You don't recognize me because they've drugged you for a long time. But somewhere inside of you, you know me. If you stay with me, the drugs will wear off and you'll start to remember. You'll start to understand that what I'm saying is true.' He became overwhelmed by his own words, by the enormity of the situation, because even if he managed to convince her, he had no idea how he would get them out of there alive. In the distance he heard the voices, Lenny's and the others', receding in what Anders hoped was the direction of Lenny's room. He had very little time.

'Will you please trust me? Please come with me?' He was crying a little bit, and the tears fell onto her cheek and dripped down into her ear. 'I've been looking for you. There was a motorcycle accident, they told me you'd died, but . . .' He remembered the tattoo. 'I can show you, in the bathroom, in the mirror.'

Her eyes flickered with a flash of confusion. He reached for the skirt in her mouth and waited for some evidence of agreement not to scream if he removed it. He felt the slightest release in her muscles, a nod of acquiescence with her eyelids.

To his surprise, she didn't even speak when he pulled the fabric out. Even as he climbed off her, and she accepted his hand to help her up, she remained silent. But she kept her eyes trained on him the entire time, throughout their tentative walk from the bed to the bathroom. She hadn't stopped fearing him; she'd merely decided her best chance at self-preservation was to stop fighting and do as he asked.

In the bathroom he switched on the light and stood behind her. They continued to stare at each other in the mirror.

'Here.' He gently touched her shoulders to turn her and she

flinched. 'It's okay,' he assured her, and then resumed, reaching to lift the hair from her neck, working his fingers to uncover the tattoo. It was so hard to be so close to her, sharing the small space and touching her like this, yet knowing she didn't feel the same sense of intimacy that threatened to crush him.

He opened the smaller medicine cabinet mirror so it reflected off the larger sink mirror. 'There. Can you read it?' He turned her a bit more so she stood at the right angle.

She finally looked away from him and into the mirror. She made a noise, a short intake of breath upon seeing a word inked into her skin. She reached up and felt her neck.

'Can you read it?' he asked again, hoping that the backwards sight of his name on her body would bring back the memory of getting the tattoo, and thus convince her.

She nodded; her fingers trembled at her neck. 'It says Anders,' she whispered.

'Olivia?' She lifted her eyes to him. '*You* had that tattoo put there. You never told me; I didn't even know about it until you were in the hospital, after the accident. A nurse discovered it and showed me. And this injury –' As he spoke, he gently touched the spot on her skull where her hair was growing back. 'This is from the accident.'

Her eyes went back to the mirror. He could see her mind working, trying to make sense of it all, trying to decide what to believe, what was a lie. For all she knew, the tattoo would wash off with her next shower.

'Wait.' He also remembered the item he'd carried with him since the accident. He dug in his pocket and pulled out the necklace. She gasped and covered her mouth with one hand upon seeing it. 'You lost this when you were thrown from my bike . . . I found it on the ground.' He hesitated. Her face was blank; she recognized her jewellery, but otherwise she had no idea what he was talking about.

He opened the clasp and held it up, as if to say *May I?* She gave the slightest nod and he took a step closer and reached around her neck. Their cheeks were inches apart; her nervous breathing filled his ear. He thought of how, when he'd believed her to be dead, he'd seen her standing with the necklace before the dresser at the beach, and wondered now if he'd had a premonition.

'Time is short. I don't know if you even know where you are. We're still in Kenya.' She nodded; that much she understood. 'We're in a hotel on the outskirts of Nairobi. If we don't get out of here fast, out of the country, we're doomed. I don't know the battleground like they do.'

The tiny space filled with silence. He waited, feeling every second pass and their chances for escape diminishing.

'But this is my home,' she whispered. 'I don't want to leave it.'

His heart sank. *No, home is in Florida*, he wanted to say. He told himself it was the drugs talking. She wasn't really fighting him anymore, only questioning why this was happening to her. She'd loaded so many questions into the two simple statements, but the answers weren't simple, and if he took the time to explain more, they would risk their chance to get away.

'There are things they didn't want you to know, to remember. They took you away from me, and when I came looking for you, I learned about these things. I've also been told that Brent might kill you.'

She started crying then, tears dripping slowly down her cheek. He knew it was all too much for her to take in at once. How could she possibly decide to place her life in the hands of an unknown man without more information?

'Please, there's so much to explain, and I will eventually, I promise you. But I need you to trust me for now.' She needed to know she had a choice, though he questioned what he might do if she made the wrong one. 'What does your gut say? You once told me that you always listen to your gut. Does your gut tell you that you can trust me?'

Her gaze turned once more to the tattoo. 'And *you* are this Anders?' she asked, a lilt of hope at the end of the question.

'Yes, yes.' With that encouragement he went for the wallet in his back pocket, but he moved too abruptly and his motion startled her; she backed away from him and pressed herself against the sink. 'Here.' He handed his driver's licence to her, an offering.

She looked at it, but shook her head. 'I want your passport.'

And just like that she'd made a demand that required *him* to trust her. His mouth opened, but no words came.

'I want your passport,' she said.

'Okay,' he said. 'Sure.' He stepped slowly out of the bathroom, keeping an eye on her as he went to his bag and pulled out the passport. She followed him out, and he handed it to her, keenly aware that he'd now placed his life in her hands. Maybe that meant they were even. Maybe that's what she had intended.

She opened it, staring first at his picture in the front, and then leafing through the mostly empty pages. Her hands shook; despite her assertion of control, she was still terrified.

'It's brand new.' The world traveller pointing out his lack of experience, his inadequacies.

He raised one eyebrow at her. 'I never had a need for one until now.'


HE OPENED the door and was temporarily blinded by the bright, harsh sun. He placed one arm across the door opening, blocking her exit in case his own gut was wrong and she planned to make a run for it. A glance down the walkway toward the door to Lenny's room told him they were still here. Two Africans stood in the open doorway; Anders could make out the butts of rifles hung from straps on their shoulders. He edged back into the room in case they happened to look over.

'I told you,' came Lenny's voice from inside the room, 'he's halfway to the airport with her by now.' He'd spoken loudly, intending for Anders to hear every word.

'Then *you* will come with us.' The command issued by one of the men in the doorway sent a chill down Anders's spine. If Lenny was forced to accompany them as insurance, he'd end up dead when they discovered he'd lied. Anders was certain of that. He heard the shuffling of boots and guns, and he leaned out again just in time to see the men enter the room and slam the door behind them.

What followed, the sound of large men struggling and yelling, didn't sound good. Lenny wasn't going willingly.

He glanced back at Olivia and wondered how in the hell he and Lenny had ended up in this situation. She met his eye; she'd been listening, too. But her look revealed nothing to him.

For a moment he felt like the stranger he'd become.


HE GRABBED their bags and took her hand, and they edged out of the door against the wall towards the opposite end of the building. As they made their way down the stairs to Leng's room at the back, he made a silent thanks to God that the guide had insisted upon staying with them until they were safely on a plane to the States.

'They've found us,' he announced when a sleepy Leng opened the door. 'And they've got Lenny.'


IN THE Land Rover, Leng explained his plan. Olivia sat in the second row with Anders but maintained her distance.

'You will fly from Dar es Salaam instead of Nairobi. We will drive all day, and tonight you will stay at the home of a friend of Makena. You will fly on the first plane in the morning.'

Anders was about to say, 'I'm not leaving without Lenny,' when Olivia interrupted him.

'Makena?' She leaned forward and directed her intense stare at Leng. 'Did you say Makena?'

Leng turned and smiled his large smile, nodding. 'Yes, Makena has many friends.'

She suddenly looked at Anders and began to finger the necklace at her throat. He knew at that instant she was finally starting to believe.

# 21

ANDERS RELAXED only slightly when they crossed the border into Tanzania. Though it felt like another obstacle to their escape had been scaled successfully, he couldn't quell his fears about Lenny. Leng assured Anders that he'd put out a call for help to find him, and by the amount of time he spent on his phone speaking in Swahili, Anders had to believe him.

They finally arrived at the home of Makena's friend Halima just before dinner. They were greeted warmly by the family: Halima, her husband, Andwele, and their two children. All of them, including Leng, sat down together to a large feast with breads, rice, various vegetable dishes, and curries, and he wondered if it was typical or had been prepared for their benefit. Olivia chatted affably with their hosts throughout the meal, making the children laugh with stories in a language he didn't understand.

After dinner, Halima showed them to their sleeping quarters. The bedroom belonged to the two children, who'd been displaced to the floor of their parents' room to make space for the guests. The room was small and spartan, with a double bed, a dresser, and a frayed armchair and small footstool in the corner. Staring at the one bed, he realized Makena hadn't advised their hosts of Olivia's memory loss. It didn't matter. Sleeping in the armchair might not be as comfortable as the night before, but they'd be much safer here than back in Nairobi. He wondered again where Leng would sleep, and if Lenny would have the chance to sleep at all.

From his spot on the bed he'd created with the chair and

footstool, he watched her when she returned from the hallway bath. The scent of soap and the warmth of steam floated into the room behind her as she closed the door, her hair twisted high in a towel. She was wearing one of his T-shirts and the sarong he'd bought for her from an outdoor market where they'd stopped briefly for lunch that afternoon. The way she'd tied it around her waist accentuated the slight swell of her stomach, but she was oblivious to it.

She leaned forward to towel-dry her curls, and then stood in front of the dresser and combed them out carefully with his comb. Everything about the scene felt so familiar to him, so reminiscent of their life at the beach, yet he no longer knew the woman in front of him. When their eyes met he quickly looked away, ashamed for staring at her, though a part of him felt she was purposely teasing him, paying him back for the hell she thought he might have played a part in causing.

'Why do you look at me like that?' she asked.

'I'm sorry ...' He hesitated. 'It's just that today ... and tonight, at dinner ...'

She sat on the edge of the bed and waited.

'I ...' He sighed. They really hadn't spoken much since leaving Nairobi. He'd tried to explain more to her about what had happened in Florida, and he'd even broached the attack at Jimmy's. She'd listened and asked a few questions, but her reaction had seemed remote and clinical. Even doubting. He believed Leng's earlier mention of Makena was the real reason for her cooperation. He'd hoped as the day lengthened they'd grow closer, despite the drugs, but that had never happened. Instead, he'd spent the afternoon and evening with an unknown Olivia, one who chatted in Swahili with the vendors at the market and discussed the status of Zimbabwe politics at dinner with their Tanzanian hosts. 'I'm just seeing an Olivia I never knew,' he said.

'You told me we were lovers.'

'Yes.' He looked at the floor for a moment, not entirely comfortable to be talking of such subjects with this unknown woman. 'On the day of the accident, I had planned to ask you to marry me.' He met her eye then, curious as to how she'd take this news.

She studied him sadly, as if she felt pity for him but could do nothing to help. It wasn't the response he'd hoped for.

'Yet you feel you don't know me?' She seemed genuinely confused.

He opened his mouth to speak, but in his frustration let out only a small grunt.

'Why didn't you?' she asked.

'We were in the middle of the woods, at a swimming hole, and there was a noise in the trees. It spooked you.' He gave her a small smile. 'After that, the mood was broken.'

'That doesn't sound like me.'

He stared at her. She was right. The Olivia he'd come to know in Africa was fearless. If the stories of her past were believed, she was a woman who revelled in the sight of lions, the closer, the better. A woman who walked into a tribal village and made strangers her friends. By all indications, there should have been nothing in the Florida forest to scare her. Nothing except a black Mercedes.

'No, you're right. It doesn't.'

They sat in the silence of the small room, listening to the sounds outside the door of their hosts gathering the children for bed. They heard footsteps in the hall, and then the creak of the bedroom door next to theirs as it closed.

After a moment, she said, 'I'm sorry if you feel there was a part of me I didn't let you see. I don't have an explanation for you, at least not right now. Maybe, eventually, I will.'

He swallowed his sadness. He closed his eyes and tried to find a comfortable sleeping position in the chair as he listened to her pull the covers back from the bed and turn out the light. And then her silence in the dark except for an end of the day sigh.

He didn't know how much time had passed when she called to him; he only knew he hadn't fallen asleep.

'Are you still awake?'

He opened his eyes, but he couldn't see anything. 'Yes.'

'I just wanted to tell you . . . I'm sorry about your friend.'

'He'll do okay. He can hold his own.' He knew neither of them believed that.

'Come sleep in the bed.'

He didn't move.

'It's all right. Really.'

'Are you starting to remember?' he ventured, hopeful.

'No. I don't think so.' She paused. 'But you're probably not too comfortable in that chair, and my gut tells me I'm starting to like you.'

He smiled slightly. He rose from the chair and fumbled in the dark until he reached the bed. He lay on top of the covers, still fully dressed, a good two feet from her. 'Thank you,' was all he said, and closed his eyes, willing sleep to come so he wasn't so aware of her at his side.

'It's okay to get under the covers. I trust you.'

The last three words almost caused him to weep and without a word he worked his way under. He fell asleep thinking of the sound of the surf and the smell of salt in the air, how the moon reflected on the ocean on their late night walks, the caress of the breeze on their faces. He felt a fragile sense of security he hadn't felt in a long, long time.


SOMETIME IN the middle of the night he woke with a jolt to the sound of her muted screaming. Convinced they'd been discovered, he shot up half asleep and already swinging, ready to fight to the death to keep Brent or his henchmen from taking her again. He quickly realized he was battling air.

And then he knew what was happening. All those nights at the beach and only now did he understand.

'Olivia!' he whispered, shaking her gently. She continued to make the strange noise. Not quite a scream, but more like a scream trying to escape.

He flipped on a light and saw her sweaty figure tangled in the sheets, her contorted face as her arms struggled to push something away.

'Olivia!' he said again. Without stopping to think, he did what worked at home when he'd thought she was merely having a bad dream. He reached for her, cupped her face in his hands to hold her head still so he would be the first thing she'd see when she finally opened her eyes. And then, one last time: 'Olivia!'

When her eyes opened, he watched the fear ease, and then, transform into something else.

'It's you,' she said.

He suppressed a gasp. Had he detected a shadow of recognition in her tired eyes, in the intimate way she breathed the words? He waited, willing the creeping relief inside him to be still.

But then she tensed in his grip, and he knew whatever glimpse of memory she'd just experienced had slipped away, sucked into the wake of her departing nightmare.


AT LENG'S request, their hostess woke them before dawn to head out for the airport in Dar es Salaam, and Anders didn't have time to consider whether the night before made things more awkward between them or less so. Neither mentioned the nightmare, and he wondered if she even remembered.

They arrived so early that the doors to the large room housing the ticket counters were still locked. They loitered in the open area outside, gazing at magazines and cheap souvenirs through the dirty glass cases of decrepit kiosks. Like the airport lobby, the kiosks, too, were locked, so they couldn't even buy a magazine or newspaper to pass the time. Leng left the two of them alone and carried on idle conversation at the kerb with taxi drivers waiting for the first flight of the day to arrive.

When the armed guards finally opened the doors, shouting out directions in Swahili to the small but growing crowd, they followed the lead of others and filed in. The room was cavernous, but dark. There were lights above their heads but for some reason no one turned them on.

Anders approached the ticket counter for Emirates Air and endured the suspicious eyes of the single ticket agent when he paid for their tickets in cash. She was a young Middle Eastern woman wearing a modern suit but also a scarf wrapped elegantly over her head and much of her face. Even Olivia gave him a curious look when he pulled out the wad of foreign currency.

They were forced to wait again before being allowed to approach security. Leng insisted on staying with them. Though he wouldn't be allowed past security, he claimed he would remain at the airport until he saw their plane's wheels leave the ground. When Leng's phone rang, he stepped aside to answer but raised one finger to indicate he wasn't going anywhere.

Anders's unease about leaving Lenny grew as the line snaked slowly toward the X-ray machine. Leng had assured him he would find Lenny and ensure his safety, that he and Olivia needed to leave while they could, but Anders wasn't convinced. As soon as he had her safely on the ground and ensconced in a hotel in New York, he would turn back around for his friend.

His hand trembled when he handed his and Olivia's passports to the security guard. The man stared him in the eye for a long moment; Olivia received the same treatment and more, as his eyes took in the full length of her. Anders swallowed and held his tongue, praying the man would just let them pass. He was certain safety lay just on the other side of the scanner.

'Step aside, both of you,' the guard ordered.

At first Anders turned around and looked at the line behind him, thinking the guard had to be speaking to someone else.

'Step aside,' he said again.

He took Olivia's hand and did as the man asked.

'Is there a problem?' He tried not to sound smart.

'Tell me, sir, what was the purpose of your trip?'

'We're going home.' He recognized he hadn't answered the question, but he hoped his feigned confusion would appease the man.

The guard wasn't having any. His already stern face hardened. 'I asked, what was the purpose of your trip? To Africa.'

Anders glanced at Olivia and hoped she would go along with things. 'We were on safari.'

An interminable length of time passed as they watched the man leaf slowly through their passports. Though they'd eaten well that morning, he felt weak.

'Mr Erickson, is it?'

He nodded.

'Your passport was issued only days before you departed the United States.' Anders's heart began to pound like a bass drum in his chest. He hadn't thought this through, not in the least. 'Your lovely companion here,' he eyed Olivia again, 'was in Kenya for quite some time before your arrival. And *her* passport is well worn, I notice.'

Anders blinked and didn't respond. His mind charged through various explanations he could offer, but none seemed plausible. Plus, why did it matter to this man? Yet he knew there didn't have to be a reason for the harassment; maybe this was how the guy got his jollies. He only knew he didn't want to give him an excuse to extend the interrogation. So he kept silent.

Suddenly Olivia spoke but he couldn't understand her because she'd switched to Swahili again. Whatever she'd said, it didn't have the intended effect.

'Are you trying to patronize me?' The man bellowed at her in his heavily accented English, and she stepped back in fear.

'No, sir,' she returned to the language Anders could understand, 'I was only trying to explain that he met up with me later.'

With his thick arm, he grabbed her at the elbow and both she and Anders flinched. 'You think I'm stupid? You think you can speak a different language to me and that I will forget to do my job?'

'No, sir, I didn't mean any disrespect.'

The guard readjusted the rifle on his shoulder and motioned with his head away from security, in the direction from which they had come. Anders felt like his breakfast was quickly making its way back up in the wrong direction. The two of them waited for what they knew was coming.

'You will come with me now.'

He scanned the area for Leng as the man led them to a long hall on the other side of the terminal. Where the hell had he gone? The hall was dark and barren, and their three sets of feet echoed on the dingy tile floor as they made their way to a door at the end. He felt like a condemned man being led to his execution. He believed it wasn't unrealistic to think this might well be the case. And he knew the extinguishment of his life in some remote part of the world wouldn't merit more than a tiny, one paragraph blurb in the back of US newspapers.

Anders and Olivia exchanged a look as they waited for the

man to unlock the door. His tried to apologize; hers screamed *do something.*

'She's pregnant,' Anders blurted. 'She needs to eat soon or she'll be sick to her stomach.' Olivia didn't react except to glance at the guard, to gauge *his* reaction. There wasn't one.

'Come on,' the guard bellowed and pushed them into the room. It was nothing but a storage facility filled with boxes, some small canister tanks of some sort, and what appeared to be aeroplane parts. When they were instructed to sit, they made their way to a few dusty boxes in the corner and lowered themselves onto them.

The guard slammed the door without another word and they heard him lock it from the other side. Anders wondered if they were waiting for something or someone, or whether they would just die there from eventual starvation.

'Somehow, I thought if I perished in Africa it would be at the hands of a wild animal.' He was trying to make her smile, but she didn't even look at him or acknowledge she'd heard.

The silence between them returned.


ANDERS WASN'T sure what he expected when he heard keys jangling on the other side of the door many hours later. Whether he thought death was imminent, or rather just felt relief that something, anything, was about to happen, he couldn't say. He was thirsty – the room was hot and had no circulation – so maybe he was hoping they were bringing their prisoners water. He knew he'd drink it, even straight from the tap. Maybe he would demand a phone call to the American embassy; he hoped he was brave enough to make such demands. He only knew that the two people who walked through the door when it opened were the last two people he expected to see just then.

'Daddy!' said Olivia, and she bolted from her spot next to

him and flung herself into Lawrence Mayfield's arms. Makena stood next to him. If Anders hadn't been sitting, he would have collapsed from the shock. Even the blow of seeing Makena there and knowing she'd betrayed him didn't approach the paralysis he felt from hearing Olivia use 'Daddy' as a term of affection.

Anders stood as Mayfield finally met his eye. With a slight nod of the head, Mayfield said, 'Mr Erickson.'

Anders glared at the man across the room. 'No *Andy*?' he wanted to say, but he didn't. At his stony silence, Olivia seemed to remember why Anders had come to Africa and she stepped slightly away from her father in what Anders thought was a lame show of support. He reminded himself that she really didn't know him, that her response wasn't that odd, but logic couldn't trump his fear that she was about to walk willingly into a trap.

Makena took the lead. 'Anders, please don't be angry with me. I—'

'Why would I be angry with you, Makena?' he said, suddenly lashing out, his voice loud. 'Because I trusted you, and you obviously relayed everything I told you to this bastard?' He thought of Brent's words then, how he'd claimed Mayfield had manipulated Anders all along. Maybe Brent *was* a crazy son of a bitch, like Matt had said, but so far he seemed the most honest of all of them. 'Where's Leng? He seems to have disappeared. Did you use him, too, or was he also in on this?'

Makena's face displayed pain but Anders refused to see it. 'I didn't—'

Mayfield touched her arm to interrupt her. 'Leng is waiting outside for us, Mr Erickson.' His statement was made with so much assurance, so much finality, as if to suggest that the man possessed knowledge of things Anders couldn't even hope to understand. 'Now, why don't you calm down, take a seat again, and let me explain why you were detained?'

Anders felt Olivia's gaze, all her doubts about everything he'd told her resurfacing.

'No.' Anders looked at Olivia as he spoke, even though his words were meant for her father. 'Not until you tell her the truth. Tell her the truth about Florida.'

Mayfield just stared at him as if trying to decipher what, exactly, Anders wanted him to tell his daughter.

'Tell her who I am and what you did.'

All of a sudden his face took on the cold, condescending expression Anders was familiar with. 'What I *did*, Andy?'

'Tell her who I am, dammit!'

Olivia's eyes moved slowly from Anders to her father. But Mayfield didn't acknowledge her look; he continued to focus his stare on Anders.

'Okay. You are the man she lived with in Florida.'

'That's it? That's all you can tell her about me?'

Mayfield glared. 'You are the man who was driving the motorcycle she was thrown from. You are the man who let her ride without a helmet on her head.'

Anders grunted, shaking his head, and looked at Makena with pleading eyes.

'Larry.'

When Mayfield heard Makena's quiet, but commanding, voice, he glanced at her and she shook her head in reproach. The transformation was subtle, but his next words were evidence of her powerful influence over the man. Makena clutched Olivia's arm as if she knew what he was about to say.

'You are the man she claimed to love.'

Anders swallowed at finally hearing the admission from him, even if he did qualify it. He searched Olivia's face for a reaction; she simply gave him the same sad look she'd given him the night before. But at least now she knew he'd spoken the truth. He turned back to her father. 'And *you* are the man

300

who took her away and gave her drugs so she wouldn't remember me, aren't you?'

He nodded, ever so slightly, even as he attempted protest. 'It wasn't the only reas—'

'And you told me she'd died, and that I killed her, didn't you? And you threatened the nurse at the hospital, and others there, too, didn't you, to keep me from learning the truth? You even paid off some cops to scare me, and throw me off your trail. And the more I think about it, you probably paid off someone at the hospital, too, to keep me out of her records.' He paused, and because he still couldn't believe it, his voice rose an octave when he spoke the next words. 'All so you could get her back with Brent Campbell.'

Mayfield only stared at him, but as far as Anders was concerned, his failure to deny the allegations served as his confession to everything. Olivia must have agreed, because she now looked at her father as if seeing him for the first time and not liking what she saw. Her eyes began to swell with tears.

'But you almost killed her in the process, didn't you, when you had us run off the road in—'

'No!' Mayfield cut him off. 'No, I had nothing to do with your accident. His thugs are responsible for that mistake. I should never have trusted him to bring her home. I took advantage of it' – he appeared pleased with himself as he admitted this – 'but I didn't cause it.'

The two men stared at each other as Anders weighed whether to believe him.

Makena's low voice fractured the silent stand-off. 'Please, Anders, let him explain. That's why we are here, why we stopped you from getting on that plane.'

Anders leaned against the wall and crossed his arms. Waited.

'You're right in one respect. I was trying to get her back with Brent. I had my reasons for doing so, but—'

'Maybe you should tell me what they were.' Olivia's voice startled everyone, especially her father. He looked surprised that she was demanding information from him. 'I mean, if everything he told me about Brent is true,' she motioned at Anders, 'then I really need to hear those reasons from you. And they'd better be good ones.'

Mayfield stared at his daughter for a moment, but to Anders's surprise, he turned in his direction as he began to speak, as if Anders was the person he needed to convince.

'I didn't know Brent was behind what happened at Jimmy's. I was only trying to honour her mother's wishes.'

Olivia scoffed at that. Anders could tell she didn't like his excuse, and she also didn't like that he spoke about her as if she wasn't in the room. 'I'm right *here*.' She waited until her father looked at her. 'What does that mean? Her *wishes*? Somehow I don't think Mom would have intended for you to force us together at all costs.'

Mayfield turned to her and for just a moment his entire body seemed to deflate like a dying balloon. 'I never thought he'd hurt you, baby.'

For the first time, Anders thought the man might be speaking honestly.

As if she'd read Anders's thoughts and wanted to capitalize on them, Makena spoke up. 'I told Olivia's father everything you told me, Anders, because if what you said about Brent was true, I knew he'd help you.'

'Help me?'

'Mr Erickson, I have more resources at my disposal, in case you haven't noticed.' Mayfield stood straighter and shook his head condescendingly, letting Anders know that despite his daughter's feelings for him, and despite the fact that he'd risked his life to save her, he still hadn't earned her father's respect. 'What were you thinking? You'd whisk her back to the States, and he'd just forget about her? He's a man obsessed with getting what he wants.'

Anders wondered if Mayfield realized he could have been speaking about himself. But he also knew the man was right. Anders hadn't thought that far ahead; he'd only been concerned with getting Olivia out of Africa safely. He hadn't thought about how he'd avoid a repeat of Florida, assuming Brent had something to do with the accident, as Mayfield had suggested.

'I want him brought to justice for what he did to her,' Mayfield said.

It sounded too easy to Anders. He was still sceptical, despite Mayfield's suggestion that they now shared the same goals. Hadn't Brent suggested the same thing? His sense that he was a pawn in some unknowable battle between the two men grew larger.

Yet even if Anders accepted everything her father said as true, why did he stop them from getting on the plane? Why not, at least, let Anders put more distance between Olivia and Brent?

'Is it true about the drugs?' Olivia's small question interrupted Anders's thoughts.

A shadow of guilt dropped over Mayfield's face like a veil, and Anders believed that somewhere, deep down, perhaps the man felt love for her. But it wasn't enough.

'Daddy?' she persisted.

'I was trying to spare you the pain of what those boys did to you.'

'But you let them get away with it!' she yelled. Anders wondered how much angrier she'd be when her memory of that night returned. For now, her anger was limited to being lied to about everything. She possessed, second hand, the knowledge of what had happened, but she didn't yet *feel* it.

'I told you, I didn't know he was involved, baby. I—'

'*So what*?' Her question echoed Anders's thoughts exactly. She rubbed at the corners of her eyes, trying not to cry. 'What did that matter? The others weren't worth your efforts?'

Mayfield's face went steely; his lips tightened into a straight line. The man from the hospital waiting room had returned. When he spoke, his voice had lost its apologetic tone. 'There are things I can't explain to you just now.'

Olivia grunted, a look of sheer disbelief on her face. She turned to Makena. 'You knew about ... Jimmy's?'

'No, honey, I didn't know near as much as I thought I did until Anders came to me.'

Olivia looked at Anders then, and for a moment it felt like they were alone again in the room, except now she didn't despise him. She believed in him. Now if only she would love him again, too.

'Mr Erickson, if you want to see your friend again, I suggest we get moving.'

'You know where Lenny is?'

'I know that you left him behind when you escaped with Olivia from your hotel in Nairobi.'

Mayfield's words stabbed at him. Just as he'd blamed Anders for causing the accident in Florida, he'd just accused him of abandoning Lenny. But this time, Anders resisted the mind game.

'And you can help me find him?'

'When I find Brent, I suspect I'll find your friend, too. If he's still alive.'

Anders's jaw tensed and he clenched his fists. He hadn't allowed himself to think that Lenny might be beyond rescue. 'When *we* find Brent,' he clarified.

'No. I will do this without you. I don't need you in my way. I have quite a network in East Africa, and I don't want your amateur heroics to undermine that. You will stay with Leng.'

Anders laughed, but not with amusement. 'You've got to be kidding. I almost had her on a plane. But for your interference, we'd be safely in the air by now. I still haven't heard a good explanation for why you didn't let us go. You don't need us on African soil to find him.'

Mayfield shrugged. 'Perhaps not you. But I do need Olivia.'

'Why?'

Now it was Mayfield who laughed, throwing his head back slightly in mock pleasure at Anders's naivety. 'She will be the lure, of course.'

Anders was incredulous. If not evil, the man was insane. 'I see.' His voice started low and quiet, but escalated as he talked. 'And you expect me to just let you walk out of here with her? After everything, I'm supposed to *trust* you?' He came close to Mayfield and got in his face. 'Well, *fuck* that.'

Mayfield didn't flinch. His eyelids dropped halfway and he regarded Anders with hardened eyes. 'You don't really have a choice. You can't stop me. You have no one.'

He wanted to know what Olivia thought of her father's plan. He wanted so badly to glance at her, to communicate with her on some other level, but he knew if he looked away just then he'd be admitting to the weakness of which Mayfield was so certain.

'Okay. I'll stay out of your way.' He looked hard at Mayfield, to let him know a contingency came with his agreement. 'But only if Olivia stays with me.'

'Now *you* are kidding, sir. I'm not going to let my daughter out of my sight, now that I'm here and can ensure her safety. I came over seven thousand miles to save her.'

'So did I, *Larry*. And I didn't rob her of her memory to do it.' He waited for him, and hopefully Olivia, to register the difference. 'If you want my cooperation, she stays with me. If she's your lure, then it doesn't matter where she is.' Only then did he turn to Olivia, because he knew she held all the power in the room just then. 'That is, if she's willing to stay with me.'

Mayfield glanced at his daughter. She looked at the ground, unable to meet her father's eye. She then met Makena's gaze briefly – for courage, Anders thought – and lastly, she looked at him. He took her hand and pulled her aside for privacy.

'Remember what we talked about in the hotel the other night?' he asked, whispering at her ear. So close, he could smell the soapy scent from last night released in her sweat and he had to fight against the easy intoxication of it. 'What does your gut say?' He squeezed her hand and saw her swallow. They were both so thirsty.

'Olivia,' he said insistently, 'what's your gut say?'

# 22

THEY MET up with Leng outside the airport and once again climbed into the Land Rover. After they left the city, they travelled through small towns on their way back to the bush. Anders stared at the crowds, at the many vendors and stalls lining each town's single street, the young boys in the fields guarding cattle, the women with children at their feet and baskets on their heads, and he knew that Mayfield was right. He'd never find Lenny without an army, and his small army – Leng and Makena – had suddenly defected to the other side. Except when Leng explained he would be taking them to a distant manyatta in the bush, Anders exchanged few words with the guide. He still smarted from the apparent betrayal, and he wouldn't be ready to consider whether they might have done right by him until he was safely back on US soil with both Lenny and Olivia at his side.

As they drove over primitive roads, leaving the small towns behind, Anders held Olivia close and this time she wrapped one arm around his waist. Her sudden attachment to him was his only comfort. Though he tried to hide it from her, his guilt over Lenny was quickly overwhelming him. Any relief he'd felt that first night away from the camp, when they'd finally rescued her from Brent, had been replaced with a despair so deep that he found himself questioning if he hadn't unwittingly struck a Faustian bargain to get her back. As the sun descended behind the trees, and the sky grew darker and larger above them, he closed his eyes and leaned his head against the roll bar. He begged silently for sleep to come and quiet his thoughts.

ANDERS WOKE several hours later to the sound of Leng's voice whispering quietly to a man standing outside the driver's side door. Like so many of the conversations he overheard, he couldn't understand the words being spoken. He tried to gently reposition a sleeping Olivia as he edged up from a semi-reclining position and pulled his numb right arm from where she'd trapped it against the hard armrest.

Leng noticed that he'd woken.

'Anders, please, I introduce you to Solomon, the manyatta chief. He will provide a bed and food and will assure your safety until you can leave.' Leng briefly shone his flashlight in the direction of the entrance to the village, and Anders caught a glimpse of the small mud huts that Olivia had described to the French girl at the camp.

*Until you can leave.* It sounded as if they were being held captive. He couldn't help but wonder if indeed they were.

'I hope to find a nearby camp for you,' Leng added as if reading his thoughts, 'but for tonight, the chief welcomes you.'

The chief nodded to Anders. He returned the gesture and said, 'Thank you, sir. It's a pleasure to meet you.'

He responded in a foreign tongue and Anders looked to Leng for translation.

'The chief speaks very little English, but he expresses his joy at having you as his guest, since you are a friend of Makena.' Leng motioned to Olivia, who had just begun to wake from her slumber. 'Please, if you both come, he will show you where you can sleep for a few more hours.'

\*

THE OPENING that led inside the hut forced them to bend at the waist to enter. Once in, he still had to hunch his shoulders to avoid hitting his head on the ceiling. The interior consisted of one small rectangular room – he estimated it to be no larger than eight by ten feet – and two smaller sleeping alcoves on either side. The sleeping surface was stretched canvas tied to wooden posts made from the large branches of some tree. A small fire pit was smouldering with a dying fire in the middle of the room, but there didn't seem to be anywhere for the smoke to escape. The embers provided the little light existing in the room. A few tin pans and plastic cups were stacked on a wooden rack on the opposite wall between the two alcoves.

The chief spoke and then Leng said, 'He would like to introduce you to one of his wives, Loiyan.' Only then did Anders notice a woman huddled in one of the dark alcoves. She looked at them without any expression of emotion. 'And he invites you to sleep for a few more hours.' The chief smiled and motioned to the other empty canvas.

Olivia began speaking to the woman in Swahili. She was now smiling warmly at Olivia and offering her hand. Anders managed a weak smile as he watched the exchange.

After Leng and the chief left the two of them alone with the chief's wife, he lifted Olivia's backpack from her shoulder and placed it on the dirt floor under the canvas, as far away from the fire as possible, and then did the same with his own bag.

They worked their way onto the small canvas. To fit, he spooned her, both sets of their legs curled up into the foetal position, and he thought it was a good sign when she didn't object.

'I feel like we're in a coffin,' he mumbled.

Within moments the chief's wife began to breathe heavily and then snore, and Olivia giggled quietly. Something about the sound of it reminded him of the old Olivia, the one who knew him, and his mood lifted, however slightly.

'What did you say to her?' he asked, whispering in her ear.

'I asked about her family, whether she had any children. I was afraid we were taking the kids' bed.'

'And?'

'She's one of four wives. She has two children with the chief. They're with him in a different hut, with another one of his wives.'

'Hmm.' He grinned a little, though he faced the back of her head and there was no way she could see. Still, she elbowed his stomach and he grunted. She *had* to be on her way back now; he was sure of it. It was as though a cloak had been lifted, as if her real personality, the one he remembered, had returned. But he hesitated asking her. Instead, he merely responded to her playful jab with an innocent, '*What?*'

'It's perfectly common here. Completely acceptable for a chief.'

'I didn't say anything.'

Suddenly she turned to face him and, to his surprise, she intertwined her legs with his. Their noses almost met. He reached up and touched her face and felt tears.

'Are you scared?'

'No.' She shuddered; he didn't just feel her tears then, he could hear them.

'What is it? What's the matter?'

'Nothing's the matter.' She scooted even closer, gripped him tightly.

'Olivia . . .'

'Shh, shh. I remember,' she said, grabbing at the back of his head. A short cry of relief caught at the base of his throat just as she covered his mouth with her own and began to kiss him. He pulled away just long enough to see her face, to know if she spoke the truth. Through her tears she gasped, 'I remember you,' and in that instant, he knew she did.

AFTERWARDS, THEY lay in the dim light of the dying embers. She finally asked him if he'd like to see the sunrise, and when he expressed reservations about going out alone and unarmed with the wildlife, she grinned a little and said, 'We need to get you used to the bush.'

Relieved to escape the smoky confines of the hut, he followed her outside, still amazed by how the same woman who had been so freaked out by a simple noise in the woods of Florida was now fearlessly trekking on foot across an open field in Africa, just before dawn, no less. He imagined being stalked by desperate lions whose night-time hunt had reaped no results and would willingly accept either of them in exchange for a full stomach before bedding down for the day.

Once she'd located an acceptable spot at the top of a small hill under a lone acacia tree, they sat and leaned close to wait for the show. He wrapped his arms around her and gave her an appreciative squeeze. The relief of having her back, all of her, made it easier to believe Lenny was alive and that soon they'd all return to Florida to resume life where they'd left it.

'If you close your eyes,' he said, following his own instructions, 'it's not too hard to imagine that we're sitting on the dune behind our house.' He laughed gently and added, 'Just pretend the calls of the monkeys are the cries of seagulls.'

'Open your eyes, Anders.' He did as she asked. 'Look at that.' They stared at the gold shafts of light that seemed to explode from the earth as the day made its arrival on the horizon. 'Why would you want to pretend we're anywhere else?'

*

HE ASKED her to tell him about her childhood.

'What do you want to know?' she asked, her tone resigned.

He gave her a look. And so she began to tell him her version of the past he'd first learned about from Matt and Makena, a somewhat different version from what she'd shared with the guests at the camp. Despite her initial reluctance, once she began to talk, the words gushed like a dam breaking.

She told him how she and Brent Campbell had been thrown together at a young age because of the business relationship between their fathers. How her family spent months at a time in Africa; how his spent summers with the Mayfields on Nantucket. How, as a result, he'd been her best friend growing up; at times, even, he was her only friend. As they entered their teens, they spent long days in the bush chasing after wildlife on the savannah, or on the beach scouring for shells and sea glass. By the age of fifteen they were lovers.

His stomach wrenched when she made this admission.

'At first it was just innocent, experimental type stuff, you know? We were just two curious, hormonal kids with a lot of time on our hands and parents who looked the other way because they had more important things to do. I think they thought we'd be married eventually, anyway, so in some strange kind of logic, they figured it didn't make any difference.' She paused, thinking. 'But it did. Things got weird. *He* got weird.' She looked Anders in the eye. 'This is going to sound odd, but it was as if he thought they'd *given* me to him, in the same way they'd given him cars and trips and everything else he wanted. He began to have a sense of entitlement to me.'

'It doesn't sound odd at all, from what I've seen of him.'

'My mom was crazy about Brent; he could do no wrong. She'd been a surrogate mom to him.' This confirmed what Makena had told Anders. 'I don't know, maybe that's why she was blind to his faults. And because my father cared more about the business than the family, *he* did nothing to disabuse him

312

of the notion. He wasn't going to do anything that might upset the relationship with Brent's dad.'

'What *was* the relationship with his dad?'

'His dad's company handled the distribution for my father's company throughout Africa and the Middle East.'

Anders thought about Brent's claim that he worked for Olivia's dad.

'But Brent said he "apprenticed" with your dad? What was he talking about?'

She grunted. 'That's the fancy way of saying he worked for my dad for a few summers during prep school. It was his way of being near me.'

'What about Makena? I'd have thought she would have protected you.'

'Well, except for those few summers, Brent and I spent much more time together on this side of the ocean. Especially when we were younger. And my father never let Makena accompany us when we came to Africa.' She laughed bitterly. 'He was probably afraid she'd stay, and they'd lose her.' She sighed. 'So I don't think she realized what was happening. The picture she received had been drawn and coloured by my parents, so she just thought we were two kids who were sweet on each other.'

'And you never told her differently?'

'No. In case you haven't noticed,' she laughed sadly, 'I tend to keep everything in here,' she pointed to her heart and then to her head, 'and here.'

He wondered if there were still things she didn't remember, like that first day at the beach, because she hadn't kept everything in then, not by a long shot. But she'd never really told him any more, either, not really. And he knew now there *was* more. There'd been so much more.

'If I don't talk about something, then it must not exist, right?' she added, though it sounded as if she was talking to herself.

'So what happened? How did you get to where we are now?'

'He went to the military academy and I went to university. When I got to school, I finally began to lead a somewhat normal life. I made some friends, went to parties, dated some guys. By the time I saw Brent again the first summer, I'd changed. I was ready to move on, but he wasn't too happy about it, and neither was my father. I guess I screwed up everyone's plans.'

'He really thought you guys would stay together? That's crazy.'

'Yeah, to most people. But he wasn't most people.'

'What about your mom?' A part of him felt guilty for using Olivia to test Makena's honesty, but he needed to know whom to trust.

'She passed away when I was sixteen.'

'I'm sorry, Olivia.' She lowered her eyes and simply nodded. 'So what did you do?' he asked. 'I mean, about Brent, and your dad?'

She took a deep breath. 'You won't understand.'

He leaned away to see her face better. 'Olivia?'

'You won't, Anders.'

'Give me a chance.'

She turned her face from him, pretended to watch something in the distance. He looked up briefly and saw giraffes crossing in front of the rising sun. It *was* magnificent. He couldn't deny her that.

'Olivia,' he whispered, practically begging, 'please trust me.'

'My father came down on me hard. He told me how selfish I was, how spoiled. He talked about how much Brent loved me, and that I was breaking his heart. He insisted that I appease him, at least.'

'What did that mean?'

She shrugged, but she curled in tight against him, hid her face in the hollow between his chest and shoulder. She was

314

embarrassed about something. 'See him on holidays, travel with him a little during the summers.'

*And fuck him*, he wanted to add, and was immediately ashamed of himself for having the thought. Instead he said, 'And having no interest in the guy, you were agreeable to this . . . why?'

'He didn't give me much choice.'

'I'm not following.'

But she merely twisted some more in his embrace and didn't respond.

'Olivia?' he said again.

'Not every nineteen-year-old is equipped to defy her father and live in a trailer, Anders.'

His muscles tensed and his skin went cold. *Money matters to everyone.* He could still hear Matt's voice, his dismissal of Anders's naive belief in Olivia's strength.

'I know that.' He felt her shudder. He knew she'd just had the same thought he'd had: her father had essentially prostituted her. He reached his hand to her face and wiped the new tears away. 'Hey,' his voice was soft, his lips touched her ear, 'I *know* that.'

She nodded but she still wouldn't look at him.

'Did he threaten to disinherit you or something?'

'It wasn't even that. He just threatened to pull me out of school. Without him, I had no way to pay for it.' Between her crying, he could barely understand her. 'But school meant so much to me. It was the only place I . . .' Her voice trailed off, but he understood.

'Why do you think it was so important to your dad?'

'What?'

'To give Brent whatever he wanted. I mean, a parent might hope he can somehow influence his child's choice of mate, but my God, didn't it seem strange to you? The lengths to which your father was willing to go to keep him happy?' Mayfield had claimed he was 'honouring' her mother's wishes, but Olivia clearly didn't know about the supposed deathbed promise. He wondered whether to tell her about it. 'Do you really believe what he said? That he was only trying to honour your mom's wishes?'

'I don't know! When we were younger, she loved that we were together. But she wasn't around when Brent got really crazy. I can't imagine she would have supported my father's efforts. I mean, looking back now, they were ridiculous. But I didn't know any different. My father controlled everything. That he would try to control my love life didn't seem that unusual. And I'm ashamed to say it, but the trade-off wasn't so bad. Brent was like an obnoxious relative I put up with at Christmas and weddings but didn't even think about the rest of year. That's what he had become to me. A mere nuisance. Even after we both graduated, I saw him only a few times, because he was stationed out of the States. It wasn't until the war started that he began to put more pressure on me.'

'That's when he asked you to marry him?' He remembered the article being more recent, though.

'Well, that's when he started talking about the idea. But he didn't love me. He's pursued me for so many years only because I'm the one thing he's never been able to have, not on his terms, at least. That's when I really started outright resisting.' She grunted. 'Or fighting back, I guess you could say.'

'But at some point you agreed to marry him.' It came out sounding more like an accusation than a question.

'No.' She shook her head. 'No. He proposed a couple of years ago, after he'd left the regular service and entered the reserves, but I turned him down.'

'There was a newspaper article.'

Finally she looked up at him again. He couldn't read the meaning in her narrowed eyes.

'I saw it. It was in that shoebox of yours, on the closet

shelf. Along with the ring and . . .' He stopped. They still hadn't talked about what had happened to her in the bar, not since her memory had returned.

'And what?'

'The matchbook.' He waited to see how she'd react. But he couldn't read the look on her face. 'It's how I found you.'

If she'd been upset that he'd gone through her things – he still couldn't tell for sure and he hoped she would understand his desperation at the time – any anger melted upon hearing his words. Her eyes welled up again and he tightened his grip on her.

He asked gently, 'When did you first remember?'

'Not long after I arrived in Florida. I stopped taking my medication as soon as I left Connecticut. It was just like this time. I had little spurts of memory, more like shadows of familiar feelings, and then, not long after, it all came back.'

'You never told me.'

She waited a long time before answering. 'I intended to, eventually. But I was afraid. I didn't want to lose you.'

He squeezed his eyes shut. *How could you think that?* he wanted to ask. But he just sighed and let the silence speak for him.

'That article was just another ploy by my father to pressure me. He must have known Brent planned to propose. He must have contacted the paper within days of the whole thing. That story about me receiving the ring on the same day I'd been mistakenly informed of his death? I think they must have planned that in advance to play with my emotions. Because it worked, for a bit. I *was* upset when those soldiers came to our door to tell me. I mean, I didn't love the guy, but I *had* known him for years, and spent a lot of time with him. So when I thought he'd died . . .'

'I always thought those guys only showed up at the homes of spouses, or parents.'

'Yeah, me too. I'm guessing the soldiers who came to my door had been paid to do so, if you get my drift.'

Just like the cops who'd shown up at the beach.

'But you screwed up their plan when you eventually turned down his proposal.'

'Yes.'

And Brent decided to retaliate.

'Olivia?' She looked up at him. 'How did you end up at Jimmy's?' He asked the question as gently as possible so she'd understand he wasn't questioning her judgement.

'I thought I'd been invited to a party to welcome him home from Iraq.' She sighed and used her index finger to wipe under each eye. 'Of course, Brent never showed up. I knew, I just *knew*, he was behind it.'

They stopped talking for a while. Anders had no intention of forcing her to relive the nightmare at the bar, and he didn't really know what else he could ask her that wouldn't lead to that.

As if she knew he still had questions but didn't want to ask them, she said, 'Jimmy found me the next morning, curled into one of the booths. I think I was in shock. I didn't tell him what happened, but he could tell. He took me to the hospital. They started medicating me before I was even discharged. I'd been told they were antidepressants.'

'Jimmy's as bad as the rest of them,' Anders said angrily. 'Why'd he let it happen in the first place?' The question was rhetorical, but she thought it was meant for her. She shook her head.

'He wasn't there. He'd let them have the place for the night. That happened a lot with those guys. He might have owned the place, but trust me, they called the shots.'

He thought of Matt's comment: *You really have no idea how things work in their world, do you?* 'Then he's an idiot, for letting them.'

His anger seemed to upset her; she covered her face with her hands. 'I'm sorry,' he said. She nodded but wouldn't look at him. 'I just . . . it just makes me so mad . . . that no one did anything, even afterwards. How could Jimmy—'

'Please don't,' she said. 'Please don't talk about it anymore, okay?'

Her words had been like a verbal slap, and he resisted the urge to lean away from her. 'Okay. I'm sorry.'

The sun was fully awake now and it began to burn off the morning mist clinging to the ground. He could hear voices floating up the hill from the manyatta as its inhabitants began the day. He'd hoped to finally ask about her pregnancy but now he couldn't; he'd already upset her enough. But why hadn't she mentioned it to him? He knew it had to be his; she hadn't been with Brent long enough to get pregnant by him *and* start showing. Something was causing her to withhold the information from him, and that same, unknown 'something' made him afraid to ask.

'Anders?' Her voice was small, but it told him she harboured no resentment for his small tirade. She lifted her head and her eyes glistened from unspent tears. 'You think my father knew Brent was behind it, don't you? Even though he said he didn't . . .'

He hesitated giving an answer. He'd never heard such sadness in a voice. In spite of everything, she didn't want to believe the worst about the man she called *father* instead of *dad*.

'And you also think he had something to do with the accident.'

'I don't know who was responsible. Brent, like he said, maybe. I just don't know, Olivia. Maybe your dad simply took advantage of the situation to get you back home, to get you on the drugs again. To help you forget what had happened to you.' He didn't believe it himself, but what was he supposed to say?

'But to send me right back into the arms of . . .' She let out a short wail. 'If my father knew Brent was responsible for . . . what happened at Jimmy's, why would he cover for him?'

He thought then of Brent's words, when Anders had suggested it was Olivia's father that Brent might be afraid of: *You've got that backwards.* And he knew then that Brent had something over Lawrence Mayfield. Something big. Something that forced him to sacrifice his daughter's life to save his own.

'I don't know.' He met her stare, saw the craving in her eyes. 'I just don't know.'

# 23

BY LUNCHTIME, Leng reported he had located a nearby camp that could accommodate them for whatever period of time it took Olivia's father to find Brent and, Anders hoped, Lenny. Olivia was reluctant to leave the manyatta, which she preferred to a camp, and only allowed herself to be persuaded because she didn't want to cause the chief's children to be evicted again from their regular sleeping spot. After lunch, lengthy goodbyes, and promises that she would visit the nearby school each day to help with the children, they took off once again with Leng at the wheel. By mid-afternoon, they'd been shown to their tent by the camp manager and had settled down on the bed together for a badly needed nap.

They passed several days just waiting. Leng kept in contact with Makena, who had stayed with Mayfield, and he provided Anders with updates on the search. Most of these reports were, in Anders's opinion, worthless, and only made him more anxious. As promised, Olivia kept busy at the school, and usually Anders accompanied her. One of the camp guides ferried them to and fro, and sometimes she brought children back to the camp as a sort of field trip. He noticed she seemed happiest, or perhaps lightest, when she worked with the kids or in the village. At least, he thought, it was a more natural way for her to forget what had happened.

He noticed, too, that as the days passed, her abdomen shrank a bit, and he began to fear that he'd caused her to lose the baby. Did she know it, too? Is that why she hadn't said

321

anything? The issue was present between them at all times, yet he thought each was too afraid to touch it.

It also didn't escape his notice that, in any other circumstance, being in such a place with her would have constituted the vacation of a lifetime. But as much as he savoured having the old Olivia back, he couldn't completely surrender to it. Not while Lenny remained at large.

ON THE fourth morning, he awoke with a start.

He lay on his back, and Olivia nestled against him with her head in the crook of his shoulder. One hand caressed his chest.

'We'll hear something today. I can feel it.'

'You think?'

'Yeah.' She flung one leg over both of his.

He closed his eyes and listened to the dawn. With her help, he was beginning to recognize the difference here between the call of a bird, the chirp of an insect and the whistle of a tree frog, something he had no problem doing at home. 'Black-eyed bulbul,' he announced, and she laughed at him. 'Am I right?'

'Yeah, you're right.' She propped herself up on her elbow and waited until he opened his eyes and noticed she was staring at him. 'What do you think of this place?' she asked.

Somehow he knew she meant Africa, not the camp. It reminded him of the day at the beach, when she'd asked his opinion about whether she should stay. That day now felt like another lifetime.

'I think it's incredible.'

She was silent for a moment, and then she said, 'But?'

He laughed a little. 'But? Did I say "but"?'

'No. I heard it, though.'

He gave her a small smile and quick kiss. 'There's no "but". I do think it's incredible. It's magnificent. And I understand what you love about it so much.'

'But it's not Florida?'

'No,' he said, laughing again, 'I don't think anyone would ever confuse it with Florida.' When she didn't laugh with him, he looked at her sideways. 'I'm not following. Is it supposed to be?'

She sighed. 'No, of course not. I just ... I don't know, I want you to love it, too.'

He rolled over so they were face to face. 'I know you do. And I do love it, I guess, but—'

She let out a small 'told you so' grunt.

'– it's just that I haven't really experienced it under the best of circumstances—'

'I know, I'm sorry, I—'

He put a finger to her lips. 'Shh, don't apologize. You're the last person to be apologizing for anything. I'm just saying that once Lenny is back, then ...' He stopped. What if Lenny never made it back? What if Mayfield never found him, or he found him, but it was already too late? Anders suddenly felt restless. Had he let her father manipulate him again? He should have been out there, looking for his friend. But what about Olivia? He reminded himself why he'd stayed behind, that she needed him here. If Mayfield failed, Anders was her last defence against Brent Campbell. 'What matters is that I love *you*, okay? Everything else will work itself out.'

She didn't look convinced. And, really, neither was he.

AFTER BREAKFAST, Leng came to Anders, excited with the news that Brent's plane had been spotted not far from Arusha.

'*His* plane?' The name of the place meant nothing to Anders, but this was the first mention of a plane.

'Yes. Mr Campbell is a pilot.'

'Is this a good thing? I mean, isn't he probably long gone, then?'

Leng's forehead wrinkled. 'No, I think not. Not if you believe he will not leave without Ms Mayfield, as Mr Mayfield believes. And Arusha is not far.' At seeing Anders's obvious doubt, he added, 'I will try to get more information for you. Maybe after lunch?'

Anders thanked him and took off to find Olivia. He located her in the library, a small tent near the edge of camp that housed a small collection of books, games and puzzles. She sat cross-legged on the floor, her skirt spread out over her lap, and she had a smattering of young girls circled around her who listened intently as she translated a picture book from English to Swahili. Three goats sat on the floor outside the circle as if they were dogs guarding their little masters.

She set the book down when she saw him and, after saying something to the children that he couldn't understand, rose to meet him at the opening of the tent. Each wide-eyed face turned in their direction.

'What is it? What's wrong?'

'Nothing.' He almost said 'Just stay close today' but he didn't want to scare her. 'I just wanted to make sure you don't take the kids back without me, okay?'

'Okay.' She touched his forearm. 'Why? Is something the matter? Have you heard something from Leng?'

He forced a smile. 'No. Nothing's the matter. I'm just bored and want to go with you.'

She relaxed. 'Too long without your motorcycle, huh?' She laughed. 'We'll have to see if we can't wrangle one up for you.'

'Yeah, I guess so.' He nodded at the kids. 'Your little charges are waiting. I'll be around, okay?'


HE LEFT Olivia with the children and the goats, and after an hour or so fidgeting on their bed with a magazine he'd found in the lounge, he made his way over to the camp manager's tent. The flaps had been tied back to form a wide opening and he could see her inside sitting before a small writing desk. She must have heard his footsteps in the dry grass because she called his name before he'd even stepped onto the canvas porch.

'Come on in, I'm just catching up on paperwork.' She motioned to the opening. 'As you can see, my door's wide open, literally.' She gave him an inviting smile to match her words.

Her tent looked similar to theirs, though not as luxurious. It was smaller and much more lived-in. She'd attached photos to a fishing line strung across the top of the dresser mirror – friends and family from less far-flung corners of the world, he presumed. Her name was Tory, and she was American. She was younger than him, perhaps only two or three years older than Shel. He wondered if she had a boyfriend back home, wherever home was, and if it got lonely out here after a while, if the employees formed unlikely relationships that would never last in the glaring light of the real world. Or maybe the bush *was* her home, her real world, as it had been for Olivia long ago.

The bed was unmade and when she realized he had nowhere to sit, she jumped up and straightened the covers a bit. 'Here,' she said, patting the mattress, 'sorry about that.'

'You don't get many visitors back here, do you?'

She laughed. 'No, it ruins the illusion.' When he just gave her a small grin, she asked, 'Have you heard anything?'

She knew only that they'd lost contact with a friend, that they thought he was in danger and were trying to locate him. 'Not much. Leng said maybe he'd know more after lunch.'

'Sorry, Anders. I know you and Olivia must be going out of your mind. I guess it'll sound like a cliché to ask this, but is there anything I can do to help?'

He glanced around the tent but didn't see what he was looking for. He saw her vest hanging from a mahogany coat rack in the corner. Her well-worn boots rested on the floor underneath it, ancient soil clinging to the soles and sides. 'Yeah . . . I was just wondering . . .'

'Yes?'

'Well, Leng makes all these contacts, somehow, you know? I mean, the cellphones don't work out here, do they?' He felt like an idiot.

'Some do. Depends on the phone.' She saw his embarrassment and smiled to assure him that his questions weren't as stupid as he thought they were. 'But most of us, Leng included, use a satellite phone. It's a bit more reliable in the bush.'

'That's the yellow phone I see you using sometimes?'

'Yes.' She tilted her head. 'Did you need to make a call?'

'Well . . .' He hesitated. 'It's not really an emergency.'

She raised her hand as if she were a traffic cop. 'Don't say another word.' She went to the vest, dug into the large front pocket and pulled out the phone. 'I'm not sure how much battery is left.' She winked as she handed it to him. 'Just don't let the other guests know, okay?'


HE SAT at the top of the hill she'd recommended for the best reception and listened to the faraway rings from half a world away. From his elevated perch he could see Olivia standing in front of the library tent and talking to one of the camp guests. At least five or six children hovered close; one clung to her skirt.

'Hello?' The groggy voice at the other end of the phone broke his reverie, and he suddenly realized that it was something like three or four in the morning in Florida.

'Shel?'

His one-word enquiry met with silence and if he'd known what he'd planned to say before, it all slipped away in that instant of uncertainty.

And then, out of the sky, 'Anders?'

He breathed a sigh of relief. It had only been a delay in transmission.

Next, his 'Did I wake you?' spoken simultaneously with her 'Is that you?' More silence and then they both laughed. It would take some practice getting used to the delay. He waited for her to go first.

'Where are you? Are you okay? Did you find Olivia?'

He imagined her sitting up in bed in the dark, rubbing the sleep from her eyes while her black cat, Bagheera, mewed insistently at the end of the bed for its breakfast.

'I don't even know anymore.' He could hear the exhaustion in his voice; he wondered if the distance amplified or minimized it for her. 'Somewhere in East Africa. We started out in Kenya, but we're in Tanzania now. I'm okay, and yes, we found Olivia, but . . .' He stopped. After what had happened at the beach house, what she'd said to him about Lenny, how could he now tell her he'd placed their friend's life in so much danger?

His hesitation allowed time for his words to reach her, and she responded before he'd figured out what to say next. If she'd heard his lingering 'but' she didn't acknowledge it. 'Oh, God, Anders, that's such good news.' It sounded like she was crying, though he couldn't be sure. 'I'm so happy for you, I really am.'

By all indications, she'd forgiven him everything. He could so easily just accept it, just pretend he'd forgotten what had happened or, at least, put it behind him. Pretend that the only reason for his call was to let her know they were okay. Though even that wouldn't be accurate.

'Shel, listen, I need to tell you something.'

He spotted Olivia walking with the children out to the line of Land Rovers. Leng and one of the other Maasai guides accompanied the group, and to his surprise, the second guide opened the passenger side door for her and she climbed in. While the children took their places on the bench seats in the back with the goats at their feet, the two guides loaded several large baskets onto the rear and tied them down with a deft skill that caused Anders to momentarily forget his anxiety over Olivia's imminent departure. Leng then took the driver's seat next to Olivia. *Where the hell was she going?* Why wasn't she waiting for him as he'd asked her to?

'I'm here,' Shel said, and her sleepy voice pulled him back to Florida. He heard something in it he'd never heard before. Poise.

'What happened at the house, what I said to you ... and the stuff with Crystal ...' He sighed. Just what, exactly, was he trying to say? He felt it, but he couldn't articulate it. Some part of him just wanted to tell her he missed her, her easy companionship, her complex simplicity. Explain that she was his friend – his best 'girl' friend, as she'd said – and he was sorry for how he'd treated her.

'No, everything you tried to tell me was right,' she said. 'I just didn't want to hear it. It's okay, believe me.'

He sighed again. 'It's not okay. I didn't—'

'Wait, Anders, before I forget. About Crystal' – she paused, and even across the ocean, he knew from the sound of her voice she'd just straightened her posture for courage – 'she called, trying to find out how to reach you.' It didn't come close to what Anders thought Shel might say about Crystal. 'She said it's urgent, that she has some information for you.'

'And she called *you*? Did you tell her Olivia was alive?'

'Yeah, but she said she'd found out something really important, something you would want to know. She said it was confidential. Do you need her number?'

He couldn't believe how calmly she spoke of Crystal to him. How *magnanimous* she was being.

He gazed down at the camp. The Land Rover was pulling away. He had the inexplicable urge to run down the hill and stop it. 'No,' he said quietly as he refocused on her question and remembered his phone call to Lenny from Connecticut, 'I have it.'

'Hey, I took your advice. Did Lenny tell you what I did?' The pride Lenny had described oozed through the phone line.

He chuckled in spite of himself. 'Yeah, he told me. You rock, Shel.' It was one of the phrases she used and he teased her about. 'Sounds like you're kicking that professor's figurative butt.'

'I am. And now all these other women are coming forward with similar stories. There's an investigative hearing next week and we have to testify.'

'You'll do fine, I'm sure of it. Wish I could be there.'

'Oh, no, it's closed to the public.' And then she added, 'Thank God.'

He smiled silently; she didn't even get it. The phone beeped at his ear; Tory had warned him about the low battery. He had mere minutes left to finish and he still hadn't gotten around to telling her about Lenny, much less the original point of the call.

Shel kept talking. 'I'm terrified, but you know what? He's just a weak, pathetic person who turned tail as soon as I reported him. So I'm actually looking forward to the hearing. It's all sort of liberating.'

'Shel, my battery's low.'

'Oh. Okay.' From her tone he knew she thought he was cutting her off, but if that was the case, she wasn't going to let it bother her.

'No, it's not okay. Listen, I don't know when we'll be back, and I just need to tell you, what I said about us, I–'

'What do you mean, you don't know when you'll be back? I thought you said you found Olivia?'

'We did, but–'

'Are you staying there?'

'Staying here? In Africa?' His voice pitched high, suggesting the absurdity of the idea.

Yet even as she asked the question and he acknowledged it, he realized that's where this whole thing was heading. He could see it in Olivia's eyes, her love for this land, this life. He'd seen it immediately at the first camp, even before she knew him as someone other than Joe Miller, and it had only grown after the night spent together in the tiny, hot, smoke-filled hut. He'd expected the return of her memory to be followed by the memory of – no, not just the memory, but a *longing for* – their old life, but instead, *she'd* expected the polar opposite: to Olivia, that first reunion had been some sort of initiation of Anders to the ways of the bush, to the life she loved and hoped he would adopt as his own. She hadn't spoken of this to him directly, not really; everything they'd done since showing her the tattoo had been geared ostensibly towards escaping Brent's reach and now also recovering Lenny, but he knew it nevertheless. And somehow, thousands of miles away, Shel had known it, too.

The phone beeped again. If he could say it out loud, hear it for himself, then maybe it would be easier when the in-evitable discussion with Olivia surfaced.

'No.' He hesitated, not quite understanding the import of his own words. 'No, we're not staying in Africa.'

HE RAN down the hill to near the tables where the staff worked busily in preparation for lunch. He caught sight of Tory talking to a guest and waited impatiently for the conversation to con-clude. Despite his nerves, he remembered she didn't want the other guests to know of the favour she'd granted him.

'Did you talk to Olivia before she left?' he asked, still breath-less, as he mindlessly handed the phone back to her.

Her expression conveyed concern, but it wasn't for Olivia.

It was for Anders. 'Yes, she was looking for you, and I told her you were making a phone call. She said to tell you she's taking the kids back to school, that she wouldn't be gone for long,' she laughed a bit, 'and then you'd have her full attention.'

When he didn't laugh with her, she said, 'Anders? What's the matter? You look upset.'

'I don't like her going out alone like that.'

'She's not alone; she's with Leng.'

He nodded, trying to tell himself that she was right. There was nothing to worry about.

She motioned to the food being brought out. 'Why don't you have some lunch with us, and I'm sure by the time you've finished she'll be back.'

BUT OLIVIA still hadn't returned by the end of lunch, which he hadn't touched.

'Can you radio Leng?' he asked when, sensing his increasing distress, Tory came to his tent a short while later with a cold beer.

'No problem. I'll go do it right now, and as soon as I hear back, I'm sure we'll find out everything's fine. I'll stop by as soon as I have some information for you, okay?'

The words reminded him of Shel's message during their earlier call. So before she left, he asked her if the phone had been recharged yet, and if he could use it a second time.

HIS VOICE caught in his throat when Crystal answered. The emotions he'd felt that day at her house – first the shame, and then the rage – came rushing back at him when he heard her lilting voice. He hoped he wasn't about to fall into another one of her traps, so often placed and set, he thought, merely to further boost her inflated ego.

'It's Anders,' he said, keeping it short.

'Oh, Anders, thank God! Shel said she had no way to contact you.' She said it as if they were the closest of friends, as if he hadn't almost snuffed out her life the last time they'd seen each other.

'I called *her.*'

'Oh.' The silence that followed suggested she was confused by that. 'Aren't you in Africa?'

'Yeah.'

'Is Lenny with you?'

He hesitated. He was unwilling to give her any more information than necessary. 'He came with me.'

Crystal didn't respond, as if waiting for him to say more, to explain. He told himself it was none of her business, though he knew that wasn't true. Lenny was her son's father. But his patience with her was waning already.

'Forgive me for being so abrupt, but I'm sure these phone calls aren't cheap and I'm using the camp's phone, so what do you want?'

'You called *me*, Anders.'

He grunted. Nothing had changed. 'Don't fuck with me again, Crystal! Shel said you needed to talk to me.'

The dead air that followed his outburst made him wonder if she'd hung up. Or maybe she was just deciding whether to play with him a bit more.

Finally, 'I'm sorry. You're right.'

The tension in his shoulders eased at her change in tone, but if she was waiting for praise from him, she'd be waiting a long time. As if realizing it, she continued, 'I have some information about Olivia's dad.'

'You mean something more than an empty file?'

Though thousands of miles and an ocean separated them, he thought he heard her swallow.

'Look, I'm sorry about that. I really am. But I did risk my

neck for you.' He almost smiled; she didn't even hear the irony in her statement. 'It wasn't my fault everything was gone.'

'It was your fault you waited until –' he stopped himself, not sure how to word what had happened between them '– you waited to tell me.'

'Hey, I did the job, I was entitled to payment.' He knew if he could see her, she'd be giving him one of her shrugs, as if to say *Oh, well*. 'Anyway, I like you, Anders. I've always liked you.'

As if that explained everything.

'I'm listening,' he said then, reminding her of the reason for the call. There was no use arguing about what had happened.

'Last week there was talk around the hospital, something about a big shake-up at the top. Apparently the FBI and the DEA have been sniffing around.'

'What's this have to do with me? Or Olivia's dad?'

'Did you hear me? *DEA*. Do you know what that stands for?'

'Yes, I know what that stands for.'

'He owns a pharmaceutical company, doesn't he?'

'Yeah,' he said slowly, as he started to see some connection. 'Mayfield Pharmaceuticals, I think it's called.' But how did she know that?

'Well, I did a little research. You're not going to believe this, but it seems the hospital might be involved in the import of illegal drugs into the US.'

'How do you know this?'

'Oh, let's just say I have friends in high places. You don't need to know how I worked my magic. Anyway, guess what name also came up in this?'

His mind had already begun to process the information she was feeding him, trying to figure out how it fitted into the pieces of the puzzle he'd already linked, but her next words stunned him, and not for the reason she thought they would.

'Mayfield-Campbell Imports. Is his first name Lawrence?'

'Did you say Campbell?'

'Well, yeah,' she laughed a little, 'but I thought the name Mayfield would be the one to interest you.'

It did, he wanted to say, but it was the name Campbell that surprised him. That thrilled him, really, because he was starting to understand some things that had previously been inexplicable.

'Is her dad's name Lawrence Mayfield?' Crystal asked again.

'Yeah, yeah.'

'Well, he's the one then. Supposedly this company imports African art and furniture into the States, but it's all just a front. The real business is drugs, illegal prescription drugs. You know, the drugs our government hasn't approved. Mayfield's company has been supplying a network of hospitals all over the country, with the hospitals' apparent knowledge and cooperation, I might add. Heads here are going to roll.'

Anders remembered Brent's words: *I know things that can send him away for years.*

'Anders? You still there?'

'Yeah.'

'Well, they think he knows they're on to him and he's up and left the country. In other words, he's considered a fugitive.'

'Lawrence Mayfield? You're sure about this? Olivia's father?' He couldn't believe it.

'Yep.' He could hear her self-satisfaction right through the phone. 'He's the guy they're looking for.'

*And I'm the guy who knows where he is.*

# 24

OLIVIA STILL hadn't returned by the time the staff began setting out the cups and saucers for afternoon tea. Even Tory seemed worried now because Leng had never responded to her radio call, and when she tried to make phone contact after Anders returned her satellite phone, he also failed to answer his phone. She couldn't even offer to have someone drive Anders to the school because all the other guides were in the bush with guests.

'But what about a spare vehicle?' he asked. He refused to wait any longer. He was prepared to cross the savannah on foot if necessary.

'I have one, but I don't have anyone to drive you.'

As if he hadn't understood the first time.

'Tory, I know this is asking a lot, and I wouldn't ask if I didn't think her life was in danger, but could I please drive myself?'

'Her life is in danger? What—'

'Please, I don't have time to explain.' What he needed was time to think, time he didn't have. 'Can I take it?'

'Yes, yes . . . of course.'

He stared at her, trying to think. He had to get this right. He couldn't just take off half-cocked without a plan like he had so many times before. He had the sense that whatever he found at the school would determine their future – his, Olivia's, Lenny's.

He grabbed Tory's wrist, and she gasped, alarmed by his urgency. 'While I'm heading over there I need you to make some calls for me. They're very important. I need you to call Olivia's father. He's the emergency contact she gave you when we arrived. Tell him I think I found Brent and tell him how to get to the school.'

'Brent?' She couldn't understand, because they'd told her only that they were looking for someone named Lenny.

'Tell him to get there right away, as soon as humanly possible, okay?'

She nodded nervously.

'And then I need you to call the American embassy in Dar es Salaam. Tell them I've located Lawrence Mayfield of Mayfield-Campbell Imports. Make sure you give them that name. Lawrence Mayfield of Mayfield-Campbell Imports. Tell them to send the police –' he shook his head in confusion '– or whoever they send to pick up fugitives. Tell them to hurry.'

'Mayfield? Fugitives?' He could see her thinking, tying the Mayfield name to Olivia. 'Anders, you're scaring me. What's going on?'

'Tory, please, I just need you to do this for me, okay?' He gripped her harder. 'And listen, this is important: when you talk to Olivia's father, don't breathe a word about the call to the embassy. Not a word.'


HE GUESSED that as the crow flies, only five or six miles separated the school from their camp, but because of the rough condition of the dirt roads and the roundabout way they were laid out, it took a good forty-five minutes to get there. He located it easily, though. When he spotted the school from a distance and saw it was as vacant and silent as a ghost town, he swerved abruptly off the path and gunned the truck straight for the building, despite Tory's injunctions against leaving the road. The violent pounding in his chest warned him in the same way the flashing yellow lights of a roadblock warn of danger ahead.

He slammed to a stop at the open entrance to the school and jumped from the vehicle into the dust kicked up in the wake of his frantic driving. Dusk would be upon him soon, but for now it was still light out, and through the square holes that served as the school's windows he saw the children's empty seats. He reminded himself that the grounds were empty because the school day was over and all the children had already gone home. He told himself that Olivia must have talked Leng into stopping by the manyatta before heading back to camp, that he'd find her there if only he could figure out which road led to the small village.

All his attempts to rationalize the truth away ceased when he crossed the threshold of the doorless entrance into the dim classroom. There, in the corner, beyond the miniature desks and chairs, beyond the free-standing chalkboard with the lessons of the day still scrawled in a foreign language on its powdery surface, beyond the small bookcase with its sparse collection of worn books, sitting stiffly in a chair at the teacher's desk with his eyes wide open, was Leng.

Anders stared at the guide, his legs weakening beneath him, and muttered two words: 'God no.'

He didn't need to step closer to know that the man had been murdered. A trail of coagulated blood marked the side of his head and neck, and even from across the room Anders could see the gaping, though remarkably even, wound from the bullet. His jaw hung slack, and blood had also dripped from his mouth and over his chin. His strong arms hung at his sides.

A piece of paper had been pinned to his chest.

Anders's heart rate soared. He stepped into the classroom and slowly approached the desk. Every step required immense effort; each lift of a foot added another weight to his ankles. He heard a noise outside, the caw of a bird, and he halted, jerking to look around the room. But the classroom had no corners in

337

which to hide, no tall shelving behind which someone could take cover. He was alone, for now.

He went only as close as necessary to make out the scribble on the paper, which he knew was meant for him even before reading it: *Welcome Anders!*

He swallowed the lump in his throat to stave off the tears and the fear. He succeeded only with the first.

Outside, he tried to catch his breath. Bending at the waist, hands on thighs, he talked himself through the shock. He told himself that Olivia and Lenny hadn't suffered the same fate. Just as he'd always had a nagging suspicion that Olivia hadn't died at the hospital in Florida, he told himself he'd know it, he'd *feel* it, if Brent had murdered them now.

When he'd settled his nerves enough to stand straight and walk, he circled the classroom building carefully, glimpsing around each corner before proceeding. Once at the back, he spotted another, smaller building tucked under a cluster of fever trees. He crossed the yard, his eyes darting in every direction as if watching for a sniper. A crude sign had been nailed to the wall next to the open doorway. On it was painted a word he couldn't read, followed by the English in parentheses: Storage.

'We're in here, Anders.'

The voice reached his ears from somewhere inside. He stopped upon hearing it.

'Come on in,' it beckoned. 'We've been waiting for you.'

Still he didn't move. With the fading sunlight on his face, he knew Brent could probably see him, but all he saw was blackness through the doorway.

'I guess he doesn't want the chance to say goodbye.' Brent spoke softly this time, and in some twisted logic Anders felt relief because he understood the comment had been directed not at him, but at Olivia, and it told him she was still alive. But from the short cry that immediately followed, he knew he'd caused her physical pain, and the sound compelled him to step forward into the darkness. Just as her captor must have intended.

Anders's eyes adjusted to the dark, but he couldn't make out much more than the outlines of their bodies. Suddenly a light shone in his face and he averted his eyes until the beam was redirected upward. From the sound of things, something was placed on the ground then, and when he turned back, a large, boxy flashlight illuminated the middle of the room from a spot near Brent's feet. Brent sat on a long crate with Olivia in front of him, his back supported against the hard mud wall, and they both faced Anders. One arm encircled her neck in a chokehold and the other held a pistol to her temple. Her eyes screamed her terror, and he had to look away. Those eyes might cause him to do something he'd regret.

He just stood there, frozen.

Thinking.

Finally, 'What do you want, Brent?'

'Did you see the gift I left for you in the schoolhouse?'

'What do you want?' he repeated.

'The same thing you want.' He tightened his arm around Olivia's neck and she winced.

Anders clenched his fists and told himself to remain calm, to wait for the right moment, which would eventually come. Which *had* to come. 'It would be easier to believe you if you'd stop hurting her.'

Brent shrugged. 'Unfortunately, your presence has forced me to do things I would have rather avoided.'

Anders wanted to remind him that he wasn't around when he'd offered her up to his friends with as much thought as one gives to tossing a dog a bone. But he knew sarcasm wouldn't advance his cause.

'I'm not forcing you to do anything. I'm just asking you to

let up on her a bit, get the gun away from her face. The gun is just making the situation worse.'

The man laughed. 'You think I'm an idiot, don't you?'

'No, not at all. I've been apprised by several people, in fact, how clever you are.'

'And what did they tell you? Play nice, and he'll give you whatever you want? You think I'm just going to let her stand up and walk out of here with you?'

'No. I'm not an idiot, either. I only want you to move the gun so we can talk.'

'We have nothing to talk about. I want Olivia, you want Olivia.' He looked at her then as someone looks at something very precious. 'No compromise is possible.' He dragged the barrel of the gun slowly along her cheek and stopped at her mouth. She moved her head to the side to avoid it, but he forced her lips to accept the gun's caresses for a moment before returning his aim to her temple. Anders merely watched because he knew it wouldn't help her to react. He waited until Brent turned his gaze back to him.

'You're wrong. I want Olivia's happiness. I want her safety. I want her to act of her own free will. But she's not a possession that you or I can just *have*.'

Brent laughed. 'God, you bloody Americans. *Life, liberty, and the pursuit of happiness*, is that it? Always harping on happiness.' He leaned his face in close to Olivia's and spoke the next words to her. 'But I almost forgot, babe, your Florida boy hails from the happiest place on earth, doesn't he?'

'Didn't realize you'd renounced your citizenship, Brent,' she said. It was the first time Anders had heard her talk back to him and he took pleasure in it, though his meagre enjoyment was short-lived because the comment angered Brent and he jerked his arm to twist her neck. She cried out and the sound of her pain stabbed at Anders.

'Stop hurting her.'

His voice came out sounding louder, more authoritative than he'd expected. If Brent didn't have a gun in his hand, it might have even sounded menacing.

But still he stood rooted to the ground, his body unable or possibly just unwilling to make the move his brain wanted to make.

When Brent looked back at him, Anders saw the same ruthlessness he'd seen in the lion's eyes as it ripped at the zebra's heart. If Leng's murder hadn't already convinced him, the emptiness staring back at him was all too familiar and erased any lingering doubts as to the man's humanity. In his life he'd known only two men he was certain lacked a conscience. One had been his own father; the other stood before him now.

'If you cared about her happiness,' Brent said, 'you would have left us alone. Because she *was* happy. You saw her at the camp. But you insisted on pursuing her when you should have walked away.'

'I've pursued her safety. I haven't harmed her. I haven't drugged her or lied to her.'

'No? One man is already dead. And right now you're placing her life, and another life, in jeopardy.' He briefly lowered his eyes in the direction of Olivia's stomach.

Anders continued to stare at Brent, he couldn't look away, not now, but in his peripheral vision he perceived the faintest change in Olivia's expression. Curiosity had carved out a tiny corner for itself in the space of her fear. Though she couldn't have seen Brent's face, she suspected, on some level, he wasn't talking about Lenny. What neither Brent nor Olivia knew was that Brent had also just reminded Anders of the other life he'd once placed in jeopardy. Whatever courage he'd possessed when he entered the small building began to wane.

Brent lowered the pistol and placed it against Olivia's leg. He used it to edge her skirt up, slowly revealing her knee and then her thigh. She wriggled in his grasp and cried out,

'Anders!' but Brent squeezed her neck again and she stopped. The gun continued to inch upward along the inside of her leg. She began to whimper.

'Stop it, Brent.'

Brent ignored him and the black barrel crept closer and closer to its destination. When it reached the top of her leg, he worked the tip of it under the elastic waistband of her panties and reversed his direction.

'Stop it!' Anders lurched forward but halted when suddenly he faced the end of the gun. *Better than where it had been heading.* He started talking – 'Just tell me what you want' – just saying anything to keep Brent distracted from what he'd been about to do. 'I'll do anything you ask if you'll just stop hurting her.'

Before Brent could respond, a low moan came from the far corner to Anders's left. He allowed himself to look away from the weapon pointed at his face and for the first time saw a hulking figure crumpled in the shadows. A small gasp escaped his lips when he realized who it was, and only then did he accept some part of him had clung futilely to the hope that Lenny might be his ace in the hole.

He turned back to Brent, his intense fear transforming to fierce anger. 'What did you do to him?' he demanded.

Brent laughed at the change. 'Only what was necessary to persuade him to talk. He was quite a challenge. Despite what *you* did to him, he's very loyal to you.'

Anders fully understood the implication of what had been left unsaid.

Movement came from the corner, and all three pairs of eyes turned to watch Lenny struggle to sit up. His hands were tied behind him and his feet bound at the ankles. He tried to say something, but unintelligible sounds came from his bloodied lips. Anders saw his feet were bare and caked in blood and orange African dirt.

'What did you do to him?' he asked again, his tone more despondent than demanding this time.

'You know, Andy – he calls you Andy, doesn't he? – I really didn't know you had it in you.' He made a clucking noise and shook his head. 'Shagging your best friend's wife under the guise of finding Olivia.'

Anders glanced at Olivia; she stared back at him. The curiosity that had previously grabbed a toehold was now firmly planted alongside the fear.

'Ex-wife.'

Brent grinned at that.

Lenny made a noise again, and then mumbled, 'Don't let him play with you.'

Brent adjusted the direction of the gun as if he was trying to decide where to aim it. Anders realized that Brent's uncertainty could provide the opportunity he needed. He had to rattle him somehow, just enough to cause him to make a mistake, but not so much that he decided the only way out of the situation was to dispose of them all.

'She's not pregnant,' Lenny muttered. His voice was getting stronger, but his grimace told all of them that he spoke in spite of his pain, not in place of it.

At first Anders was confused. He didn't know if he'd referred to Olivia or Crystal, and from the puzzled look on Olivia's face, she too assumed he meant Crystal, but then Lenny managed to add, 'Side effect, the drug.'

*Of course.* Why she'd appeared slightly smaller to him as time passed, why she'd never mentioned it when her memory returned, as he'd expected. A trace of regret passed through him.

'Sorry, mate,' Brent said, training the gun back at Anders with a small shrug. 'But you were so much easier to play when you thought you were a daddy.'

Olivia began to cry silently as she grasped the joke Brent

had played on Anders. He knew then that she'd attributed her swollen stomach to something else entirely.

Lenny shifted and let out a tortured grunt. Anders thought he might be dying right in front of him from injuries Anders could only guess at.

'He needs a doctor.'

Brent waved the gun in Lenny's direction. 'Take him, then. He's all yours. I already got what I wanted from him.' He kissed the back of Olivia's head, eyeing Anders from behind her untamed curls. 'But she stays. We have unfinished business.'

'You're going to let us go? Just like that? As long as I leave her with you?'

'Sure. Olivia and I will be long gone before you even get to a doctor. I'm not worried about you, or anyone else finding me later, if that's what you're thinking. Plus, I think once your friend gives you the details of our visit together, you'll have an extra deterrent against doing anything stupid.' Anders glanced at Lenny's feet again and wondered what other injuries existed that he couldn't see. 'I generally have to send my message only one time. Too bad I couldn't relay it to you directly.'

'What about Olivia?' he asked, playing along. 'You'll just ply her with drugs again?'

'Well, it's a bit more involved than that. Some hypnosis, maybe even some shock treatments, will be required at the beginning, you know, to manage which memories she loses, but, essentially, yes. I do intend to resume her medicine.' Anders cringed every time he referred to the drugs as *her medicine*.

'And she won't remember any of this?'

Brent grinned. 'That's right. She won't remember any of this.' Using the hand that held the gun, he caressed her hair. 'After all, we want her to be *happy*, don't we?'

Anders hoped Olivia would understand what he was about to do. He took a step in Lenny's direction, testing the offer.

'No!' she cried out, her one word begging him not to leave her there.

But Brent just stared at him, so he continued on. When he reached Lenny, they exchanged a silent look, and Anders kneeled down, moving for the rope that bound his feet.

He heard Brent rack the slide on the gun, and he froze.

Brent laughed loudly. 'Oh, come on. Be serious.'

Anders turned and stared at Brent. He wasn't sure what to believe. Was he reneging on his offer, or was he just telling Anders that Lenny had to stay tied? He pretended to think the latter.

'How are we supposed to leave if I can't untie him?'

'That's your problem. But I can assure you he won't be able to walk, anyway.'

Anders looked to Lenny for confirmation and the slightest nod told him, on this point, at least, Brent spoke the truth. He felt sick, wondering what suffering his friend had endured at the man's hands.

He tried to think, to strategize, but the situation was deteriorating before his eyes. He'd hoped that once he had Lenny outside the hut, he could somehow fake a departure and then double back and take Brent by surprise. But he couldn't lift Lenny, he knew that much. Lenny was six feet tall and 230 pounds of pure muscle. And Brent knew it, too. He'd offered to let them go only because he knew they couldn't.

'Guess you've run out of options,' Brent stated matter-of-factly as Anders stood to face him again. He repositioned his aim and pointed the end of the barrel a few inches from Olivia's temple. She began to sob quietly.

In his despair, Anders resorted to the same useless appeal he'd made earlier. 'What do you *want*?' he pleaded. He tried to see if the gun's safety was on, but the dim light made it impossible. 'I'll do anything you want if you'll just leave her alone.'

Something passed over Brent's face, a glimmer of recognition, and for a miraculous moment Anders thought he was about to proffer his terms.

'Is that what you told your dad when he beat up your mom?'

Brent's question slammed Anders like a club to his gut, knocking the breath out of him. He took at step backward to keep his balance as his world briefly went silent and his vision suffered a blackout.

Brent laughed, obviously pleased with the reaction he'd provoked. Anders stared at him and tried to refocus, to figure out what he knew and how he'd found out, but his father's voice raided his brain. '*Get my rifle, Anders.*'

'What'd you promise your dad, Anders?' Brent persisted. 'What did you say to *him* so he'd leave your mom alone?'

He struggled to listen to Brent's questions, to make sense of them and determine what answer he could give to help Olivia, but the other voice wouldn't let up. '*Get my rifle, Anders.*'

'Tell me. Tell me what you said to your father.'

*He'd come home from school to find his dad in the middle of one of his tirades against his mom, against the world, and Levi whimpering on the floor, cowering against the leg of the coffee table. He knew the dog was hurt, and he knew who'd hurt him.*

Brent rested the pistol right against Olivia's head and she gave a short cry.

'Please stop,' Anders whispered.

Brent pressed harder, forcing her head to tilt to the side. 'What was that? Are you asking *me* to stop? Or is that the answer to my question?'

'You.' He swallowed, but his mouth was too dry, his breathing too rapid. 'I'm asking you to stop.'

*He ran to the dog, and when his mom tried to run to him, his dad stopped her. Physically. With force. He didn't merely yell, or restrain her. He swiped her hard and knocked her against the wall, shocking Anders. He'd always known, but it was the first time he'd witnessed the abuse.*

'That's too bad,' Brent said, 'because I wanted an answer to my question.' Olivia's sobs grew louder, more desperate. She attempted to move, but when Brent gripped her neck tighter and whispered something into her ear, she stiffened.

'*Get my rifle, Anders.*'

*He'd resisted the instruction, and when his mom spoke up in his defence, his dad hit her again, cutting her lip open and painting her mouth and chin with an unusual amount of blood. So he acquiesced and retrieved the gun from his parents' bedroom closet, thinking the only way to protect his mom was to do as his father asked.*

'*Bring it here.*'

*He stood silent at the entrance to the family room, holding the Winchester in one small hand and the bullets in the other, his head down but his eyes looking up with hate at the ogre across the room.*

'*Bring it here!*' *The second time the command was so loud, so sharp, that he jumped.*

'I'll tell you if you stop,' he said. 'I'll tell you anything you want to know.'

Brent grinned with satisfaction. He eased up on the pressure, and Olivia closed her eyes in brief relief.

*His hands were shaking when he handed over the rifle. He dumped the few bullets into his father's sweaty palm.*

'*You remember how to use this, don't you?*'

*Of course he did. It had been drilled into his head during their one failed hunting trip. They'd never taken another because Anders had been incapable of shooting at anything alive. His father had been disgusted with him.*

*He stared at the floor in front of him and answered with the slightest nod. He watched from the corner of his eye as* his father loaded the rounds into the rifle and levered one into the chamber. When he finished, he held it out to Anders.

'I'll bet you never told Olivia much about your father, did you?'

Anders gazed at Brent. 'What do you want to know?'

'Actually, I already know everything I need to know.' Brent shrugged. 'I just want to hear you say it. Olivia should hear it, too, don't you think?'

'*What?*' His shallow breathing was making it difficult to get air into his lungs. The walls of the hut began to undulate. 'Hear me say *what?*'

'I want you to tell Olivia what you said to your father so he'd stop hurting your mother. What did you do to save your mom, Anders? And the dog. What did you do to save the dog? Hmm? I think Olivia would find it quite relevant. After all, I think she still believes you might just save *her.*'

*'I want you to take the dog outside and put it out of its misery.'*

*He jerked his head up in disbelief as his mother cried out, 'Peter, no!' He made the mistake of looking into her eyes in the same instant his dad reacted to her objection by smacking her across the face again. The force of his assault was so strong this time that her head hit the corner of the wall with a sickening thud before she fell to the floor.*

*Something broke in Anders when she cried out and then hit the floor. Some fear rose up in him that his father would murder his mother if he didn't stop him, and he lunged for the man in a rage. At twelve years old, he was no match for him, but in the ensuing scuffle, the gun discharged twice. The first bullet ricocheted off the tile floor and, unbeknownst to either of them, hit his mother in the leg.*

'Tell us, Anders.'

*The second bullet hit Levi, killing him instantly.*

'I . . .' The words stuck in his throat.

'Andy.'

He looked briefly at Lenny, who'd muttered his name to get his attention.

'Tell us,' Brent insisted, pulling him back. 'Tell us and I'll move the gun away from Olivia's head.'

'I . . . I didn't do anything. I didn't stop him.'

Brent smiled. 'Hear that, babe?' he said at Olivia's ear. 'He didn't do a damn thing to save his mom.' And then, just as he'd promised, he readjusted his aim. At Anders. 'In fact, you killed the dog, didn't you?'

Olivia gasped, and Anders made the mistake of looking at her directly. She regarded him with horror.

'I . . .' he began quietly, shaking his head at her. But words wouldn't come.

'Andy!' Lenny tried again. 'You're smarter than him! Don't let him play games with you!'

Brent kept on, relentless. 'And you helped him shoot your mom, didn't you? You might have even shot the bullet that hit her.' How did this man know these things? Even Lenny didn't know these things. 'Aren't I right, Anders? It was mere luck that you didn't kill your mom, too, wasn't it?'

Suddenly Brent's tone changed and he leaned forward. His voice was so soft that Anders had to strain to hear him. 'Well, guess what, my friends. Anders's *luck* has just run out.'

A wave of nausea gripped Anders's stomach. He tried to battle the thoughts invading his head. Tried to think. He kept seeing the family room of his youth, with its bright white walls splattered in blood and the Florida sun streaming through the windows, mocking them. The *family* room, his mom had always called it, and at times he'd despised her for that.

*You're smarter than him.* Lenny's voice played in his head. *Don't let him play games with you.* It had taken Anders years to understand that everything his dad did was just another play in the power game, another chance to demonstrate his control over others, but he *had* finally understood. He'd learned.

But he'd forgotten what else he'd learned. He'd forgotten that sometimes it wasn't simply a matter of stopping the game. He'd tried that back then and he'd tried that now and both times he'd failed miserably. If he couldn't stop the game, he had to play it. He knew how. He'd learned that, too, though he'd never wanted to admit it. And he'd learned from one of the best.

*Don't let him play games with you.* Anders stared at Brent and studied the man as if seeing him for the first time. He'd been working under the mistaken assumption that Brent might take Olivia's life and, quite possibly, his own, if Anders didn't stop him first. Yet Brent, too, viewed everything as a game, one he believed he would always win. Anders realized now that as long as he did nothing to disabuse Brent of this notion, Olivia would be safe. Brent might have killed Leng, but Leng was disposable in Brent's mind. He wouldn't kill Anders, though, not yet, not if he believed Anders had something he needed, and he most certainly wouldn't kill Olivia because she was the prize. Lenny was still a wildcard. Anders believed he could save them all if he simply played the game and kept it going until either Mayfield or the cops showed up. *If* they showed up.

He also believed – no, he *knew* – he was smart enough to play it better. Luck would have nothing to do with it.

He took a step forward and left doubt at his back.

Brent sensed the change. He still had the gun trained on Anders but his arm was tighter, his expression had dropped the smirk. But Anders looked right through the ready weapon and peered into the man's eyes.

'What will you do when you can't get the drugs anymore?'

The question wasn't at all what Brent was expecting and

Anders saw him relax again, just slightly. He didn't bother answering, safe in his belief that Anders was the ignorant one.

Anders took another step.

'Back off.'

'What will you do when you have no way to wipe out the memory of what you've done to her?'

'That's like asking me what I will do when the sun goes out.'

'Won't ever happen, is that it?'

Brent just blinked slowly.

'You've got too much on her father, right?'

'I have no idea what you're referring to.'

'No? You obviously had more champagne than I did back in Kenya.'

Brent laughed, but it lacked the self-assuredness of earlier.

'You must not remember your response when I asked you if you were afraid of her father.' Brent waited for more, stone-faced. 'You said I had it "backwards".'

One more step.

'I said back off, mate.' Brent tightened his grip on Olivia. 'I'll kill her.'

'No, you won't.'

Olivia began to moan.

'I have no plans to back off, Brent. So kill me now.' He motioned to Lenny. 'Kill both of us. Take her and take your chances.'

'Anders, stop it!' she cried. 'He'll do it.'

He continued to stare at Brent as he answered her plea. 'He won't kill you. He might kill us, but he won't kill you. Will you, Brent? Because then she's all yours, and no one will catch you. Like you said, you'll be long gone.'

Even as he walked closer, Anders questioned why he was taunting the man. There was a fine line between participating in Brent's game and causing him to abandon the whole thing in anger, frustration and, if Anders wasn't careful, desperation. But something told him he still had a distance to go before he crossed that line.

'But think very carefully before you do it. Because what happens if you kill us, and then you find out I knew more than you did. I knew things were no longer *backwards*? What happens if the odds aren't in your favour anymore? If you suddenly discover you no longer have anything hanging over Lawrence Mayfield's head? And your drug supply comes to a screeching stop?'

He could see Brent thinking, trying to assemble the puzzle pieces.

'Are you curious as to what I'm talking about?' He took one last step and now he stood mere feet in front of them. He was close enough to take the gun if Brent allowed him to. 'I've learned a lot since our conversation in Kenya. Give me the gun and I'll tell you everything you need to know.' He raised an eyebrow. 'Before it's too late.'

He reached out his hand, almost believing Brent might just let go of the weapon suspended inches from Anders's grasp. Almost, but not quite.

'I will always have something hanging over his head. I'm the brains behind his empire.'

'Really? Give me the gun and maybe I'll forget you said that when I testify at his extradition hearing.'

Olivia gasped, causing Brent to cast a fleeting glance at her. Without stopping to debate the merits of his decision, Anders reacted and grabbed for the barrel while he simultaneously tried to push it to the side and out of the line to his heart. But in the instant he went for the gun, Brent pulled the trigger. Olivia let out a high scream and began to kick and flail to escape Brent's inattentive grasp. The bullet ripped through Anders's left shoulder and knocked him to the ground, but with his right hand he held tight to Brent's wrist and brought him off the crate and down onto the dirt with him. The flashlight tumbled onto its side.

Anders fought to force Brent to release the gun so Olivia had a chance of grabbing hold of it. He and Brent wrestled on the ground, each struggling to gain the advantage. He could see Olivia climbing to her feet. 'Be ready!' he called to her. As his warm blood soaked the sleeve of his shirt and the burning pain of the bullet wound reached his brain, he tightened his grip, twisting, as he dug his fingers into the underside of Brent's wrist to cause his hand to open reflexively. Brent grunted just before the gun dropped to the ground.

As if she'd been waiting for the moment her whole life, Olivia picked up the gun without hesitation and pointed it at Brent's head. 'Get away from him!' she ordered.

But both Brent and Anders ignored her. Brent, perhaps, because he didn't think she'd shoot, and Anders because his success at forcing Brent to drop the gun had given him a euphoric sense of power that left him craving more. He suddenly wanted one thing, and one thing only: to inflict on Brent the same pain Brent had inflicted on Olivia. His brain had harnessed his surging adrenalin and pooled it with years of bridled rage, and Brent became the target for their simultaneous release.

With both arms he let loose and pummelled the momentarily surprised face beneath him. Brent quickly began to fight back, but Anders's assault was unrelenting and brutal. Whatever supernatural force had taken hold of him rendered Brent incapable of meaningful defence. Anders's lighter weight was not an obstacle; his mangled shoulder and injured rib were not obstacles. With each strike his strength grew. In the periphery of his mind he heard Lenny calling to him, ordering him to stop – 'He's not your dad!' – but the mention of his father, the speaking of it out loud, only fuelled his rampage.

It was Olivia's voice, louder and stronger this time, that brought him back.

'I said, *get away from him*!'

Anders stopped mid-swing, stunned. The command had been meant for him.

Suddenly a shot rang out and both entangled men started from the sound of it. Dried mud sprinkled to the ground from where the bullet had hit the ceiling, and Anders felt Brent give up the struggle.

With his good arm he pushed Brent away and scrambled to his feet. Olivia glanced at him, at his shoulder, but just as quickly refocused her attention on Brent. He'd sat up and was attempting to stand. She took a step closer and, with the hand holding the gun, motioned at the crate. 'Go sit down.' She delivered the words with eerie composure.

Brent complied, staggering a bit. Yet when he collapsed sitting on the crate and raised his bloody face to them, the lingering confidence remained. The discharge of the gun might have convinced him to do as she asked, but he still wasn't afraid of her.

Anders moved slowly to Lenny and laboured to untie his hands and feet with only his right hand. He was all too aware now of the fierce pain shooting down his left arm and through his back.

'You might want to say your prayers, if you have any left.'

Anders stopped and turned at Olivia's words.

She stood several feet in front of Brent, far enough away where he couldn't try to pull the same stunt Anders had just pulled. She held her arms straight out in front of her, both hands on the pistol as if she'd been holding such weapons her whole life. He guessed she probably had.

'Olivia?'

'This is between me and Brent, Anders.'

Anders glanced at Lenny, but if he had an opinion, he wasn't sharing it. He lowered his eyes as if he was just trying to endure his pain one minute at a time.

'Don't do it, Olivia.'

He saw her swallow, he saw her thinking.

'It's self-defence.'

'No, it's not. You don't have to do this for us to leave here alive.' Despite his own actions a moment before, he added, 'It won't make you feel better.'

Her eyes widened and she nodded. 'Yes, actually, it will.' She'd given it some thought.

'I don't think so.'

'He deserves it. *I* deserve it.'

'You're right. But if you do it, you'll have to live with it forever. Don't let him do that to you. Don't let him hurt you one more time.'

For just an instant, she directed her angry stare at him.

'Shut up, Anders! You're wrong! If he walks the earth, I'll never rest.'

He glanced at Brent and saw the truth of Olivia's words in his eyes. They lacked fear. He wasn't afraid because he didn't believe she had it in her. He thought he still controlled her and when this ended, he still would.

Anders knew then she was right. Even sitting in a prison somewhere, Brent would pursue her. Somehow, some way. Who was Anders to tell her she didn't have a right to set herself free? If she'd been held physically captive, no one would question her right to kill her captor to escape. Why was this any different?

Brent stood. He cast a brief glance in Anders's direction and his wrecked face wore the smug look of a victor. Olivia stepped back. 'Sit down!'

'Olivia!' Anders said her name this time as a warning. He rose and started toward her, to get to her and the gun before Brent.

'Let's end this now, babe.' Brent moved closer to Olivia as he talked. 'You have no intention of shooting me, so let's do this the easy—'

Anders saw her eyes squeeze shut immediately after he heard the crack of the gun beneath her scream; Brent's head jerked back, a crimson spot bloomed on his forehead, and he collapsed in a crumple to the ground. She dropped the gun as if it burned her hand and covered her face just as Anders reached her. He clutched at her, encircling her with both arms and using his good one to push her head into the hollow of his uninjured shoulder. She let out an excruciating howl, and the pain in his shoulder was nothing compared to the sound of her anguish in his ear. Together they lowered themselves to the ground, where they remained, clinging to each other, until the bulb in the flashlight died out and they were plunged into darkness.

# 25

SHE CONTINUED to cling to him, silently, throughout the remainder of the ordeal. When her father and Makena arrived, she didn't acknowledge her father's presence. When Makena tried to comfort her, she didn't speak. When Makena ministered to Lenny in preparation for getting him to a hospital in Dar es Salaam, she didn't watch. When Makena also tried to tend Anders's shoulder and he stubbornly refused, she didn't insist that he accept Makena's care. Even when, to Mayfield's surprise, officials from the American embassy showed up and, with the help of the Tanzanian police, took him into custody, she didn't seem to notice his blustering departure. Even as the authorities began to question the three of them – Anders, Lenny, and Olivia – she appeared not to hear their voices. He knew she did, though, because when they suggested talking to each of them separately, she tightened her grip on his waist. Fearing that his friend was much worse than he let on, Anders insisted that Lenny be treated before he endured further interrogation, and they acquiesced.

She clung to him even as he trailed the makeshift stretcher that carried Lenny out to a van.

'We're going to follow you,' he told Lenny as they loaded him in. But Lenny shook his head and said, 'Just finish with them and get back to camp with her,' referring to Olivia as if she wasn't right next to Anders listening to every word. 'I'll be okay.' Anders understood the words to mean *she needs you more*.

'What did he do to you?' He wanted Lenny to tell him something, anything, to let him know he'd see him again.

Lenny motioned to his feet. 'This is the worst of it, Andy, trust me.' Seeing it wasn't enough, he added, 'He cut the Achilles tendons clean through.'


SHE CLUNG to him when they returned to the storage hut to finish making their statement to the Tanzanian police. He baulked at going back inside because he knew it would only make her worse, but she wouldn't leave his side and the cops claimed it would 'be best' for getting the details right. From the way they said it, he took that to mean he didn't have a choice. To his relief, Brent's corpse had been removed. He assumed Leng's had been taken out of the classroom by then, too.

He did all of the talking about what had happened. He emphasized several times that she'd had no choice but to fire the shot that killed Brent, that she'd done it in self-defence, but when they tried to confirm this with her, she wouldn't respond. She wouldn't even look at them.

In the end, he didn't think it mattered. They didn't seem too upset by Brent's demise.


ON THE ride back to the camp, she sat with him in the middle row as Makena drove. She leaned in close with one arm still around his waist and appeared to be staring at his bloody shoulder. He tried to talk to her, but still, she didn't speak.

Tory greeted them with a nurse and a first aid kit, and at Makena's continued urging, Anders finally let the nurse treat and dress his wound and give him antibiotics. He knew a bullet wasn't lodged in his shoulder, the cops had confirmed they'd found all three that had been fired in the hut, but he thought Olivia needed to see the wound being stitched and know that he was okay.

In the tent, after having already asked Tory to get the bucket filled, he gently suggested she take a shower. She nodded in agreement, but made no move to make it happen. He knew, psychologically even more than physically, she needed one. He took her hand and led her to the back of the tent, to the dark corner where the showerhead delivered its weak spray onto the concrete drain pad. Slowly, carefully, he unbuttoned her shirt and removed it, and then grasped at the bottom of the clingy camisole underneath and lifted it over her head. Like a child, she cooperated, moving or raising her arms at the appropriate time but otherwise offering no assistance. He found the zipper at the side of her skirt, lowered it, and then worked the skirt and her panties down her hips. He'd barely touched her calf, but in the way a horse shows its hoof at a similar touch, she took it as a signal and lifted one foot and then the other to step out of the garments. His throat tightened and he fought back tears.

As he rose, he turned her around so she wouldn't see his face. He worked the handle of the faucet, turning it just slightly until he'd confirmed the water temperature wasn't too hot, and then he twisted it to open fully.

She stood mute and motionless as the water cascaded over her head and down her skin. He reached for the shampoo, his movements slowed by the weight of his grief. He shampooed her hair, choking up again when he saw the tattoo, and then he lightly soaped her body with a washcloth and watched the dirt slide down her skin and into the drain. He remained behind her as he worked, not wanting her to see how close he was to breaking too, yet at the same time he willed her to turn around and speak just one word to him. One word was all he needed. She did neither.

Once finished, he shut the valve to save what water remained for his own shower after he'd put her to bed. He towelled her dry and slowly combed the tangles from her hair.

He pulled a clean T-shirt from his bag and lowered it over her head. Again, she did only what was necessary to get her arms through the holes.

Makena had given him some sedatives to help her sleep, and he looked at them now on the bathroom sink. If she noticed him considering them, she gave him no indication. In his mind's eye, he imagined handing her the pills and a bottle of water, and he knew she would obey and swallow them down without protest. But he couldn't do it. Perhaps sleep was what she needed, and the sedatives might guarantee sleep, but he simply couldn't do it. He couldn't ask her to swallow another pill.

He walked her to the bed, pulled back the covers and, after she'd lain down and curled up into a ball, he tucked her in. He bent down next to the edge of the mattress and looked at her face, inches from his. With one hand on the back of her wet head, he leaned in and kissed her forehead. She didn't say anything, and her blank expression otherwise showed no movement, no indication of pleasure or pain, but much to his relief, she finally raised her eyes and met his. He bit his lip and held in the violent shuddering that threatened to consume him, until a moment later, when she lowered her lids and pretended to drift off to sleep.

NOT LONG AFTER, he did break. He should have seen it coming, but he didn't. It caught him completely unawares.

He waited until she fell asleep before wriggling out of his wet clothes to take his shower. Even though the nurse had dressed his injury well, he had to scrub his skin to remove the dried blood that had found its way to other parts of his body. He became angry at having to work so hard at erasing the evidence of the night's horror. At some point, the anger dissolved into tears and they flowed unbidden, mixing with the water running down his face. He was powerless to stop them, though at first he tried. Overwhelmed by his despair, he finally fell to his knees on the hard, wet floor and, burying his face in a soaked towel to muffle the sounds, just let them come. When the water ran out, he sat there, shivering and cold, and sobbed some more.

If someone had asked him later what, exactly, he'd been crying about, he probably wouldn't have been able to name just one thing. Of course he was crying for Olivia, for what she'd done in the storage hut and what she'd have to live with because of it. Her victim might have been her captor, but at one time, long ago, he'd also been her best friend. And of course he was crying for what they'd all done to her – the rape, to be sure – but also the pills, and the lies, and how they'd used her as a pawn in their own warped games.

But he was also crying for himself, and he felt miserable and selfish for it. He thought of what he'd done to Lenny, and Shel's biting words – *it's like you handed her a gun to shoot him with* – and how Lenny had stuck by him nevertheless and suffered even more for his loyalty. He pictured Shel in the doorway to the beach house, her face open and vulnerable, unable to mask the pain he'd caused her and yet always willing to give him another chance. He cried harder at the image because she was probably the one person who was capable of truly comforting him just then, and she was a world away.

And finally, he was crying for his mother, and his stubborn refusal to understand her, and his inability to save the one thing that gave her comfort when she had no one else: Levi.

THE CHILDREN from the school came to visit Olivia the next day, bearing wildflowers and gifts of handmade beaded jewellery. That morning, though she still moved numbly about the tent, she did so of her own accord. She tried to whisper apologies to him for her catatonic state the night before, but he merely took her in his arms again and refused to hear them. After dressing herself and braiding her hair, which he found odd because he'd never before seen her wear her hair in a braid, she held his hand and walked with him to the breakfast grove. She greeted the children and their teacher with smiles and subdued conversation. Coffee in hand, he watched her *ooh* and *ah* over the gifts and ask the kids about the day's lessons. When they didn't understand because she'd forgotten to switch languages, and she let out a genuine laugh and started all over in the tongue he didn't understand, he tried to pretend he wasn't on the verge of more tears.

He'd known it from the first day at the camp in Kenya, but only now did he admit the truth of his knowledge.

He was witnessing the one thing that gave *her* comfort, and despite what she might argue, it wasn't him.

HE RETURNED to the hill where he'd talked to Shel while he'd watched Olivia walk into Brent's trap. This time he planned to call the third woman who mattered to him. He neglected again to account for the time difference when he placed the call, and he winced when he heard his mom's groggy, anxious voice. Of course she sounded anxious. Her youngest son was in Africa and her phone was ringing in the middle of the night.

'Mom, it's me.' Not wanting her to worry any longer than necessary, he added quickly, 'I'm just calling to tell you I'm fine, everything's okay. I found Olivia.'

'Anders? Oh, honey, is that you?' Her words were staggered because she hadn't anticipated the delay. 'You're okay? Are you sure? Olivia's okay? You're still in Africa?' She was rambling, still half-asleep.

'Yeah, I'm still in Africa, and we're all okay. I just wanted you to know that. I didn't want you to worry.'

It was quiet for a moment; she'd already learned to wait. Then, 'Oh, thank you, baby. I'm so glad you called. I was sick with worry.'

'I also wanted to tell you something else. I—'

'What is it?'

'I wanted to say . . .' He took a deep breath. How to explain from so far away, and so long after? 'I wanted to tell you I'm sorry—'

'What are you talking about, Anders?'

'I don't know, for not being more patient with you, I guess. And for—'

'What? Baby, are you sure you're okay? What are you talking about? You're always patient with me. You are the kindest, gentlest man I know. You're more than a mother could ever ask for.'

His ribcage expanded with years of pent-up emotion. For years he'd resented what he thought of as her ability to deny the past, but now he knew she hadn't denied it; she'd merely decided long ago to move on and not let it ruin her future. And she'd convinced herself that he'd done the same.

'I'm talking about Dad,' he blurted. 'I'm sorry I didn't stop him that day. I'm sorry I wasn't able to help you. I'm sorry I didn't save Levi. And I'm sorry I've been mad at you ever since. And mad at myself.'

The line was silent for a long time, much longer than any transmission delay.

When she spoke, her voice had taken on a breathy, stunned tone; it was so soft, he barely heard her. She simply said, 'Anders.' She said his name as if it was the answer to a long-held question, though not the one she'd been expecting. Then, when he didn't speak, she whispered, 'What in God's name has happened over there?'

\*

EVERY MORNING, and then again just before dinner, he called the hospital in Dar es Salaam for updates on Lenny. Lenny's room had no phone, so Anders didn't have the opportunity to speak with him directly. By all accounts, though, he was steadily improving and, with the proper assistance, would soon be able to manage the long-distance travel back to the States.

The inability to talk to Lenny made Anders anxious to leave the camp, but he tried to hide his feelings from Olivia. After a few days, she resumed her teaching activities with the children from the village, though she stayed onsite and let their teacher bring them to her. Anders could see she benefited from their visits, and he figured she was better off busy at the camp than bored in Dar es Salaam, sitting in the waiting room of a hospital with too much time on her hands.

But when he called the hospital on the eighth day, and they informed him Lenny was almost ready to be discharged, he recognized it was time to go home.


AFTER DINNER, after all the other guests had retired to their tents for the night, he asked her to sit with him on the elevated deck where earlier they'd all watched the sunset. He didn't plan to broach the subject there; he intended to wait until the privacy of their tent. Maybe he was stalling, or maybe he just wanted to immerse himself in the beauty of the African night one more time before leaving it behind.

The embers in the fire pit still glowed bright and warmed them. It reminded him of the fire pit on their deck at the beach, and he wondered if in the silence she'd had the same thought. Closing his eyes, he reached for her hand and tried to imagine they were there. He tried to imagine if things would ever feel the same between them again.

'Anders?' Her voice drifted over through the still air, and

he opened his eyes to meet her stare. 'What was he referring to, about Crystal?'

It shouldn't have, but the question surprised him. In the past week, neither had mentioned anything remotely related to what had happened at the school. He knew she'd eventually want to talk about it, indeed, would *need* to, but he didn't think the subject of Crystal would be high on the list. Certainly not the first topic to be discussed.

'I thought you'd died,' he reminded her. And then he slowly took her through all the steps he'd taken to get information after the accident. All of it he'd already explained many times, but he thought she needed to hear it again to understand how bad off he'd been when he succumbed to Crystal's demands. 'But I kept thinking to myself, what if you were alive? What if they'd all lied to me? Lenny suggested I ask Crystal for help. She works at the hospital you were in, in billing.'

Olivia waited. He tried to read her face for signals, but she wasn't giving any.

'But she wouldn't help me unless . . .' He shrugged. He didn't need to say it. She wasn't stupid. 'I wasn't in my right mind. I'd reached a point where I didn't know what else to do, and I let her get to me one day. She claimed she had your files, but she wouldn't give them to me. I lost it. I tore up her house looking for them, and when I didn't find them, I gave in. I was ready to do *anything* at that point to get answers.' He paused. 'I don't know what else to tell you.'

'Did Lenny know?'

'Well, he knew what she wanted in exchange for her help. I'd told him. But no, he didn't know it finally happened, not until afterwards.' He remembered again the look on Shel's face on his doorstep, when she'd told him Lenny knew.

They still held hands and Olivia surprised him by giving his a squeeze.

'Did *you* tell him?'

'No, she did.' He sighed. 'I'm sorry. It's not something I'm proud of.'

'Don't be sorry.' As if to answer the astonishment on his face, she added, 'Like you said, you were going to do whatever it took to get answers, and you did. You found me.' She knew the folder had been empty; he'd told her that before, too. She knew it was the matchbook that led him to her.

She scooted her chair so their knees touched and they faced each other. 'Anders?' She took both of his hands in hers and waited for him to look her in the eye. 'You saved my life. No one else was willing to do that for me. *You saved my life.*'

THEY LISTENED to the bellows of hippopotamuses as the beasts made their way up from the river to the grassy areas at the edge of camp. It'd happened every night since they'd been at this camp, though this was the first time they'd concentrated so intently on the sound.

When it died down, she said, 'Makena said he's not going to fight extradition.'

He looked at her. She'd said it the same way she might have told him her plans for the children the next day. 'Really?' He waited, afraid to ask what more Makena had learned.

She nodded slowly. 'She said he probably won't even fight the charge when he gets back. He's going to admit to everything in hopes they'll cut him a deal.'

'When did she—?'

'She went to see him. For some reason, she still has sympathy left for the man.' She let out a small, sarcastic laugh. 'He told her that he'd been importing drugs on a small scale for years, but Brent discovered what he was doing back when he'd worked with him during those summers, and he helped him grow it into something much larger and much more lucrative.' She shrugged. 'Doesn't surprise me too much. Brent always *was* a lot smarter than my father.'

'Brent was blackmailing him.' He'd stated it, but she treated it as a question.

'Yeah. He still claims he didn't know Brent was behind –' she stopped and took a deep breath '– Jimmy's. He says he immediately began receiving anonymous threats warning him against pursuing the guys involved, and the threats led him to believe that both he *and* Brent were at risk. Apparently some of the guys in the bar had helped with the drug-running.'

Anders thought about Mayfield's predicament. It made sense, his decision to experiment with the Cranitex. If he could make Olivia forget what had happened, he'd spare her the trauma and, at the same time, save himself and Brent. And it also explained why he'd let Brent try to take her out of Florida, once he realized she'd stopped taking the drug.

'So our accident *was* an accident?' he asked, thinking out loud.

'I guess. He says Brent wanted to handle getting me back to Connecticut, and that the man he paid to do the job botched it big time. I wasn't supposed to get hurt.' She carefully touched her index finger to the bottom of each eye, wiping at tears that hadn't yet fallen. 'But like he said at the airport, he took advantage of their screw-up. They got me back before I ever had a chance to tell you what had happened.' She turned and gave him the sweetest, warmest smile he'd ever seen. 'But they misjudged us, didn't they? They miscalculated my taste in men.' She laughed a little, a genuine laugh this time, and it told him she was going to be okay.

He reached under her hair and rubbed the back of her neck where the tattoo was, then pulled her close and kissed her.

'I need to get to Dar es Salaam. They're going to discharge Lenny soon, and I need to be there to help him.' He hesitated, but thinking of how well she'd reacted to the incident with

Crystal, how composed she'd been relaying all the information about her dad, he plunged into the next question, the one he'd intended to save for the tent. 'Will you come with me?'

She nodded slowly. 'We should leave first thing tomorrow morning.'

'Really?' He'd thought if she agreed, she'd need a few days, at least. 'Tomorrow? You're willing to go so soon?'

'Of course. You need to get there.'

He was so pleased with her answer that he grabbed her head and planted another kiss on her lips, this one loud and dramatic. 'I can't wait till we're home. I can't wait to walk through that door and have you there with me again.'

She went stiff, and as quickly as he'd made his assumption, just as quickly he realized it had been the wrong one.

'Is that your way of saying you don't want to stay here?' she asked, eyes down, as he released his grip.

He lightly rubbed the tops of her hands. He didn't know how to answer. 'What I *want* is to be with you.' She watched his fingers with vacant eyes, as if she was a bystander and someone else was the recipient of his caresses.

'But you'd prefer that to be in Florida, right?' When he sighed, she added, 'I guess that's a yes.'

'Olivia,' he lowered his voice to match hers. He wished he hadn't brought it up. He, too, had misjudged; she was still too fragile. 'Florida is my home. But if you need us to be here for now, then we'll be here. We'll get Lenny home and we'll come back.'

She grunted and gave him a look of disbelief. 'Do you know what you're—?'

'The place doesn't matter.'

'Oh, it matters all right. I don't want you to stay with me out of obligation, out of some misguided pity.' Her eyes welled up and it scared him. This conversation was definitely happening way too soon. She was in no condition to handle it, and he wasn't too sure he was, either.

She turned to stare into the fire and the single tear that fell slowly down her cheek glistened orange in the light. 'Look at me.' When she did, he wiped it away with his thumb. 'You need to separate out what we're talking about, okay? Wanting to be with you is not the same as wanting or not wanting to be in Africa. Do you understand?'

'Of course it is. This is my home, just like Florida is your home.'

He opened his mouth to speak. He wanted to say, *No, Connecticut is your home*, but he knew it wasn't true. She had nothing there, not really. She'd been born in Africa, though even that, he knew, wasn't why she felt as she did.

'Well, by your logic, your not wanting to return to Florida is also the equivalent of not wanting to be with me. Neither one of us loves the other *enough*, is that it?'

Her mouth fell open. 'Anders,' she whispered.

He suddenly found himself asking her the questions that had been haunting him since Connecticut. 'If you love this place so much, why didn't you talk about it more? How come you never told me you wanted to live here?'

Her despair hardened into anger. 'I could ask you the same thing.'

'What do you mean? What are you *talking* about?'

As the conversation escalated, he realized they'd never had an argument of this magnitude; they'd never even had an argument at all that he could remember.

She answered his questions with one of her own. 'What I mean is, why didn't you ever tell me about your dad?'

The question stunned him, and in his shock he just stared at her. What could he say? Because I didn't want to scare you away? Because I knew any woman in her right mind would run screaming from the son of such a man?

When he failed to answer, she looked up at him, almost

apologetically, and slowly shrugged. 'I just need to stay here.'
She sounded weary. Incredibly weary. 'I just need to be here.'
He'd risked his life for her, but maybe it still wasn't enough.
For either of them.

HE OFFERED to stay longer until she knew where she would
go and what she would do, but she had Makena and so she
declined. In the brief period before his departure, they quickly
transformed from reluctant ex-lovers to exceedingly polite
friends, and it broke his heart. He believed it also broke Olivia's,
and even Makena's. Maybe Makena's even more.

When she first heard he was leaving, she paid a visit to
their tent while Olivia was in the library with the children. He
tried to busy himself with packing his few possessions, but she
stood with her arms crossed and waited patiently for him to
finish and give her his full attention. He finally sat on the bed
and waited for the lecture he knew was coming.

'This is the wrong thing to do.'

'She essentially asked me to leave. What am I supposed to
do?'

She sat next to him and took his hand. He let her pull it
across to her lap. 'Stay.'

He sighed.

'She needs you.'

'I don't think so.'

'I know so.'

'She's convinced I'd be staying only because I feel sorry
for her or something. "Misguided pity" I think she called it.'

'Is she right?'

'No! Of course not.'

'Then convince her otherwise. She needs you to say it.'

'I thought I did.' He stood and walked to the opening in the
tent, gazed out over the dirt path and beyond it, at the tall

grasses blocking the view of the riverbed where the hippos gathered. *Could* he stay here, in her world? He couldn't even imagine what he'd do, how he'd spend his days. They couldn't be camp guests forever. Where would they live? How would they support themselves? She might be independently wealthy – though even that, now, was questionable – but *he* wasn't, and he wasn't willing to sponge off her the rest of his life. Would his life be spent on the edge of hers, always wondering what she was saying when she spoke in Swahili, always the outsider? Had she already asked herself these questions about him? Is that why she'd pulled away so quickly? He didn't understand how things could have changed so much in the span of a few weeks. They'd been so happy together in Florida, before the accident. He didn't understand why she couldn't just come back with him. He didn't understand why she couldn't be happy there again.

Makena rose from the bed and came to stand next to him, as if waiting for him to reach a verdict. He finally met her eye. 'I need to help Lenny get home.'

She touched his shoulder. 'As you should. But then you should come back. She *needs* you to come back.'

AT DAWN on his last day, he stood with Olivia at the side of the Land Rover, waiting for the guide who would drive him into Dar es Salaam. He shuffled his feet in the dirt; she stood about a foot away and pretended not to notice.

'Do you think you'll go see your dad before they take him back to the States?'

She shook her head. He waited, and she said, 'I have no desire to see him ever again.'

He nodded. To avoid looking at each other, they both watched the subdued commotion of the kitchen staff getting ready for the first meal of the day in the grove. The figures in the distance appeared to them as nothing more than shadows through the morning mist, but the noises of dishes and silverware being set out reached them easily.

'Olivia?'

She glanced up at him, a look of hopeful anticipation in her eyes.

'I think . . . after Brent found out what your dad was doing, and worked his way in deeper over the years—'

She looked away angrily; whatever she thought he'd been about to say, what he'd just said wasn't it. 'Don't make excuses for him. It's inexcusable.'

'I'm not. It *is* inexcusable. But—'

'Did you know my father and Brent investigated you?' she asked, her eyes narrowed. The question took him by surprise for its content, but also for the sudden, sharp tone in which she asked it. 'Did Makena tell you?' He shook his head slightly. 'That's how he knew about your mom and dad. They'd gotten hold of the files, so he knew everything. He knew the state stepped in. He knew you and your brother and sister had been in foster care for a few weeks.'

His mouth fell open. Even Karina and Stephen had never really known the real story of what had happened that day. Anders had refused to talk about it, and his mother told them the whole thing had been an accident. Her good intentions had backfired, though, because they'd always blamed Anders for the family's split, and had let him know it in the subtle way that kids can. 'But those records aren't public,' he stammered. 'They're supposed to be—'

Olivia scoffed, and he stopped talking. Of course Mayfield would have found a way around such protections.

He sighed. It didn't matter now. 'I only meant . . . I do think he loves you.'

She rolled her eyes.

'I think he simply didn't see a way out.'

'Yeah, well, neither did I.'

372

A rustle through the trees signalled the approach of the guide. He stopped when he saw them. 'Oh, excuse me, Ms Mayfield, Mr Erickson.' He nodded his head at Anders. 'Tory thought you were ready to depart.'

'Yes, I am. We're just ...'

The guide waved his understanding and stepped back to give them another minute.

'Well, you'd better go,' Olivia said quickly. She hugged him, the hug of a sister, and had difficulty looking him in the eye.

He refused to leave her like that.

He reached behind her neck, under her hair, and rubbed the spot where she had the tattoo. 'What about this?' He gave her a tender smile, wanting so badly for this last moment not to be awkward between them.

'I don't know. What do you think?' She grinned, a bit bashfully. Despite everything, she was trying, too. He could see that.

'Well, everyone who comes to Florida leaves with a souvenir.' With his other hand he touched the small of her back and pulled her close so that she pressed into him. 'I think you should just consider it your souvenir.'

He debated his next move. They'd barely touched each other since their conversation on the sundowner deck, but he felt it would be wrong to pretend everything before had never existed. He lowered his head, giving her time to protest, and when she didn't, he touched his lips to the side of hers, and her mouth found his. She whimpered a bit as he kissed her. His kiss was long, and hard and soft at the same time. It was deep, and desperate and sad.

And it was nothing like the kiss of a brother.

# 26

ANDERS'S SECOND visit to the airport in Dar es Salaam differed in every way from the first. The American embassy provided an attaché to accompany him and Lenny until they literally stepped onto the plane, or in Lenny's case, rolled onto it in a wheelchair. At each step along the way, airport personnel treated them like royalty, moving them to the front of lines and rushing to help with their luggage. At the gate, the ticket-taker informed them they'd been upgraded to the bulkhead in first class.

'You arrange all this to appease your guilt, Andy?' Lenny quipped when the attaché stepped aside to take a call on his cellphone. The comment didn't contain a trace of anger or even sarcasm, but still, it unnerved Anders. He stared down at Lenny, fumbling for a response. He was about to speak, to say 'I think we have Makena to thank' when Lenny beat him to it. 'It was a joke,' he said, his voice deadpan, convincing Anders it wasn't.

THEY ARRIVED in Dubai just after 11 p.m. for a three-hour layover and were on their own until they boarded the next flight to JFK at 2 a.m. Anders pushed Lenny down the jetway into the terminal; even approaching midnight, it buzzed with activity. Weary Europeans stood in line at a much too brightly lit McDonald's or huddled in groups on makeshift beds on the floor, clutching paper cups of coffee and talking rapidly in their native languages. Anders thought one group was arguing until they burst into laughter. A group of Arabs napped under a large tent on the upstairs level. He did a double take at the sight of a goat at the edge of their canvas mat until he realized it wasn't real; whether it was plastic, or possibly stuffed, he couldn't tell.

Unable to find a spot away from crowds, he finally chose a seat not far from a small cafe and coffee bar in case Lenny decided he was ready to eat. He propped his feet up on the wheel of Lenny's chair, crossed his arms over his chest and closed his eyes to rest them.

'You think Shel would be willing to pick us up in Orlando?' he asked.

'Don't really know.'

Lenny's level voice caused Anders to open his eyes to see the expression on his friend's face, but Lenny just stared vacantly at a luggage shop three storefronts down the terminal.

'I'll call her when we get to New York.'

'You do that.' A second later Anders's feet fell to the floor as Lenny began to wheel himself away. 'I need to take a piss.'

'Oh.' He swung his backpack over his shoulder and rose to follow him. 'Okay.'

'Alone.'

Anders sighed. He didn't argue, but he followed Lenny anyway, knowing *alone* was impossible.

Lenny had to have known Anders trailed him, but it wasn't until they were both inside the empty men's room that Lenny acknowledged him again.

'What the hell. Did you hear me?' His muscular arms bent at the elbows, his large hands still gripped each tyre of the wheelchair.

'Yeah, I heard you.' He unzipped the backpack.

'I'm not using that, Andy.'

Anders held out the small plastic urinal. 'You're not supposed to stand.'

'Fuck off.' Lenny passed the wall urinals and wheeled down to the last stall. It lacked a door, but was larger than the others. Anders followed him and dropped the container into his lap.

Lenny grabbed it and flung it back at him. It nicked Anders's right ear and tumbled to the tiled floor. 'I said, I'm not using that!'

A middle-aged man entered the bathroom and stared at them unabashedly before unzipping his trousers at the wall. Anders glared back at the man with the anger meant for Lenny. 'What are *you* staring at?' he mumbled as he bent over to retrieve the plastic urinal.

The man responded but, once again, Anders couldn't understand a single word. He just wanted to be home, though he wondered where home was. The beach house no longer qualified.

When the man left, Anders turned to Lenny. 'What's the matter with you?'

'What do you think's the matter with me?' Lenny was still shouting. 'Why are we here, huh? Where the hell is Olivia, Andy?'

It took Anders a moment to respond. 'I told you, she stayed at the camp.'

'I don't mean physically, you idiot!'

Anders grunted and looked away.

'Look at this!' Lenny motioned to his wrapped feet and Anders couldn't help but do as ordered. 'Just tell me it wasn't all for nothing.'

'I'm sorry, man. What do you want me to say? I'm sorry!' Now Anders was yelling, too. 'I'd switch places with you in an instant if I could.'

The room fell silent and the loudspeaker announced the boarding of a flight to Nairobi.

'What are you gonna do, Andy?'

'*What?*' He grunted again and threw up his hands in frustration. 'What are you talking about?'

'When we get back.'

'I don't know!' He took a step forward and offered the urinal again. 'Do you want this or not?' His tone suggested it would be the last time he'd ask, though of course it wouldn't be. They both knew he'd never let Lenny stand.

Lenny's deep-brown eyes searched Anders's face as he held out an arm to take it.

'I'll wait outside.'

'You didn't answer my question.'

Anders let out a sarcastic laugh. 'Which one?' But when he looked at Lenny, he knew. And he thought he answered truthfully, even if he didn't quite yet understand the answer himself.

'No.' He shook his head. 'No, it wasn't all for nothing.'

# Florida

# 27

ANDERS SAW Shel before she saw them. He and Lenny had just come off the train that took them from the gates to the main terminal, and as they entered the glass-walled corridor that led to the opposite side of security, he spotted her on the other side of the wall. She was engaged in an animated discussion with an elderly couple. The man pointed to Shel's shirt – she had the Tinkerbell tank on – and her grin widened and her arms began to fly as she launched into some tale. He could guess the situation: they were probably waiting for a grandchild to get off a plane, and Shel was giving them her expert opinion of how best to 'do' Disney World with their little charge. It wouldn't matter that they were locals, too; Shel was Disney's self-anointed biggest fan and her word was the gospel.

At the end of the corridor, Anders stopped pushing Lenny's wheelchair. He waited and watched to see how long it would take her to notice their arrival. But she saw them out of the corner of her eye almost immediately. She squealed, causing everyone in the vicinity to look, and issued a quick apology to the couple before dashing in their direction and knocking Anders back with the force of her hug. Lenny received a similar embrace; because he was seated, it lacked only the momentum of the running start.

'Oh my God! Oh my God!' She kept touching each of them, as if to confirm they existed in the flesh before her. Anders hadn't said much on the phone from New York when they'd called to ask her to meet them at the airport in Orlando, but he suspected Lenny had been more forthcoming about their harrowing days in Africa.

Shel handed over her keys to Anders in the parking garage and asked him to drive so she could talk to them about the trip. Anders smiled at that; as if the two activities were mutually exclusive.

She kept her word, asking so many questions that the fifty minute drive to Lenny's Deltona apartment felt like mere minutes. Though Olivia's name surfaced numerous times as they talked – she'd been the point of the trip, after all – somehow they all avoided the fact that she hadn't returned with Anders.

The nurse they'd arranged for Lenny was waiting in her car in the parking lot, and she popped out and took control as soon as she saw Anders unfold the wheelchair from Shel's trunk. Anders eyed the woman; her shapely figure modelled an otherwise staid uniform like it was the outer layer of a stripper's costume. 'He's gonna be just fine,' he said to Shel, and she laughed.

Her name was Isabel, and Anders and Shel spent a good hour showing her around Lenny's apartment and helping her to get him situated. All conversation between the two friends came to an abrupt halt, though, once they'd left Isabel and Lenny behind in the apartment and pulled back onto I-4 towards the beach. Shel now sat behind the wheel.

'Thanks for picking us up,' he said, desperate to break the awkward silence that seemed to have climbed into the car with them.

As they raced down the highway toward the beach, he watched the sabal palms and longleaf pines pass by in a blur outside his window. He knew the drive from Lenny's apartment to the beach like he knew the contours of a longtime lover's body. He knew what stretch of the highway still boasted forest on each side, and he knew where nature had already been stripped away to expand the concrete jungle. His relief that everything looked the same, that no new parcels of land had been razed during his absence to make way for another large housing development or new strip mall, was cut short when he saw it, on the east side of the highway, just before the New Smyrna Beach exit. He had to twist to see better, since the message was tucked into the trees and was meant for the westbound traffic, but even so, he couldn't miss it.

A new billboard.

'Coming Soon!' it exclaimed. 'New homes from the low 100's, from Paradise Builders. Get a piece of paradise for yourself!'

He looked at Shel then to see if she'd noticed it. She hadn't, but she must have felt his stare, because she gave him a smile. 'Glad to be home?'

She kept her eyes on the road and didn't press for an answer when he failed to respond.


IT WASN'T until her car rolled into the driveway, with the crunching of shells under the tyres officially announcing their arrival, that he realized how difficult it would be to go inside the house. Makena had generously offered to let him stay as long as he wished, but upon seeing it he knew he would stay just long enough to find something else. He wondered if his old landlord had a vacancy at the trailer park.

'Well, here you are.' Shel kept one hand on the steering wheel as she cut the engine. 'We didn't have any hurricanes while you were gone, so lucky for you the house is still standing.' She laughed a bit, but she looked at her lap and then out the window, belying her levity.

'Yep, everything looks the same.' The interior of the car fell silent, but he didn't move to get out. His eyes were drawn to the side-view mirror as two teens in wetsuits walked along Atlantic Avenue with surfboards under their arms. He became aware of the gentle sound of the surf from just a few hundred feet outside the car. He'd missed that sound. He closed his eyes and absorbed it. He felt her gaze then, and when he looked over she was studying him, eyeing the last remnants of the bruises on his face.

'Someday you'll have to tell me what really happened over there.'

He nodded slowly. 'Okay.'

She waited as if she thought he might start talking about it right then, but when he remained quiet she slapped her palms lightly on the steering wheel. 'Well, I guess I should let you get some sleep. You must be so tired.'

She reached across his knees and opened the glovebox to press the button that released the trunk. They each exited the car, and after he'd retrieved his bag, they stood together near the driver's side door.

'Thanks for the ride.'

'No problem.' She waved off his gratitude and reached for the door handle.

'Shel? Would you like to come inside for a while?'

She paused for only an instant before opening the car door.

'I'd like it if you would,' he added.

She scratched her eyebrow and shifted her weight from foot to foot. She tucked her hair behind her ear, though it simply fell forward again. Finally she took a deep breath and looked him in the eye, shaking her head. 'No, I don't think so. I really should get home.'

He hesitated, and then he pulled her closer and lightly kissed the top of her head. Her hair smelled of coconuts.

'Okay, then. Thanks again for the ride.'

She simply nodded and climbed into the car. He watched as she started the engine and readjusted the rearview mirror. She put the gear in reverse before looking out the window at him;

her posture was perfect in the seat but her left hand trembled as she attempted to tuck her hair behind her ear one more time.

Wagging a thin finger in his direction, she smiled big as if they hadn't just had the umpteenth moment of awkwardness. 'Don't forget. Welcome back party at my place tomorrow night.'

He waited until she'd pulled off before turning towards the empty grey house.

A STALE smell greeted him and he knew then the only proof of Olivia's time there would be her possessions and his memories. He flung open the doors to the deck first thing and stood for a long time watching the two surfers, the same ones, he presumed, he'd seen walking behind Shel's car. After he'd taken a shower, unpacked and started a load of laundry, he rummaged in the kitchen for something to eat, but except for canned soup he couldn't find anything that hadn't spoiled or grown mould. On the counter near the refrigerator he saw the carton of cigarettes he'd purchased before taking off for Connecticut, and though it still had five or six packs inside, he tossed the whole thing in the trash. He thought of Shel, then, and retrieved it.

He called his mom's house and breathed a sigh of relief when her answering machine picked up and he was able to tell her in a message that he'd made it home safely. He wasn't ready to explain that Olivia hadn't returned with him.

He finally collapsed on the sofa and flipped on the television. Five minutes later he flipped it off and sat in the silence until the light in the room began to fade. Only when dusk arrived and a mosquito landed on his arm did he rise to close the doors to the deck. He retreated to the bedroom and forced himself to lie down on the bed. Even on the sheets her scent had dissipated, and he knew that was probably a good thing. He was grateful for the impending dark because it allowed him not to see her things. The hairbrush and clips on the dresser, the camisole draped over the chair in the corner. That same strip of four small pictures clinging to the seam in the mirror frame.

The doorbell rang. He rose quickly, sure that Shel had reconsidered. He opened the front door in anticipation; it faced west and a faint glow from the departed sun still burned pink on the horizon.

But it was only a neighbourhood kid, on his last rounds trying to sell candy bars for his soccer team.

Anders bought the whole box.

# 28

ONCE HE'D finally fallen asleep, he didn't wake until close to one the next day. Hanging around the house just long enough to take another shower, he wheeled the sport bike out of the garage and within minutes had left the beach at his back. After a brief stop at the bank, he pulled into the Harley dealership around two fifteen. By three he'd picked out a model to replace the bike mangled in the crash and was signing the necessary paperwork to transfer the registration. He was only halfway to Shel's by four, though, because it'd been much too long since he'd enjoyed a wide open ride through the back roads of his beloved Florida.

By the time he arrived, the sun had already dipped behind the trees and dusk was imminent. The heavily wooded trailer park absorbed the darkness more quickly than the house at the beach, but to his surprise he saw her yard as soon as he turned down the narrow dirt lane. It literally glowed.

She'd decorated the entire front yard of her trailer with white Christmas lights. They hung from the live oaks as if challenging the Spanish moss to a beauty contest; they draped from frond to frond on the small Robelini palms near the steps to her door. She'd strung them from tree branch to tree branch, illuminating the tables and chairs she'd set up for the party. Even the umbrella to her Wal-Mart patio furniture was wrapped in the delicate twinkling lights. The sight brought back the memories of the first night on the Maasai Mara, the flickering candles on the long dinner table and the hurricane lamps in the fever trees, and he was forced to slow the bike until he'd managed to swallow the emotions rising in his throat.

He spied Lenny sitting at one of the tables drinking a beer, his feet propped on a chair and the empty wheelchair at his side. Joey was behind it, pretending to pop wheelies. Lenny waved to him but otherwise continued his conversation with some of their co-workers from Palmetto who sat at the table with him. He spotted Sergio. There were others scattered throughout the small yard, too; some he recognized and others he didn't.

Shel was talking to Samuel at the barbecue grill but she paused her conversation and came to greet him as soon as he shut down his engine.

'Did I get the time wrong?' he asked, giving her a short hug and nodding in the direction of the small crowd. He wondered if she'd given him a later time because she didn't want to be alone with him again.

'No, you're just in time.'

He pulled the carton of cigarettes from his backpack and offered them to her. He'd save his other gift for later. 'Here. I almost tossed the whole thing in the trash but then I thought you might want them.' She looked at him curiously and he realized his brief stint with smoking had occurred entirely outside her presence. He laughed and said, 'Long story.'

She took the carton but said, 'I quit, Anders.'

He stared at her. 'Wow.' Then catching himself, he added, 'I mean, congratulations. That's great, Shel.' Instinctively, he bent down and with his hand pulled the top of her head close as if to kiss it, as he had the day before, but when he just sniffed her hair, she giggled. He remembered that she hadn't smelled like cigarettes yesterday either, nor had her car. And she hadn't moaned about needing a smoke.

'I'm sure someone else will want them. Come on,' she said, taking his hand and pulling him in the direction of the party, 'I have a few people I want you to meet.'

The few people turned out to be some of the other women from her school who'd joined in her fight against the English professor, and a guy named Josh whom she'd met in her American history class. Josh wore a baseball cap backwards and a concert T-shirt of some band Anders didn't recognize.

'Looks like Shel finally found some friends her own age,' he said to Lenny later. He'd joined him at his table near the edge of the yard and was now playing tic-tac-toe with Joey on a paper plate. The party was dying down, and Joey had been begging Lenny to go home for the past half-hour, but Lenny was still nursing a Budweiser, so the game had been Anders's way of distracting the boy for him.

Lenny grunted an unintelligible response and took a swig of his beer. 'What are you gonna do, Andy?'

Anders looked at him, unsure of his meaning.

'Are you just gonna piss away all that money your mom gave you?' He tilted his head toward the new Harley. 'I see you've already spent a good portion of it on a new Softail.'

'No.' He sucked on his own beer and watched Shel and Samuel laughing at something Josh said as the three of them began to clean up. 'The insurance money will pay for most of it.'

Lenny merely nodded, acknowledging his mistake.

Anders marked a final X on the plate and drew a line through the latest game. 'Joey, man, didn't your dad here ever teach you the foolproof way to win this game?' He pulled a clean plate from underneath the one they'd drawn on and scooted his chair closer to the boy's. 'Come here, let me show you.' In between explaining tic-tac-toe strategy to Joey, he slipped in to Lenny, 'I'm thinking of going to school.'

Lenny landed his bottle on the plastic table with a thud. 'No shit?'

He glanced at him out of the corner of his eye and shrugged.

'You're too old for school, Andy,' Joey said, and Anders laughed.

'College?' Lenny asked, just to be sure.

'Yeah. I mean, it's not like I plan to be a doctor or a lawyer or anything like that. But, you know, maybe I'll study forestry, or horticulture, or environmental science or something.' He shrugged again. 'I don't know, something that might help pull this state out of the crapper before it's too late.'

He could feel Lenny staring at him as he finished out the game with Joey, who finally won.

'You're serious, aren't you?'

'Yeah. I think I am.'

Lenny shifted in his chair a bit. 'Well, then maybe you should consider a degree in African Studies.' He said it as though he'd just commented on the weather.

Anders drew a new game grid without looking up, without acknowledging the remark in any way. His leg began its shaking. After a long pause, he said, 'Yeah. Maybe.'

'Andy?'

When Anders glanced at Lenny, the beer was at his lips and the hand holding it trembled.

'He kept pressuring me to tell him something about you, some weakness he could use against you.' It was the first time Lenny broached what had happened to him during the time spent in Brent's captivity. Anders knew *pressure* meant *torture*. 'It took me a long time to decide what I could say to appease him without hurting you.' Anders shot a quick look at Lenny's feet; he wondered at what point in Lenny's decision-making Brent had decided to cut the tendons. Would Lenny have suffered less if he'd given up something, anything, sooner? 'I finally told him about . . .'

He stopped and nodded in Joey's direction; they both knew he'd been about to speak Crystal's name.

'It's okay,' Anders said. 'She wasn't too upset about it. That wasn't the problem.'

Lenny grunted and shook his head impatiently. 'Don't you

get it? There were a lot of things I could have told him to make him stop, but I told him about that for a reason.'

Anders waited.

'I wanted him to understand that you'd do anything, *anything*, to save her.'


WHEN THE sky started to sprinkle, Josh helped Anders get Lenny and his wheelchair into Samuel's SUV for the ride back to Deltona while Joey, with Sergio's assistance, pushed Anders's new bike under the carport.

'You sure you don't want me to follow?' Anders asked Samuel, ignoring Lenny's eye roll. He knew Lenny didn't like being reliant on others, but he also knew Lenny had many months of physical therapy ahead of him and he'd never heal if he didn't stay off his feet. Samuel, at sixty-two years old, might not have an easy time getting Lenny into his apartment, even with Joey and Isabel to help.

But both Samuel and Lenny insisted he stay and help Shel clean up.

When they pulled off, Anders was left alone with Josh and Shel, both of whom were traipsing back and forth from yard to trailer collecting empty bottles and trash. Though some part of him knew he should head home and just give her the gift later, another part of him hoped he'd be able to talk to her alone.

A clap of thunder signalled the start of harder rain. Anders closed the umbrella and grabbed the last of the leftovers before dashing into the trailer. He found the two of them standing in Shel's tiny kitchen drinking beers. Shel stood in front of the sink; Josh leaned against the fridge. He'd finally removed the baseball cap, revealing a mop of blond curls that rivalled Goldilocks.

'God, you're soaked!' Shel darted past him, returning

quickly with a towel. He accepted it and then hauled himself up to sit on the counter.

'I guess I'll have to wait until the rain lets up,' he said. Shel knew his bike was his sole means of travel; he rode in the rain all the time.

Josh piped in. 'Yeah, you could get yourself killed.' And Anders knew then that Shel hadn't told him much of anything.

'Wanna beer, Anders?' she asked just as Josh said, 'So Shel says you just got back from Africa.'

'Yeah, I did,' he said, but shook his head at Shel.

'Cool. Were you on safari?'

He stared at Shel a moment before meeting Josh's gaze. 'Yeah, I guess you could call it that.'

They all jumped when a crash of thunder shook the trailer. The lights flickered and then went out, plunging the trailer into darkness. From the window Anders could see the entire neighbourhood had suffered the same fate.

'I guess I ought to head home,' Josh said finally when the darkness made the threesome even more awkward. Shel protested, but it was clear her efforts were all for show. The party had been for Anders and Lenny, and her new friend recognized that, at least for the time being, he was the odd man out.


THE LIGHTS came on minutes after Josh left. As they walked back to the kitchen, Shel muttered, 'You plan that, Anders?'

But darkness once again enveloped them just as she was about to blow out the candle, and she grunted.

He laughed at her and said, 'So tell me about this Josh.'

'There's not much to tell.'

When he didn't say anything, she said, 'We're friends, from school. I told you, he's in my American history class.' He still didn't say anything, just looked at her sideways. But she knew what he was thinking. 'We're *just* friends.'

'For now.'

'Maybe, maybe not. Anyway, what's it to you?'

He shrugged. 'I don't know. I guess it'd make me happy. He seems right for you.'

She opened the refrigerator and reached in the dark interior for a bottle of water. Twisting at the cap, she took a long, thirsty guzzle as she eyed him from behind the bottle.

'I've got a gift for you. From Africa.' He unwrapped the necklace from the tissue and silently placed it around her neck.

'It's very long,' she whispered, remaining still as he worked to fasten the hook in back.

'Well, it's supposed to be. On the Maasai women it comes only to their knees,' he winked, 'but they're much taller than you.'

She looked down at the red, blue and green beaded piece that almost reached the floor.

'It's gorgeous.'

'It's called a wedding necklace.'

She nodded with her eyes down and reached around to attempt to unfasten it herself. She knew she wasn't meant to wear the heavy, elaborate thing.

'Here,' he said, touching her shoulder to twirl her around, 'I'll get it.'

Together they wrapped the necklace back in its tissue, with Shel thanking him a little too emphatically and promising to find a spot to hang it later.

'Sounds like the rain has let up,' he said.

'There's still lightning.'

But he ignored her fears and dug his keys out of his jeans as he reached for his helmet on the kitchen table.

'Anders, wait. Are you okay?'

'Yeah, I'll be fine. It's not that far and there's barely a sprinkle now.'

'No, I mean ... you know ... do you want to talk now about what happened over there?'

He looked at her a long time. *Yeah*, he wanted to say. *Yeah, I really do.* He heard the rain, coming harder again. He finally just shook his head.

He turned for the helmet once more, and when she realized he intended to leave, she grabbed his arm. 'Please, don't go out in this storm on your bike. You can stay on the sofa bed.'

She must have understood how badly he dreaded going back to the empty beach house. So he let her lead him into the family room with the candle. He let her give him a pillow, and a blanket, and he played along when she tried to make light of everything by carrying Bagheera over and dropping the cat on the sofa with him. 'For company,' she said. He called goodnight to her as she headed for her bedroom, the room into which, in the past, he'd always been welcome.

He fell asleep hours later listening to the remnants of the distant storm and thinking about what Lenny had said.

# 29

HE KNEW the rain had stopped when he opened his eyes to sunlight streaming through the room's only window and the chatter of birds in the trees outside the trailer. The cat must have heard him stir; it jumped onto the couch and nuzzled hard at his neck as it kneaded its paws against his shoulder. He rolled over to pet it as he mimicked its heavy purring.

Shel came out of the kitchen holding a box of cat food. She shook it and Bagheera quickly abandoned him.

'Fair weather friend.'

She grinned. 'Sorry. He's got his priorities.'

'I'm hungry, too. Let's head to Osteen to get some breakfast at the diner. I'll give you a ride on the new bike.'

'Tell you what, why don't you take your shower while I finish cleaning up the kitchen from last night, and then we can go.' She motioned to the other side of the trailer. 'The clean towels are in the bedroom closet.'

As if he hadn't been there a hundred times before.


THE TOWELS were high up on a single shelf. Just as he lifted an arm to reach for one, a flash of emerald green from the corner of the closet floor caught his attention. He stopped, one arm still stretched and resting on the shelf, and peered down. It was just a sparkling sliver peeking through a pile of laundry, but he knew immediately what he was seeing. He knew without a doubt. His heart began to beat frantically in his chest as the meaning of it sank in.

'Anders?' Shel called in to him, oblivious. And then, immediately after, 'Oh God!' She sprung through the doorway but halted in the middle of the room, watching in horror as he used a foot to push the clothes aside to reveal the helmets. His old black one, and the green metallic one he'd bought for Olivia to match her eyes.

'It's not like it looks.'

He couldn't take his eyes off the helmets. He couldn't move. He couldn't swallow. He couldn't even think of Shel standing behind him because he was afraid of what he'd do to her if he acknowledged her presence in the room with him. In his mind's eye, he saw her sitting at the table at the Ocean Deck, her hand shaking as she tucked her hair behind her ear, her eyes glassy from tears. *I'm really sorry about Olivia*, she'd said. He'd been surprised by the strength of her sympathy. For a moment he felt weak, and dizzy. He held on to the shelf until it passed, and then he turned and faced her. She gasped when she saw his face; her hands flew to her mouth.

'Oh God,' she said again, but this time it came out as a wail.

He simply shook his head at her as he moved to the other room to retrieve his things.

'Anders.' She reached out to touch him as he walked by her but stopped before she made contact, as if she knew he was a powder keg about to ignite.

She began to sob as she watched him work his shirt over his head.

'Anders, please. Please let me explain.'

He pulled on his boots and stood.

'Anders, please!'

He turned to her, finally. 'What the fuck could you possibly say to explain?'

She dropped onto a chair at his shouting, and like the tears in her eyes, words began to fall uninhibited from her lips. 'I was at the beach that day, that morning. I'd volunteered to pick up the fish for the restaurant. I went by your place, just to say hi.'

He stared, waiting for her to say something to exonerate herself, but knowing nothing she might say would succeed.

'I pulled up to the house just as you and Olivia were pulling away. I waved, but you didn't see me . . .' She began to cry harder. 'If only you'd waved . . .'

'*What?*'

'I don't know! If you'd seen me, I wouldn't have . . .' She cried out in frustration. 'I don't know,' she said again, louder, 'I just found myself following you!'

'You *followed* us?'

'At first it didn't feel intentional. I mean, you were heading for the mainland and so was I, but then when you turned up toward Route 40, I knew where you were going. I just *knew*. You were taking her to the springs, and it upset me.' She'd been speaking hurriedly, on the defensive, but the next words came out as an accusation. 'That was our spot, Anders!' she cried, and then she bent forward and covered her face, as if she realized she sounded childish or like she was blaming him, and that was the last thing she wanted to do just then.

'It was sick, I know. I kept asking myself – *what are you doing, Shel? You're acting like some sort of stalker* – but I couldn't stop myself. I just couldn't stop myself.

'I waited until you'd turned off the road, and when I was sure you were far enough ahead, I followed. I saw your bike at the trailhead. I kept trying to talk myself out of following you all the way to the spring, but I couldn't. It was like you had some magnetic pull on me.' He grunted with disgust at that, but she kept talking. 'I got there just as . . .' She stopped herself from saying it out loud.

Anders closed his eyes and shook his head. He didn't want to hear any more. He knew from the look on her face what she'd seen, and if things had turned out differently on their way home, he might have almost felt sorry for her just then. But they hadn't, and he didn't. Fury burned inside him.

'Please,' she begged. 'Please try to understand. I was so upset and angry with you—'

'*You* were angry with *me*?' he shouted, and she flinched and leaned back farther as if she thought he was about to hit her. 'God damn it, you almost killed her!'

'No, no! I swear it wasn't like that. I never meant for either of you to get hurt. I never thought you'd be in danger. You're such a good rider. I just—'

'You just *what*? What, Shel?' he said. 'What could possibly have motivated you to do such a thing?' His hand made a small motion in the direction of the bedroom.

She sobbed loudly. 'I don't know! I guess I just wanted to make you mad. I wanted to ruin your day. I don't know.'

'Yeah, well, congratulations. You ruined my day. *You ruined my fucking life.*' He marched into the bedroom, picked up the helmets, and marched back out. After grabbing his backpack and the newer helmet in the kitchen, he headed for the front door. Just when he'd thought he'd banished the rage for good, just when he'd convinced himself that he'd purged all evidence of being his father's son, it reared its ugly head and reminded him it lived in his veins like dormant bacteria.

'Anders, please try to understand!' The door banged behind her as she followed him outside. 'I didn't know someone would run you off the road!'

He couldn't steady his hands as he unfastened the bungee cord and tried to find a way to attach two of the helmets to the back of the bike. She grabbed for his arm but he shook her off.

'Leave me alone, Shel!'

'*Please.*'

He ignored her; he thought she was pathetic in her begging,

but in his anger the helmets kept slipping and Olivia's finally fell to the ground.

He cursed under his breath and stood still, trying to regain his composure, his calm, so he could get the job done and get out of there.

She squatted down to retrieve the helmet.

'Don't touch it,' he demanded, and she froze with her hand on the surface. 'Don't touch anything of mine. Don't ever do anything for me again, you got it?'

She lifted her tear-streaked face to him and her bloodshot eyes met his angry ones. He saw her swallow; her jaw seemed to tighten. She rose with the helmet in her hand and held it out for him as an offering. 'I didn't ruin your life. I did something stupid that caused you a lot of pain, and I'm sorry. I truly am sorry. But I *didn't* ruin your life.' Her voice was strong; all vestige of begging had evaporated like the evidence of last night's rain. He looked at the helmet but didn't move to take it from her. 'If she's the one, you should have stayed in Africa with her. You shouldn't have come back.'

He yanked the helmet out of her hand and worked to secure one to the helmet lock, the other with the bungee cord. She stood watching but he ignored her.

She stepped back when he climbed onto the bike and started the engine. As he lifted his older helmet onto his head, she said his name one last time, and though he heard her, he pretended he hadn't.


HE RODE the new Harley out to the springs, opening it up on Route 40 without a thought to whether he was breaking any laws. The bike performed as promised, taking the curves well, but he almost wished he was on his sport bike, because all he cared about just then was feeling speed. A lot of speed.

He didn't think about why he headed to the springs. He just knew he couldn't return to the house at the beach. Other than that, his brain was on autopilot as far as riding was concerned. It was too occupied with other things. Like Shel, and Olivia. And whether he'd made a colossal mistake in leaving Africa without a fight.

He slowed briefly as he passed the spot where the accident had occurred, though no evidence of that day remained except in his head. Had Shel seen the accident, too? He'd been so angry with her he hadn't thought to ask the question, and she hadn't said. He refused to believe she had, because that would require accepting that she'd not only stolen the helmets, she also hadn't come forward with information about the car. Information that might have answered a lot of questions long ago. Information that would have saved him a lot of grief.

His cellphone vibrated in his back pocket just as he pulled onto the dirt road leading to the trailhead. He continued on, ignoring it. If it was Shel, he had no desire to speak with her.

At the trailhead, he shut down the engine and sat on the bike, listening to the sounds of the forest, the slight breeze as it whistled through the trees. Only then did he begin to question why he'd come. What, really, did he expect to find? He told himself he just wanted the mental solitude that he couldn't seem to get anywhere else. The beach held too many memories. But then, so did this place, didn't it?

IT TOOK only a few minutes to walk down the trail to the pool. He sat at the edge and tugged at his boots and stripped bare. He didn't even hesitate before diving in. He knew how cold the water would be, but he craved the shock it provided. It didn't fail him.

He swam freestyle laps, trying to focus his mind on his form and the feel of his muscles under the skin as he cut through the icy bath. When he'd exhausted himself, he climbed out of the pool and onto the same wide rock he'd lain on with both of them, Shel and Olivia. The sun had heated the smooth surface and it warmed him as he stretched out flat against it. He turned his head and looked at the other spot they'd used, the bed made of scrub pine needles from above and dead leaves from nearby water tupelos. He closed his eyes.

Olivia had asked how many other women he'd brought to the spot. *Just one, but I didn't tell her I loved her*, he'd answered. And he'd been truthful.

His cellphone rang again. He reached for his jeans on the ground and retrieved the phone. When he saw it was Lenny, he answered.

'Shel stole the helmets,' he said, skipping 'hello'.

'I know.'

'*You knew?*' The anger he'd managed to let go on the ride and during his swim crept back.

'No, no,' Lenny said quickly. 'I mean, she called me. Just after you left her.' When Anders didn't respond, he added, 'I've tried a couple times to call you.'

'Sorry. I was on the bike. Couldn't hear it.' It wasn't the full truth, but it wasn't entirely a lie, either.

'Where are you?'

Anders hesitated. 'The springs.'

'Near Ocala?'

'Yeah.'

Lenny was quiet and Anders could hear the judgement in his silence.

'You gotta get your ass back over there,' he said finally. 'She's going out of her mind.'

Anders watched a sandhill crane walk along the water's edge at the far side of the pool. 'You mean like I did the last couple of months?'

'Oh, grow the fuck up!' Lenny exploded. 'Get over yourself

already. She didn't *cause* the accident. You've gotta stop messing with her. You're killing her.'

'*I'm* messing with *her*? I didn't abscond with her helmets! I'm not the reason Olivia almost died from head injuries.'

'You *are* messing with her. You can't just pick up where you left off, using her while you wait for something better to come along. You're making me think you and Crystal are more alike than I'd thought.'

'Fuck you. I'm not using her.'

'She said you gave her something called a wedding necklace.'

Anders grunted. 'Oh, please. It's a souvenir. *Olivia* helped me pick it out.'

'Bad choice, Andy.' At Anders's silence, he said, 'She said you stayed there last night.'

Anders heard the wind from large wings cutting through air and looked up to see the crane's mate coming in for a landing. Despite its size, it landed gracefully next to the first one.

'Were you there last night?' Lenny asked.

'I stayed on her couch, for Christ's sake. I'm not using her.'

'Then I think maybe she's the one who needs to hear that.'

Anders closed his eyes and shook his head. 'Did she tell you what she did? She followed us all the way out here! And all that time, she played dumb. They almost charged me, and still she didn't say anything.'

He could hear Lenny sigh at the other end. 'You're conveniently forgetting that they never intended to charge you. And you're also forgetting that Shel is right. But for Olivia's sicko boyfriend – who, I'll also remind you, no one knew about – the lack of helmets would have been nothing more than an inconvenience that day. She acted like a lovesick teenager, but that was her only real crime.'

Anders ignored his last sentence. 'But she didn't know they weren't going to charge me!'

'So what? Put yourself in her shoes. Let's say she had come forward and admitted she stole the helmets. You would have been royally pissed off at her, but would it have made any difference in your decision to go after Olivia?'

He didn't answer.

'If anything, from her point of view, it would have just made you more miserable. Did you ever think of it like that?'

'What if she saw the accident? What if she could have helped the cops find the car?'

'She didn't.'

'How do you know? Did she tell you that?'

'No. But I just don't think she would have kept something from you that might have helped your search.'

Lenny stopped talking for a moment, and Anders stared at the water. He had an overwhelming desire to set the phone down and slip in again, to lose himself in its frigid depths. Lenny's voice pulled him back to the surface.

'That girl would give her life for you, Andy, even though she stood by as you were willing to give yours for someone else.'

# 30

HE OWED her an explanation. He owed her that much, at least.

He found her sitting on the small front stoop to the trailer, Bagheera in her lap. The cat didn't look happy about the rumble of his bike or the interruption of its massage; it leapt quickly to the ground. Shel didn't move.

He didn't pull into the drive. He remained in the lane, sitting on the bike with the engine still running, his feet on the ground to balance himself. Even from across the yard he could see she'd been crying.

She didn't stand and run over to him. She didn't smile, she didn't frown. She simply looked at him, and he looked back. He finally shut down the bike and went to stand in front of her.

'I need to say something to you.'

She didn't make room for him to sit. Her chest heaved as she took a deep breath.

'That day when you came to the beach and helped me clean, and I was so horrible to you—'

'You weren't horrible to me.'

'I was trying to explain something, but I didn't do a good job of it. And I tried when I called you from Africa . . .'

She waited, willing to listen.

'Look, you were mad at me about what I'd done with Crystal, and you were right to be. Both you and Lenny were right to be. But . . .' He sighed. He knew he had to get it right this time. 'You were mad at me because I betrayed Lenny, and

I did, I know. But you were also mad because you couldn't understand how I could do that with *her*, and yet I rejected you, right?'

Her eyes glistened in the sunlight. She remained fixed as a statue.

'It's because she meant nothing to me. If I had any feelings about her, it was hate. So in my mind, it wasn't a betrayal of Olivia. Do you understand?'

She sucked in a small sob, trying desperately not to cry.

'But if I'd done what you'd wanted that day ... don't you see? It *would* have been a betrayal of Olivia ...'

She covered her mouth with one hand and hunched over as if to hide from view; the old Shel was still in there and she didn't want him to see her. When she was unable to stop a few tears from coming, she began to apologize. 'I'm sorry. It's okay. I'm okay.' He moved to sit next to her and this time she scooted to the side to let him.

He touched her arm and gently pulled her hand away so he could see her face. 'What I'm trying to say is ... I *do* have feelings for you, Shel. I always have. But they're not the same ones you want them to be. Do you understand?'

She nodded, wiped at her eyes. 'I do understand. I do.'

'What you said, about how I should have stayed in Africa if she was the one ...'

She turned to him, anticipating his next words.

'I think I made a big mistake, coming back. I—'

'Anders,' she cried. 'Why *did* you come back?' Her resigned tone told him that she knew, she'd known all along, that she'd lost him to Olivia. And then she implored him to answer the question she'd asked him three days in a row. 'What happened over there?'

He took a deep breath and tried to muster the courage to put the experience into words.

'Please? I'd like to know.' She lifted the tail of her shirt and used it to dab underneath her eyes as she talked. The new Shel pushing the old Shel back in her place. 'And it would be good for you, you know, to talk about it.'

He owed her an explanation. He owed her that much, at least.

And so he talked. And he told her everything.

He explained about Brent's lifelong obsession with Olivia, and how he helped Mayfield build his drug import business. 'Once he did that, he had Mayfield in his pocket. Olivia didn't even know there was a business relationship between the two of them. She thought it ended when the apprenticeship ended.' He explained about the Cranitex, how her father's company had developed the drug and how he'd used it on his own daughter, first to block her memories of the rape and then, later, to block certain memories of Florida.

When she heard about the rape, Shel questioned, just like Olivia, how a father could let his daughter's attackers get away with such a crime.

'Brent had been blackmailing him for a long time to get at Olivia, but when she was raped, her dad didn't know Brent was involved, or even suspect it. He thought they were *both* at risk of being found out.'

'Sounds like Brent beat him at his own game,' Shel said quietly.

Anders thought back to how he'd let Mayfield manipulate him, and how, in his first conversation with Brent outside their tent, he began to suspect that Brent, in turn, was manipulating Mayfield. *He's got money, and power, but he's not half as clever as he believes himself to be.*

'Yeah,' Anders said slowly, 'for a long time, he did.'

But he and Olivia had out-manipulated them both, hadn't they?

*Hadn't they?*

His vacant stare caused Shel to eye him cautiously. 'What

happened in Africa?' She hesitated, speaking softly and choosing her words carefully. 'I mean, to you and Olivia?'

'Lenny and I went after her. We showed up at their camp pretending to be someone else, but it backfired. One night Brent invited me to their tent for a drink.' He explained how Brent played dumb until Olivia went to bed, and then how Lenny intervened when he saw Brent had a gun and was about to use it. 'Brent knew all along it was me.' He told her how Brent's thugs captured Lenny, how Olivia's father showed up at the airport and promised to help find him, how Anders had no choice but to accept Mayfield's help, and how eventually Anders ended up at the school and in the storage hut. He told her what happened in the hut, how he'd almost collapsed under the weight of his past.

And finally, he told her what Olivia had done, how she didn't hesitate to take Brent's life at the moment of decision, and how, even though he believed she'd had every right, he was still having trouble with what had happened.

Shel was uncharacteristically quiet when he finished. He glanced at her, and she was crying again. But this time, he knew, she was crying for Olivia.

'You're not being fair to her,' she said.

'What do you mean?' But she didn't answer. 'What do you mean, Shel?' he asked again.

'It's not fair, holding that against her.'

'I'm not—'

'You just said it, in so many words. You know, for the longest time you held it against your mom that she didn't do something about your dad. Or at least you didn't think she did. And you didn't respect me, either—'

'That's not true. I—'

'No, it's okay. I *know* it's true, and I understand why now. I really do. I earned your disrespect.' She laughed a little, a sad laugh. 'I'm not saying that excuses you ...'

He nodded, accepting her indictment.

'But now you're holding it against Olivia for doing exactly what you'd wished your mom had done, or I had done.'

'*What?*'

'Look, I don't mean literally. I'm not talking about taking a life. I'm talking about getting a backbone. I just mean ... she took control of her destiny finally, you know? And from the sounds of it, she had only one way to do it. Don't punish her for it now.'

She'd grown up so much while he was gone. She'd learned to protect herself better, and she now recognized another woman's attempt to do the same.

The cat rubbed against his legs and he reached down to pet it. 'I'm not. There were other issues.'

'Lenny said you came back because you didn't want to live in Africa, and she didn't want to live here. But that can't be right. That can't be the reason.'

When he didn't respond, she asked softly, 'Anders? Had she ever told you she'd been raped?'

He shook his head. 'No.' He realized now, in hindsight, she'd inadvertently left him clues. 'She said she'd intended to, but she was afraid.'

'Of what?'

Shel spoke the question so quickly after his response that he turned, and her piercing eyes told him she already knew the answer; she was simply reminding him of it.

He looked away and stared at the trailer across the lane. There was a 'For Rent' sign in the front yard. She saw him looking.

'There's talk of a developer buying the land,' she said in a quiet voice. 'Taking out the trailer park and putting up McMansions. It's just a rumour, but I guess some people are getting out now, before it becomes reality. But I can't believe Gus will do it.' Gus was Shel's landlord, and at one time Anders's; he owned the land and many of the trailers on it. He was a Florida boy through and through.

'Why not? It'll make him a rich man.'

Shel sighed at his caustic tone. She stared at him, then, until he met her gaze. 'Was he right?' she asked, referring, Anders knew, to Lenny.

Anders shrugged. 'Yeah, he was right. We faced down a sociopath together, but we couldn't manage to decide where to live.' He laughed sarcastically. 'And that's why I came home to Florida.'

'You might be back in Florida, Anders, but I don't think you're home.'

# Home

# 31

HE SPENT a few days closing up the house. He packed up his things – there wasn't much, clothes mainly, and Olivia's things, which consisted primarily of clothes, books, some CDs, and her box – it would be up to her to decide what to do with that – and made arrangements to have everything shipped to Dar es Salaam. The furniture he'd leave for Makena.

Even though hurricane season had passed, he covered the windows and doors with plywood because he didn't know Makena's plans, whether she'd let the place sit empty as before, or whether, now that it was renovated, she'd rent it out or sell it. He wondered if she even realized its value.

After officially giving notice that he wouldn't be returning to Palmetto – ever – he went to the library with Shel, and she showed him how to search the Internet to find a shipping company for his bikes. He suggested he could simply call the Harley dealership and they'd steer him in the right direction, but she insisted. He realized once they got online that she had an ulterior motive: she created a free email address for him and informed him that she expected him to keep in touch.

'I doubt I'll have access to a computer in the middle of Africa,' he protested.

But she'd already done her research and determined that wireless broadband could be found in the major cities. 'Spend a few bucks on a laptop to take when you make trips into town for supplies, and you're set.'

When he learned how much shipping the bikes would cost him, he made the decision right then and there to give up the sport bike and take only the Harley. Shel became the lucky recipient of his impulsive donation.

On his second to last day, he stopped at the hospital to thank Carrie. She told him that Crystal had tracked her down after hearing the Mayfield name being connected to the illegal drug imports, and that's how Crystal determined the man Anders had complained about so much – Olivia's father – was the same man being sought by the Feds.

He also paid a visit to his mom. They'd spoken over the phone earlier in the week and he'd told her of his decision, but he needed to see her before he left and he knew she needed to see him.

And, finally, he stopped by Lenny's apartment, but anything that needed to be said between them had already been said, so they had a beer or two and talked about Joey and Gators football until Lenny's physical therapist showed up.

It was a toss up which was harder: the teary, touchy farewell his mom offered, or the stoic, acting-like-they'd-see-each-other-at-work-the-next-day goodbye exchanged between the two friends.

HE MADE all of his plans as if he'd already spoken with Olivia and knew she'd welcome him back with open arms. He'd considered trying to reach her by phone. He knew the name of the camp, and he figured he could somehow relay a message for her to call him. And he knew she would. But in the end he decided the only way to convince her of his intent – his *desire* – was to demonstrate it. And the only way to demonstrate it was to leave Florida without an obvious safety net. He couldn't talk about leaving it all behind.

He had to actually do it.

*

HE ARRIVED in Dar es Salaam near half-past three, but this time he hired a driver to take him into the bush right off. They'd be travelling for several hours after nightfall, and for that he had to pay a premium, but if he was lucky he'd arrive at the camp just as the guests were finishing dinner.

On the long ride it occurred to him that she might have moved on to a new location, but he resolved not to worry about it; he'd deal with that problem only if it came to pass. Tory could tell him where to find her, if need be.

They approached the camp just after nine. He saw the glow of the grove campfire in the distance telling him the meal was over, and that most everyone would be sitting around the circle sharing stories from their day. As soon as the truck rolled over the dirt into the main drive at the front of camp, where, but for the headlights, darkness still prevailed, Tory came running out to meet the unexpected night-time visitors. She gasped when Anders stepped down from the passenger seat.

'Does she kn–?' she began, and he put his fingers to his lips and shook his head to silence her.

He paid the driver as Tory retrieved his small bag from the back seat.

'She's at the fire,' she said, letting him know there was no chance of Olivia overhearing their conversation. As the truck pulled away and he began to walk with her, she asked, 'What are you doing here?' Her voice was slightly giddy.

He continued down the dark path through the trees, silent, intent on reaching his destination. When he reached the outer edge of the circle, still cloaked in the shadow of night, he reached for the ring in his pocket and said to Tory, but loud enough for all to hear, 'There's something I forgot to do.'

Olivia's face opened like a moonflower as she turned at the familiar voice, and he emerged into the light.

# Author's Note

When I first considered using a memory-blocking drug to banish Olivia's memories, I worried about the credibility of such a plot device. I began researching chemically induced amnesia, hoping to find something that would work for her particular story. Little did I know that the use of drugs like the one I envisioned is – frighteningly or fortunately, depending upon your viewpoint – just on the horizon.

According to a 30 June 2007 article in the London *Telegraph*, researchers in two different studies have made substantial progress in the use of so-called 'amnesia drugs'. One study reported in the *Journal of Psychiatric Research* explained how researchers at McGill University and Harvard University used propranolol, a drug typically used to treat hypertension, to 'dampen' the memories of trauma victims. After treating accident or rape victims for ten days with the drug, researchers found that subjects exhibited fewer signs of stress when later asked to recall the traumatic events. In another study at New York University, scientists used a drug called U0126 to erase a single memory from the brains of rats while leaving the rest of their memories intact.

Memory-blocking drugs similar to the fictional drug in this novel are still, to my knowledge, at the research stage, but they appear to be real indeed.

# Acknowledgements

Writers spend many hours alone in front of the computer with only their characters (and their cats – thanks Smokey) to keep them company, but the final product of any book reflects the abundant help generously given by many individuals.

I am forever indebted to the great folks at Macmillan and St Martin's Press, who gave me my break and have nurtured my budding writing career in ways that some authors can only dream of. Sincerest thanks to Maria Rejt, Kelley Ragland, Sophie Orme, Matt Martz, Anna Valdinger (now down under), Sophie Portas, Hector DeJean, and so many others on both sides of the pond who've helped bring this novel to fruition. A special thanks to Richard Evans. I love it!

Many, many thanks to Jamie Morris, who entered my life as my Orlando AWA workshop leader but soon became a wonderful friend, too. A master at getting to the heart of a story, she also knows just when a needy writer needs praise and a stubborn one needs critique. I was fortunate to have Jamie at my side from the very beginning on this one.

Because I've moved several times, I'm lucky enough to have mentors in two cities. Alison Hicks, my AWA workshop leader from Philly who was instrumental in my first novel, also had a hand in this one and deserves my gratitude for her continuing guidance and friendship.

Numerous people gave assistance and answered questions along the way. Trish Celano and Melanie Tamsky helped with my medical questions; Jeff Davis (the coolest cop ever) patiently explained police procedure and gave me several tutorials on guns; Anthony Grossman, Nathan Ginn, Mike Philpott and Bunny Ernst all helped with my motorcycle questions (both for the novel and when I decided to join the ranks of bikers myself); Debbie Williams gave a name to my fictional town in Connecticut; Robin Harvey explained the ins and outs of chloroform and its alternatives; and Greg from Berklay Cargo Services willingly shared his knowledge about shipping bikes even though he knew his customer was fictional and didn't have a penny to his name.

So many others have been incredibly supportive throughout my journey and helped spread the word: my in-laws Sunny and Bill Combs and their amazing friends, the members of my Orlando writing workshop, Faith Fortin, Lisa Fuller, Diane Reed and the rest of the Bookwormers, Sheila Kramer, Joseph Hayes, Jennifer Greenhill-Taylor, Margaret Reyes Dempsey, and the booksellers, librarians and, most importantly, the readers of *Tell No Lies* who took a chance on a new author. (A special thanks to the many readers who wrote and asked when the next one was coming; those emails were the ultimate encouragement.)

Once again I must thank Jo Bicknell, who, in addition to everything else she's done for me, never fails to ask how it's going.

My acknowledgements would not be complete without a nod to Africa; I couldn't have written the Kenya and Tanzania scenes without seeing it for myself. Thanks, also, to Nina Wennersten, whose expert planning made the trip go off without a hitch, and to the incredible people we met during our travels. Whether it was camp staff, guides, the Maasai, market vendors, people we met on the streets and in the villages, or even other travellers from around the world, each and every one supplied an essential ingredient – some a pinch, some much more – for this novel.

Lastly, and above all, love and appreciation to Rick, Jessie and Sally. You three are what matters most.

extracts reading groups

competitions books new

discounts extracts extracts

competitions discounts

books new events

events books extracts reading groups

reading groups

extracts new

books titles reading groups

interviews events

books extracts events

extracts discounts new books interviews

new books events books

events new events

discounts extracts discounts interviews new books extracts

**www.panmacmillan.com**

extracts events reading groups books

competitions books extracts new